Shadow of the Rock

Eileen Haavik McIntire

Happy traveling!
Eileen Haavik McIntire

Library of Congress Control Number: 2011904495

Publisher's Cataloging-in-Publication
(Provided by Quality Books, Inc.)

McIntire, Eileen Haavik.
  Shadow of the rock / by Eileen R. Haavik.
  p. cm.
  Includes bibliographical references.
  ISBN-13: 978-0-9834049-0-3
  ISBN-10: 0-9834049-0-9

  1. Women--Fiction. 2. Identity (Psychology)--
Fiction. 3. Jewish art--Fiction. 4. Adventure stories,
American. 5. Historical fiction, American. I. Title.

PS3608.A2365S53 2011   813'.6
                    QBI11-600058

Cover design by Six Penny Graphics.

Published by Amanita Books, an imprint of Summit Crossroads Press, Columbia, Maryland, USA.

4/3/2021 .50
(TB) Goodwill
Dundalk

Acknowledgments

The grandmother of David Levy Yulee, Florida's first senator, was captured by pirates and sold to the vizier of Morocco. That's the story according to Florida folklore, and it's often mentioned in Florida history books. It's an enticing tidbit, but a credible Florida historian claims it is a fabrication. What is the true story?

The question intrigued me. To find an answer, I spent countless hours in various libraries, drove the back roads of Florida, and explored ancient cemeteries in St. Thomas and Gibraltar. I walked the planks of the frigate, *USS Constellation*, and toured the kasbahs of Morocco. One fascinating fact led to another, building such a mass that I was crushed by the weight of it until my friend Betty Myers said to me, "Just write a good story that people will want to read."

This is a work of fiction. All the characters are imaginary except for the impressive adult figures of Moses Elias Levy and his son, David Levy Yulee. The facts provided about the lives and accomplishments of these two men are documented in Florida's history.

The character of Eliahu ben Youli is taken from Samuel Romanelli's book, *Travails in an Arab Land*, first published in 1792. Details of life in Morocco in the 1780s and 90s come from many sources but especially from Romanelli's *Travails* and William Lempriere's *A Tour from Gibraltar*, published in 1793.

Many people have contributed information, suggestions, corrections, and support to me in the writing of this novel. First is my husband Roger McIntire. Without his creative comments and encouragement, this novel would have remained unwritten.

Chris Monaco, author of *Moses Levy of Florida*, and Judah Cohen, author of *The Sands of Time – A History of the Jewish Community of St.*

Thomas, Virgin Islands, both were generous in providing authoritative and useful information about the Levy family. I first met Judah in the ancient Jewish cemetery in St. Thomas and will always remember him sitting on a stone bench in the hot sun looking up Moses Levy in his laptop files.

Harry Ezratty, Katina Coulianos and many others helped along the way with facts and insights into Florida, St. Thomas, and Jewish history. Readers Pam McIntire, Lorien Haavik, Pat Groller, Marilyn Magee, Stan Haavik, Larry Haavik, Lucy Steinitz, Judy Rice, Pat Threadingham, Amichai Heppner, and others offered excellent advice. My thanks also go to mystery writer Loree Lough, the UUCC writer's group, the Maryland Writers Association, the White Oak Writers, and the Columbia Fiction Critique Group.

Any errors in this book are entirely my own.

Chapter 1

Off the Coast of Morocco, Africa, 1781

Rachel closed her eyes to enjoy the sea breezes playing with her hair, for once free of hijab. After a moment, she leaned forward on the rail to peer back toward the horizon, squinting to make out the ominous silhouette of a ship's tall sails behind them.

A sailor sauntered across the deck toward the gunwales, passing close to Rachel. "Aye, you're a pretty lass, you are." He winked at her.

Rachel ducked under his attempt to pat her on the head. She lifted her chin. "You may not address me that way," she said. "And don't treat me like a . . . a child."

She was, after all, fifteen years old and almost a woman. Head held high, she raised the hem of her skirt slightly to pick her way across the fittings and lines on the deck to the hatchway. This time, she limped with her left foot turned inward. She hoped that would stop the men on deck from watching her out of the corners of their eyes. She refused to be frightened by their stares.

"Come, Papa," she said to the reed-thin gentleman emerging from the darkness below.

She watched him trip on the simple black djellaba he wore over tan breeches and stockings as he stumbled onto the deck to join her. With one hand he held a black kippah on his head against the following wind that lifted their ship gently over the swells.

Rachel took her father's hand, at once aware of the broad sails soaring over them and the immensity of the sea surrounding them. For a moment, she felt imprisoned by the ship's rigging that enclosed them all in an enormous web spanning the deck to the mast tops. She heard the pigs and chickens snuffling and scratching in their pens behind her, and even here on the open deck she could smell their stench.

She smiled up at her father. "I cannot wait until we reach America, Papa. I want so much to see Esther and Ada." She looked back at the sea, shading her eyes with her hand. "I wish we could have sailed to America with them two years ago."

"You miss them." Moses glanced down at her. "But they are safe enough, although the war drags on."

"America must be a thousand times better than living in Morocco." She pulled a miniature American flag out of her pocket. She had sewn it herself, piecing together thirteen red and white stripes and a blue square with thirteen stars in a circle. She spread the flag out against her dark green skirt and sash.

She noticed another sailor staring at her. She stared back with crossed eyes and stuck her tongue out at him. The sailor turned his attention elsewhere, hiding a laugh. Seeing this, Rachel thought that perhaps she had overdone her gargoyle expression. After all, she wanted to repel, not amuse, the men who found her so interesting.

Rachel peered again at the dark and distant silhouette on the horizon. "There's another ship behind us."

"I've been watching it for some time, and it seems to be gaining on us."

"How can we ever reach America if we are stopped again and again by other ships?"

He shrugged. "We are fortunate, my dear. We've only been delayed for official reasons and by friendly powers. The French and Spanish have no quarrel with America, and we sail on an American ship, although. . . ." He leaned out over the rail to stare back at the ship behind them.

Rachel glanced up at him. "Although what, Papa?"

"Our ship was built to transport goods, not to. . ." He stopped there. His salt-and-pepper beard quivered in the breeze. "Be patient and pray that all ships we see are privateers from friendly nations."

"But, Papa, I wish we were in America now!" She pouted and then leaned out over the rail to take another look at the ship behind them. She knew her father would not speak of his fear. She was old enough to realize that consequences much worse than being late to America could befall them. Her father had told her this trip could be dangerous, with Britain the enemy and American ships so vulnerable now without British protection or a strong navy. Then he'd said, "All of life is a risk, and I would not have succeeded as I have without taking a risk or two."

Rachel stared at the ship behind them. "We passed through the Straits of Gibraltar and left the Mediterranean two days ago," she said. "Surely they will not stop us so far out on the open ocean, Papa. I know we have much to be thankful for, but I will be so relieved to be there and not here."

"And so will I, my dear." Moses adjusted his kippah.

The light winds were a disadvantage to their gargantuan, slow-moving hulk. It creaked and wallowed in lazy rolls while its pursuer sliced the water far off their stern. The wait dragged on. Rachel and Moses stayed at the rail, peering through the haze at the other ship.

At last, the following ship drew close enough so they could distinguish a long, low hull and two masts raked back toward the stern. Captain Moore joined Moses and Rachel at the rail and peered through a spyglass. Rachel heard him growl a string of curses under his breath before turning to bark orders at the first mate. The bosun blew his whistle. At once, the ship crawled with sailors darting from mast to line and back again, all of them urging more speed out of the reluctant sails. Consternation shadowed every face. Rachel felt a quiver of fear as her father pushed her back against the gunwales to keep out of the sailors' way.

Rachel gripped his hand. Even she knew their ship was under-manned. Their captain had been willing to risk all their lives to increase his profits, removing weapons needed for protection on the high seas and filling the space with cargo. But the permissions were so long in coming that once her father had fought his way through that hurdle, he booked passage on the first ship heading for America that presented itself.

"We need to go below." Moses grabbed Rachel's arm and pushed her ahead of him toward the hatchway that led down to their cabins.

Reaching the lower deck, they hunched along under the low ceiling, passing three sailors gulping the last mouthfuls of food out of bowls as they rushed to the top deck. Behind them, the sailors' hammocks swung from the ceiling like white bats.

Rachel's eyes followed the sailors up the steps, at once glad and fearful that they had ignored her. Then her father pulled her through the common quarters that served as dining room, parlor, and barn for the passengers, crew, and an additional lot of pigs and chickens. Rachel could barely see her way. The dark planking on all sides swallowed any daylight eking through the portholes and gun ports. Even the gimbaled lanterns could not dispel the dreariness.

Below this deck lay the cargo, mysterious crates and barrels stowed in long rows running the length of the ship. *That's what they want.* Rachel bit her lip.

As Rachel hurried past the captain's cabin, she heard a scared meow from Jezebel, the ship's cat and vermin-catcher, who crouched under the bunk, staring at her with wide eyes and twitching ears.

A woman flung aside the curtain across the doorway of her cabin and poked her head out to peer over at Rachel and then up at Moses. Her unruly gray hair spread out in all directions like, Rachel almost laughed, a basket of uncombed wool, and she clutched a shawl slung haphazardly across her shoulders.

"I hear such activity above, Mr. Levy," she said. "Is anything amiss?"

The only other passenger on the ship, Annie sat on the edge of her bunk taming her hair with a tortoiseshell comb. She looked inquiringly at Moses as she worked.

"The ship behind continues to approach us, and we fear it is not a friendly one," Rachel blurted.

Annie pressed her lips together as she patted her hair back and covered her head with a bonnet. She smoothed the folds of her skirt. The grim look that crossed her face made Rachel shiver.

Annie peered at Moses out of the corner of her eye as she said to Rachel, "Come here, my dear. Let me arrange your hair."

Rachel sighed, resigning herself to Annie's attempts to show gratitude. Annie was the widow of an old friend and in desperate circumstances. Papa had paid for Annie's passage on this ship so she could rejoin her family in America.

Rachel again heard the bosun's whistle and then feet pounding on the steps up to the top deck. The sailors' hammocks in the bow swung empty. All hands had been rousted and called topside.

Annie gave Rachel's hair a final pat and picked up a scarf to cover it. Rachel pulled away irritably, but her eyes widened when she saw her father's somber expression. "What is it, Papa?"

He did not speak at once, but she saw him clench and unclench his jaw. Rachel felt gooseflesh on her arms.

"I thought that once we passed through the Straits of Gibraltar into the Atlantic, we would leave those murdering thieves behind," Moses said. "I fear that I was wrong."

The vague, undefined dread that had crept through Rachel took shape. She had thought that an unfriendly ship might delay their passage, perhaps steal the freight onboard. She glanced at the heavy trunks stowed under their bunks. Everything she and her father owned was packed in those trunks.

"Are you sure, Papa?"

Her father put an arm around her and drew her to him. "Their boats are distinctive. They would not dare this ocean in them if the wind had been fiercer, but you can see yourself that we barely move with the breeze."

He stroked his beard. "They should wait for dark to sneak aboard." He stopped, and Rachel heard him mutter, "But this ship is not built to fight pirates." His mouth twisted as if he tasted bitter fruit. "And they know that."

Chapter 2

Spain, 1941

Ruth stood in the darkness under the boathouse eaves, her body tense, eyes narrowed into slits, mind willing the boat to appear.

Her journey depended on the darkness of the new moon, but she gazed up at the stars and clamped her lips into a tight, straight line. Tonight the stars beamed on the earth like tiny searchlights across the cloudless sky.

In the distance shallow night sounds—a squawk from a night heron, the drone of a lone car following the coastal road—broke the silence. Ruth listened for the hum of a muffled engine and thought of the rocks and dead trees that could wreck the boat and their mission.

She shivered, hugging the metal case close to her chest as she paced the silent pier. Her walking shoes swished on the planks. The brown suit and hat she wore made her look much older than her nineteen years, but they camouflaged her body in the darkness so her pale face seemed to hover weightless.

Three men sat on the boathouse bench, watching her. They had brought her here and now waited with her, still protectors, still transporters, their eyes focused on the case. The smell of their sweat sharpened her awareness of danger.

Ruth felt the precariousness of her own position. Alone on this pier. The three watching men. What would they do if the boat did not come?

It must come. She had no place to go if it did not. She glanced down at the metal case. She dare not leave it unprotected. For a moment, the responsibility of it seemed too heavy to bear.

Chapter 3

Chesapeake Bay, 1998

Sara Miller stopped her red Civic at a lonely crossroads in southern Maryland and contemplated the weathered sign for a "Bait Shop and Marina." Was this the right place? The sign pointed down a potholed gravel road to the right.

The summer warmth and exotic scent of flowering honeysuckle lured her onto the gravel. The honeysuckle gave way to poplars, their shade encroaching on each side, emphasizing the isolation around her but adding a sense of the mystery she craved. This was so much better than another tedious day in the office.

The woods opened onto a dirt parking lot. Ahead of her stood the marina with bait shop, boat ramp, and three piers extending like fingers over the water.

Sara parked near the ramp and walked toward the piers. She swept back her short, brown hair and paused to stretch, breathing deeply of the sea air, but the humid, muggy air had the smell of rot in it. Sara peered at the debris washed up on shore. Dried seaweed and dead fish.

The morning sun cast brilliant sparkles across the ripples of the wide river before her. The glare blinded Sara for a moment as she strolled onto the pier, passing three old fishermen fussing about in a weathered motorboat.

She gazed east out of the river's mouth to the Chesapeake Bay and felt glad that she'd taken the day off for this little adventure. At twenty-two, she was too young to die of boredom in a dead-end job. But what to do instead? She had to make some sort of decision and move on with her life.

She heard pounding of steps on the pier boards behind her. Then laughter and wisecracks caught her attention. She looked back.

A sunburned man about thirty or so wearing white shorts and an unbuttoned black shirt now leaned against a piling, arms folded, smirking down at the fishermen. It was Tony. Sara felt a rush of excitement and nervously straightened her tee shirt.

"You don't think you're gonna catch anything with those rigs, do you?" he said, grinning.

"More'n you will on your ragboat," one of the fishermen answered, glaring at him from the runabout, his feet squishing water that had seeped through the leaky floorboards.

Sara walked back toward the man leaning against the piling. "I was wondering if you would be here," she said.

He looked at her and grinned. "Well, well, well. Sara, isn't it?" He pushed himself off the piling and walked toward her.

She nodded. He'd remembered her name. "Hi, Tony. I enjoyed talking with you at Barbara's the other night. . . ." She stopped and took a breath to calm and lower her voice. She hoped she didn't sound nervous. "Thought I'd run down here and see your sailboat." He looked much handsomer by daylight.

"Sure." He walked alongside her to the end of the pier where a trim sailboat floated. Its stern was angled their way so she could read the boat's name: *Buccaneer.* Underneath in smaller letters was the homeport: Miami, Florida. *Buccaneer.* Miami. The romance of the words filled her with yearning.

He smiled at her.

Sara smiled back.

"So what do you think of my boat?"

"It's beautiful. You take good care of it." She hoped he'd ask her aboard.

"Yeah. A lot of work but worth it. Looks like you enjoy sailing as much as I do."

Sara hesitated but then admitted, "I've sailed a little."

"I thought so." He folded his arms. "You kinda look like a sailor. You look like you could have been born to it. Like me."

"No, not at all." Sara gazed at the boat. She imagined herself a sailor traveling the world over on just such a boat. A vision of exotic ports flitted through her mind. Now there was adventure for you.

"I've sailed up and down the coast here and all over the Caribbean in my little boat," he said, as if reading her thoughts. "Speaking for myself," he glanced at her, "maybe you too, I couldn't stand to live out my life on land."

The words touched a chord in Sara's soul. He was right. She was too adventurous to live the boring life she'd fallen into. She needed to move on.

He gestured back toward the bait shop. "You here by yourself?"

Sara hesitated, and then sidestepped the question. "Actually, I was looking for a beach, but I remembered you talking about your boat the other night so. . . ."

"How about a sail instead?" he interrupted.

Just what she'd been hoping for. Sara stole a look at him.

"For an hour or two," he added. "I promise, but maybe you're afraid."

The words were a challenge. "Certainly not."

Tony had been a lot of fun at Barbara's the other night. People knew him. He certainly seemed nice enough. Spending this glorious morning sailing on the Chesapeake was just the sort of serendipitous adventure she dreamed of. She barely knew this man, and her mother would be shocked at the idea. Her girlfriends, on the other hand, would be right behind her, pushing her forward. She couldn't say no to this new experience.

He stepped onto the boat. "Come on, we'll have a good time, and I'd like the company. I dropped my Aunt Mae off to buy groceries. She'll be a couple of hours, so I have some time to kill before I have to get back here." He cocked his head and once again smiled at her.

Anyway, he had to get back for his Aunt Mae. "Sure." She jumped onboard.

He caught her hand as if she needed help, then moved his hand up her arm to steady her on the rocking boat.

She smiled back at him, feeling pleased with herself. "It is a beautiful morning," she added, glad she'd taken the day off, glad she'd driven out here to see him.

"Yep, sure is."

She took a deep breath, tottering on the rocking boat, and sneaked a glance from the dock to the river's mouth, gauging its distance. She looked down the pier at the other boaters. The fishermen had finished checking their own gear and were heading out to the bay.

Tony lowered an outboard motor into the water. "Help me get the lines off, will you?" He gestured to the ropes tying the boat to the pier.

Sara sprang forward to obey, hoping she wouldn't do anything stupid. The activity and the bright morning sun chased away a vague sense of misgiving. They'd be out on deck, visible to people on shore and in the other boats. There'd be witnesses if he tried anything. Not that he would, of course.

She sat down. Jumping overboard was always an option too. Her tee shirt and shorts wouldn't be hard to swim in, and sea nettle stings weren't that painful.

Sara watched him press a button to start the outboard. It roared to life. He looked up at her.

"This little motor knows who's boss," he said.

Once away from the pier, Tony turned off the outboard, raised its propeller out of the water, and grinned at her. "Hold the tiller, while I get the sails up."

Sara slid over to the tiller, and in a few moments they were tacking down the river toward the Chesapeake. The soft morning breeze felt exhilarating. She could smell the salt in the air.

"I'll take over now." He ran his hand over hers as he took the tiller.

Sara smiled at him and then looked back at the spreading wake of the boat. Tony sat against the gunwales and squinted up at the sails. Silhouetted against the sun, only his eyes, sparkling like the bay, could be distinguished in the shade under his broad-brimmed hat. Two gold chains gleamed against the dark fur of his chest. The diamond stud he wore in his left ear glinted as he turned his head. He reached over and stroked her hair with one hand and then dropped his hand lightly down the front of her shirt, touching her breasts.

"Nothing like sailing, is there?" he said.

Sara slid away from him, trying to appear casual, but she didn't like the way he touched her. A slight quiver of fear dampened her good spirits. She didn't know this man that well.

He grinned at her and sang, "Yo, ho, ho and a bottle of rum."

Sara winced. "You don't look much like a pirate," she said.

"No? I'll have to work harder."

"Not on my account."

"I can show you my whole bag of," he winked at her, "tricks."

"No thank you." Sara sat up. His cockiness irritated her.

They were drifting—the breeze was light and shifting—through the water toward the bay; but the dock was still clearly visible. In the distance she could see other boats pushing their way through the water on their own pursuits.

Sara noticed Tony throwing calculating looks her way. He didn't seem as nice as he was at Barbara's party. He'd made her laugh with his jokes and she'd liked him. A lot. Now she detected an underlying nastiness. Her stomach turned. She gripped the seat. His gaunt figure against the sun cast sharp shadows across the cockpit, and the gulls circling overhead seemed to be warning her with their cries of "skreak, skreak."

"Do you keep your boat back at the marina we left?" she asked.

"Oh, no, I'm just passing through. I'll get you back there, though. Don't you worry."

Passing through? She'd gotten the impression that he lived here. "How did you meet Barbara?"

Tony's attention was on handling the sails. "Friends of friends."

Sara forced a smile. "You have to pick up your Aunt Mae soon."

"My Aunt Mae?" He laughed and turned his head to look over the bow. Like a nightclub in the harsh morning light, Tony now seemed tawdry, jaded, and no longer fun. Watching him, Sara decided that the diamond in his ear was only a piece of foil-backed glass. Fake.

Like him. Damn it. When would she ever learn? Obviously there was no Aunt Mae. Once again, she'd followed her impulse in a foolish search for some kind of adventure and once again, she was in a dubious situation, but this was worse than getting lost on back roads in her car. Who was this man anyway?

"I see you're from Miami, Florida," she ventured.

"Oh, I am? Where did you see that?" He looked puzzled.

Sara waved at the stern. "On the stern."

"Oh that." He laughed. "Yeah. I thought Miami sounded like a good port to be from."

"You're not really from Miami?"

"Maybe so." He pulled on a rope as Sara saw him study her in the speculative way a wolf watches a lamb.

Sara shivered and thought about all the ways a man could use a rope. She slid closer to a boat hook attached to the cabin and settled back to wait. If they came closer to land, she'd jump overboard.

Sara glanced at her watch. "We've been out here more than an hour. I need to get back."

"Not so soon. We just got out here." Tony steered the boat into the breeze and let the sails luff, then he dropped the mainsail. He sniffed the air. "Maybe the wind'll pick up in a little bit."

Sara turned around to look back at the marina. She could see the piers. Her car sparkled in the sun. "We're in the middle of the river."

"Yeah, but we're not in the channel. I thought I'd anchor here aw-hile and do some fishing. You can fish too, if you'd like."

"I hadn't planned to be out so long . . ."

"We won't be long. I promise. There's my Aunt Mae, you know." He winked at her. It made Sara cringe. She wanted to run. "How about going below and bringing up some beers."

"I don't want anything," Sara said. Nothing to prolong this.

"Yeah, but I do." He was cutting a small fish into strips with a long knife. "Go along now and help me out."

Sara hesitated, not wanting to leave the open deck, but he seemed engrossed in baiting the hook, and she'd be quick. Kitchens, that is, galleys, had knives too. She was probably imagining things anyway. She stepped down into the cabin and opened a small refrigerator. Then the cabin darkened as his bulk blocked the doorway.

Before she could turn around, he leapt into the cabin, pushed her forward against the refrigerator, and pinned her arms against her body.

Chapter 4

Off the Coast of Morocco: 1781

Moses heard their captain's shouted orders and the firing of the small cannon above them. He stepped away from Rachel and began pacing back and forth, head down. Four sailors leapt down the hatchway ladder and pushed the three passengers aside to ready the big cannons. Using heavy ropes and squealing pulleys, the men strained to roll the cannons into place at the gunports.

Moses stood by helplessly, watching Rachel and Annie at the table puttering in a meaningless rearrangement of tin cups and plates, wiping off the scraps of food that were a focus for complaint only an hour before. He noticed Rachel slip a paring knife into her pocket and fear clutched his stomach. Such a pitiful weapon against pirates, but the ship's arsenal was just as pitiful.

"Four big cannons," he muttered to himself. "Two facing out each side of the ship, so only two will be useful. Two small deck cannons above. I wonder how many muskets?" He studied the muskets, bayonets, and pistols as they were hauled out of wooden chests and passed up to the sailors on deck. Most of the weapons were rusted. The gunpowder was probably wet and useless too.

Moses peered out the gun port along a cannon barrel and saw the other ship approaching fast, its cannons—Moses counted five aimed at them—lined up and ready for firing. The pirate ship seemed overloaded with men, all carrying pistols or swords. "We're outnumbered three to one," he muttered to himself.

The sailors pushed Moses aside and began an intricate dance to load the cannon barrels and prepare to fire. He grabbed Rachel and Annie and pulled them back to huddle behind the table and away from the ship's sides. He watched the sailors fire the cannons, one by one, scrambling out of the way as the cannons recoiled. The smoke and acrid smell of gunpowder clouded their quarters, immersing them in a gray fog that stung his eyes, adding the sounds of coughing and choking to the chaos.

Moses' confident manner eroded away. The deck gun fired again at the other ship. He heard a cannon ball crash into their ship's hull near the gun ports. He cringed, then laughed to cover that reaction, reproaching himself for the madness of thinking that in these perilous times, he and Rachel could safely make such a radical change in their lives.

Moving to America was part of the same insanity that had propelled them out of the safe harbors of England to the frustrating maelstrom that was Tangier. Then he had read Tom Paine's pamphlets. Because he revered the American Declaration of Independence and, he forced himself to admit, because he was bored and restless, he had selfishly made the decision that now jeopardized his daughter's life, his own and that of an innocent friend.

Madness.

The shouts around them, the cannon booms, the gunfire, grew louder, more frequent, and more terrifying. The smoke spread out like fog so they caught only glimpses of the frantic crew running up and down in confusion. Moses wrapped his arms around his daughter, and she buried her face in his cloak. He had already dismissed any hope of the crew's fending off the attackers.

"Papa, they are thieves. Will they bargain with us?" Her voice was muffled, but Moses heard the tremor in it.

He hugged her more tightly. "We will give them what we have and tell them we can get more to pay our ransom, if we are," he couldn't help the fear in his own voice, "unharmed." Then he added, "We must remain calm and act," he took a deep breath, "as if we have bank vaults behind us. After all, they are thieves, perhaps they can be bought." It was a small hope but better than none.

"At least," Annie said to no one, touching her bonnet, "pirates won't want me for. . . ." She stopped and changed course. "I have no money." Then she added in weak sarcasm, "I expect they'll make me empty their chamber pots." Her mouth trembled.

"But Papa, can we think of any other way?" Rachel asked, lifting her head. "All we own is in our sea chests, and we must have it for our new life in America."

"America," Annie mumbled. "I would settle for Tangier now."

"Hush," Moses said. "We are not in Tangier, and there will be no new life if we are killed. We must turn to our faith now." He peered through the smoke at their quarters, seeking possible weapons and hiding places.

"I don't see how prayer will help us." Rachel waved her hand impatiently.

"I didn't mean prayer. I meant faith in our own people. The synagogues have treasuries to aid victims of piracy and persecution, and I have contributed many times over the years. They will surely help us."

He could see that this prospect of help on some later day didn't calm Rachel or Annie.

"But I am Christian," Annie said. She paced back and forth, wringing her hands.

"Ah, yes, but you are also American. Do you not think that America, or perhaps your relatives in America, will ransom you?"

"I wouldn't be in this dilemma if I weren't an American on an American ship. Other countries have paid tribute to the kings of these barbaric countries to prevent . . . ." Moses shot her a warning glance. She caught it, looked at Rachel, and concluded in a lower tone, "piracy."

The pirate's ship now lay a hundred yards off their ship. As if to answer Annie's accusation, the pirates fired two more cannon balls at their prey, ripping through the already tattered sails above. Moses could hear the panic of the sailors on deck as they shouted and screamed. Another explosion caused the entire ship to shudder. Water seeped through the planks above them. He turned to the two women. "Quick. Change into your oldest, simplest, most worn clothes. They will strip you of anything finer." He retreated to his own compartment to do the same.

As cannon answered cannon, the blows and recoils of the guns rolled their ship as if it were pushed back and forth by a giant's hand. Cups, plates, and boxes tumbled about, spilling their contents underfoot. Thunderous crashes were followed by the cracks of splitting wood. Water splashed through gaping holes onto the bedding and clothes. Then the attacker's ship closed the last few yards, swept alongside their ship and thudded against the freeboard. With savage yells and whoops, the attackers boarded. The gunfire, the screams, and the pounding feet mixed in a brawling, bloody stew. Scarlet now tinged the water seeping from above.

Feet appeared on the steps as the savages crashed down to confront the passengers.

Moses reached for Rachel and saw her choke back her terror and cringe against a post, her eyes flitting from corner to corner like a panicked bird.

Annie mutttered, "Dear God," as she slumped on her bunk.

Moses faced the rough and filthy men who stank of dirt and sweat and blood. All were shirtless, their breeches bloodied and stained, but each one sported a fancy bit of lace or other adornment. Moses swallowed as he realized the odd bits of finery were souvenirs of past conquests. The pirates waved pistols, axes, and knives, pushing him back. At that moment, despair and terror filled his soul. He could be killed in one rush of blades and tossed aside as they reached for the real treasure, his beloved daughter Rachel.

The pirates hunched under the low ceiling, their swords lifted for the blow that would kill him. Moses shut his eyes and gritted his teeth, preparing to die, when a harsh voice from above the broken hatchway barked a command. The pirates halted. The command was repeated.

Moses opened his eyes to see the pirates fall back a step, and then he was yanked and prodded along with Rachel and Annie toward the ladder to the top deck.

Chapter 5

Spain, 1941

"My brother's late, isn't he?" Ruth said, glancing at the men sitting on the pier.

One of the men nodded. Another spit and said, "He has to go easy, Miss, careful."

Ruth turned back to stare at the sea. If the boat did not come tonight, where could she go? She could not return to the farm with the men.

Did they wonder at all who she was? Did they know anything about this . . . adventure, beyond the limited scope of their role? What were they thinking as they sat there? Ruth studied the metal case, long, narrow, and more likely to hold weeds than roses. Yet it contained a puzzle that even she did not understand.

She heard a murmur behind her, then the low put-put of a distant motor. She peered out along the dark shoreline in the direction of the sound. A black hulk, running lights off, pushed its way through the water towards the pier. Silent ripples lapped the shore behind it. Relief swept over her.

A fishing boat crept into the dock. One man turned the wheel in the cabin while another caught the pier, pulled the boat alongside, and gestured to Ruth to jump aboard. He waved to the farmers in the shadows on the wharf. They stared back, unsmiling.

Ruth snatched her valise in one hand, tucked the metal case under her arm, and jumped onboard, then joined the tall man in the cabin. "Thank goodness you're all right. I was getting worried, Samuel."

"Hid in a creek while a patrol boat passed." He winked at Ruth, then looked at the case and cocked an eyebrow. She nodded in response as she set the valise on the deck and turned to watch the other man push the boat away from the pier. He then took his seat in the cockpit as he waved at Samuel to move forward.

Chapter 6

Chesapeake, 1998

Sara ripped out of the man's grip and reached into the refrigerator for a beer bottle to use as a weapon, but he jerked her away.

"I thought of something I'd rather have," he said.

"Get off me!" She struggled to push his arms away.

"Nah. You know you want this." He dragged her towards one of the bunks. She reached for a cabinet handle, yelling for help but knowing no one would hear her.

He was all arms, and they were as tough as anchor chain. They squeezed her body like a python as he dragged her backwards to the bunk. He wrenched her right arm back, close to breaking it. Then he wrung it tight when she kicked at him. She could taste his sweat and the smell of it sharpened her fear.

Sara let her body go limp, hoping he would loosen his grip, but that made it easier for him to push her forward toward the bunk. She slammed her head back into his face but missed. He twisted her around and pushed her onto the settee, using his body to pin her there like a bug skewered to a board. The settee covers smelled fresh and clean against the stink of his sweat. He clawed at her body, tearing her tee shirt, and then tugged at her cut-offs.

His weight left her struggling to breathe. She felt him spread her legs and settle himself between them. Her kicks hit only the bunk and the air. Bending one of her arms backward, he used his other arm to push his shorts down. She screamed for help in terror but knew the screams were futile and only fed his violence.

As his paws tugged at her clothes, she freed one arm and stretched it out behind her to the galley countertop. Her fingers ran across the varnished wood, feeling for a weapon, and fumbled on a corkscrew. She seized it and, without a second's thought, stabbed her attacker in the back. He shrieked with pain, and as he rolled off her in agony, she stabbed him again, aiming for his neck, then she kneed him. Blood spurted into her eyes, turning the cabin red.

She leapt off the bunk, eluding his hand as it grabbed for her, and ran up the steps. She slipped and fell forward into the cockpit. She didn't stop to see if the brute was behind her, but in one fluid motion, pulled up her cut-offs, grabbed her purse, jumped over the side, and began the long swim toward shore and the green haven beyond it.

Her strokes were shaky at first as she fought off the terror. The saltwater stung in her eyes. She could see the sycamores and oaks and poplars on shore, but even though they waved their branches at her like friends, they shrank into the distance as she swam toward them. Risking a look back at the boat, she saw with relief that her attacker was not on deck. She clamped down hard on her feelings and put her energy into swimming. The water felt cold but cleansing. The purse, now saturated and heavy, dragged her down. She fished out her car keys and let the purse sink to the bottom.

She concentrated on her strokes, counting them to keep her mind occupied. She could feel the panic, knew it could overwhelm and incapacitate her, struggled to keep it at bay. As she swam, her eyes filled with tears. She tasted the salt of them as they mingled with the water of the river. Sara knew she wasn't a powerful swimmer, but she could last a long time with sidestrokes and long glides. If she kept from panicking, she ought to make it to shore, but the trees that waved at her were still far away.

Pausing to raise her head, she glanced back at the sailboat. It remained where it was, bobbing peacefully. When she searched the shoreline far ahead, she could just make out the piers and her car down the beach to her left. She swam toward the closest point of land. She would feel safer in shallow water where a sailboat could not venture. Once near shore, she could wade up to the beach and walk the shoreline around to her car.

How long had she been swimming? Her arms, clogged with fatigue, moved like pistons. Sara felt as if she had spent an eternity in this surreal world where she never moved forward and the trees never got closer. When she tired, she paused and floated for a moment, listening for the sound of a boat motor but hearing none. Her body was covered with the stings of sea nettles—she could not avoid them. As she neared the shore, she swam into a crabber's pot lines and hung onto the floats, treading water to rest.

At last she felt mud and seaweed under her feet. Then she touched the bottom. She stood up and waded along the shoreline toward the piers and her car. Her clothes clung oddly to her body. Two young boys on a pier stopped dipping their crab nets to stare at her.

As Sara staggered to the marina, she noticed that none of the fishermen had returned, and the dock attendant was occupied inside the marina office. She trudged along the shore to the boat ramp and then dragged herself up the ramp to her car.

She took one last look at the bay, blue and serene in the sunlight. Sails dotted the water here and there, but the *Buccaneer* still floated tranquilly. Alone, off the channel, and seemingly innocent.

Sara brushed her hair out of her eyes and shook her head. How badly had she hurt him? Had she killed him?

She opened the car door, slid behind the wheel and locked the door. Despite the warm day, Sara kept the car windows closed while she sat in the heat and shivered. When the shadows of the nearby sycamores crept across her car, she started the motor and stole back to Martinsburg and the quiet safety of her apartment.

That night, Sara showered five times. She made the water as hot as she could stand, but it was not hot enough. She rubbed herself dry at last, but she did not feel clean and lurking under the fear was the terrible question. Had she killed him?

Chapter 7

Off the Coast of Morocco, 1781

Moses squeezed Rachel's hand as the pirates prodded the three captives toward the ladder. He attempted a reassuring smile at Annie, who clung to Rachel, sagging and terrified.

As they climbed the ladder to the upper deck, Moses turned back to whisper, "They are pirates and thieves but think of them as businessmen. They want money. We can bargain." He drew a deep breath and pulled himself together to appear calm and strong and was gratified to see Rachel do the same.

They emerged on deck, pausing at the hatchway to peer through the smoke of gunpowder. The smell of blood, urine, and sweat assailed Moses. Annie covered her nose and mouth with her shawl. Rachel retched and threw up onto the deck. Moses put his arm around her and held his other sleeve in front of his mouth. If only he could have spared her this horror.

A swarthy man sat on the gunwale, peering at them through black, bushy eyebrows, a sword resting on his knees. He fondled an ornate silver pistol set with pink coral cabochons and spat over the side as he silently regarded them with one eye. The other eye had crusted shut with dried mucous, and scabs covered the thick muscles on his arms. He wore a blue sash around his waist and on his head the frayed and soiled hat of a French naval officer.

The man pointed a bony finger at them and gestured for them to come forward. They struggled toward him trying not to slip in the blood and bits of flesh that splattered the deck.

The captain of their ship, usually so proud and arrogant, had been pushed to his knees and knelt on the deck, pleading for his life. His eyes turned to Moses and silently begged him for help, but Moses could only stand by as one of the filthy thugs hacked the captain's arms at the elbows and then silenced his screams by running him through the heart. Moses shielded Rachel as much as he could, but his thoughts turned to the miserable four cannons and rusted guns.

Another sailor, whose mutilated body lay at their feet, left a bloody trail as he was dragged to the gunwale and thrown overboard. His body floated in a crimson sea. A third sailor was nailed to the deck—his body impaled on a marlinspike.

The rest of the defeated crew, men Moses recognized from his walks around the deck, cringed in the midst of the carnage. None of them moved. They all stared down at the deck, shrinking in their bodies as if to become invisible. Moses could smell their fear.

The women also shrank into meek ghosts as they hid behind Moses. He looked at Rachel as she gestured to the paring knife hidden in her pocket. He shook his head—any attempt to use it would be suicidal.

Moses studied the repulsive beast who confronted them from his seat on the gunwale. He must be the leader of this band of scoundrels. He aimed his pistol at Moses, then lowered it and stood to survey his captives like a shepherd counting his sheep. His spare body leaned toward them, and he growled in an odd mixture of Spanish and Arabic. Moses understood some of the words but could not shield the women from the malevolent, gloating tone.

Moses looked over at the other pirates, a ragged assortment of men whose skin ranged from dark tan to mahogany. He shook his head at the irony. Ferdinand and Isabella had forced the Moorish ancestors of these men, like his own, out of Spain and confiscated their property and possessions. These men had turned to piracy to survive.

The brutish man stretched a large and filthy hand toward Rachel and moved it in an outline of her body. She shivered.

Moses protested, "Keep your hands away from . . . ." He got no further as the pirate's other hand caught Moses in the face and felled him to the deck.

"Kill him," the pirate captain said. Another pirate stepped forward, sword in hand. Rachel threw herself on her father and looked up at the pirate captain. "Money! We have money!" she cried. The savage hesitated, waiting for his captain's word.

"We have friends with money to help victims of pirates," she stammered, parroting her father's earlier words.

The pirate sneered at her. "You dare speak to me? Maybe I take back only your head!" He grabbed her arm and pulled her toward him.

Moses knew that Rachel did not understand the pirate. "She meant no insult, she is only a child," he blurted in Spanish, sputtering blood from the blow to his mouth.

The captain turned on him and snatched him halfway to his feet. "You have money? Here?"

"A little. But we can get more. A fine ransom."

The captain dropped Moses to the deck. And then leering at Annie, he said, "I think we have a little fun with this one first. Then we take what they have with them and later, maybe our king or his sons will reward us, before he takes the rest of this fool's money."

The captain's men laughed and one snatched at the worn and faded djellaba Rachel wore. The captain knocked him to the deck. "Leave her alone. We can sell this beauty for a princely sum. Even the king and his sons would find this one a prize if she is untouched. Otherwise, we will get next to nothing and may lose our heads as well."

"Take them below, but you," he growled in English, pointing to Annie, "you stay." Annie choked a whimpering noise as Rachel and her father were pushed back down the steps. Her father fell to the planks and lay there half sitting. Rachel sank to her knees beside him.

A pirate followed them down and sat on a barrel, watching them. Moses gave him a fleeting glance as Rachel examined his wounds with anxious eyes.

"Papa, are you all right? I did not understand what they said. They almost killed you."

"You were quick to think of the money—you saved my life."

"But why did he stop that man from hurting me? What will happen to Annie?"

"Hush. We can only wait."

"Wait? He may kill her. He may . . . oh, no, we must do something." Her eyes darted around the room. "Why did he put both of us back down here?"

"He's . . . he's saving us." Moses slumped over and reached for Rachel's hand. "I told you. He may be a thief, but he is also a businessman. He means to profit from us." He watched her as she thought about this.

She gazed down at him. "You mean the money and the ransom." The words were innocent, but Moses saw the fear growing on her face. She was young, but he knew she had seen the sailors' interest and the pirates' lustful glances at her.

"Yes, that too." He spoke slowly as he sought to choose his words.

"What do you mean? What else can it be?" He knew that she demanded the truth from him.

Moses looked at her a long moment. What should he tell her? Words that no father should have to say, that no woman should have to hear, but she must be prepared for what Moses now feared was all too inevitable. He shook his head.

"You, my dear." Moses sighed.

"Oh no," Rachel whispered. Her hand flew to her heart. She sat next to her father.

And because he could think of no way to say it that would soften the tragic truth, Moses put his arm around her and took her hand in his. He said it plainly. "He plans, I think, to sell you . . . to some wealthy man in Morocco, possibly to the king or one of his sons."

Chapter 8

Spain, 1941

The three men on the pier had already disappeared into the darkness. Ruth heard them start the truck and turn it around to head back the way they'd come. A smile of relief flitted across her face. That part of her journey was over. She turned towards Samuel.

His tall body was hunched over the wheel in the narrow confines and low overhead of the cabin. He shoved the gear into reverse to ease the boat away from the pier and then into forward, peering out at the dark water as he steered the boat away from the shallow water and hazards along the shore.

Ruth patted his arm with affection, but his grim expression didn't change. He seemed so much older now and tired. Their efforts were no longer a lark for either of them.

"It's more and more difficult to travel anywhere in Europe," she said. "Who are friends? Who are enemies? And how can we know for sure?" For a few moments on the pier, her fear that Samuel had been caught—or worse—had almost overwhelmed her.

Samuel glanced at her. "You are a fool to trust anyone."

Ruth watched him pull a handkerchief out of his back pocket and wipe his face. The grimy pants and shirt he wore made him look like a young Spanish farmer. He tucked the handkerchief back into his pocket. "You should go home. This work is too dangerous."

Ruth did not respond. He had no right to order her around, even if he was two years older, and she was too tense to start an argument. She was quite old enough to make her own decisions and just as intelligent and capable as he was. He was like their parents, wanting to keep her protected and safe at home. She would have laughed if the situation weren't so grim. Whatever happened, she would not go home. She would not be the kind of silly, frivolous woman they wanted her to be.

Chapter 9

Martinsburg, West Virginia, 1998

Sara did not go to work the next day or the next. She couldn't sleep and spent most of the time watching television in her apartment, but she couldn't remember what she had watched. When she thought of her trip to the Chesapeake, her fingers trembled and she felt queasy.

She was right to protect herself against that attack, but surely a corkscrew couldn't actually kill a man. Sara scrutinized the Maryland newspapers every morning for days after the attack but saw no mention of a dead or wounded body found on a small sailboat.

She could not make herself report the attack. She had escaped without injury except to her pride and self-esteem. What if she had killed him? Would they arrest her for murder? Would those fishermen remember her or her car? She left him free to attack someone else, but maybe he had learned a lesson. If he was still alive. She shivered.

Probably nothing much could be done even if she did report the incident. It was her word against his. And then everyone would want to know the details. She would end up appearing foolish and having to listen to everyone's opinion about it.

All rationalizations. Sara knew it, but as much as she tried to forget the trip on the bay and deny the attack, the memory stalked her, shadowing her with nightmares, self-doubts, recriminations—and a cold, unrelenting anger.

She returned to work but spent joyless weekends at home rather than attempt the adventurous outings she used to enjoy. Her smile disappeared. She felt as if two people hid in her body—one an automaton that walked through the day performing as expected; the other a seething cauldron of anxiety and anger.

One day she asked Barbara, the paralegal in the office, how she had met Tony.

"Handsome, isn't he?" Barbara said. "I forget who invited him along, but he sure was a lot of fun. Seemed like a nice guy."

Sara bought a small Beretta handgun and kept it in her purse. Occasionally, she'd drive out of town and practice shooting at tin cans on a fence. She signed up for a self-defense course in martial arts.

At first, Barbara and Shana and other staff in the office would catch her in the hall or the restroom, and they all asked the same question. "What's wrong, Sara? You used to run ahead of the rest of us. You seem so depressed. There's no spirit there anymore."

Sara had no answer for them. Anyway, as long as she did her work, the job was secure. Unchallenging and oppressive and safe, but better than being terrified on a sailboat. For now, anyway.

Her mother, Amelia, told Sara to "buck up" but never stayed around to sympathize or ask questions. For that Sara was grateful. She had never felt comfortable enough with her mother to confide in her. They saw things too differently. Her mother would be horrified.

Grandma Ruth had always been more perceptive and understanding. A spark in both of them connected, but Sara could not bring herself to share her ugly secret, even with her grandmother.

Whenever Sara thought of the assault, she felt ashamed. *How could I have been so stupid? And now I may be a murderer.* Terror dogged her, gnawing away in her stomach. Still she smiled and tried to appear normal as she deflected her grandmother's concern.

"Sara, something's wrong. How can I help?"

As the months passed. Sara's life took on a boring sameness as she coped alone with the assault and possible murder. Even her high school sweetheart Peter was back in her life. She'd left him behind when she went to college, but somehow they had found each other again a couple of months ago. Sara needed the quiet evenings she spent with Peter.

She grimaced. They certainly were quiet, all right. The word "boring" flitted through her mind. She usually made dinner, and he usually brought videos to watch. She supposed marriage was like that. Certainly her parents' relationship had settled into a routine of dinner and TV . She shouldn't expect more than a safe harbor, a loving man. Should she?

Love. Sara shrugged, thinking of her date that night. Another quiet evening spent with Peter. Sara fidgeted with the buttons on her blouse as she waited for him. She had stopped at the cemetery on her way home from work, soaking in the peacefulness at her father's gravesite, and the pall of somber thoughts still hung over her. When she got home, she showered, but the water felt as if it were beating down on her. She selected beige slacks and white blouse to wear. Peter had promised to take her out to dinner tonight for a change.

Barbara at work had asked her about him that afternoon and showed her enviousness by adding, "When's the big date, Sara?"

Sara knew Barbara thought Peter was quite good-looking and nice. Sara supposed he was and buried her growing impatience. What did she want in a companion? Was she expecting too much? Peter refused to run with her after work. He refused to go to the gym. He didn't like traveling and ridiculed the whimsical weekend trips she used to enjoy, but he had always been around. He was familiar, and now he seemed like a bastion of safety as well.

Sara felt numb inside, but she tried to please him. She stuck through ball games in the hot sun and hid her boredom; joined in on his office picnics and smiled until it hurt; went to church with him and buried her impatience. Nothing she did was true to the Sara she used to be, but that Sara made stupid decisions and may have killed someone.

She heard Peter's heavy shoes stomping up the stairs and opened the door.

Peter stepped in, carrying a bouquet of yellow roses, but his smile turned to a frown as his eyes swept over her. "I thought maybe, just this once, you'd wear something a little, uh, sexy, maybe."

She looked at him in surprise. "I'm not wearing jeans."

"Please, wear something pretty tonight, will you?" He handed her the roses with a smile.

Sara took them with a slow dread. He'd never given her flowers before. Her stomach hurt. She did not want to deal with whatever this meant. "My clothes are fine, and they're what I'm going to wear."

"I thought we'd go someplace nice for a change." He grinned at her. "Tonight."

"These are fine for wherever." She made her tone indifferent. She walked to the door.

"But. . ."

Sara was already out the door. Peter followed.

Peter drove to a candlelit restaurant in downtown Martinsburg where a table in a secluded nook had been reserved for them. Sara looked at Peter and thought of corrals and cages.

"We've known each other a long time and been back together again now for several months," he began. He covered her hands with his.

She stared at the tablecloth. She did not want to look at Peter. Her mind ran in circles chanting safety, security, a loving man.

"So what do you think?"

Sara could find nothing to say. Her eyes darted around the room as if seeking escape.

"It's time for both of us." He pulled out a small black box with silver trim. "I thought you would like this." He offered it to her.

Sara dropped her napkin and reached down to retrieve it. Peter set the box on the table and opened it in front of her. The ring's solitaire diamond beamed its message.

"House in the suburbs," she said. Her stomach ached and now her head hurt. She glanced at Peter's open, eager face. She felt like a fraud as she grappled with the fear and guilt that now controlled her and nodded.

He smiled. "I knew you'd say yes."

This was all wrong. She couldn't do this. It wasn't fair to Peter or to herself. Sara let Peter slip the ring on her finger while her head buzzed with conflict. Her heart sank as she saw Peter's beaming face.

The next morning she drove to work, looking east into the bright, early morning sun. The glare reminded her of sparkles on the waters of the Chesapeake. Her hands began to tremble and her heart to race. She felt nauseated and dizzy. She pulled over to the side and stumbled out of the car. Feeling as if her mind were floating away, she raised her hands to her head, knowing that somehow she had to hold her head together or her brain would evaporate, and she would lose whoever she was. The feeling terrified her. She had to run. She trotted along the road, away from the harsh glare of the sun, to distract herself from the panic.

In the days after that first panic attack, Sara tested herself cautiously, experimenting with short trips at various times of day. Early morning trips facing the sun most often triggered the suffocating shortness of breath, racing heart, dizziness, upset stomach. She changed the route she drove to work, but she could not explain the panic and chose to deny and ignore it.

She could not deny the recurring nightmares and the vague, undefined fear that forced her awake each morning and propelled her joylessly to work. Her job was as stifling as ever. She was officially engaged but could not name a date or visualize a life with Peter. She felt paralyzed with fear and indecision.

Each day, she felt as if she could not stop the force that lifted her feet one by one to trudge farther down a path that would kill her.

Chapter 10

Off the coast of Morocco, 1781

Rachel stood as if her body had turned to stone. The vague hints that she had not grasped suddenly became harsh reality. Her head buzzed with the effort to reject her father's ugly words. The pirates would sell her like a. . . .a head of cabbage?

Her father patted her hands and held her tightly. Her legs were too weak to hold her, and she sank to the floor. Finally, she whispered, "But I am a Jew."

Moses sat down with her, his arms still around her.

"Yes, my dear." His voice broke. "But whoever might buy you, Muslim or Christian, will force you to convert."

"I will refuse."

"You must do as they say. They will be more powerful than you. Your refusal will give them reason to punish you, and their punishment will be harsh. You must survive, and we must find a way out of this."

What would they do with Papa? She swallowed. "They can't do this to us, Papa, they can't."

Moses squeezed her. He shook his head.

A new thought occurred to her. "I will never see Esther and Ada again, will I?"

Her father did not respond, which was even more frightening.

"I was so looking forward to America, Papa," Rachel said through her tears. "Everything had seemed bright and beautiful when I thought of our future there. Now I am afraid, and I see no future."

"We will find our way out of this nightmare," Moses said, but Rachel saw the pity in his eyes. "Do not give up hope."

"I won't, Papa, but I will resist, and it will not be easy for them."

After a long pause, Rachel said, "What will happen to Annie?"

"Annie is older. She has been, ah, Annie has been married, so she's not . . ."

"A virgin?" Rachel said outright, ignoring her father's surprise. "Annie is not a virgin, so she is up there, and I'm down here because he's saving me to sell to some man as a . . . a virgin. He plans to sell me! Me!" Rachel repeated the words in disbelief. "It's impossible!"

"I know, my lovely little girl. And the pirates believe that I will bring in much money for a ransom, and perhaps the Americans will ransom Annie so once we get to a port, she will be imprisoned until money is paid for her release."

"Oh, Papa." Rachel's sigh was heavy with tragedy. "Is there nothing we can do?"

Her father, usually so competent, so in control, only shook his head. "I don't know," he said. "I wanted so much more for you than an arranged marriage, the kind of marriage expected of our family as Jews in Morocco. I wanted you to be happy and not just a pawn in my business relations. Now even that kind of marriage looks better than. . ." He stopped.

Rachel stared at the floor, struggling to control her tears and her fear. She frowned at the trunk under her bunk. It contained no jewels, no silver, no gold, only the necessities for living in a new country.

Moses squeezed her hand. Rachel could feel his despair.

She heard the pirates on deck toss the bloodied, dead bodies overboard, and then their shouts as they began scouring the ship for everything of value.

She thought of the ship's crew. The pitiful men who had survived the brief losing battle would no doubt be searched and stripped. Then they would be left with rags to wrap themselves, destined to be sold as slaves if they remained healthy, to be killed if they did not. She glanced at their guard who sat watching them, licking his lips as his eyes strayed frequently toward the noises overhead.

Rachel reared back as two of the thugs, half-jumping, half-running, rushed down the ladder, flicking their eyes like rattlesnake tongues at her and Papa. She watched the pirates ransack the staterooms, passing their trinkets, coins, belts, purses, pistols, knives, and anything of value up to those on deck.

The trunks under the beds were hauled out. Rachel and Moses gripped each other's hands as the pirates pawed clothes and books with dirty fingers. They filled their pockets and then closed the trunks and hauled them up the ladder.

Their guard gazed enviously at his comrades. He called over to them, begging for a replacement, but they ignored his pleas while taking every cent and every trinket. Rachel and Moses wore ragged, faded burnooses over ragged underclothes, but the pirates tore off the burnooses, snorted in disgust at the rags, then went for the trunks, ripping out the linings of the finer clothes and laughing as they removed and counted the coins stitched there.

"You're getting nothing," Rachel said to their guard. He scowled at her. "Tell him, Papa. They will take everything; he will get nothing. Tell him, Papa."

Moses relayed in Spanish what Rachel said.

"Tell him we have money, we can get money. Tell him Annie is an American and has money, tell him she can get money, too, if she is not harmed."

Moses chattered on, interpreting all of Rachel's half-lies for the miserable man.

Their guard looked up the ladder. Rachel could see he was anxious to get his share. She pressed on. "He could tell the captain about Annie's ransom. The captain would be pleased and would let him go up to join the others. Tell him, Papa, hurry!"

Moses continued to interpret, and the man moved to the ladder and yelled. No one came or answered.

"Tell him again, Papa, tell him about Annie's money and what is in the pile up there."

Moses went on, embellishing Rachel's story, and the man stepped halfway up the ladder and yelled. When he yelled again, the captain's voice yelled back at him in a Berber dialect.

"You'll get your share," the captain said.

"But the old woman, she's worth something too, they said."

"She may bring something at the slave market. We will see what we can get."

"No, no, they say she has money, others will pay for her."

"Money? She doesn't look rich. They're lying, just to save her scrawny neck."

"She's an American. She could have friends with money."

"Take her below, I'm through with her anyway."

Moses stood near the ladder. He interpreted this exchange for Rachel as she tugged at his torn burnoose. "I think he's going to bring Annie down. I . . . I think she's ill."

A guard appeared holding Annie at the open hatch. As he pushed her down the steps, Rachel and her father rushed to catch her. The guard laughed as all three fell in a heap on the planks.

Rachel hugged her, feeling her pain and terror. "Oh, Annie, how awful for you. They are horrible. Did they . . . hurt you? What can I do?"

Annie sat, stunned and silent. She didn't look at them but drew the rags that now were all that remained of her clothes, tightly around her as if to protect her soul. Rachel folded Annie into her arms to quiet her shivering. Annie gripped Rachel's arms and lifted her tear-stained face to Moses, but her eyes remained closed. She moaned softly to herself, as if she were keening the death of a loved one. Moses came forward and patted her on the back as Rachel rocked her back and forth, cooing to her.

As Annie's shivering quieted, Rachel looked up at Moses. "What will happen now, Papa?"

Moses held a finger to his lips. They listened as the noises above took on a steady rhythm. "They are consumed by their search," he said. "They have no interest in us."

The three captives sat quietly, arms around each other as if to form a barrier against the pirates. Finally Annie whispered in a grim attempt at humor, "I guess I was wrong about the chamber pots. This old gray head made no difference."

She put aside Rachel's hands and, pulling herself up with the post, she rose, with Rachel's help, to her feet. Then she took Moses' hand and Rachel's, and all three stood in solidarity.

Rachel considered how they might help themselves. She watched her father study every detail of their plundered quarters as he searched for any vulnerable avenue for escape or negotiation.

Moses walked to the ladder and stared up through the hatch. "The pirates understand my Spanish, and I know something of their customs. I could bargain with them, if there was anything to bargain with, but so far, only money seems to provoke a reaction, and they have stolen all that we possess."

Rachel saw him cast his eyes at her and bite his lip. She sensed how powerless he must feel. He could not save her from the pirates, and they would not stay away from her for long. She faced a grim future. Her legs felt as if they would collapse under her with the terror. With all the strength she could muster, she quelled the terror by considering strategies for escape. She would not be able to turn to Papa or even Annie. She would probably be taken from them. She must not expect help from anyone. Escape from whatever fate the pirates planned for her would depend on her own resources.

She looked at the devastation around her. Ripped bedding lay strewn across the floor along with fragments of cups and plates. Cannon balls had crashed through the planking, leaving sharp pieces of wood protruding into the room and gaping cracks in the side.

Moses turned to Rachel and gestured toward the holes. "We certainly have more air and light down here now." He laughed with a grim face.

Rachel nodded. "And fortunately, the seas are calm or we would be drinking seawater." The pirates had made no attempt to repair the cracks in the hull.

Rachel stumbled across the debris to peer through the gaps. She watched as the pirate captain and most of the men scrambled over to their own ship and released the ropes that kept the two hulks together. As the boats drifted apart, the remaining pirates set the old ship's sails to follow their captain.

For the prisoners, the view became only glimpses of open sea.

Chapter 11

Spain, 1941

As Samuel steered the boat down the Spanish coastline, Ruth peered into the dark night, noting lights twinkling here and there, like flashlights, and the solid black blot of the land that distinguished it from the gray rippling water. She turned her head to stare out at the sea where the faint running lights of distant ships revealed their presence. Squinting, she could make out the specters of other small boats running without lights and wondered if their errands were anything like hers. She raised a settee cushion, set the metal case in the hold underneath, covered it, then lay down to fall asleep.

The trip to La Linea took two days and nights. They hugged the coast, and the two men took turns at the helm. Ruth joined them in scanning for patrols or other trouble, but they were lucky and arrived without mishap at dawn in Spanish waters near Gibraltar. Samuel dropped the anchor.

Ruth picked up her precious case and the valise. She looked at Samuel. "So you leave tomorrow for Marseille. Let me know when you're ready to return."

"Of course. The usual signal."

She sighed. "We can't make many more of these trips. We push our luck every day we remain in Europe."

"There's too much to do. I've got to keep working as long as I can."

"And I have to take care of this," Ruth picked up the case, "then I'll be ready for the next trip." She pushed back the growing fear that she would never be back and there would be no "next trip."

Chapter 12

Martinsburg, West Virginia, 1999

Sara stepped through the days like an irritable sleepwalker. She could not reconcile herself to the idea of marriage and yet she continued the relationship with Peter. Her job bored her, but she showed up each day. Panic attacks plagued her, yet she refused counseling.

Months passed but then a tragedy struck that changed everything. Amelia called Sara at work, an event so unusual that Sara answered the phone with trepidation.

"I'm at the hospital," Amelia said. "I have terrible news."

Sara gripped the phone. "Are you all right?"

"Grandma Ruth was hit by a car this afternoon. She died on the way to the hospital." Amelia spoke the terrible words quietly and without tears, but Sara could hear the sad disbelief behind them. She couldn't quite grasp them herself. Grandma was dead?

"They've called for transport to a funeral home." Amelia stopped with a sob. Then she said, "Can you call your brother? I'd like us to be together tonight."

Sara shook herself. "Yes, Mom. And then I'll get to the hospital as fast as I can."

"Thank you, dear."

Sara hung up the phone, still in disbelief. She called her brother who was as shocked as she was.

"How's Mom?" he asked first. "Can you pick her up at the hospital? I'll be home for dinner."

"I'll bring Mom home," said Sara. "It's Friday, you know."

As Sara drove to the hospital, she remembered a thousand little contradictions about her grandmother, puzzling things since they sprang from a woman who had no past. Really. She seemed to have appeared out of nowhere to marry Sara's grandfather.

Ruth presented to the world a hard, solitary shell, but Sara remembered how Grandma had dried her tears, given her treats, and kissed her forehead time and again.

Her mother was not at all like Grandma. Amelia was more like a vanilla pudding, seeking only to keep things peaceful and pleasant at home, ignoring anger and strife and confrontation.

Sara looked at herself. How had she handled the attempted rape? With passive denial . . . just like her mother would. The realization scared Sara. She wasn't like either her mother or her grandmother. They wallowed in the ordinary as if there were no mysteries, no universes, no dark continents.

Sara sighed. Thank goodness she had told no one that she could be so stupid as to go out on a sailboat with a man she knew nothing about. And, anyway, it happened more than a year ago.

She was beyond all that now.

As she drove her mother home from the hospital, Sara considered all the things she did not know about her grandmother. Grandma had lived a long life, but for what? She had no friends, no accomplishments, only her family. Now her life was gone, and no one knew anything about her and how she had ended up married to their grandfather.

Sara glanced over at Amelia, took a deep breath, and asked a question that had lurked in her subconscious for years.

"Remember that day we got lost on a trip," Sara began, "and Dad stopped to ask a police officer for directions?"

Amelia sat up, startled. "That was a long time ago."

"Why was Grandma so upset about that? We hadn't done anything wrong." It had all seemed innocent enough to Sara, but her grandmother had begged Dad to drive on in a voice too bitter and angry to ignore. That experience was so odd that it remained in Sara's mind as the essence of her grandmother.

If only Grandma could have channeled that anger into something constructive. Helping the underprivileged, for instance. Or fighting for justice. Activities that meant something. Instead she had remained a homebody, touching no one. *Except me.* Sara knew her grandmother had some kind of secret, but what could it be?

Amelia had no answers. "She told us that she wanted to look forward, not back, but," Sara's mother added firmly, "she was a normal person and lived a normal life. There's no mystery. She just didn't want to talk about her early life or her family."

"But how did she meet Grandpa?"

"You know he was in the military. You've heard the story before. They met in Europe right after the war."

"What was Grandma doing there?" asked Sara.

"I don't know. Helping out somehow, I guess. They met, got married, and moved to Martinsburg. Your grandfather needed the VA medical services here, and they just stayed. That's all there is to know, Sara."

"But haven't you ever wondered. . .?"

"No." Amelia was quite firm. Sara glanced at her and saw that her mother had clamped her lips shut. What was her mother thinking?

Finally Amelia said, "There isn't anything else, Sara. I know you always had a vivid imagination, but this is real life. People are ordinary."

They walked into the house and Amelia pulled an apron off a hook and tied it around her waist. She looked like the Betty Crocker on a box of cake mix. Nobody wore aprons nowadays. Home-spun West Virginia. *Home and family works for Mom, but it's not for me. Not with Peter.*

Amelia took a roast chicken out of the oven and piled broccoli into a pot. Sara began peeling potatoes. She risked another question.

"What about her family? Shouldn't we contact them about. . . ." Suddenly Sara couldn't speak.

Her mother put an arm around Sara and hugged her. "We'll miss her, won't we?" She went back to the stove. "She mentioned once, a long time ago, that she had a brother who was killed in the war." Sara heard her mother's voice break.

Amelia turned around, threw down a potholder and sat at the kitchen table. "I don't feel much like cooking, but I had begun all this for tonight. I was hoping your brother would come by."

"He will, Mom," said Sara. "We need to be together tonight." The roasting chicken smelled delicious. Her mother must feel so sad and here she was, cooking dinner anyway.

"Could Grandma's brother have lived after all? Could he have just been injured?" Sara watched her mother, again searching for evasion.

Amelia shook her head. "If that's so, I never heard anything to suggest it."

Sara could detect nothing but honest puzzlement and sadness in her mother's expression.

Amelia shrugged. "She was a loving, ordinary person. Just like you and Dave and Peter. Where is Peter anyway?"

Sara gave up. Trying to get anything but the most obvious out of her mother was impossible. Still, it must have been hard growing up in such a strange household. Her grandparents were loving, but they were also grim. They seemed to be practical and down to earth, but there was always something else, something they weren't saying.

"Where is Peter, honey?" her mother repeated.

"I don't know," Sara said. The response was automatic. "Busy, I think."

She remembered the time her older brother Dave rescued her from two bullies down the street—even though it cost him a bloody nose. Her grandmother must have loved and missed her own brother. Why hadn't she ever mentioned him?

Sara surveyed the simple dishes and the familiar blue tablecloth and felt overcome again with sadness. Warm memories of her grandmother and grandfather, Mom and Dad, flooded her mind. Suddenly she found it hard to breathe. She dreaded another panic attack. She closed her eyes and willed herself to be calm. When she opened her eyes, she took a moment to stare out the window and breathe normally.

The attack passed. She heard the front door open and Dave's usual call, but it was somber tonight, "Mom, I'm home."

He stomped into the kitchen in the heavy farm boots he wore when he was drawing on his West Virginia roots. Most of the time he sold insurance in a conservative suit and Rockports. Sara wished she could reach out and make his life better for him, but she didn't even like her own job.

Dave walked over to his mother and hugged her. He seemed embarrassed, perhaps by the emotion that hung in the air. "I'm so sorry about Grandma. I'll miss her a lot." He poured himself a glass of wine and looked at Sara. "How's Peter?"

"Okay." She waved at his jeans and boots. "Did you take off today?"

"Nah. Just had to talk to some clients way out of town. Thought I'd never find their place down that dirt road." He took a long sip of wine and heaved a sigh. "I felt bad not being here when you were at the hospital."

Sara nodded. "It was a terrible shock."

As was their family's custom on Friday evening, they shared a moment of silence before the meal. Sara remembered how her grandmother had always presided at the Friday dinnertime. The silence went on too long. Finally, Sara asked, "How are things going at work?" This was one subject that absorbed her brother's interest.

"Just fine," said Dave, spooning a large helping of potatoes onto his plate. "And I've been going to a church in town. I really enjoy those people." He mumbled the words and looked down at his food.

No one spoke, then Amelia said, "That's nice, dear." She picked at her food. "Church is a good place to meet a nice girl."

Dave smiled. "I have met an interesting girl. Good-looking, too." He reached for the chicken. "I do have to get involved in the community, make contacts, that sort of thing. It's hard to make friends after you've left school. Most of my buddies are married or they've moved on."

Sara felt his nervousness. She put words to his concern. "Grandma wouldn't have liked this sudden interest of yours."

"I know. She'd blow a gasket." Dave sat back. He was calmer now and looked like a dog who'd hidden a bone. "Never did understand why she detested an institution that's supposed to do good." He sighed.

Dave finished his dinner and dropped his napkin on the table. He looked at his mother. "You going to be all right?"

She stood to begin clearing the dishes. "Of course."

He glanced at Sara, nodded, and then he and his farm boots stomped out the back door.

Chapter 13

Morocco, 1781

Early the next morning, Moses squinted into the sun to see that they were approaching a scattering of windswept, rocky islands off the mainland. The largest bore the crenelated ramparts of a small fort. Cannons from the fort were aimed their way, and the silhouettes of guards stood against the sky.

As the ship sailed past the islands into a bay, he scanned the shoreline and the watchtowers and ramparts of a walled city far to the left on the mainland. "Mogador, I think," he muttered. After all the months of looking westward, toward the land of freedom and opportunity, he felt the bitter blow of thwarted dreams. They had returned to oppression and ignorance. He feared for them all with a growing dread.

He looked back at Rachel and Annie from his vantage point beside the ragged gap in the ship's side. "I think we're coming into Mogador, Morocco. It's the king's new city, but I believe the Arabs now call it Essaouira."

Rachel and Annie rose from a vandalized bunk and stepped over the debris to join Moses. They stared through the gap for a few moments at the town with its minaret in the distance and at the camels on the beach in front of them. Then Rachel turned away.

"Morocco," she said. "We are back in Morocco." Her mouth twisted in distaste. Watching with concern, Moses attempted to counsel her about what might happen, but Rachel refused to listen and turned her back to him, as if that would make the horror go away.

Moses knew Rachel had only a vague understanding of slave-trading pirates and arrogant men of political power. The thought of her being sold into the harem of some man wealthy enough to buy her, even if he were the king or one of his sons, was too repulsive to imagine, but it was about to become a reality. He watched Rachel pull the miniature American flag out of her pocket and kiss it.

Annie turned to Moses. "You and I know how badly women are mistreated in these Arab countries. We must use our wits and scheme to gain even slight consideration from any man of influence here. And I am Christian, and you and Rachel are Jews, which gives them all the more reason to oppress us."

Moses knew what she had left unsaid. Once back in Morocco, Annie and Rachel, as women, would have a difficult time ever leaving it again. Even he, as a Jew and a single man, would find leaving difficult. They would all become slaves at the mercy of the capricious misuses of power that pervaded the cracks and corners of daily life in Morocco.

At last, the pirate who had convinced the captain to let Annie return below, came halfway down the ladder and peered at them. "Up on deck," he said in English, gesturing toward the hatch. Rachel looked at her father with a raised eyebrow at the pirate's use of English. How much English did he know? Moses thought back to what they might have said around him.

They emerged from the hatchway onto the deck, staring out at sea rather than facing the leers of the pirates. Moses knew the pirates were considering greedy plans as to how they might market not only the beauty they had snared at sea but him, Annie, and the other captives as well. He scrutinized the captive sailors. They had all once been proud men. Now they were forced to huddle on the deck, ankles tied one to the other, not daring to look up or speak.

Moses stood straight, his expression stern and his bearing confident, hoping that a show of bravado would keep the pirates from handling them as cruelly as they had the other captives.

Rachel hid behind her father. Moses held her close, knowing she was afraid and unsure.

Both ships were moored in a small bay just inside the rocky barrier islands. The water was calm here, but the high, grim walls of the city stood at least a mile away. The actual port where ships were docked must be around the point, Moses decided. He knew that the king had officially opposed piracy in his efforts to increase trade with Europe. Moses supposed that the king's position simply meant that the pirates had to barter their booty in secret rather than open negotiations.

Moses scanned the shore searching for possibilities to escape. He could see fishermen on the beach spreading their nets and tending to their drab little boats, but he was allowed only a few moments before the pirates gestured to Moses and the two women that they were to climb down a rope ladder to a dinghy for the long row to the town wharf. The pirates released the other captives to follow Moses, but cocked pistols were aimed at them all.

Moses feigned confidence to help Rachel and Annie suppress their growing terror. He took their hands as they sat together with the other captives in the bobbing, overloaded dinghy for the trip to the quay. As they approached the town, the oars brought up stinking clumps of sewage, rotting fish, and vegetables at every stroke.

The pirates maneuvered the dinghy among the fishing boats to reach the quay and then pushed their captives onto the ramp up to the wharf, prodded them down the quay, through open double gates under an ornate stone arch, past guards holding muskets, and into the customs house. Moses, Rachel, and the other captives stood helplessly by as their future was tossed back and forth in the intense haggling between the pirates and the officials. At last, money exchanged hands, and the pirates left without even a backward glance. Meanwhile, one official used a flax reed to scrawl rapidly in a large ledger resting on his knees. Another motioned to the captives to follow him.

The guards marched them out of the customs house and halted them briefly in a broad square that seemed to be the center of activity for the town. Along one side of the square were the stalls of the fishmongers, each one grilling fish behind the displays of fresh-caught shrimp and squid, flounder and haddock. All the captives inhaled the aroma as if that might feed them.

"I am so hungry, Papa," Rachel whispered.

"So am I," said Moses and Annie in one breath. He could not help staring at the fish stalls. The pirates had thrown them only a few biscuits and oranges since the ship's capture. No one here would concern themselves with feeding the prisoners.

To keep his mind off his hunger, Moses studied the square in which they stood, again searching for possibilities to escape. Along each side were two- and three-story buildings, each one glaring white in the brilliant sunshine. Elegant arches decorated in blue-checkered designs offered intriguing glimpses down dark, narrow streets. In scanning the walls, Moses came across a plaque labeling this square as the Place Moulay el Hassan.

He nudged Rachel. "I think this is the main square. See that clock tower?"

She looked up at the tall building standing behind the souks at the southeast corner of the square while a great mosque stood off the square in the opposite corner.

"Watch for any sign or landmark," Moses whispered, "that can help you know where you are. We must rely on our wits to escape."

The guards interrupted Moses' survey and forced them down a narrow street through the swarming mass of humanity—Berbers, Bedouins, Arabs, Africans, and even some Europeans —and the camels, donkeys, mules, and goats that crowded them as they walked. The captives stopped only once as a strange character covered in stinking, poorly tanned animal skins worked the crowd with a cup. He mockingly pushed his cup at Moses, but Moses did not have the spirit to muster even a smile, and the beggar was shoved aside by the guards.

Donkeys laden with sacks of olives, nuts, and dates pushed them to the walls as their drivers herded the beasts forward. The heavy aroma of olive oil mingled with the resinous fragrance of the thuja wood piled in the doorways they passed. Here and there a craftsman paused in his carving to stare at the procession. Moses thought of the ivory inlaid thuja wood casket he had left in Tangier, but his reverie was broken by a prod on his back.

The prisoners were taken down another side street where fruit, vegetables, and leather goods were set out for sale. In each stall sat a vendor, cross-legged, with his wares on both sides and behind him. His customers stood in front, pointing to one thing and then another in his store. Craftsmen worked their tools in open doorways.

The pebbled streets were filthy with garbage and dung which the prisoners could not avoid. Around them the brays, snorts, clops and claps, haggling, yelling, and gossiping merged in a deafening cacophony.

As they walked, Moses memorized the buildings they passed, seeking to find the Jewish quarter from which surely they could seek help if they were allowed any way to contact the Jews there. He looked down at the stained and ragged burnoose he had worn to escape the attention of the pirates. Now it only served to make him appear as powerless and ignorant as the rest.

He reached over and put his arm around Rachel. She stared back at him with empty eyes. He looked over at Annie. She raised an eyebrow and nodded at Rachel. She understood what he was trying to say. Annie would have to protect Rachel now because soon the two women would be separated from the men.

Moses clenched his fist and turned for one last look at the ocean behind him.

Chapter 14

Spain, 1941

The boat bobbed gently in quiet waters off a deserted Spanish beach. Ruth and Samuel stood side by side on the boat deck, scanning the shore for any sign of habitation. They saw none.

Samuel nodded at the metal case in Ruth's arms. "Will you be sending that as usual?" He spoke softly.

"No, not this time." Ruth studied it thoughtfully. "I have an odd feeling. . . . I'm not sure I trust the people who gave it to me."

"Whatever we think, it was given to us in good faith. It must be returned."

Ruth lifted herself up on her toes and kissed him on the cheek. "I just want more time to consider how to handle it. It will be returned to the proper owners when they are safe and able to receive it. Stop worrying."

"I'm not worried. I know you'll do the right thing. Just be careful, that's all."

Samuel lowered a small dinghy into the water and rowed Ruth to shore. They clambered out onto the sand and hugged each other, then he pushed the dinghy off the beach, hopped in, and began rowing back to the boat. He paused and saluted his sister.

Ruth smiled and returned the salute before raising her gaze out to the sea beyond. In the distance across the water, the mountains of Morocco rose from the desert. Stories of Morocco were woven into her family tapestry. Scores of her ancestors had fled the Spanish inquisition and found Morocco a refuge. Two ancestors had found it a prison.

She shivered and took a reassuring breath of the oleanders in the gardens behind her before scurrying up to the road and walking along to join a group of workers joking, laughing, and flashing papers through the checkpoint before passing into Gibraltar.

As they walked by an unpretentious British hotel, Ruth ducked behind it and let herself into a small apartment. Dropping the valise, she flung off her hat and laid the metal case on the table.

Exhaustion crept over her, and she yearned for the quiet, spacious comfort of a bed on land. Instead, she made a cup of tea and sipped it as she sat staring at the case. Finally she sighed. She had shopping to do and someone to meet. She knew exactly where to go for the materials she needed to protect the case for a long wait.

She had to find out more about this particular piece before she sent it on. And she knew the perfect place to hide it until then.

Chapter 15

West Virginia: 1999

Her mind burdened with sadness, Sara helped her mother clean up after their meal. Amelia seemed subdued and thoughtful, but she was often that way, expecting others to take the lead. Sara glanced at her, as stable and unassuming as usual, wearing the apple-blossom print apron over a plain dress the color of West Virginia granite.

As Sara finished drying the last plate, Amelia took off the apron and walked out of the kitchen. She stumbled over to the sofa. Sara sat alongside and took her mother's hand.

"I can't believe she's gone," said Amelia.

Sara stared at the wall, feeling the irrevocable finality of death, but the tears wouldn't come. She hugged her mother and together they sat in the dark on the living room sofa, sharing memories. Sara felt closer to her mother than she ever had.

The next morning they prepared to visit the funeral director to make final arrangements. Dave brushed off Sara's plea for help. "You know what to do. You always do," he said.

Sara and Amelia stood in front of Ruth's crowded closet, seeking the best dress for Ruth's final appearance. A lavender scent wafted toward Sara from the closet, and Sara had to choke back the tears as she studied the dresses and blouses hanging in front of her.

All of them had long sleeves. Even the summer clothes. Too cold, too windy, too sunny—whatever the reason, Sara had never seen her grandmother in anything with short sleeves. How odd, but then Grandma always felt cold, even in midsummer.

Just before they left for the funeral home, Peter came over to help.

His presence irritated Sara, but you had to hand it to him. Peter was dependable.

"I'll go with you," he said.

Sara looked at her feet, unwilling to meet his soft, brown eyes. After a long pause, she took a deep breath. "Thank you, Peter, but we must do this ourselves."

Then not caring what he thought, she rushed out the door, leaving Peter to her mother, who locked the front door and walked out to Sara's car. Peter trailed behind and then trudged over to his car.

In the end, Sara made every decision. The interview with the funeral director was just as painful for Sara as she expected, and she faced it with her mother who maintained a stoic reserve. Sara knew his questions were necessary and at first felt relieved that the funeral home would put together the obituary and notify the newspapers. The relief turned to embarrassment when Sara found so many of the questions unanswerable. Even her mother did not know enough about her own mother to answer them.

"Where was she born?" asked the funeral director.

"I don't know," Sara said. She thought a moment. "I don't think my grandmother came from West Virginia."

The director looked at Amelia. She nodded. "I don't know where she was born."

The director studied them both, his pen poised above the paper. "Okay. So when was she born?"

"I don't know," Amelia replied, "but I guess it must have been, maybe, 1921, 22?"

The director pursed his lips. "All right, perhaps you know where she went to school?"

Sara waited for her mother's reply, but Amelia stared at her hands and said. "No, I don't know."

"Occupation?"

With relief, Sara seized on a question she could answer. "She was a homemaker. Both my mom and my grandmother never had any interest in working outside the home." She glanced at her mother, wondering if she would make any comment about this assessment, but she said nothing. Sara saw the director note this on the form.

Her mother and her grandmother too, both of them, Sara thought, would have been better off if they'd had jobs. She had seen them both become less confident and less involved as the years passed.

"All right," the funeral director continued, bringing Sara back to the task at hand. He shuffled the papers. "And at least we also know her religion might have been Jewish."

"Jewish! Why would you say that?" Amelia protested.

"I don't understand," Sara said. "We didn't discuss religion at home, but I always thought she had been brought up in some fundamentalist church. Anyway, she never went to church, and, actually, I don't think my grandmother had any particular belief." Sara didn't want to mention her grandmother's fiery contempt for organized religions.

Amelia nodded in agreement.

The funeral director sat back and studied Sara as if wondering how to continue. Finally, he took a deep breath. "But, ma'am," he said, "when we removed the clothes, we noticed serial numbers tattooed on her arm. I've seen them before. She must have been in a concentration camp during World War II."

Sara felt as if she were standing on quicksand. She gripped her mother's arm.

"Oh no," Amelia whispered.

Sara had never seen her mother so pale, so. . . shocked. As shocked as Sara felt herself. Could her mother not have known about this? Was that possible? Sara fanned Amelia's face with her hand. "Are you all right?"

"I just realized. . . ." Amelia held her hand to her mouth. She seemed to be talking to herself. "I only saw it a couple of times when I was little. How could I have known? She wouldn't tell me what it was."

She looked at Sara. "I asked her about it, but she only shook her head and after that she took to wearing long sleeves all the time, and I," she shook her head, "I forgot about it."

Chapter 16

Mogador, Morocco. 1781

As Rachel picked her way through the piles of waste with the other prisoners, she kept her thoughts on the hope that her father would be able to reach their friends for the ransom and that it would come soon. But her next encounter made her despair of an early rescue.

Two women, shrouded in black, and a short, pudgy black man confronted the procession and gestured that Rachel and Annie were to accompany them. Rachel turned to Moses and clung to him, but one of the guards seized both her and Annie and shoved them toward the shrouded women. They took over and, with the little man behind them, led Rachel and Annie down a crowded alley through a courtyard to a narrow room that ran along one side.

They were handed large, poorly sewn haiks of rough, black wool. The shrouded women motioned that Rachel and Annie were to undress and cover themselves with these rectangular pieces of cloth.

Rachel wept as she and Annie shed their clothing under cover of the haiks, since the odd little black man stared unblinkingly at them. Then Rachel watched the two women snatch up each piece and chatter while they examined the materials. Their eager hands ripped the hems and linings of the caftans and undergarments searching for coins but found none. If she could speak their language, Rachel could have told them the pirates had picked them clean.

One woman found the flag Rachel had hidden in a pocket, stared at it puzzled, and then tossed it onto the pile of clothing. Rachel gasped and stepped forward to retrieve it, but the black man barred her way. Annie's rags were kicked aside. The three captors left their prisoners huddled, frightened, and clinging to each other in this barren room to wonder what humiliation would come next.

Rachel silently prayed that her father would find help. She steeled herself against the fatalistic advice she felt Annie would offer. She glanced at the older woman and saw the pity in her eyes. Rachel turned away. She needed strength and courage now, not pity. She paced the floor, knowing that Annie wanted to help but could do nothing.

Hours passed. Rachel stopped pacing and gestured to the haik she clutched around herself as she looked at Annie. "No one would know us in this. We are women, prisoners, alone and powerless. They will think we are stupid and ignorant, the way they keep their women."

Annie reached over to put an arm around Rachel.

"My father knew better," said Rachel. "He understood and he sympathized with me. He knew all the stupid rules I was supposed to follow just because I am female, and he helped me make fools of them all. Oh, Annie," she suddenly broke down and sobbed, "Where is he now?"

Annie held Rachel close and stroked her hair. "Your father is a learned man. He must have friends who will help," she whispered.

Rachel pushed Annie away. "Yes, and he is also compassionate . . . and daring. I know that he will find a way to free us. If I were not a woman, I would be with him, the way I was in his teaching."

Annie looked down at her. "He would let you?"

Rachel wiped her face on a rough corner of the haik. "It was his idea. I wanted to go with him, but a girl would be most unwelcome, so we made it a game. I would dress as a boy and he would show me how to conduct myself as a scholar. I listened and learned something new every moment I spent with him." She clenched her fists. "I cannot bear to be caged like a pigeon and served to whoever wants me."

In her misery, she stared down at the tiled floor. An odd piece of broken blue tile caught her eye. She stooped, picked it up, and hid it in the folds of her haik. She fingered it, feeling its shape and size. *This bit of glazed pottery is like me. Lost, broken, but still strong and unique. It has survived. I will too.*

She felt Annie's arms around her. "We must take this, whatever happens now," Annie whispered, "one day at a time. We will get out of here. You must have hope."

Rachel let herself feel Annie's warmth. Perhaps she had misjudged the woman. Rachel looked around at the bare, windowless walls, the blue-and-white checkered tiles on the floor, the locked door with only a small, grated window to let in light and air. She consciously willed herself to stand proud and confident.

She studied the door. How could they get out of there? How could they escape?

Darker questions forced their way into her mind. Would they ever find their way out? Would Papa?

"Oh, Annie," said Rachel, "I hope my father is unharmed and alive. What can be happening to him? Surely he can bargain for his release." If they did escape, how would they ever find him? Would he be able to find them? This town was a maze of confusing alleys and streets.

"He is a fine, intelligent man." Annie said. "He will know what to do."

"Yes, I am sure he is doing everything possible." She paused. "But what about us? What will they do with us?"

Annie stroked Rachel's hair and began to braid it.

About to protest, Rachel stopped as she heard footsteps outside, then the key turning in the lock. The door swung open and the little black man who had accompanied them from the dock stood in the doorway. Behind him lurked an elderly man wearing a kippah. They stepped into the cell.

Rachel would have run to the older man begging for help and protection—surely he was Jewish—but his forbidding expression stopped her. The little man muttered some words in a language Rachel did not understand, then grabbed Rachel's arm to force her closer to the older man who shook his head and, smiling slightly, reached out to stroke Rachel's cheek.

She was astonished. Perhaps this man would help them. Did he speak English? Before she could speak, Annie ran forward and stepped in front of Rachel. At the same time, the older man muttered a few words and turned to leave. The short little man pushed Rachel back and she fell to the ground. He stepped over her to follow the older man out the door. Rachel heard the key turn in the lock, and they were left alone.

Annie helped Rachel to her feet and held her close, crooning to her, "There, there, my little one, my sweet little girl, now, now."

Rachel shivered in the heat of their prison and her teeth chattered. She leaned against Annie, feeling her warmth and drawing on her comfort.

"What did they want?" she finally asked, her voice muffled in the folds of the haik.

"I don't know," Annie said. "Maybe they are deciding what work we will do." Rachel heard the tremble in Annie's voice, betraying her dread of another brutal ravage.

"I can do work," Rachel said, but she remembered the touch of the man's hand on her cheek. She looked at Annie. "Why didn't the Jewish man help us? Why was he here? What did he want?"

Rachel knew some plan for her was in the making, but she trembled to consider what it might be. She vaguely understood that scrunching her face to repel obnoxious attentions was not the thing to do here.

She left the comfort of Annie's arms, walked to the grated door, and hit it with her fist.

Chapter 17

Martinsburg, West Virginia, 1999

Sara endured the memorial service, appalled at its impersonality. The service could have been about anyone. She couldn't remember much about her father's or grandfather's services, and perhaps she was too young to have an opinion, but shouldn't the readings and the sermon recognize the individual human being and his or her life? No one in this service today had spoken a word about her grandmother except her name.

Sara studied the faces of the people around her. Too few for someone who had lived almost eighty years. Her mother, brother, Peter. A few of her coworkers. Some of her brother's coworkers. Peter's parents. A couple of relatives on her grandfather's side.

She drifted through the small reception that followed the service, teacup in hand, listening vaguely to the chattering around her, hearing no words that could comfort her and not once a remembrance of her grandmother. She felt a gulf separate her from the others milling around the room.

As if from a great distance, she saw with new eyes that her mother handled the funeral and this small gathering with polite dignity. She played the role well, even to the cookies, cakes, and snacks she had prepared for guests.

So far her mother had said nothing about what they had learned from the funeral director. Sara also was not yet willing to share what must have been her grandmother's big secret. How much had her mother known? Several days before, when she and Dave and her mother had met to plan the funeral arrangements, the discussion had bloomed into a gentle debate.

"We should keep it non-denominational," Sara said, testing the waters. "You know how Grandma felt."

"Oh, no," her brother protested. "It has to be Christian. We have our friends and family to think of, you know." Sara studied her brother, but he evaded her eyes.

"My minister can conduct it," he added. "We can have it at my church."

So in the end, the funeral had been Christian. Her mother said it was best that way, but Sara felt that her grandmother would have detested the whole business. Sara was now aware of possible deep and secret reasons for her grandmother's opinions. Out of curiosity, Sara had checked the phone book for a synagogue; but there was only one in Martinsburg, and it was the only one in her part of the state. Had she known anyone who was Jewish in her school? She didn't think so.

Sara still felt the shock of the discovery. How could her grandmother be Jewish, and the family not have the barest hint of it? How could she have lived in a concentration camp and not once spoken of it? Why had she not told them about her dead brother? Was the past so terribly tragic that looking forward was the only recourse for her? How could she have lived a lie for so long?

And now, she's still living a lie, buried as a Christian in a Christian cemetery.

Her grandmother had denied her past, which gave her a safe, secure life—and a brief obituary and an off-the-shelf funeral. Now Sara followed in her footsteps, seeking safety, security, and a life without terrifying adventures on sailboats.

The heat of the room began to suffocate Sara. She could not face her brother or Peter or the rest of them a moment longer. She left by the back door, took a long walk, and then, for the first time since the assault, drove her car out into the country where she deliberately turned onto back roads she did not know. She returned home late that night, feeling more centered and happier than she had for months.

The day after the funeral dawned clear and sunny, lifting her spirits. She called her office, excusing herself again. Of course they understood.

Then she called Dave. As she and Dave had done for years, ever since their father died, they carried on as if they were the heads of the family, bypassing their mother who usually found ways to distance herself from the day-to-day negotiations.

"I'm concerned that we may have missed letting some of Grandma's friends or relatives know about her. . . death." Sara gripped the phone and swallowed. "We shouldn't leave it to Mom. She's suffering much more than we are from the loss, but someone has to go through Grandma's things." She stared out the window at the dull frame houses of Martinsburg and waited. She heard a long sigh.

"You're right, I guess. We'd better find out if there are any bills or something else that needs taking care of. Wait until I get there, Sara."

"I'll wait, but something else has come up. Something important."

"Did Grandma give us a bundle in her will? Did she have a will?"

"It's not that. It's just something I think all of us in the family should know. When can you get to Mom's house?"

"Sounds mysterious." Sara heard papers rustling. After a long silence, Dave replied, "I suppose I can get there in an hour."

Sara willed herself to drive slowly to her mother's house, but her heart was racing. Questions filled her head. Who was their grandmother anyway?

At her mother's house, she let herself in and climbed up to her grandmother's room. She paused at the door, feeling the sadness and barrenness of the room. Then she walked in and sat on the bed, hoping to feel her grandmother's spirit and the bond they had shared. The pervasive, old-fashioned scent of lavender enveloped Sara like the sleep of death.

She contemplated Grandma's massive bureau. It seemed to guard the room, squatting in place like a huge, malevolent toad. The somnolent feeling that had stolen over her in this room faded away. Sara wondered where her grandmother could have found such a monstrosity. Sara stepped over to it, ran her hand over the smooth surface. She pulled at the drawers, but they were all locked. Where would Grandma have hidden the key?

She studied the bureau, then felt underneath the bottom drawer and found not one key, but two, both held in place by tape.

The larger key was iron and as gothic as the antique bureau itself. The other key appeared plain and official. Sara hid the keys in her pocket and walked down the stairs into the kitchen. Her mother stood at the sink, staring out the window.

"Mom, I need to talk to you." Sara pulled out a chair and gestured for her mother to take it. Sara sat facing her across the table.

"What's this all about, Sara?"

"Can you remember anything, anything at all, about Grandma's past? I mean her childhood? Growing up? Her parents? Anything?"

Amelia folded her hands and stared at the tablecloth. A minute passed before she lifted her shoulders with a sigh. "No. I told you. She seemed so uncomfortable and pained when the subject came up, that I felt it was something that shouldn't be discussed. She never wanted to look back, and I forgot about it."

Sara watched her mother, wondering if she would be upset about their plans. Sara broke it gently. "Mom, Dave is coming over. We thought we should take a look at Grandma's room in case there's something that needs to be taken care of."

Amelia did not respond. A tear dropped to the tablecloth. She swept it away.

"We're going to have to open the bureau," added Sara. "I found the key."

Amelia brushed her eyes and looked up, showing real interest at last. "You found the key? Where?"

"Taped underneath."

Amelia nodded. "I suppose it was there all along. I can't imagine that the bureau has anything more than underwear and old keepsakes."

"Probably. Dave and I thought Grandma might have some bills or notes about friends or family that we should notify."

"I guess you're right." Her mother turned away to end the conversation. "Your grandmother was as close-mouthed as a fencepost. You never knew what she was thinking."

Sara stared at her mother, thinking that the same could be said of her. Glancing out the kitchen window, she saw Dave's car pull into the driveway. She tapped on the glass. Dave looked up, waved, and used the back door into the kitchen.

"Okay. I'm here," he said. "Let's take care of it."

Sara heard the subdued eagerness in his voice. It saddened her because she didn't think he would like whatever they found in the bureau. Together, the three walked up the stairs in a solemn procession to the room that had been their grandmother's preserve for so long.

Sara selected the larger of the two keys with shaking hands, fitted it into the keyhole at the top of the bureau and turned it with difficulty. They heard a loud click. Sara reached to open the top drawer, but Dave was first to the handle. They took a quick look through the top two drawers, turning up undergarments, scarves, jewelry and an assortment of odds and ends.

Dave glanced at Sara. "No personal papers of any kind."

Then Sara opened the bottom drawer. Dave probably hoped for an inheritance, but she hoped for answers.

They found neither. A stained, brown valise filled the drawer. Dave lifted it out carefully and laid it on the bed. They stared at it.

The valise was made of some heavy fabric fragile with age. It opened at the top by separating two handles, but the handles were locked together.

"I have a vague memory of seeing this," Amelia said. "Years ago."

Sara handed the second key to Dave. He fitted it into the keyhole in the handles and took a deep breath as he turned the key. They heard the click, then Dave picked up the handles and separated them. They peered inside at a lumpy, blue cloth cover and, peeking up at one side, a large brown envelope. Printed on one side were the words: "For Sara."

Sara pulled out the envelope while Dave whisked aside the cloth cover. Underneath lay objects wrapped in more blue cloth. Dave picked up one oddly shaped bundle and unfolded the cloth wrapper.

"What is this?" He held up a golden candelabra with nine golden arms, each decorated with blue stripes.

"Oh for goodness sake," their mother said. "I believe that's a menorah."

"A menorah? Like for Hanukkah?"

Sara leaned over to look at this symbol of Judaism.

"What was Grandma doing with a menorah?" Dave radiated disbelief.

Sara picked up a small oblong bundle and uncovered it. "What about this?" she said, holding up a rectangular piece of tile that was as long as her hand and half as wide. It was decorated with colorful Hebrew letters and had a recess in back. They all examined it, but no one knew what it was.

"And look at this." Dave pulled out what appeared to be a shawl with Hebrew characters woven into the design. At least, the letters looked like the Hebrew letters Sara had seen before and if Grandma were Jewish. . . .

Underneath the shawl were an Old Testament in Hebrew, a prayer book, and a photo album.

Sara reached for the album. Her fingers tingled as she leafed through it, scanning each page for clues, but the photos had cryptic, unreadable notes under them. She didn't recognize anyone in the photos and in many cases, names or other writing were obliterated with a line of thick, black ink. The last pages were filled with photos of unframed paintings and small sculptures. Each photo was labeled with a number. She handed the album to Dave.

He flipped through the pages for their mother. "Do you recognize anything in these pictures?" he said. Amelia shook her head.

Sara turned to the envelope. Grandma had addressed it to her, writing Sara's full name in bold cursive letters. How odd. Why?

"Did Grandma tell you anything about this?" Dave's tone became overbearing.

Sara flinched. "No. I'm as surprised as you are. Maybe what's in this envelope will explain it."

Dave grabbed for the envelope, but Sara held it out of his reach.

He stuck out his lower lip. "We aren't Jews. Anyway, you know how Grandma stayed away from the churches around here. She didn't like any of them."

"So what if we are Jews?" Sara said. "And you don't know the rest."

"What rest?"

"Grandma had been in a concentration camp."

"Oh come on." Sara could hear the scorn in Dave's voice. "She would have told us about that."

Sara held up the prayer shawl. "The funeral director told Mom and I about the Nazi branding on her arm."

"Ridiculous!" Dave stepped back. "Anyway, all kinds of people were put in those camps. And don't you go spreading stories about this. What if my girlfriend hears about it? I don't know what she'd think." He sounded angry.

"I'm sure it wouldn't bother her, Dave," said Sara, annoyed at his reaction.

Dave groaned. "I don't think they'll elect a Jewish person around here."

Sara ignored him and turned to her mother. "Mom, are you sure that Grandma or Grandpa never said anything about being Jewish?"

"I know Grandpa wasn't Jewish," said Dave. "He was born in the middle of West Virginia."

Amelia folded her arms and shivered. She spoke softly as if to herself. "His family was Methodist," she said, "but we weren't. My mother made sure of that. She told us no religions were good enough. They always had to hate or oppress somebody."

She sighed and smiled up at Sara. "Many times I wanted to go to church with my friends. I was curious, you know, and nobody seemed to agree with my mother."

"Not around here they wouldn't," Sara said, patting her on the shoulder. Dave gaped at his mother and, for once, had nothing to say.

She took Sara's hand and pressed it to her cheek. "I know, but her attitude kept us out of the community, and she let everyone know her opinions. Whenever anyone tried to shut her up, she would argue that any true religion would encourage questions. She said none of us needed to go around protecting God."

Sara remembered the fierceness of her grandmother's attacks on Mormons or Jehovah's Witnesses or anyone else who came to the door pushing religion.

"But she did honor some things that I guess you might say were spiritual," added Sara's mother with a slight smile. "Friday evenings, for instance. We always had a special quiet time on Friday before supper. And then, you know, we never had pork or ham when she was around. She said she didn't like it."

"I know that," said Dave, his belligerence returning. "But Grandpa didn't care much for pork either, and his folks were pig farmers."

Sara pulled out a sheaf of papers from the envelope. Among the notes and scraps of paper, they found a blue bank passbook. Dave grabbed for it, but Sara got it first. She opened it to the inside cover and caught her breath.

"What is it? Is there anything in there?" Dave said.

"It's for a savings account with my name on it."

"Only your name? It's got to be for both of us."

"No. It just has my name, and the balance in the account," Sara could not believe it, "is $50,000." She read it again. "$50,000." She stared at her brother and mother in shock. "I can't believe it," she whispered.

"That's impossible." Dave frowned. "Why would Grandma leave you $50,000?"

"I don't know," Sara could barely speak. She felt dizzy as visions of what $50,000 could mean danced through her thoughts. She looked back at the passbook. A brief letter and a faded scrap of flimsy yellow paper were clipped to the cover.

She scanned the yellow scrap first and held her hand up for attention. "This seems to be a receipt for something, I can't make out the writing, but it's signed by someone named R.Yulee and dated 1941."

"She doesn't say anything about me?" Dave asked, grabbing at the receipt.

Sara turned away from Dave, holding fast to the yellow scrap. "No, she doesn't."

"What does the letter say?" asked Amelia.

Sara skimmed through it, and then read it out loud. "'Dearest Sara, I am leaving this to you in case I cannot carry it out myself. You are old enough now and smart enough.'" Sara looked up. "This must have been written recently. She goes on to say, 'I have learned that there is safety only in secrecy, but to lose one's heritage is a terrible thing. I have lost my family and my brother through fear. And I have left undone my last assignment, and this has blighted my life. I am asking you to find my brother, Samuel E. Yulee, if he is still alive, and give him the enclosed receipt so he can complete the last delivery. This will be difficult for you, my dear, but you have the skill and courage to do it. I have long thought my brother to be dead, murdered in the most heinous way, but perhaps I was mistaken. If he is alive, he would wonder about me as I have long wondered about him. I do not have the energy to take on this task, but you are young. I write this to you now, but I hope to tell you my story. Whatever happens, please find him and finish what I could not complete myself.'"

Sara choked through the last few words and stared at the letter. After several minutes during which none of them spoke, Sara looked up. "All these years she has hidden this secret."

"She never told us about any of this," her mother whispered. "Never."

Sara shook her head. "I guess this means that the 'R. Yulee' on the receipt is our grandmother. All these other papers appear to be receipts too and shipping statements." Sara shuffled quickly through the papers. "They're all dated around 1939 . . . 1940 . . . . Here's one that was 1938."

"That's all? Somebody's shopping list?" Dave said. "And what's this about a brother? You mean we have a long-lost great-uncle?"

"Maybe," their mother said. "I always heard he had been killed during the war—must have been World War II—but for some reason she began thinking recently that he may still be alive."

"Yeah, but that sounds like a long shot to me," said Dave, frowning at the letter.

Sara nodded. "We don't know anything for sure. If he is alive, where is he? Who is he?"

Sara leafed through the scraps of paper. "These notes are all pretty cryptic. I can't make them out. Just numbers, dates, and what looks like descriptions, I guess. Weird."

Their mother shook her head. "You'd think she would have given you some names and addresses. How does she expect you to do this with no real information about who and where anyone might be?"

"She wasn't finished," Sara said in a low voice. "She was killed before she could pull all the information together for me."

"I know one thing." Dave's voice became menacing. "We've got to keep this quiet. Nobody else needs to know about this. Sara, that goes for you, too. You don't have to say anything about this to anyone. After all, we don't really know what this is about."

Sara shrugged. She would have to discuss this with somebody—she didn't know who that might be yet—just to carry out her grandmother's request. But she would be careful, because of the money and the secrecy that surrounded this discovery.

Their mother stared at her hands, saying nothing.

"Good. I'm glad you agree." He stopped and focused again on the bank passbook. "Are you sure that isn't meant to be shared?"

"Yes, I'm sure." She showed him her name. "Grandma left it for me."

"It's not fair. I should get half."

"But you don't, Dave. That's clear," Amelia said. "Now leave Sara alone. You make enough money."

Dave shook his head, grumbling, "I can't believe our grandmother left $50,000 for Sara and nothing—nothing!—for me."

"She wasn't finished," Amelia said. "I know she must have meant something for you too."

Sara looked away. She would like to help Dave, but then she thought of her grandmother, so angry, so bitter . . . and so secretive. A new thought struck her. Her grandmother had been afraid and that made her life seem so sad. If she had only sought counseling or at least shared the burden she was carrying, perhaps she, all of the family, could have been so much happier.

A vague thought fought its way through to Sara's consciousness. She let it flicker to the surface. Maybe her own life would be happier if she talked to a counselor about what happened to her on the Chesapeake. Sara submerged that thought and replaced it with another. She would make it up to Grandma. She would find the brother and discover what this was all about.

She supposed she could request an extended leave without pay from her job. They may not like that or they might like it a lot. She had no heart for the job and should just quit, but quitting was such a scary proposition.

And there was Peter. The house in the suburbs. She would be giving all that up too. Was she willing to let go of every lifeline to a safe, secure life?

No one knew who her grandmother was. The obituary had been painfully short. Sara wondered how she would want her own obituary to read. She shivered. For just a moment she felt as if she were drowning in the cool water of the Chesapeake. She could feel the beginning of a panic attack and took several deep breaths.

Her grandmother had handed her a tough challenge but had believed in Sara enough to trust her to carry out this difficult task. She must find Samuel E. Yulee for her grandmother, for her family, and, Sara took a deep breath, for herself.

The first step involved no risk at all. She needed to find someone to translate the notes in the album. There might be a clue there. And she'd check the Internet for a Samuel E. Yulee and for Yulees in general.

Was Samuel E. Yulee alive? Did she really have a great-uncle that she'd never met? What did the letter and the receipts mean? Sara pondered these questions a moment as she realized the immensity of this project. She could not let her grandmother down, but how was she going to proceed? For a moment she felt overwhelmed, then bursting through the anger, depression, and sadness of the last year came a low giggle that erupted into a laugh. This was going to be fun!

Chapter 18

Mogador, Morocco, 1781

Moses stood helplessly by as Rachel and Annie were herded away. He stared after them until they disappeared around a corner, then a guard pushed Moses forward with the other captives. He was just one link in a chain of ragged men prodded through the dung-covered streets of Mogador, Morocco. His tears dropped to the dust unseen.

As Moses stumbled along, he searched his memory for incidents involving the captives of Barbary pirates. He had heard the story of Theodore Cornut of Avignon, a French captive who was a skilled architect and engineer. Twenty years before, the enslaved Cornut had been used to design and rebuild Mogador at the king's whim, but Cornut had died of some plague before the project was completed. An English renegade finished rebuilding the city.

Moses saw "renegados" everywhere. He was puzzled at this but watched them as he walked and finally realized that these soldiers of fortune were employed as garrison guards. Most were black, but a few here and there were white. He heard several speaking English as they passed in the streets, a fact he tucked away in his mind as a possibility for the future.

He felt weak from hunger. The dust permeated his skin and clothes. Pebbles pierced and burned his bare feet. The pirates had stolen his sandals. Moses sighed ruefully. It was just as well. If he still wore them, he may not have been given time to remove them as required for Jews when passing a mosque. Despite his captivity, this error might have been seen as an offense and an excuse for torture or forced conversion.

"At least," Moses muttered to himself with a grim laugh, "I am spared this concern."

A cadaverous sailor behind him heard the comment. "We ain't being spared much, I'm saying."

Moses looked up as they walked by the grand mosque and heard the muezzin's loud, monotonous call. The guard prodded the captives away from the mosque as men drifted in from all sides to wash themselves in the mosque fountain before prayer.

The constant wind hammered the heat at them. Moses squinted at the white of the walls that blinded him with reflected sunlight. Only the blue shutters and tiled arches added some relief from the stark buildings.

Arabs in white djellabas, their heads covered by hoods or tarbouches, paused in their bargaining to gawk at the miserable procession of ragged men. One onlooker shook his head and turned away while another hurled loud insults and derisive laughter. Urchins threw stones and then ran down alleys only to reappear a few streets later. The captives trudged on while flies buzzed around their heads, attacking their eyes, ears, and wounds, adding yet more misery.

Moses shook his head to discourage a buzzing insect. He felt the tears, but they would do nothing to help Rachel and Annie. He needed to observe and plan, look for the possibilities in this impossible situation. They were all still alive and not likely to be killed, even though an unpleasant slavery might be their fate until—yes, until—he found a way to release them.

Moses kept his thoughts on remembering their route through the maze of alleys and streets of Mogador. He could see that they were heading toward the far walls of the city. The guards herded the captives through another arch with double gates, and they arrived at a barren courtyard next to the ramparts. The guards prodded them past stinking, open privies along the inside of the city walls until the procession reached a doorway built into the wall. The captives were pushed forward and then down stone steps to a dark and barren cell with dirt floor. The guards shoved the captives into this dungeon and locked the door. One tiny, grated window in the door admitted air, and the heat drove them to the ground exhausted. They lay there panting to breathe.

A sailor turned to Moses. "I've heard about this king, you know. He sends his—what do you call them?—his men, his courtiers, so to speak, down the coast to claim shipwrecked sailors and passengers. I don't know what he claims them for, and I'm wondering what he does about people like us, captured by pirates."

"I don't know," said Moses, but the thought raised his hopes slightly. He knew that the king's courtiers were likely to be Jewish and might be prepared to help a fellow Jew, but no one could count on a king who ruled by caprice and was swayed by the scent of money.

Moses forced himself to focus on the possibilities of his circumstance instead of his misery. Saving his precious Rachel had to be his only purpose now. His own skills would most likely be commandeered to enhance the trade and profit of the king and his retinue.

"You're English, are you now?" the sailor said.

"Yes, but I have lived in Tangier for several years," Moses said.

"Almost all of us is American. I'm hoping the king will be told that. Could help. The king, his name's Muhammed ibn Abdullah." The sailor drawled the name. "He knows about America, you see. He's kind of a friend to us. He's the first ruler on this whole continent of Africa to say as how America is a new country and that was a few years ago. Wait until he finds out we're most of us Americans, that's what I say."

"We can hope that will be true." Moses replied. He knew that the king was thought to be a pious and peaceful man, but Moses had heard many stories of the king's arbitrary use of power and his outright thievery. Moses kept to himself the thought that only financial gains would influence this avaricious monarch.

Moses doubted that mere acknowledgement of America by the king would result in better treatment of American citizens in Morocco, especially if they were captives and had no money or power. His mind, unlike his fellow prisoners, was set on his own negotiations and reaching prominent Jews in this part of the world for help.

Moses was not a wealthy man, but he had always managed to earn or barter enough for a comfortable living, and he had traveled widely. In Tangier, he and Rachel had moved among the interstices of the intricate pattern woven by the powerful Jewish, Christian and Muslim forces in this part of the world. He knew that several prosperous Jewish merchants lived in Mogador. Perhaps he could count on them for help. He had skills and knowledge they would find useful. Perhaps he could bargain with them for the concessions he needed to release Rachel and Annie.

The captives murmured among themselves, at first speculating on hopeless plans for escape and then on more immediate needs. Would they be given water and food?

A red-faced, beefy sailor sat on the dirt floor next to Moses and looked over at him. "Sorry about you and your women. We just didn't have the guns and the men to . . . to do much."

Moses shrugged. "You fought bravely. I thank you for that," he said.

The sailor laughed grimly. "We hoped to save ourselves. I've heard the stories. They'll force us into hard labor at the port or the mines. The farms maybe. I would not mind that." He shrugged. "Did they tell you where they took your daughter and the other woman?"

"No. They just pushed them down some alley." Moses choked back the tears and motioned vaguely with his hand.

After a long silence, the sailor said with awkward formality, "I am Horace Billingsly, from Yorkshire," and put out his hand.

"You are English," Moses said, shaking Horace's hand, "but on an American ship." He immediately remembered that the king of Morocco reviled the English and, in fact, favored other countries over England in trade agreements. Perhaps that was why he was so quick to recognize the new country of America.

"If anyone inquires about us," Moses said, "you must insist that they notify England."

Horace shook his head. "I've been signing on with American merchant ships. Now that the war's gone sour, his majesty's government won't have much use for the likes of me. More likely they'd thank these Arabs for saving them the trouble of hanging me on an English rope."

"I hope not. None of us knows what will happen next," Moses said, but he thought his new friend's pessimism was quite right.

"No papers, no identity. They know we would say anything, so they believe nothing."

The only door to their cell opened to blinding sunlight. An Arab burdened with an enormous clay urn struggled through the opening. A guard with musket stood behind the Arab, protecting him from the prisoners as he let the urn drop on the floor. The water carrier left and soon returned with a battered tin cup. He set it down beside the urn and grunted a few words, but before anyone responded he was out again. The guard followed him, and they heard him latch the door on the outside. Moses waited his turn as the men, too dispirited to compete for the cup, drank from it and then passed it to the next man.

Later, a shallow clay bowl of watered-down couscous mixed with bits of squash was pushed into their cell along with flat pieces of bread. The men all ate from the bowl with their hands, brushing away the flies and picking up the couscous with the bread to stuff the soppy mess into their mouths. Moses wiped his hands on his clothes and ate like the rest.

Moses and the other captives were locked in their dark prison for two days. Moses listened to the general speculation and fear but did not join in. He stared at the stone walls and considered the possibilities. Perhaps he could be a part of the trading at the dock. He would still be a slave, but he might find ways to discover where Rachel was held.

He sighed. He would have to be careful in inquiring about Rachel. His guards might have no knowledge of Rachel or Annie, and he didn't want to stir their imaginations. Even with those who might know where she was, an attitude of indifference would be his best negotiating position and the safest approach for both Rachel and Annie.

He must use all his wits to make sure they were both rescued unharmed. If only he could be with them. Moses picked up a clod of dirt and clenched it his hand until it disintegrated. What was becoming of them as the hours passed?

He knew from their encounter with the pirate captain that Rachel had good instincts in dealing with her captors, and the Arabs would not expect her to be educated. First impressions could mean life or death. Moses hoped his beautiful young daughter would be aware of the possibilities in first impressions of her, but she must apply her skills with caution. How Annie would react, he didn't know.

Moses sat back, working out in his mind a plan of the city as he remembered it from their walk through the town. He would not think like a slave, enduring hardship and hoping for a miracle. He would build his own miracle.

Chapter 19

Martinsburg, West Virginia, 1999

Sara's mother leafed through the phone book. "There's one synagogue in town, but I don't see any others listed in the area."

"I have to start somewhere, Mom," Sara said, "but I don't want to go to one so close to home. It's a small town. Everyone knows everyone else's business."

"I still think you're being foolish."

"I'll find one on the Internet."

The Maryland suburbs were not too far a drive. Sara selected a synagogue at random located in Rockville. When she called for an appointment, the secretary gave her a Rabbi Siegmond. He sounded young and seemed friendly enough, and he was receptive to talking with her. She didn't elaborate on the reason for the appointment, and the rabbi didn't ask. Sara relaxed her grip on the phone and took a deep breath as she penciled in the time and date on her calendar.

She felt like an interloper imposing on such an austere stranger as a rabbi. She wasn't Jewish and certainly not a member of his congregation. Did she have any right to ask for his help? Should she offer him money for his time? Was she supposed to genuflect or something when she met him? Kiss his ring? Brought up with no religious training, she had no idea what to expect, but her grandmother's bequest propelled her into these uncharted waters.

She found the synagogue in Rockville, outside Washington, D.C., with no trouble. The building was a massive block of stone with the name in large letters incised in gold over the front entrance. The building awed her. She opened what she guessed was the main entrance door and asked a woman standing in the vestibule for directions to the rabbi's office. The woman pointed to a paneled hallway. Sara walked down the hall and knocked at the door with the rabbi's name on it.

A tall man with sympathetic eyes opened it and smiled at her. "Sara Miller?" he asked.

Sara nodded and walked in as he stepped aside. Two armchairs stood in front of his desk. He gestured at one for Sara and took the other. A worn, red and blue oriental carpet covered the wood floor.

His eyes were blue, Sara noted with surprise, despite his dark coloring. She had expected brown eyes. She sat down in one chair as he took the other. His good-humored smile reassured her, and the faded brown sweater over white shirt and tie made him seem relaxed and human. On his head rested a black yarmulke trimmed in silver. Sara had expected him to wear a black robe, like in the movies. Instead, he seemed to be an ordinary human being. On the wall were two framed posters, one from the sixties announcing a civil rights march and one from the seventies advocating the farmworkers' union and grape boycott.

Sara stared at them.

"My father's heritage," the rabbi said. "Would you like coffee or tea?"

Sara smiled at him. "Hot tea, please. If it's no trouble."

"Not at all. Just a moment." He left the room for a few minutes and returned with two cups of tea and a bowl of sugar. "No lemon. Sorry."

"I don't use lemon," Sara said. "Thank you."

"So how can I help you?" The rabbi dumped two heaping teaspoons of sugar in his cup.

Sara did the same.

"I'm not sure," she began and then stumbled through the story of her grandmother and the items in the valise. When she came to the photo album, she stopped. "I just don't understand why she kept her past such a secret, Rabbi Siegmond."

"I have talked with many survivors of the Holocaust, Sara," the rabbi began. "Some have felt great shame and tried to keep their past a secret—especially if they had been in a camp. Some of them have gone through years of counseling. Perhaps your grandmother also felt that shame but refused to seek help."

"But why would she feel shame? None of that was her fault." Sara felt a slight quiver of guilt as she thought of her own reaction to the attempted rape.

"Yes, if you are being reasonable, but emotions aren't governed by reason. Tell me, where did your grandmother come from?"

"I don't know."

"You don't know?"

"No. None of us knows anything about our grandmother's family or history or . . . or anything except that maybe she had a brother who was killed in World War II. Even my mother doesn't know where her own mother was born or where she went to school." The words rushed out.

"And just before she died, my grandmother decided that her brother, who would be my great-uncle, I guess, is alive after all. She wants me to find him, but she was killed before she could give me any information about him or herself."

The rabbi sat back and studied her. Sara stared at her hands. Did he believe her? She knew how bizarre the situation was. She picked up the valise, set it on the coffee table in front of them, and opened it.

"The only clues we have are in this valise," she continued, "and my grandmother is no longer here to explain any of it."

"It certainly looks like it's been through the war." He ran his fingers across the fabric. "It must be ancient."

Sara pulled out the envelope and laid it aside, then the menorah and placed it beside the valise. She held the valise open toward the rabbi. "Look through it yourself."

The rabbi rummaged through it, pulling out the other items and laying them side by side with the menorah. Then they both stared at the array.

"As you say," the rabbi said, "the valise contains what appears to be a collection of receipts, an album, and some Jewish artifacts."

"Yes, it does." Sara clasped her hands together and sat back, looking at the rabbi. "There was also a bank passbook clipped to another receipt and a brief letter."

The rabbi cocked an eyebrow as he drew his eyes up to Sara's face. "A bank passbook?"

Sara nodded. "Yes, with a balance of $50,000 and the account is in my name."

He sat back and pursed his lips. "Did the letter or receipt offer any clues?"

"The receipt was signed by someone named R. Yulee. It's dated March 15, 1941. I can't make out what it says other than that." She rummaged through her purse for the letter and receipt.

"So you don't know what it's for and who this R. Yulee is?"

She handed the letter and receipt over to him. "My grandmother died suddenly and unexpectedly. She told us nothing of her past. I guess she was beginning to change her mind about that when she was killed.

Her name was Ruth Rachel so if her brother was Samuel E. Yulee, then maybe the R. Yulee was my grandmother's name—before she married my grandfather, I mean."

The rabbi studied the two documents and began reading the letter.

Sara leaned toward him. "You see the letter says I should find this Samuel E. Yulee and return the last delivery, whatever that means. He may not even be alive now, and I don't know anything more about him than his name." Sara paused. "My grandmother had left something with him for safekeeping. The bank account is to help me finish the delivery by finding her brother."

"But why would she ask you alone and not your brother?"

She hesitated. "I work in a law office and maybe she thought I was some kind of investigator, although . . ." Sara thought a moment. The rabbi waited, a quizzical expression on his face. She cleared her throat. "This sounds silly, but I think my grandmother . . . that is. . ."

How could she say this? "We were close. I think we connected on some level." She put her finger on it. "We could talk to each other." Yes. That was it. They understood each other. Sara could tell her grandmother about those back road drives, about her adventurous exploring—except not about the sailboat—and her grandmother responded with interest instead of the criticism her mother and brother dished out.

The rabbi waited a moment before replying, but Sara was not going to fill this inviting silence. She was finding him comfortable and easy to talk to, and he was just a little older than she.

"Not much to go on except that your grandmother was serious about this." He handed the documents back to Sara.

"Yes, she was. Too bad she was so secretive."

"And what about this album?"

Sara opened it for the rabbi. The thick pages were yellowed with age and cracked at the binding as she turned them. Sara pointed to the captions under the photographs. "I think at least some of the writing is Hebrew, but I can't read it."

The rabbi peered at the page, trying to decipher the cramped handwriting. "That might be Ladino, a kind of Spanish Hebrew spoken by Jewish exiles, but most of these photos are of art."

"Yes." Sara sat back and watched as the rabbi studied page after page.

"Looks like they're all numbered. There's probably a master list somewhere, but I guess you don't have that?" He looked up, and Sara shook her head.

"These other photos are perhaps friends or family. Most of the names are scratched out although some of the writing is legible. I don't have the time to give this the study it needs, but I can have someone go through and translate it for you. Even so, that might not get you any useful information, since the names are all first names."

"I wondered about that. I was hoping for names of towns or places. On most of the pages, it looks as if maybe the last names and other words have been scratched out so you can't read them."

"It certainly appears that she was hiding anything that might identify her—or the people in the photos. That's understandable if she had this in Europe during World War II."

He leafed through a Rolodex on his desk. "How about calling Elaine Steinitz? She helped displaced persons find their families after the war, and she knows Ladino. She'll probably enjoy helping you with the album."

Sara smiled at the rabbi. "That would be wonderful. I'll be happy to pay her for the translation."

"Well, you talk to her about that." He wrote down the name and phone number. "It might take some time. It does appear to be a family album, and some of the names are Spanish or Portuguese. Probably your grandmother came from a family of Sephardic Jews."

Sara leaned forward. She had never heard of them. "Sephardic Jews?"

"I guess you don't know much about Jewish history."

Sara shook her head.

"I'm sure you've heard about the Catholic Inquisition. It persisted all over Europe for centuries to persecute Jews and heretics. The Rabbi leaned back in his chair and folded his arms.

"I have heard of Torquemada," Sara said. "Wasn't he associated with torture and murder?"

The rabbi winced. "Yeah, that was his legacy, all right. Ferdinand and Isabella of Spain hired him to become their Inquisitor-General. Then in 1492, they issued an edict expelling all Jews from Spanish territories. Several years later, the Portuguese followed suit." He paused to take a deep breath, and then continued.

"Jews were forced to leave these countries or convert to Catholicism. The Jews who left and their descendants are called Sephardic Jews. The Jews who stayed and converted were still subject to discrimination and abuse, since they were 'new Christians.'" He shrugged. "Many of them hid their Jewish connection and held their rituals and meetings in secret despite the risk of torture and death if discovered."

"Do you suppose that's part of my own heritage?" Sara said.

"It could be." The rabbi leaned forward. "That's why separation of church and state is so important."

Sara felt pushed back by his intensity. This idea must be important to him. A fragment of a news story surfaced in Sara's memory, something about a fundamentalist demonstration against a quiet Baha'i meeting in a town near Martinsburg. That happened recently—not more than two years ago.

The rabbi picked up a pencil and tapped it on his desk. "Frankly, I agree with Thomas Jefferson—'Religion with power in its hands is the worst kind of tyrant.' I wouldn't trust any leader who exploits religion."

Sara thought about her grandmother in a concentration camp.

"The fact that conversos were forcibly converted Jews was lost in some families over the generations, leaving only a few Jewish customs lingering on." He pursed his lips and studied Sara. "Did you have any customs in your family that seemed unusual?"

Sara stared down at her hands and thought of their Friday evening dinners. She felt too stunned and overwhelmed to talk about her own family. She needed time to absorb all this.

As if sensing Sara's need, the rabbi leafed through the album. "You did notice that most of the settings in the photos are tropical? Palm trees. Hibiscus and bougainvillea flowers."

She looked up. "Yes, I did. I never heard of our family having any southern connection. But does the name Samuel E. Yulee sound at all familiar to you? Do you have any suggestions?"

"Yulee is an unusual name. I don't think it is Jewish or an adaptation of a Jewish surname. And I suppose you don't have any kind of identification for him. Birth date? Social Security number? What about his middle name?"

Sara shook her head.

"That's the kind of data you'd need to research public records. You have a tough job ahead of you. I suppose you might contact an experienced genealogist."

"I know it will be tough, but I don't want to go to a genealogist. At least, not yet. I don't think I have enough information about him."

"The only other thing I can suggest is that perhaps you could search for Yulees on the Internet. It's not a common name." He snapped his fingers. "I do believe there is a Florida town named Yulee."

"I've already checked the Internet. Didn't find any Samuel E. Yulees, and almost all the other Yulees I turned up live in Florida, which makes sense, I guess, with all those palm trees in those photos. But that is a very old receipt and a very old album."

"What about the other papers you have there?" He nodded at the envelope Sara had laid on the table.

"They're all receipts, too, but they're cryptic. Some of them are also signed by R. Yulee and some by S. Yulee, which I guess might be Samuel. It will take time to figure them out, and I'd have to know a lot more about this than I do now. I think they're in Ladino too."

The rabbi shuffled through the documents, and then looked up at Sara. "These appear to be receipts for things like paintings and sculptures, I think, but the notes are all so abbreviated, I can't tell for sure. They date from 1938, 1939 . . . here's one that's dated 1940. And," he held up another receipt, "here's the most interesting one and it's dated 1941. So this is all you have to go on?"

"That's right. It isn't much, I know. I'm thinking of going to Florida and visiting the Yulees who live there face to face. There's got to be a connection, and I might recognize a family characteristic."

"I see. I wish I could suggest a more helpful path for you, but I usually don't deal with this kind of thing."

Sara realized that the practical approaches would be phone calls, genealogy websites, and a genealogist. She also knew at some deep level that connected with her grandmother that she, like Sara, would be disappointed in that approach. Dave would have taken the practical approach, but Grandma did not give Dave the money and the problem. She had entrusted it to Sara, and Sara would carry it out her way.

She smiled at the rabbi. "I suppose my grandmother was trying to protect us but imagine hiding your past from your family."

"And perhaps you owe it to yourself and your family to recover it."

"I wish she had not been so afraid or at least had trusted us more."

"For a concentration camp survivor," the Rabbi said, "that can be hard to do."

Sara thanked the rabbi, and he wished her luck. She brought out her checkbook, but he waved it away. "Send the synagogue a donation if you'd like. I'm glad to be of help, Sara. By the way, according to Jewish law, our religion is passed down through the mother. If your grandmother was Jewish, then your mother, and now you are also Jewish, unless your mother or you have converted to another religion." He smiled at her. "Please let me know what happens."

Sara left with the rabbi's last words ringing in her ears. *Grandma steered us all away from any religious connection. So I'm Jewish.* The whole idea was too new. It would take time to absorb.

Sara felt a growing realization that the task her grandmother had set for her was probably an impossible one. Even so, she was determined to do her best to carry it out, but deep inside lurked another agenda.

She needed to find out if that beast on the sailboat was alive and still preying on innocent women. What she would do about this, she didn't know yet.

The first casualty would be her job. It had been her lifeline to security—via the paycheck. She had clung to the job for more than two years despite its lack of challenge. She was way overdue for a change.

She was giving herself an arbitrary three months to find Samuel E. Yulee. The search could take as long as necessary—or until the money ran out. She smiled. Eventually she would have to find a new job . . . and a new career. How long could she make $50,000 last anyway?

That evening, Sara called Elaine Steinitz.

Chapter 20

Mogador, Morocco, 1781

At dawn on the third day of his captivity, Moses woke to creaking and scraping as the guards pushed open the door of his prison. They entered the cell and prodded the prisoners out into the dark passageway.

As Moses trudged down the alleys and into the streets of the town, he studied each guard. One in particular drew his attention. Unlike the others who wore djellabas, this guard appeared to be in his late twenties with an open face too plain to be handsome. He had the features of an Arab, but he wore English dress—tan breeches, stockings, and a loose shirt with brown leather vest—and kept to the rear of the procession. Moses stumbled and fell back to the end of the line to tramp alongside.

The guard whistled as he marched, swinging his cudgel. Moses spoke to him first in Portuguese, and then in English as a test, "Where are we being taken?"

The guard stopped whistling and looked down at Moses out of the corner of his eye. He grunted, then said in English, "Keep moving." He emphasized this order by nudging Moses on the back with his cudgel.

Moses shrugged. The guard spoke like an Englishman. He was probably an English renegade. Could he draw on their English connection to get him to help them?

This time as the guards herded the captives down the street, Moses noticed that the shopkeepers idly watched the parade with indifference. There was nothing to be gained from this motley group of slaves.

Moses again fell back toward the guard. "I must speak to one of the king's agents or administrators," he said in English. The guard did not respond, but Moses saw him smile.

"You will be well rewarded if I am able to speak to him."

The guard ignored him.

Moses tried to keep desperation out of his voice. "A terrible mistake has been made. I am Moses Levy, scholar from Tangier and a special emissary of the vizier. He waits for me even now. I must return to his offices." This was the most persuasive lie he could imagine. What else could he say?

The guard glanced at Moses and smiled. "You must speak more than English if you wish to speak to the king's advisor here." Then although he did not look at Moses, he continued to step alongside.

Moses took heart at this comment. "Yes, yes, I speak Spanish and Portuguese and some Arabic." The guard only grunted in response, and they had arrived at the quay. The guards pushed the slaves toward the stacks of cargo unloaded from the ships and now piled on the dock.

Moses trudged all day along with the other slaves carrying crates and barrels from the dock to warehouses inside the thick walls. He squinted in the glare of the bright sunlight, but the temperature did not climb to the usual blistering level, and the wind continued to blow off the ocean. At last the sun sank to the horizon. Limping with blistered feet and tortured with sunburn, he staggered exhausted with the other captives up the street toward their prison. Moses whipped himself forward with the thought of Rachel and what she must be suffering. He spotted the English guard and tottered toward him.

Mustering every ounce of physical stamina that he possessed, Moses struggled to walk alongside the guard. Muttering through parched lips, Moses said, "The king's agent will reward you well if I am able to speak to him."

"I see you don't know the king's agent," the guard said.

Moses trudged onward with the other captives. This man must help them.

After a few moments, the guard added, "The vizier said perhaps tomorrow."

"Oh, you spoke to him!" Moses stopped in his excitement.

"No. He spoke to me." The guard shrugged and motioned him onward.

The guards herded the captives down the narrow back streets and then shoved them past the cell where they had been imprisoned, past more stinking privies, up steep stairs and into a cell smaller than their first one. A slit high in one wall served as a window, and a pit on the opposite side was a privy. The guard slammed the door shut. A key grated in the lock.

The heat rose from the floor in waves, and the captives were packed together like bottles in a box. Exhausted and thirsty, unable to lie down in the crush, they sat staring mutely at the stone floor. Like so much Moses had encountered in Morocco, there seemed to be nothing but arbitrary whim behind this change of cell.

After a long while, the door cracked open and a bowl of couscous covered with flies was jammed in beside them. The food tasted bland and watery. A sailor sitting beside Moses waved at the bowl. "I see they intend to work us tomorrow." Moses had not the energy to respond, but he had lived long enough in Morocco to know that the king's administrators would use them worse than donkeys. He had to escape this cell or die—not escape to freedom yet, but to a more comfortable slavery than building the king's monuments or carrying cargo to and from the ships in the searing sun and hot winds of Mogador.

Just before dawn the next morning, a guard opened the door and stood aside to let the English guard come forward. He pointed to Moses and flicked his hand at the door. Moses rose with hope and dread fighting in his heart. The English guard pushed him out of the cell and then made a show of prodding him up the steps. Moses looked back to see the other guard herding the prisoners out for the walk to the docks. He hoped he would avoid another day like the one his younger cellmates would suffer.

His guard saw him look back and said, "At least while there is cargo to move they will be fed. You should pray you will be as fortunate."

Gently pushing Moses forward with his cudgel, the guard led him across a central courtyard shaded with orange trees, then directly into a narrow chamber. The light from the open doorway reflected on the blue, yellow, and green wall tiles. The floor, plush with layers of red rugs, felt soft and luxurious under Moses' bare feet. Benches covered with red cushions lined three of the walls and a wooden desk, Spanish in design and heavy with mahogany ornamentation, sat along the fourth wall. The matching chair behind the desk had been pushed back as if someone had hurried out of the room.

As the guard left, he murmured, "I suggest you speak Spanish." Then he slipped out of the room, leaving Moses alone.

Moses crossed to the opposite wall and sat on a cushion. He waited patiently. At least he was out of the sun and not carrying cargo. He considered searching the desk, but if he were discovered, he would be at such a disadvantage that he would lose any possibility of bargaining for his release or Rachel's and might forfeit his life.

He heard the muezzin's call to prayer and wondered how long he would be sitting there. He felt sure that the long wait was planned to undermine and diminish him and any demands he might make. Finally, a quiet voice from behind startled him. "Ah, mi amigo Moses Levy."

Moses turned and bowed. "Yes, I am Moses Levy, scholar and teacher from Tangier, your Excellency," he responded in Spanish. "I am most grateful for this audience with your eminence. My family and I have been cruelly used and seek your help."

The man hobbled forward. He was older than Moses expected. A skullcap sat precariously atop his bald head, and his face was pockmarked. He unfastened the black cloak he wore and threw it over one shoulder. Underneath he wore a black tunic and a jeweled medallion that hung on a gold chain around his neck.

"So your story to the guard was not all lies. You are a teacher." The man peered at Moses out of the corner of his eye.

Moses saw the look and spoke warily. "That is true. I am a scholar and a student of many languages. Pirates captured my daughter, a friend, and myself off the coast on the way to America. I don't know where they have been taken. I beg of you to rescue us from this situation and let us continue on our journey. My daughter is young and . . . ."

"Yes, yes, yes, but . . . ah, you ask too much. My name is Eliahu ben Youli."

Moses saw Eliahu pause for Moses' recognition. Moses had heard the name before and bowed. "I am honored to meet the king's highest vizier."

Youli stood taller. "Yes, I am the grand vizier for his royal majesty, King Muhammed ibn Abdullah. You and your daughter and her, ah, friend, are now the, ah, guests of his Majesty. It does not matter how you came to be so. You are Jews, I see, as I am myself, but the king is, ah, not easily persuaded from what is best for his, ah, business."

"Yes, I am a Jew," Moses said, drawing on every link he could put forward. "My family came originally from Spain, but we have lived in England for several generations. My daughter and I moved to Tangier only a few years ago."

"So you speak English. You speak it well?"

"I was brought up in England, your Excellency," Moses repeated.

"The king needs men of your skills. I have paid your ransom, but I must be repaid."

Moses clenched his teeth and stared at the ground. The ransom had been paid, but now he—and Rachel—were indebted to this man who did not seem kind or generous.

"You will be repaid," said Moses, "but now I have nothing. All that I have was stolen by the pirates."

"I know that. Therefore, you must work here with me until you have repaid your debt. You can be most useful to me. The king seeks to improve our trading and commerce. And your fine daughter and her, ah, companion are of, ah, some value. Perhaps they could become, ah, companions in the palace, and you could be given greater liberty." He squinted at Moses.

"No, I don't want . . . ." Moses paused. He felt a quiver of fear. He must be cautious. Youli knew more about Rachel and Annie than he admitted.

"Your Excellency must not be distracted from important concerns. The women are of no interest. I would be glad to serve his Majesty for a while, if the women could be allowed to continue their journey to America."

"We shall see," said Eliahu ben Youli with indifference.

"They are women of some accomplishment and education. They will not live well in a harem."

"Enough. Perhaps I shall find out what has happened to them. Meanwhile, you will have a room here where we can discuss business. You will serve as my, ah, secretary."

"Secretary!" Youli planned to use Moses as a slave. Moses almost sighed with relief. Working at a desk with the king's vizier utilized his abilities in a kinder fashion than hauling heavy barrels on the docks.

"Yes, very well. I accept your expressions of gratitude." Youli withdrew a tiny bell from the folds of his robe and rang it. The guard reappeared. "Take Señor Levy to the corner room in the back courtyard."

A flicker of surprise crossed the guard's face but, as was his habit, Moses was learning, the guard bowed and said nothing.

Moses was certain Eliahu ben Youli knew where Rachel and Annie were imprisoned. Youli may have already planned some fate for them, but Moses had been dismissed and he could do nothing but obey the vizier and his guard.

With the guard leading the way, Moses was lost in self-recrimination as anger and frustration boiled in his heart. In his powerless position, he could not have demanded that Youli tell him of Rachel's whereabouts, but perhaps he could have asked Youli to look into her care without pushing for her release. But then Youli had only to deny any knowledge of her and the inquiries might bring attention that would be harmful. What could Moses do?

"Wait here," the guard said, as they turned a corner in the dark passageway. His face was still expressionless, but he cocked his head at

Moses and winked.

He winked! Moses was astounded, wondering what would happen next.

The guard stepped down the passageway to an archway on his right. He peered through the arch, then turned to Moses and motioned him forward. As Moses stepped up to the archway, he hid his surprise. *Who was this guard? He might mean well. Did he think we were being followed?*

A voice from the shadows said, "Mr. Levy?"

"Annie! Is that you?" Moses saw a ragged figure turn towards him from a corner of the courtyard.

Annie set two old and stained clay jars on the ground and rushed toward him. "Mr. Levy, are you all right?" Annie grasped his hands and searched his face. She wore a dirty black caftan and a black hijab covered her head.

Moses gripped her hands and stared into her eyes. "Yes, yes, where is Rachel? How is she?"

She tugged at her hands, but Moses would not release them. "We . . . we are all right . . . for now."

"Where are they keeping her . . . and you?"

"I am one of the domestic servants. I work in the laundry. It's dark when I come in the morning and dark when they take me back. I don't know the way."

"But you haven't been . . . they treat you well?"

"Yes, but I must not tarry. They will miss me." She turned to leave.

Moses released her but plucked at her sleeve. "But what about Rachel? What is happening to her?"

"She's all right for now. But, oh, Mr. Levy, we must get her out of here. This is not a place for her." She pulled away and picked up the jars.

"Wait, I need to know . . . ."

Annie disappeared down the dark passageway. Moses started after her, but the guard grabbed Moses' arm and held him back. Shaking his head at Moses, the guard pulled him towards a bench against the wall and gestured. Moses sat down. The guard sat next to him.

"Thank you." Moses fought down the tears. For several moments, they sat in silence. Then, reaching into his shirt, the guard withdrew a thin piece of paper, so stiff and yellowed that it crackled as he unfolded it. He spread it out for Moses to see.

Faded with age yet still visible was a delicate pencil drawing of a young woman with a slight smile hovering wistfully on her face. Her hair was curled under a bonnet that Moses recognized as being popular in the years he had lived in England. Moses looked up to see the guard watching him.

"That's a lovely young woman," Moses said, hoping the man would reveal something about himself. "Who is she?"

"She was my wife." The guard took the paper back, folded it and tucked it into a vest pocket. Then he rose and without the slightest recognition that anything had taken place, he said, "This way."

They walked through a doorway, then across a courtyard, down yet another passage to arrive at a courtyard more barren than any that Moses had yet seen. The guard led Moses to a small room in the corner, opened the door and with a bow and flourish, stepped aside for Moses to enter. As Moses gazed around his new quarters, the guard locked the door and left.

The dark room, windowless except for a grated window in the door, could not dampen the hope within him. Annie was alive. She seemed to be unharmed. Rachel must be nearby. He must find out where.

Chapter 21

Martinsburg, West Virginia. 1999

Sara parked in front of her mother's house and hesitated, her hand on the car door, anxious about the encounters to come. She took a deep breath, got out of the car, walked up the steps, silently rehearsing the words, and entered the house. "Mom," she called, "I'm here."

Her mother sat in the living room. She looked up from her newspaper and smiled at Sara. Sara smiled back. Her mother had changed since Grandma's death. She seemed less aloof somehow as if learning about Grandma's secrets had opened her soul.

Sara bent over to give her mother a hug. "Is there any iced tea?"

Her mother put aside the papers and began to rise, but Sara shook her head. "I'll bring it out."

Sara stepped into the kitchen, filled two glasses with ice and tea, and brought them into the living room. She set them on the coffee table and sat down on the couch facing her mother.

Feeling as if she were jumping off a cliff, Sara rushed into what she hoped would be a reassuring description of her plans, but her mother reacted with the dismay Sara expected.

"Alone? You're going to drive to Florida and all around the state alone? You've never even been to Florida." Amelia's eyes sparked. She laid aside the newspapers. "What about your job?"

"I resigned today." Sara gritted her teeth, waiting for her mother's reaction.

Instead, Amelia stared at her for a moment, then she sat back and took a long sip of tea. Sara waited as the silence stretched out too long. Then Amelia said, "You'll never track down this Yulee, whoever he is.

It's been too long."

Sara sighed and tried to placate. "I know, Mom, but . . ."

Amelia shook her finger at Sara. "And who knows what kind of Pandora's box you'll open. Your grandmother must have lost her mind."

"Yes, but, Mom, think about this." Sara stood and faced her mother. "None of us knows who she was. We don't know for sure what her name was, we don't know her family, and we don't even know where she came from. She was your mother and my grandmother, and we know nothing about her."

Amelia shook her head. "We know she was a good woman."

"Yes, she was."

"That was enough for me." Amelia folded her arms. "I'm sure she didn't mean for you to travel all over the country, Sara."

To Sara, this was exactly what her grandmother had meant. "Mom, I have to do this. I'll call you every other day or so to let you know I'm all right, okay?"

Her mother stared at the coffee table. "We were never close, the way my friends were with their mothers. I tried to be like her, but," she reached for the tea, "but I see now that I was only trying to be the person she pretended to be."

"Oh, Mom," said Sara, stunned at this revelation from her normally repressed, undemonstrative mother. Sara sat next to Amelia and put her arms around her.

She leaned against Sara. "I was copying a fake."

"And I was copying you. Who are we, Mom, really?"

"I think she saw herself in you, Sara. She told me how concerned she was about you. We all were . . . the way you've changed the past year."

"I suppose she thought a project might help," said Sara. That's why she asked me to find her brother and gave me the money." She wanted me to do it my way, the way she would have done it if she could have overcome the terror of the Holocaust.

"All the more reason why it will be a waste of time."

"I suppose so, but I still have to do it."

"I'll worry about you every minute of every day."

"I have to make this trip."

Her mother continued to frown, but Sara hugged her again and, in an effort to appease, said, "Let's go out to lunch. Then you can help me shop for the trip."

Later, on their way home from shopping, Sara looked over to find her mother frowning at her. "You've never driven on such a long trip by yourself. Florida is two days away."

Sara smiled at her. "I drove back and forth to college."

"It will be a waste of time."

"I have to do it, Mom."

Finally her mother shrugged. "You always did what you wanted to do anyway," she said in resignation. "Maybe the trip will bring back your sunny self again."

Sara did not respond. She wished that her mother could be more supportive, more optimistic. Later, as Sara drove back to her own apartment, she realized that for the first time in, yes, more than a year, since the assault, she felt excited. Her old enthusiasm was returning. She parked and danced a few steps as she juggled her packages all the way up to her apartment.

Telling her mother about the trip was the second hurdle, after resigning her job. Sara's growing excitement and enthusiasm for the task ahead buoyed her through the call to her brother.

"What? You're going to waste that money on a useless trip to Florida? Are you crazy?"

"I probably won't spend more than a couple of thousand."

"This is the most asinine waste of money, Sara."

"Still, it's what I'm going to do." Sara clenched her teeth and stared at the wall.

"I would have invested that money. Grandma didn't know what she was doing, giving it to you like that."

"Sure, invested it where, at the race track?" She was through with this call.

"Very funny."

"I'll call when I get back." Sara hung up the phone. How different she and her brother were. Her hands were trembling, but she had told her boss, her Mom, and her brother and felt at once both lighter with those three chores behind her and excited at the task she was taking on alone.

She still had one more call to make. Peter. What would he say, now that they were engaged, to her leaving for who knew how long? How did she feel about leaving him? What if he wanted to come along? He might convince himself that he had to protect her or make sure she didn't get into trouble. Yes, he would put it that way. He would want to make a quick and efficient job of the trip, hovering over her, second-guessing every decision, complaining about every detour.

Sara sat up with a start. Her feelings were clear. No way was he coming along. This was her adventure, and she needed to play it her way. She didn't want to negotiate every step of the way with anyone—especially Peter.

Would he wait for her? Sara nibbled at her fingernails. Did she want him to? He was a solid, comfortable bear of a man—and she had needed that—but he had no imagination and no sense of adventure. Sara shivered as the truth she fought became clear. She could not live the bland kind of life he offered her. She did not need security if it meant a slow death.

She waited until they were seated in a booth at a local restaurant, conscious that she had chosen the spot for the same reason anyone chooses a public place to end a relationship—to prevent a big scene.

His reaction was worse than she feared. He stared at her, mouth open.

"You can't leave now," he said at last.

"I must. I'll be gone maybe three months."

"Three months is too long. You can't go down there by yourself on an idiotic wild goose chase. Besides . . ."

Sara looked up.

"Besides," he said, "I've bought us a house." He sat back, a smug smile on his face. "I was going to surprise you."

Sara stared at him as the anger rose within her. "You've bought a house? Without even asking me?"

"You'll like it." He drummed his fingers on the table as if the discussion was over.

"No, I won't. I don't." She felt the claustrophobia that preceded a panic attack. She took off the ring, placed it on the table, and ran out of the restaurant. She did not look back.

That was the end of Peter. She spent two days dodging his phone calls, and then the calls stopped. The weak, little girl side of her nature that had surfaced after the assault whispered to her in nightmares to stay with the safe, the secure, to go to Peter, to live in his house. Then morning would come and the brightness of the new day would sweep the nightmares away and her confidence would return.

She was taking three glorious months to travel and do as she pleased. She was going on an adventure, but there would be no sailboats on this one. Sara smiled at her little joke, realizing that it was the first time she had ever found any humor in the ordeal.

The task ahead of her was daunting and probably hopeless. Still, it was worth a try even if it became just a memorial trip for her grandmother. Sara disciplined herself to plan only one step at a time. The next step: Searching for Yulees in Florida.

That evening, Sara mapped out a circle tour of Florida that would allow her to visit each of the Yulees on the list she had prepared from the Internet. As she studied the map, her eyes were drawn repeatedly to the town of Yulee, just north of Jacksonville. The first stop.

In West Virginia, summer was over and fall had begun, Sara's least favorite season. The dread of cold weather and the beginning of a new school year persisted even though the school years were behind her. Now she was heading to warm and sunny Florida, but underneath the family quest lurked a darker motive. Sara felt the Beretta in her purse. She needed to finish the chapter that had begun on the Chesapeake. Was that preying wolf alive or not? Was he still attacking women on his sailboat? Miami, Florida, was on her list.

Now she had one more call to make.

***

Elaine answered the phone on the first ring. "Yes," she said. "I've gone through the album." There was a pause. "I've made a list in English of the names and what notes I could translate, but I'm sorry, Sara, much of the writing was crossed through with what looks to me like a permanent black marker."

Sara shook her head. "I was hoping you might find an explanation in the notes."

"I don't understand why all those photos of art and sculpture should be in a family album. Do you have any idea what that's all about?"

"None. If you're through with it, I'll come pick it up."

"I'll be here."

An hour later, Sara arrived at Elaine's small, white frame home in a development near Rockville. Elaine opened the door to Sara's knock and invited her in with a smile. Elaine's pale blue pantsuit complimented her white, curly hair and golden complexion. Her soft, motherly appearance reassured Sara.

Sara followed Elaine into the living room and was startled to see that Elaine had another visitor. He rose as they entered. Elaine nodded to him and turned to Sara. "This is the son of friends, and he's visiting me for a few days. Josh Davila, Sara Miller."

They shook hands and each sat at opposite ends of a sofa behind a coffee table that held a flowered china teapot and two mismatched, fragile teacups. Elaine sat in the facing armchair. She poured the tea and handed a cup to Sara.

Sara stared down at her cup, wondering what Josh was doing there. She guessed that he was about her age, maybe a year or two older, but after breaking up with Peter, she had no interest in getting involved with another man who'd probably try to control and criticize her. She felt uncomfortable and not sure she wanted to talk in front of him.

Elaine fluttered a hand. "Josh has studied Sephardic families. Perhaps he can add historic information that I lack. Since he is staying with me, I took the liberty of asking him to look at the album and join us." She glanced at Sara. "I hope you don't mind."

Sara did mind, but Elaine was the only resource she had, so she nodded, sat back, and waited.

Elaine peered at Sara over the cup. "Good, then. Now we'd like to hear more from you about the album. It is a puzzle, isn't it? The album was from your grandmother, and you knew nothing about any of this before her death?"

Sara leaned forward. "That's right. No one in my family had any idea that she was Jewish or anything about her background at all."

Elaine smiled at her as if Sara's story was perfectly reasonable. "And you say Yulee was the name mentioned in the letter?"

"That's right." Sara brought out the letter and pointed to Yulee's name. "Here. You see? Samuel E. Yulee and there was an R. Yulee, too, on the receipts."

Elaine adjusted her glasses and peered at the letter. "Interesting. So you know nothing about any Yulees?"

"Nothing." Sara shook her head and picked up her teacup.

"I am distantly related to the Yulee family." Josh spoke for the first time. "But this album is a mystery to me."

"I worked with displaced persons after World War II," Elaine stared at the wall, "but I don't remember meeting any Yulees." She looked back at Sara. "Of course, there were so many people. . . ." Her eyes gazed off in the distance, then she shook herself and looked at Sara. "What do you propose to do about this?"

"I'm leaving in a couple of days for Florida to visit the Yulees I've located online." Sara brought out the map. "You see, I've made an itinerary here of where they are and the route I'll take."

Elaine studied the map. There was a long silence. "So you think the answer will be in Florida." She handed the map to Josh. "You know you are talking about genealogical research here. There are many historical archives you could tap, including archives of displaced Jews from World War II."

"You're right, of course, but I would rather carry out my plan first,"

Sara said. "Most of those photos have palm trees and most of the Yulees live in Florida—the ones I located on the Net, I mean."

Elaine nodded. "You could take the album along and show it to the people you interview . . . maybe someone will recognize the photos. But that album may turn up someone's family skeleton." Elaine paused and leaned toward Sara, looking directly into her eyes. "I would be careful about mentioning it to just anyone."

Sara sat back, away from those penetrating eyes. "You're right about that. I'll be careful, and I'll keep my eyes open. I might identify some of the background in the photos too as I travel around the state." She stood.

Josh also stood and smiled at Sara. "I haven't been of much help, but I am staying in Florida—Cedar Key—and conducting research of my own there. Here's my card. Contact me when you're in Florida. I may have found out something by then."

Sara took the card out of politeness. She looked at Elaine. "Thank you for your help. What do I owe you?"

Elaine refused any payment. "I was pleased to help, my dear."

She walked with Sara to her car, but as Sara drove away, she saw Elaine in the rear view mirror, staring at the car and writing something down in a notepad.

Chapter 22

Mogador: 1781

The next morning, the guard appeared followed by a stooped old man carrying food. Moses scarcely had time to eat before the guard gestured him out the door, then led him back to Eliahu ben Youli's quarters.

Eliahu barely acknowledged Moses but motioned him to follow. They walked through the courtyards and out into the maze of alleys to the docks to take possession of cargo from a ship just arrived. The officials and the clerks they met at the port and customs house treated Eliahu with deference. Then Moses and Eliahu boarded the ship to greet the captain, who stood on deck waiting for them. He handed a sheaf of papers to Eliahu, who gave them to Moses.

"Read these and tell me whether they are in order," Eliahu said.

They were written in English, since the ship was English, but the writing was strangely composed as if to disguise the ship's nationality.

Moses read through the pages and looked up to see the captain handing over to Eliahu a bulky sack that clanked as it passed from hand to hand. Moses understood that it was a bribe and remembered that the king did not welcome English trade. He ignored the transaction going on in front of him and turned back to the papers. As he studied them, he realized that he could provide a suggestion that might cement his relationship with Eliahu.

He called Eliahu aside. "See this? These porcelain imports? I have heard of these importers and know that they must be watched. It would be better to check their crates yourself."

Eliahu chewed his fingers thoughtfully. "Yes, I see that. I, too, know that they tend to go light if they think they can get away with it.

You stay here while I oversee this examination." Eliahu left with purpose in his shrewd eyes.

The captain shrugged, crossed his arms, and looked at Moses. "So you think I have not already checked those crates?" He tossed his head toward Eliahu's departing figure. "How do you know that man?" he asked.

"I don't know him. I am a slave, captured off the brig *Harmony* just days ago."

"I know that ship. I have met Captain Moore in other ports. What happened to him and the crew, then?"

"I am sorry to tell you that the captain and some of the crew were killed. The rest captured along with my daughter, a friend, and myself."

"I see." The captain stared at the deck a moment. "It is terrible, that. It was an American ship, too. They still do not make protection payments, those Americans."

"The payments should not be necessary."

"I agree, but then there it is. And so now you find yourself a slave to that fine gentleman over there. May I speak frankly with you, Señor Levy?"

"I welcome any information and help that will aid me in my current circumstances," said Moses.

"I must tell you to go careful with him." The captain kept his eye on Eliahu. "Do not trust him."

Moses squinted at the captain. "Why do you say that?"

"I know who you are. We met some years ago when you sailed to Tangier. I was first mate then, but I remember you and your daughter. How beautiful a young girl she was. Where is she now?"

Moses choked and struggled to speak. "She was taken from me when we arrived. I fear for her."

"Mark my words," said the captain, "your master knows where she is. You must be careful what you say to Señor Youli." The captain bit on his pipe. "Do not tell him anything that he can use against you."

"You are good to warn me."

"Did you ever hear of the family Cardozo?"

Moses shook his head.

"Because of that man, your master, the Cardozos have fallen on evil times. I know this because one of the Cardozos was my good friend."

"What did Eliahu do?"

"This is the story as it was told to me. The Cardozos were a wealthy family with three sons. I met them when they traveled with me to France. Eliahu knew the family and was treated as a friend. Two of the sons came here to Mogador and became successful merchants. They wrote to the third brother who had gone to London, urging him to return and join them.

"Eliahu intercepted the London brother's reply and saved part of this letter, which, without the rest, seemed to mock the king. He showed this part to the king, who was highly offended, naturally. He executed one brother and threw the other in prison where he remains. The king then claimed all their possessions and gave Eliahu a generous reward."

The captain spat. "That is the offal who is your master."

Moses did not respond at once. He watched Eliahu cross the deck and thought about what he knew of the man. Finally, he said, "A terrible story, that. I thank you for your warning and will be cautious." He looked out at sea, towards America, and added, "but I hope and pray that his power with the king will help in releasing my daughter."

"I am saying that you should seek help in another quarter."

Such a harsh assessment petrified Moses. He could not bear to lose Rachel. She must be saved.

Eliahu hobbled back to Moses and the captain and signed a receipt for the shipment, crossing out the number written there, noting a lower number and lower cost. The captain watched without comment. Then Eliahu called for workers to carry the crates ashore.

A guard and three of Moses' cellmates appeared. As they carried away the cargo, Moses whispered to one, "Where are the others? Where is Horace?"

"We don't know. We think they were sent to the mines," was the answer.

As Moses and Eliahu walked up the street leading back to the palace, Eliahu said, "Don't speak to slaves."

"I asked about my companions."

"Your companions, you say." Eliahu laughed. "They cannot help you. Ignore them."

They entered the courtyard and made their way to Eliahu's offices. Moses turned to leave, but Eliahu called him back. "Sit down, my friend, sit down." His tone was particularly oily. Moses' eyes narrowed.

Instead of heading for his writing desk and chair, Eliahu chose the couch against the wall. Moses hesitated, then he too deliberately sat down on the couch next to Eliahu.

"I want to discuss an important, ah, negotiation with you," said Eliahu.

A negotiation? Rachel? Moses did not dare to speak.

"Come, come, my friend. We are allies, no?"

"As fellow Jews, we must help each other in adversity," Moses replied.

"Yes, yes. That is what we must discuss. I have learned of your daughter. Take heart. She is well and, because she speaks English, she has become a special, ah, protégée, shall we say, of one of the king's wives, who is an English woman."

A protégée of the king's wife? What did Eliahu mean? Moses waited, dreading the next words.

"But, my friend, the harem is not a good place for her. Fortunately, neither the king nor his sons are in residence in Mogador at this time, and I have a plan that will free her from the harem before any of them return. My plan will ensure your daughter's well-being yet allow her to remain a good Jew."

"What is your plan?" Moses' composure hid the despair he felt. He was desperately afraid for Rachel but saw no way to rescue her. No opportunity, no window, no fairy godmother presented itself, and nothing could be done without money and time.

"Do not worry, my friend. It is a good plan."

Moses watched Eliahu with dread.

"I will marry her," Eliahu said. He held up a hand to silence Moses, but Moses could not be silenced.

"You cannot marry her. She is a young girl. You are an old man."

Eliahu stood up and with the quiet deadliness of a pit viper, said, "I will marry her, and you will see to it that she accepts this arrangement."

Moses drew himself up to glare down on Eliahu. "You cannot mean to make yourself a laughing stock for all of Mogador. You cannot mean that this is the only way a powerful man such as yourself can rescue my daughter."

"Yes, I am powerful. And yes, I will marry your daughter. If you seek to rescue her from the king's harem, you will agree to my, ah, proposal. The, ah, king, our elderly monarch, an old man, much older than I, may even now be preparing to visit his palace here. We can only hope that he will not come until all our arrangements are completed."

With sickening misery, Moses saw the grim trap closing around Rachel.

"If you refuse this arrangement, I cannot be responsible for what will happen to her and her friend."

Moses glowered at Eliahu.

"I repeat, my friend," said Eliahu, "this is the only way to rescue your daughter. She will have a good life with me and," he peered at Moses with shrewd eyes, "you will be able to see her."

Moses sank to the couch, slumped in defeat.

"This is the best solution to the problem." Eliahu held up a hand. "Yes, yes, do not thank me."

Ignoring Moses' distress, Eliahu smiled to himself as he tapped his chin. Then he turned back to Moses and said, "Now, you will, you must, write to your friends and acquaintances and beg for the money that I require to buy her."

Chapter 23

Florida, 1999

Early Monday morning, Sara walked down the stairs with a suitcase in each hand. She tucked the baggage into her car trunk and stopped. What was she forgetting? Her passport. She wouldn't need it for Florida, but she didn't know where her journey would take her. She might need it. She hoped she would. She ran back up the stairs and found it in the bottom of her desk drawer. She smiled at it—never used, acquired when she still planned adventures, before the trip to the Chesapeake.

Impatient to reach Florida, Sara kept to the interstates rather than explore the side roads she preferred. She passed the Florida state line after she had stopped for lunch the next day. She felt exhilarated and ready to begin the adventure.

Ten miles down I-95, just north of Jacksonville, she turned off at the exit leading to the town of Yulee and beyond. Sara zipped through Yulee, not recognizing that the town stood at the crossroads of Routes A1A and 17. She turned back. The early afternoon sun baked the stubby live oak trees in town, and the buildings appeared dusty and sleepy. She yawned, feeling sleepy herself.

Yulee was not an expensive, oceanfront resort. It resembled a backwoods Georgia village halfway through a transformation to an industrial Jacksonville suburb. A strip of the usual stores—convenience store, self-service laundry, drugstore, post office, gas station, McDonald's, Burger King—lined each side of the highway. The old and the new stood side by side, but the old didn't hold much promise. Even the town's palmettos and sandspur lawns looked as if they had given up all aspiration and hope.

How could she find out more about this town? Go to a cemetery? Library? Chamber of Commerce? Driving up and down the side streets, she found a small wooden house perched on concrete blocks with a sign over the door saying, "Yulee Historical Museum." Sara parked and walked up to the door, but the museum was open only on Saturdays, four days away. She didn't find a cemetery or a library. Where else could she go?

The post office was a possibility. Sara parked in front and walked in. The clerk at the window looked as broad as the counter. Her skin was too heavily tanned to be healthy, and her hair was dyed a bright canary yellow. She motioned with her hand, ready to take a package or letter.

Sara put on her best smile. "I'm just passing through and thought I'd stop here for a while. Wondered how I could find out more about this town."

The clerk sighed as if the question was an imposition, but she answered politely enough in a deep, whiskey voice. "What do you want to know?" she rasped.

"Where did it get its name?"

"Sorry. Can't help you. I'm from Jacksonville and got assigned out here. I can get you to Fernandina Beach—that's just down the road maybe 15 minutes—or to Jacksonville, maybe give you directions if you're looking for someplace particular."

"What's at Fernandina Beach?"

The clerk seemed to wake up. "Now that's where you want to go if you want history." She picked up a pen and used it to point toward the road. "They have a local museum that might have something for you."

Sara bought a book of stamps and, seeing nothing else that might be helpful, left the town of Yulee to head east on A1A toward Fernandina Beach. She found the town on Amelia Island, just across the Intracoastal Waterway, and parked on the main street in front of a Victorian mansion painted a pastel yellow. A sign out front announced that it was a Bed & Breakfast. Antique, book, and crafts shops lined the street, interspersed with T-shirt and souvenir shops, all of them appearing clean, swept, and prosperous.

At the end of the street Sara saw a large, colorful sign in a real estate office promoting Amelia Island's resort properties on the Atlantic Ocean. Beyond the sign, Sara caught a glimpse of a marina and the waterway. Her mood darkened. Her hands trembled as she felt the familiar pounding heart, upset stomach, and sense of panic grip her. She took a deep breath, willing herself to remain calm, and hurried down the main street, focusing on finding the museum. The panic subsided as quickly as it had begun.

Streets in this old, historic section were laid out in a grid pattern—no circles or winding lanes. The architecture in the bright sunshine mixed colonial Spanish with Victorian. Sara passed two historic saloons as she strolled down Centre Street. Then she spotted a sign for the museum pointing down a side street. She headed in that direction.

She found the museum in a square brick building with a sign in front saying that it had been the former county jail. The yard was mowed and the hedges clipped. Sara was afraid that a small town museum like this would also be closed during the week but, no, it was open daily from ten until five.

Inside, an elderly man wearing jeans and a railroad cap sat in an old wooden office chair, weaving a basket. He laid it aside when she entered and limped over to stand behind the reception desk.

"Well hello," he drawled. "Welcome to our museum. I'm your docent for the day. Amos Blackwell." He held out his hand.

"Sara Miller." She shook hands and paid the admission fee with a smile.

"I'm all you got here today and you're all I got," said the docent. "You might want to come back on Saturday for the regular tour."

"No. I need to move on, and I really just have some basic questions," Sara said.

She found that, in the absence of any other visitor on this mid-week fall afternoon, the docent was a most loquacious tour guide who appeared to be knowledgeable.

"Can you tell me anything about the town of Yulee that I passed through on the way here?" she began.

"Yulee? That ain't much of a town, is it? What did you want to know?"

"The name. Where did the name come from?"

"That's a long story," he said. "But an interestin' one."

He sat back down in the chair, picked up the basket and pointed to a scarred walnut desk chair across from him and on the other side of the door. Sara sat there. The docent wiped his brow. Even though the museum seemed to be air-conditioned, the heat and humidity penetrated the dark walls.

"Yulee is the man who built the railroad that begins here in town," he began, looking at her over his bifocals as his hands fiddled with the basket.

"Oh, so he was a railroad man?"

"Well, yes, but he was the founder of it, you know. He didn't wield a hammer." The docent chuckled at his little joke. "His railroad starts here in Fernandina Beach. You saw it out there, didn't you?"

Sara nodded. "I came across references to a David Yulee on the Internet. He was a Florida senator or something back in the early days." The reference had intrigued Sara, but David Yulee had lived a long time ago. Maybe he had sons, though, and maybe she was a descendent.

"Yes, he was but he was a territorial representative first," the old man continued. "He and his family lived here in Fernandina Beach a while." He set the basket carefully on the floor and leaned toward Sara with his hands on his knees.

Sara smiled to encourage him.

"You see, first he was a non-votin' member of the House of Representatives. That's when he started pushin' for Florida's statehood. When it finally got voted in as a state—that was in 1845—David Levy and his friend James D. Westcott, Jr., became the first senators. David was the first Jew to serve in the U.S. Senate."

"Levy? But I thought his name was Yulee."

"Well, now, hold on there. That's another interestin' story. When he was in Washington, he met the daughter of the Kentucky governor. Nancy Wickliffe was her name. They fell in love and David wanted to marry her, but we think that her family had objections—maybe because he was Jewish, you know. The governor probably didn't want to face the political baggage that came with a name like Levy."

Sara thought of her brother Dave. "Maybe their objection was just that they wanted their daughter to marry in their faith, whatever that was."

"Could be," the old man said doubtfully.

"So how did he get the name Yulee?"

"Seems that an old family friend took David aside and told him that his grandfather had been a high mucky-muck in Morocco and that his name was really Youli, that's spelled Y-O-U-L-I. David grabbed at that idea, Americanized the name to Yulee, spelled it Y-U-L-E-E, and had his name officially changed. He also started going to the Presbyterian Church. After that, the Wickliffe family withdrew their objections."

"And so David and Nancy were married. Did they have children?"

"Four. Three girls and a boy. I guess they have descendants all over Florida."

"Do you know any?"

"Naw. Never looked. I think there are a lot of Yulees, though. Remember now, that the name was originally Y-O-U-L-I. Spelling of names was pretty original in those days, you know. And some of the

Yulees may have been slaves for his sugar plantation and maybe for his railroad. They could have taken on the Yulee name when they were emancipated. Most Yulees probably aren't even connected to the senator's family at all."

"Yes, I can see how that would be," Sara said.

"Any Yulees are long gone from here, but I think there may be one or two living on Cedar Key. That's on the west coast of Florida. Yulee built the railroad to cross Florida from here to Cedar Key. "

"Cedar Key." The name seemed familiar. Sara pulled a Florida map out of her purse and opened it.

"Right here," the docent said, pointing to a dot on the coast west of Gainesville. "You'll like it. It's a real interestin' artsy town. Kind of like Fernandina. Fernandina Beach and Cedar Key are deep water ports, you see. That's why all the interest in these two towns. We got a five-foot tidal range here too. You'll see that if you stay here a day or two. Did you notice the marina?"

"Yes, I did, but I didn't go over there."

"Look around here. This is a real nice town—and it's an old town, older than St. Augustine, no matter what they say over there. Then you go over to Cedar Key and take a look around there."

Sara smiled at his enthusiasm. "I like this town." She waved her hand in a circle. "So I'll be sure to stop at Cedar Key. Actually, I wanted to find out more about the town of Yulee, because I might be related to the Yulees and know nothing about them."

"Is that so? Well, that puts a different light on it then."

"I have fifteen names of Yulees on my list so far, and they're all over Florida. The one I'm particularly interested in is a Samuel E. Yulee, but I couldn't find anyone with that name."

"Samuel E. Yulee, eh? The 'E' might stand for Elias, a name that keeps cropping up with that family. David's brother's name was Elias. That was their Dad's middle name too."

"Interesting and makes sense. Thank you." Sara stood to leave.

"So you just plan to drive around?" The docent squinted up at Sara, his hands still fiddling with the basket.

"I'm taking this trip for my grandmother—to find her brother. I think I might have a better chance locating him if I can see the people and talk to them face to face."

"Well, watch out, though, and be careful. Outa state license tags too, I'll bet. Makes you easier to spot. Sure hate to have my own daughter driving around alone. You don't know any of these people you're lookin' for and what they might want from you when you find them."

Chapter 24

Mogador: 1782

Rachel sat on the low bench around a fountain in one of the square courts of the harem. The tinkling splash of water soothed her spirits. So far she was simply a prisoner and had yet to see the king or any of his sons. She hoped never to see them. The thought left her sick with the terror that she would be imprisoned here forever.

Rachel stared up into the sky over the courtyard and breathed deeply of the orange blossoms in the trees around her. The fresh scent lifted her spirits after hours in the claustrophobic confines of the women's apartments. The rooms reeked of the jasmine and spice perfumes the harem women seemed to swim in, and the heavy odors gave Rachel a headache.

The blue and white tiles that checkered the courtyard walks felt cool to her feet. The walks led to arched doorways into the women's apartments on all sides. Polished wood balustrades and pillars carved with delicate vines and flowers shone in the common areas, and elaborate mirrors and rich floral damasks in bright reds, blues, and greens spread across every wall. Two and even three layers of thick carpets covered the floors with color, and low couches placed against the walls served for sitting and sleeping.

At night, Rachel took refuge in the barren closet allotted to her. It had been a storeroom and grains of millet clung to crevices, but someone had thrown a carpet on the stone floor. Rachel used that for sitting and sleeping.

Annie was incensed at such treatment. One morning, she stopped by Rachel's room on her way to sweeping the walks. Her eyes sparked at its meagerness. "We sleep in beds where I come from," she whispered angrily. "And sit on chairs."

Rachel stood and hugged Annie. "In England too. I feel like a poor orphan here. The harem wives insist that I not sit on the linen-covered mattresses and cushions. They are not very friendly." She smiled at Annie. "We both rank very low, but this is good. They can treat me like a peasant and a servant. That sets me apart. I do not want to belong to this place. "

Annie laughed. "I will remember your words. I also would prefer to be a stranger."

As Rachel sat by the fountain, she saw one of the men who guarded and ruled the harem cross the courtyard. Rachel debated whether she should hide from him or to stay where she was and hope he had some other errand—or victim. These men were black Africans, and their voices were high-pitched like boys. Among them was the little man who had taken her away from her father with the two women. He usually accompanied the tall man who acted as manager of the harem.

She puzzled about these men for days until she asked Annie, whom she often saw at menial tasks in the hallways and courtyard, "Who are these strange men? What is wrong with them?"

Annie had grimaced. "My dear, those men are called eunuchs. They have been altered like sheep so they can't bother the women." She picked up an orange from the doorway. "Stay as far from them as you can."

Annie was allowed some freedom as she went about her chores, but Rachel was imprisoned like the other harem women not only in a cage but also in idleness. The wives were allowed to furnish their own rooms, hire their own domestics, and do what they pleased in the hierarchy of the harem, but they were not permitted to leave without permission from the king delivered through the eunuchs.

While Rachel was given only a simple black caftan of rough cotton to wear, the other women wore silks and other luxurious materials and often draped multiple strands of precious gemstones or pearls around their necks and arms. As Rachel watched the ostentatious parade of decorated women, she realized that they measured their status and their worth by the wealth they displayed. They were a mixed group, ranging from fair to black, and there seemed to be a ranking order in which the women arranged themselves. The older wives, for instance, demanded deference from the others, and all the wives demanded deference from the concubines.

Despite the luxurious trappings, the harem women seemed to spend their days in idle gossip and petty rivalries. Rachel pitied them. None of them could read or write, so they were forced to live in ignorance. A music teacher was allowed in so some of the women used his services in occasional attempts to play the mandolin. After hours of listening to this noise, Rachel escaped one day to the courtyard for a bit of silence and ran into Annie who sat on a bench fanning her face with a leafy branch.

"What a racket," Annie said.

"I had to leave. The shrieks they call music make me shudder."

"Yes. I think the musicians," Annie grimaced, "only want as much noise as possible."

The wives received a trifling allowance and used it to purchase showy clothing, lotions or perfumes. Rachel did not understand their need for these enticements, but she was appalled at the harem women's enforced helplessness and ignorance.

Lacking intelligent conversation, Rachel longed for a book to read, but when she asked one of the odd harem men for a book, he shook his head. Perhaps he did not know English.

After that episode, she made herself as inconspicuous as she could, sitting on the floor against the walls, observing the activities of the women, and searching for any scrap of information that might be useful. She picked up Arabic words and casually practiced them with the other women, turning these simple language lessons into compliments and, since several were interested in learning English words, an exchange.

Rachel also sought the company of the domestic servants thinking that since they were allowed in from the town, they might know what was happening outside the palace walls. Moreover, the women who came in daily to sew were Jewish. Rachel often sat with them, which pleased them, and they all tried to communicate in a smattering of sign language, Hebrew, Arabic, and Spanish. Rachel felt that she was a novelty for them, but they were kind. They felt sorry for her and they tried to comfort, but they could not read or write, and they were riddled with superstitions.

She was amazed at the number of men who brought odd bundles to the harem. One day, she asked a servant in her halting Arabic what this was all about.

The servant laughed. Speaking slowly and simply so Rachel would understand, she said, "Where do you think the wives get all their finery and their jewels?"

Rachel stared at her.

"From the Europeans and the merchants and others who want favors from the king. They pay the wives to use their influence with him, but the eunuchs keep track of it all and," she laughed, "you know they get their share."

Rachel perceived the deference—and fear—of the king's wives and realized that the eunuchs ruled the harem with tightly closed fists. Nothing escaped their eyes. They assessed every move and word of the women. Rachel soon became self-conscious and said little to the eunuchs unless spoken to directly. Then she hesitated and stammered as if she were a bit dim-witted. She thought this impression might serve her best as she negotiated these dangerous waters.

"Those men are not fools," Annie cautioned Rachel. "They are managers and diplomats between the harem and the king. Do not mock them."

Rachel bit her lip as Annie added, "They expect payment for any little favor. The king's women pay for these favors out of the meager allowance doled out to them and whatever gifts they receive."

Rachel soon learned to avoid the head eunuch. He was tall and obese and spoke English haltingly in a peculiar high voice. Although his features were African, his skin was almost white. Rachel's attempts to engage his help were ignored, and she never saw him invite conversation with any of the women. She knew her name, like the others, was written in the large ledger he habitually carried with him. She couldn't imagine what he might have written there.

As the days passed, Rachel sought to understand the daily harem regime. She would have enjoyed playing with the children, but the mothers watched their children closely and jealously. Each male child was a possible future king and a rival to the others.

Eventually Rachel found two women in the harem who spoke English. One was fifteen years old, like herself, and a concubine. Rachel met her in a passageway and noticed her eyes first. They were the saddest Rachel had ever seen. The girl smiled at Rachel, finger to her lips, and took Rachel's hand, pulling her into a small, simply furnished room.

"Please sit," the girl said, "and talk to me. My name is Yosafina."

"Yosafina. What a pretty name." Rachel smiled back at her, glad to meet someone her own age and, moreover, someone who spoke English. "And I am Rachel."

"Have you been given to the king also?" Yosafina asked.

Rachel trembled as fear clutched her stomach. "I pray not. I hope to be delivered from this place."

"Ins'hallah. I was not." Yosafina shrugged. "My father was English, you understand? A renegado. He sold me to the king. It was a bargain he made. And so I am here and a Muslim. It was the king's wish."

Rachel sat speechless. Her own father would never consent to such an arrangement. How could Yosafina's father have done such a thing?

Rachel often passed the time with Yosafina but did not confide in her. Yosafina was a creature of the harem, and Rachel was not. Yosafina's casual references to her life there at first saddened, then horrified Rachel as she realized that as young as this girl was, she was still only a toy for the king.

The other woman who spoke English was one of the harem wives and seemed to have some status. Rachel cultivated a friendship with her but soon found her shallow and dull. She was consumed by her son, a man named Yazid, and sought only to indulge him. He was the eldest of the king's ten sons and so first in line for the throne.

One day Rachel motioned Annie aside. After glancing around to make sure she was unobserved, Rachel whispered, "No one pays attention to you. The harem women here say whatever they please in front of you. Can you find out about this man Yazid as you talk with the other servants and slaves around the palace? If he has even a shred of sense or kindness, perhaps I can convince him to release us . . . if I should meet him." Rachel knew it was a forlorn hope.

Several days later, as Rachel wandered down a dark passageway of the harem, she found Annie on her knees scrubbing the tiles. Rachel stooped to talk with her, pretending that she had dropped a button.

"I wish I could help you," she murmured.

Annie shook her head and continued to scrub. "You must not call attention to yourself that way." She whispered, "I have found out about this Yazid."

Rachel did not look at Annie. "What?" she asked.

"I have only to say his name and the other servants shudder. They say he is a cruel man and from what they tell me of his exploits, he sounds to me sadistic and ignorant. I think only his doting mother believes that he will become king some day."

"She speaks of him with great pride," Rachel said.

"Do you notice that she is also afraid of him?"

"Surely not."

"I have heard a terrible story about him from one of the other slaves." Annie looked both ways down the corridor. "That slave saw him set fire to a cat he had impaled on a skewer meant for roasting meat."

Rachel stared at Annie. "But that is horrible," she said.

Annie nodded. "When Yazid saw that he had a witness, he laughed and then sneered at the slave who ran away and hid. She was afraid that she would also become a victim."

"Surely such a man would not be made king," Rachel said.

"One would hope not," Annie said. "Ins'hallah." She grinned at Rachel. 'I've heard the other sons are more reasonable."

Rachel laughed. "Keep up your Arabic. We will need it," she said. Seeing two of the wives coming her way, she continued down the passageway.

Whenever Rachel encountered Annie, she would stop and pat her on the back and whisper encouraging words. "I'm sure my father will find some way to rescue us." Rachel made the words as strong as she could since neither of them had heard anything about Moses, where he was or what he was doing. In her darkest moments, Rachel wondered if he was even alive.

Annie would shrug but one day had grimly added, "It had better be soon because I'm growing old fast, and I'm running out of patience. I fear that I will talk back to one of these harem prima donnas or a eunuch and be whipped to death."

Rachel saw beyond these pessimistic words. Annie was losing her spirit and turning into a hopeless drudge. Annie's existence, like Rachel's, was not only boring and powerless but also tenuous, depending on the whim of the eunuchs who saw every move and shrewdly divined their thoughts.

As Rachel sat at the fountain, Annie entered the courtyard and walked over to her. Rachel looked up to see the head eunuch staring at them.

He called Annie to him. "I wish you to wash my feet in warm argan oil," he said. "Do as I say. Now."

Annie bowed and turned to find the oil and a bowl. She stared without expression at Rachel as she passed.

"And you. Come forward." The eunuch looked down at Rachel. "We are planning how we shall use you. You must not become harem wife. Your children must not be a consideration for the throne. Is not Jewish money coming to ransom you?"

"I do not know what has happened to my father," Rachel replied.

"Your father is now with the vizier. Do you not think he will find ransom?"

"I believe that he will, but I have not spoken with him."

"The vizier is a Jew. Do you not know that?"

"If he is a Jew, then he will help."

"Then we will hold you back for a while longer, but soon the king, my master, will arrive, and then I must tell him about you." The eunuch stopped and surveyed her from head to foot. "And he will want you."

Rachel shuddered inwardly, thinking of Yosafina, but she dared not show how repulsive this idea was to her. She said as respectfully as she could manage, "Is there no other way? I am of no use to you. None of his wives want me here. He has no need of me."

"No? It is true that you have many faults, but we cannot let you go without some . . . arrangement."

He meant money. Rachel stared at the floor.

The eunuch reached over and swiveled her face to him, pinching her cheeks together between his thumb and his forefinger. "I expect your obedience and respect."

Rachel was forced to look at him.

"You may go now," he said. He released her, and Rachel withdrew, grateful to escape. She retreated to her room. Was this to be her fate? To become another Yosafina, owned and used at whim and then stored in this . . . this . . . warehouse?

***

Eliahu sat at his desk staring at Moses through folded hands. "I have received some monies from your, ah, acquaintances but not enough."

"I have written everyone I know, begging them for help," Moses said through gritted teeth. He stood tall and straight to remove any suggestion of servitude.

"Write them again. They must know how desperate you are. You must obtain more money if I am to save your daughter."

"Save my daughter? You call a forced marriage saving her?"

"Bah! The old, I say very old, king even now travels towards Mogador. You would prefer to see her enslaved in a harem as a plaything for that very old man?"

Moses had never in his life felt so helpless. Three months had passed. Opportunities for escape were no closer. He could not hold Eliahu off much longer.

Eliahu smiled at Moses with narrowed eyes. "You realize that she is, ah, in danger. The longer she remains in the harem, the more risk that she will be harmed by the women or the eunuchs there."

Moses stared at the carpet. Despite his abilities and experience, Moses could see no way to save his daughter for the new life they had imagined in America. Eliahu mined his expertise and sought his contacts. Moses gritted his teeth. Until he developed his own network of gossips and spies within the medina and the palace, Eliahu and the English guard remained the only links to his daughter.

The guard who had first brought Moses to Eliahu was a puzzle and an uncertain ally but better than none at all. Moses always chatted with the guard if they happened to meet, but such opportunities were rare. The guard was elusive and often assigned elsewhere.

Despite his elevated position as Eliahu's secretary, Moses, like Rachel, was a prisoner. Eliahu scrutinized all communication and controlled Moses' every action. Even so, Moses found ways to expand his influence in town and his value to the vizier—especially now that Eliahu was accumulating the money from Moses' solicitations. Moses glimpsed the letters and the monies that arrived, and he knew that there was enough to release Rachel. Unfortunately, Eliahu quickly squirreled these funds away and referred to them only as Rachel's "dowry."

Even if Moses could have managed to leave Eliahu's offices and escape Morocco, he could not retrieve Rachel to escape with him. She was buried and inaccessible inside the king's palace. It was tantalizingly close—just a few narrow streets—but might just as well have been a thousand miles away.

If, by some miracle, Rachel found a way to escape the women's quarters, she would still be unable to leave Morocco, for the king had forbidden any woman to leave the country. Even men needed permission to travel and that meant money and months of perseverance to obtain the necessary papers.

Moses kept a list of the powerful Jewish merchants in Mogador, but they were immersed in their own manipulations and intrigues for money and power. Eliahu had permitted Moses to approach all of them. Moses wondered at Eliahu's largesse since he must know that Moses would ask for help in escaping the country.

All were willing to contribute to Rachel's "dowry," a move they saw as helping Moses while ingratiating themselves with Eliahu. Only one had spoken the truth to him. "We cannot risk offending Eliahu, who is a man of great power as the king's vizier. He can grant favors we seek from the king and give us the king's business. We fear reprisals if we are seen offering help directly to you."

Eliahu, in the press of business, had once sent Moses on an errand to the British vice-consul, Mr. Hutchinson. Moses set out hoping that Hutchinson would be a reasonable man who would help but arrived to find Hutchinson at his desk, shuffling papers as if he were extremely busy, so busy that the courtesy of offering tea was omitted. Moses' heart sank but after he dispensed with the errand and before he could be dismissed, he said, "Mr. Hutchinson, I am desperately in need of your assistance."

Hutchinson dragged his eyes up to look at Moses.

Moses could see refusal in Hutchinson's face but went on. "I am sure you know that my daughter and I were captured by pirates and have been forced into slavery here. We are English citizens. We seek your help in obtaining permission to leave Morocco and travel to America. My daughter so far remains untouched in the king's harem, but he soon returns."

Hutchinson's face turned red. He drummed his fingers on the desk. Finally, he said, "I am aware of your situation, but I am only here as a representative of His Majesty the King. I have no power to intervene in your behalf." He stared at the papers on his desk, as if willing Moses to leave.

"Can nothing be done?" Moses cried.

"I will certainly try to see what can be done," Hutchinson said.

"Can you at least find ransom to release the sailors who were captured along with us?"

"But they were American sailors on an American ship. I have no way to help them since our countries are at war, but I have notified the American consul of their situation—and yours." Then he added with a sneer, "Perhaps their democratic Congress will eventually agree on how to negotiate their release." Hutchinson shrugged his shoulders and turned back to his papers.

Moses left in disgust. That weak little worm would do nothing to help and sneered at the idea of democracy. Moses stuck out his jaw. The democracy of America was as much his dream as Thomas Jefferson's, and Moses greatly admired Thomas Jefferson.

Hutchinson was probably an honest man, Moses thought as he trudged back to Eliahu's offices, unlike the rogues he encountered daily as he worked for Eliahu. Moses already knew that nothing moved in Morocco without money. None of the king's courtiers and administrators received a salary. They relied on bribes and fees for their services. Even the king and the king's sons constantly sought new sources of income. They would without a second's thought confiscate the lands, house, and possessions of anyone who was so rash as to display or flaunt them. Scoundrels, all of them.

Only the press of business elsewhere had kept the king in Rabat and Marrakech and away from Mogador for so long. Now the townspeople and the palace were preparing for his return within the week. Rachel must be removed from the harem in the next day or two.

In despair, Moses went to Eliahu.

"I will accept your proposal to marry my daughter, but first I must speak with her and tell her of this decision." Moses drew a deep breath. "On such a vital matter, she must be informed gently."

Eliahu stared at Moses through eyes slit like a cat's. After a long moment, he said, "I will consider your request. I am sure, however, that, like all women, she will be pleased to be married . . . and to a man of such great consequence as myself. Even so, we will be family, so I will see what I can do."

Moses shivered, but he bowed and gave the humble reply that was expected of him, "My apologies and gratitude."

Eliahu merely smiled.

Moses stared at the floor for a moment, then bowed again and left the room. He closed the door behind him and spat on the floor. He rubbed the spit in with his slipper. He could stand tall and straight like an honorable man, but he was not honorable. Instead, his life was now spent currying favors from men more fit to live with swine than govern. He knew a thousand men more educated, more cultured, more intelligent, and more humane than any king or sultan…or vizier . . . who had managed only to be born into his position and possessed the ruthlessness and money to retain it.

Head bowed, shoulders slumped, Moses trudged down the passageway and through the courtyard to the steps leading to the roof. He climbed to the top where he could look out at the other roofs of the town. Under one of those roofs lived Rachel. What was she doing now? What was she thinking?

Moses stared out beyond the roofs to the Atlantic Ocean. Beyond the ocean was America, too many miles away. Unreachable.

Chapter 25

East Coast Florida: 1999

The docent's last words to Sara in Fernandina Beach left her feeling unsettled and nervous.

Yes, she was alone. Yes, she had out-of-state license tags, but she had lived a life stymied by fear long enough. In her core, Sara knew she was made of different stuff. That predator on the bay had terrified her and she had detoured, but Sara's spirit had lifted her off the well-worn path and propelled her forward in a different direction. She could no more go back to her old life than she could turn into a Pekingese.

Even my old job is gone. She examined her feelings and realized that she harbored no regrets. *How long would I have stayed in that job if my grandmother had not pushed me out?*

Sara turned her attention back to the road. Despite the old man's caution, she was pleased with the information she'd picked up at the museum in Fernandina Beach. She checked her watch. It was mid-afternoon and still early enough to move on. She drove back to I-95 and turned south, heading for St. Augustine where she planned to spend the night and meet the first Yulee on her list.

Sara checked into a motel and asked the reception clerk how to find the street where the St. Augustine Yulee—someone named Evalene— lived. The clerk pulled out a local map and marked the way.

Evalene's neighborhood was only a few blocks from downtown but a world apart in character. The paved street disintegrated into a path of sand, crabgrass and sandspurs that spread out across the yards. Sara found Evalene's apartment in a one-story quadriplex that had been a motel. Each unit was painted a different color—green, yellow, red, blue.

Strong colors, not pastels, and patchy in places. Sara kept away from a shaggy grove of palmettos as she walked up to the door. She knocked and could hear a baby crying within.

The door opened a crack and an eye peered out. Then the door opened wider. A young black woman stood, arms folded, frowning at Sara.

"I'm looking for Evalene Yulee," Sara said with a smile.

"What could you be wantin' with her." The woman did not return Sara's smile and spoke with an accent Sara could not identify.

Sara tried again. "Are you Evalene?"

The woman looked Sara up and down. "Who're you?"

"My name is Sara Miller," Sara began.

The woman began to close the door. "You with the state?"

"No, no. I'm not with the state. I am trying to find someone—family, that is—named Yulee. I'm just trying to help my grandmother."

"I don't know your grandmother."

Sara stammered a reply. "I guess not. I mean. . ."

The woman seemed to take pity on her. She replied in a kinder tone. "I'm the person you're looking for, but I'm not your family."

Sara smiled again, trying to be friendly. "I guess not, but could you tell me how you got your name?"

The woman stared at Sara. She did not invite Sara in. "It's my family name in Haiti. That's where I'm from." A tough-looking, burly man had come up behind Evalene, holding the baby who had begun to shriek. He was cooing to it but had one eye on Sara.

Sara backed away from the door. "Thank you for telling me," she said. "Have a good evening." She turned, willing herself to walk, not run, to her car.

A Yulee from Haiti. How interesting.

Sara returned to the motel. Her door opened onto the parking area. She had left her suitcase unopened on the luggage rack and placed the album in the center of the table by the window. She was sure she had placed it in the center. Now the album was closer to the table edge as if someone had sat there to look through it. A quiver of fear raced through her body. She studied the room. No one could hide under that bed and the bathroom door was open. She was alone.

She stared at the table for several minutes. Exactly how had she placed the album? She must have accidentally shoved it forward a bit . . . maybe hit the table as she moved around the room. Maybe the maid had come in. Sara opened her suitcase. Nothing out of place there. If a thief was after anything valuable, that's where he would look, wouldn't he?

Pulling aside the drapery, she scanned the parking lot. The sun had not yet set and in the dusk, she could see no one standing out there or waiting in any of the cars. It all appeared to be unremarkably innocent. She must be wrong, but just in case . . . . She picked up paper and pen and walked out to linger behind the parked cars, noting a brief description and the license tag number of each car.

The next day she continued south on I-95. Except for lunch, Daytona Beach was a bust. A man named William Yulee had moved from Daytona Beach to Tallahassee just three weeks before. Sara drove down to Fort Lauderdale for her next stop.

In Fort Lauderdale, she called Gregory Yulee who told her to come right on over. Sara debated this idea with herself. She didn't know this man and she didn't want to risk an attack. The self-defense classes she'd taken gave her confidence, but just in case, she carried her Beretta in her purse. She agreed to the meeting. He sounded very young.

She found Gregory in an apartment on the seventh floor of a beachfront condo. The building appeared vacant, and the security guard in the lobby yawned as she signed the log. September. Too early for snowbirds, and all the kids were back in school.

Out of the corner of her eye, she noticed a tall, silver-haired man come through the door and stop as he saw her. He snapped his fingers as if he'd forgotten something and turned around and left. The guard pointed her to the elevators.

A young man opened the door to her knock, sending out a blast of frigid air. Despite the polar temperature, he was wearing a brief bathing suit and tee shirt. He looked to be in his early twenties.

"Are you Mr. Yulee?"

"None other. Come on in." He stepped aside and waved toward the living room.

Sara hesitated at the door. Gregory left her there and walked in bare feet over to the galley kitchen. "Want a beer?" he asked, reaching into the refrigerator.

She shivered. "No, thanks." She walked into the room, keeping her hand on the Beretta in her purse. Was there anyone else in this apartment? Didn't appear to be. At least this wasn't a boat on the Chesapeake.

"Soda?" He continued to peer into the refrigerator as if searching for some magic potion that Sara would accept.

"No."

"Anything?" He straightened up and looked at her.

"Well, perhaps a glass of water."

"That's easy." She watched him fill a glass from the tap and hand it to her. She followed him into the living room. He sat down on the sofa, but Sara took an easy chair across the room and close to the door. The carpet and furnishings were white, but the apartment seemed dark to Sara. Heavy draperies drawn across the opposite wall left only a crack to reveal an ocean view. She took a deep breath. This was not the time for a panic attack.

"So you're looking for a Yulee. Will I do?" He smiled coquettishly.

"I don't think so. You're too young."

"Oh, darn."

"I mean I'm looking for someone much older. His name would be Samuel E. Yulee." Studying him, she wondered if they might be related somehow, but she could see no resemblance to her family.

"Sorry. Nobody here by that name."

"What about your parents?"

"They're in the Bahamas. They'll be home in about two weeks, if you want to come back." He leaned back lazily. "But, to tell you the truth, I've never heard of anyone named Samuel E. Yulee in our family. I suppose there might be some far-flung relative of that name, but I doubt it."

"Perhaps I could give your parents a call when they get back."

"Sure. Here, I'll write down the number for you."

"I have the number, thank you." She turned to leave, brushing off his suggestion that she hang around to go out for dinner and a movie later. He was probably just lonely, but she didn't want to spend the evening that way.

As she walked to the elevator, she almost bumped into the man she'd seen at the desk downstairs. He mumbled an apology and rushed past her, face averted. She looked back at him fumbling with a door as she waited for the elevator.

She spent the night at a motel on the Intracoastal Waterway. Her room faced west, and she felt comfortable when she looked in that direction, but when she stepped out to find a restaurant near the ocean, the inexplicable panicky feelings overcame her. The feeling was real but why? It couldn't just be some psychological residual from the attack on the sailboat, could it? There must be more to it than that. She simply had no way to account for these odd panic attacks. She chided herself for them, but the attacks persisted.

At the same time, Sara kept a wary eye on her surroundings, scanning the cars in the motel parking lot and noticing the people around her in the motel's breakfast room and lobby. The warnings from Elaine

Steinitz and the docent lurked uncomfortably in the back of her mind.

She also looked up boat yards and marinas in the Fort Lauderdale telephone directory, and that afternoon, she paid a visit to several of them on the New River—not that she expected to see the *Buccaneer*. She hadn't worked out any sort of plan as to what she wanted to do if she found the boat or learned that she'd killed him, but she had to search for it. She needed to know the answer to that terrible question.

The next day she headed for Miami, an hour's drive down I-95. When she arrived, she chose to stay at a quiet bed and breakfast in artsy Coconut Grove, away from Biscayne Bay and away from the ocean. She thought that anyone following her would find the game more difficult in the friendly atmosphere of a B&B. And it felt warmer and more protective than a motel for the darker part of her quest in this cosmopolitan and sophisticated city.

She liked the bilingual nature of Miami, but her college Spanish was barely adequate for reading signs. Three Yulees lived here. The first was an elderly man who sailed to Miami from Cuba in his youth. His name was Enrique Yulee, the Yulee being a corruption of Julio, she gathered after a long and tedious session in her meager Spanish and his broken English.

The second, E. P. Yulee, was a young woman who spoke with a soft Southern accent over the phone.

"Sure. Come on by," she said when Sara called her. "I live in an apartment over a garage in Coral Gables. Mango tree outside my door and wild parrots in the trees."

Even with E.P.'s directions, Sara had a hard time finding the apartment behind a modest home on a street of Spanish-style mansions. To get to the apartment meant a walk through a tangled jungle of overgrown tropical shrubs and trees.

E.P. Yulee was waiting for Sara on the landing at the top of the stairs. She welcomed Sara into her apartment. "My real name is Elizabeth, you know? Only I always use E.P. 'cause I don't want people to think a single woman lives back here." She swept a pile of magazines aside on a futon with a flowered cover and waved a hand at it for Sara.

"Iced tea?" she asked.

Sara grinned. "I'd love it."

Elizabeth disappeared around a corner for a moment, returning with two glasses of iced tea, which she set on the coffee table. She sat down in a wooden chair facing Sara and smiled. "Now how can I help you?"

Sara described her search for Samuel E. Yulee.

Elizabeth pursed her lips. "You know, I am a Yulee, but my roots go back to Elias Yulee, he was David Levy Yulee's older brother. David Yulee was a senator, you know?"

Sara felt her excitement growing as Elizabeth talked. At last, a real connection to a Yulee who might be a possibility. "What can you tell me about your family?"

"I don't know too much, I'm afraid. The only reason I know about Elias and David is because my grandfather told me. He was family-proud, you know? He did a genealogy of our side of the family, but he never mentioned any Samuel E. Yulee, and I know there isn't anyone with that name in my family—that I know of, I mean."

"Is your grandfather still . . . that is, is there some way I can talk to your grandfather?"

"Heavens no. He died years ago, I'm real sorry to say. I guess my parents have family papers stashed away somewhere, but they moved to California. They've got tons of boxes they've never even opened yet. In storage someplace, I guess."

Sara tucked the information away, thinking that this family genealogy might yield clues if she came to a dead end. She picked up the album. "We found this album with my grandmother's things after she died. I thought that you might recognize some of the people and places in it . . . that is, if you wouldn't mind."

"Of course not. Let me see." Elizabeth opened the album across her knees. At first she studied each photo carefully before shaking her head. After the first few pages without success, she scanned the rest of the photos more quickly. On the last page, she looked up at Sara.

"I'm as disappointed as you are, Sara. But I don't recognize anyone in this album. And even though the photos were taken in a subtropical area like Miami, I don't recognize the places. Anyway, most of the photos are of paintings."

"Well, it was a long shot." Sara shrugged. "I really think it would have been too much to hope that you would know these people."

Elizabeth closed the album. "I suppose so. The photos were taken a long time ago, too. That's a factor."

Sara sat back. "Do you have any suggestions about what I should do next?"

"Have no idea, but since you don't have a social security number or birth date for this Samuel Yulee, I would think you're doing the right thing, visiting all the Yulees here." Elizabeth handed the album back to Sara. "Sorry I can't be more help."

"I've enjoyed meeting you." Sara sipped her tea. "If I come to a dead end, I could contact your parents. They might let me go through those boxes in storage."

"Please let me know what happens." Elizabeth leaned toward Sara and smiled. "Your story intrigues me. How can I reach you if I find out anything on this end?"

Sara scribbled a note on a piece of paper. "Here's my mom's phone number. I'll keep in touch."

Even though the visit didn't give Sara any useful information, she felt so encouraged that she plunged through the jungle toward her car without thought, startling a tall, gray-haired man picking a hibiscus in the yard. He averted his face and mumbled something as he disappeared into the darkness. Sara was just as startled and ran to her car.

The next morning, she called the third Yulee on her list, Robert E., who told her to meet him at two in his law office in downtown Miami.

As Sara stepped into the office, a voice called out from a room in back, "My secretary's out. Come on back here."

Sara walked toward the voice, crossing into a large, paneled room with floor to ceiling bookshelves. A tall man, lean and tanned as if he ran marathons, sat back in his chair with his feet on the desk and hands behind his head. His tie and jacket hung on a coat rack in a corner. He appeared relaxed and sleepy as if he'd had a few drinks with lunch.

He motioned to the client's chair as he stood up and excused himself. "I could use some coffee, how about you?"

Sara called after his retreating body. "Just sugar, no cream."

He walked out into the secretary's office, humming to himself, and came back with two Styrofoam cups, handing one to her. He eased back behind the desk to his chair and gestured with his cup for her to begin.

As Sara told him about her search, he nodded his head frequently, but Sara finally realized that the head-nodding didn't convey interest but drowsiness. She must have been right about the heavy lunch.

She finished her story and prompted him with a question, "So I'm wondering if you know of anyone named Samuel E. Yulee?"

The forthright question roused him, and he stared at her a moment. Then he yawned and said, "That's interesting, but I'm sorry, there's no one named Samuel E. Yulee on my side of the family. I guess you've heard the story about David L. Yulee, our first senator?"

Sara leaned forward. "He was an important man in Florida."

"Well, I'm not related to him at all. My grandparents came from Lebanon and the immigration folks at Ellis Island made the best job they could out of our name and finally came up with Yulee. So I'm sorry I can't help you there."

"I appreciate your taking the time to see me, though. Thank you."

Sara turned to leave. He walked her to the door, and she felt his eyes on her back as she strode down the hall to the elevator. As she thought about the interview later, she decided that she had been just a diversion from the weight of his law practice. And the "E" in his name stood for Edward. She frowned as she thought about it. She didn't know Samuel's middle name. It could as easily be Edward as Elias.

Chapter 26

Mogador, 1782

Rachel woke each morning and scratched another mark on the wall of her room. She drifted through the days, hoping that she would be released and see her father that day. Weeks had passed since her imprisonment. She knew that Annie had seen Papa several days after their capture, but what had happened to him? Where was he?

At her lowest points, when sadness and fear threatened to overwhelm her, she would dream of America and the stories Esther and Ada had written of their life there. In America, she would be allowed to move freely, to work with her father, to read and to learn as she wished, and to marry whomever she pleased.

One morning she woke to find that the head eunuch had summoned her. "You are requested to appear before the vizier. You will go now."

Rachel dared not smile, but hope burned within her. At last she would see her father. She must see her father. She had heard the gossip about the vizier. The stories of his arrogance vied with the stories of the vast amounts of money he had added to the king's accounts. Whether of arrogance or financial prowess, each story was more unbelievable than the last.

She wished she could talk to Annie, but Annie was swallowed up in the back regions of the women's quarters.

Rachel bowed her head to the eunuch and turned to follow a domestic servant who led her off to a reception room. A piece of black linen cloth was tied around the lower part of her face, and she was given a black rectangular piece of cloth, a haik, with which to shroud herself.

The domestic covered herself with a haik as well, and then the two of them were met by the same eunuch who had taken Rachel away from her father when they had arrived in Mogador. He walked ahead of them out into a courtyard, down a colonnaded passageway, through the gates, past the guards and out into the dusty, narrow streets of the town.

Rachel breathed deeply. The fresh air felt invigorating. She looked around her with wonder. Even the dust that covered her sandals felt good to her. How could she bear to return to the stifling prison of the harem? She would rather die.

Three thin, flea-bitten donkeys, flicking their tails at the flies, waited for them. Rachel was pushed onto one and compelled to ride sitting on a blanket, her legs dangling on one side of the donkey for the short journey to the offices of the vizier. The eunuch and the domestic mounted their donkeys with the ease of long practice.

The procession made its way to a heavy wooden door in a plain stone wall. The lintel was carved with arabesque tracery and painted in the same blue that decorated every other gate and shutter and doorway that Rachel saw in the town. They dismounted the donkeys, and the eunuch walked to the door, knocked, and waited. A guard opened the door from within. They passed through a dark reception area and entered a courtyard lush with orange trees. They crossed the courtyard on a tiled walkway to reach another arched doorway. The eunuch paused, then pushed Rachel forward into the chamber. The domestic followed, but the eunuch withdrew to wait outside.

As her eyes grew accustomed to the dim light, Rachel scanned the room for her father but drew in her breath as she saw an elderly man peering at her—the man who had touched her face in that prison cell. Then she saw her father walking toward her, arms outstretched.

"Oh, Papa." The tears flooded her eyes and flushed her face. She yanked off the veil and ran to him. He took her into his arms, enclosing her within the folds of his djellaba.

"Papa, you are well." Her relief was so profound that she could not say another word. Her father was alive, and he did not appear ill-used. Even his djellaba was sweet-smelling, as if it had been washed in scented water.

"My dear, my dear," Moses hugged her, holding her close with one hand, smoothing her hair and patting her back with the other. "My sweet, little one."

"Touching," Eliahu said. He watched them a moment, then muttered, "I will be back shortly."

He walked past them and out into the courtyard beyond. The domestic remained, but Rachel knew she spoke no English and was of no consequence in this room.

"Hush, Rachel. We must talk quickly. He will return soon."

"What, Papa? Have we been ransomed? Can we leave?"

"No, my dear. You must listen. We have not been ransomed. But we have received some funds from our friends in the synagogue, and I have made an," he swallowed, "arrangement for you."

"But I cannot leave without you, Papa."

"You may be able to help us both, if you will agree to this plan. It will be difficult for you, my dear."

"What? What plan?" Rachel drew back from her father and looked up at him. The grimness in her father's voice terrified her.

"It is the only way to save you from the king and to get you out of the harem. I greatly fear for you in the king's harem, my dear."

Rachel's eyes widened. "But what am I to do?"

Moses sighed. He shook his head. "I do not see anything else that will be possible, and the king will arrive soon. He is on his way here. We must act quickly."

Rachel stared at him. Her legs felt weak and wobbly. Her father had always seemed so capable, so powerful. He could find a solution to any problem.

"But what is it? How can I help?"

"You must marry Eliahu ben Youli."

"Marry! Eliahu ben Youli?" She felt as if her heart had stopped. Dread shrouded her thoughts.

"He is the man you met when you walked in here."

The horror was shapeless no longer. "But he is so old. Older than you, Papa. Why would he want me? I do not trust him!"

"Nor do I. But marrying him will retrieve you from the harem and place you in a Jewish home. I will see that he also buys Annie as well. She will live with you as your servant. If you are forced into the king's harem, you will have to convert to Islam, and," he bowed his head and whispered, "I will never be permitted to see you again."

"Oh, Papa." Her words were heavy with sorrow. Rachel sank down on the divan. Her father sat with her and pulled her to him. Rachel wept. She tried to stop weeping but found she could not. Each pause was followed by a fresh spout of weeping.

All her hopes and dreams were now obscured by the dread reality that confronted her. Her childhood was over. In her thoughts, she said good-bye to Esther, to Ada, and to America.

"And if I don't? Is there no hope of rescue, Papa?"

"Possibly, but it may take years, and you must be removed from the women's quarters. The harem wives are vengeful and jealous. They will harm you if they feel threatened. "

"But Papa," said Rachel, "they seem so ignorant and dull. I don't believe they have any spirit or ambition."

"They do not want you as a rival, and they do not want any child you have to be another contender for the throne. Each one sees her own son as king and herself as king mother. They are perhaps already plotting against you."

Rachel had never imagined that the king's wives might see her as a rival. She suddenly understood that they had planned the manipulations that had buried her in sacks, kept her behind and beneath the others in the harem in an attempt to leave her feeling lowly and worthless. While she had thought the harem women were idle and foolish, they had despised her and sought every devious means to undermine her spirit.

Moses spoke urgently. "Do not underestimate them. You are in the king's palace and helpless there. You have no knowledge or experience with the intrigues and liaisons of court life surrounding you. Eliahu is an . . . able man. He is industrious and enterprising and in much favor with the king for the ways he has added to the royal coffers. And he has done much to raise the money to buy you, my dear."

Rachel considered what her father had not said. The money was raised, no doubt, from her father's friends and contacts and other Jewish sources. It could have paid for their freedom but in Eliahu's hands, it became instead her dowry and Eliahu would take all of it. Her refusal would end Papa's favored status in the medina. Unless she complied with this plan, they would lose all hope of rescue.

"But such a man. I cannot love him, Papa, and look what he has done to you." She thought with distaste of the gossip she'd heard about him. And then she considered marriage . . . with him. She had only a hazy idea of the day-to-day realities of marriage, but she knew that she would be expected to share the man's bed . . . and whatever happened there. She could not suppress the shudder. She sat silently with eyes closed for a long time, leaning against her father, holding his hands.

She thought back to her quiet life in England and then to her travels with Papa in Tangier. She had survived the pirates' attack and life in the harem. She was intelligent, capable, and strong. Now she faced an uncertain future alone. She would need every resource she possessed to endure this . . . marriage, but they would escape this place. All of them. Papa, Annie and her. The resolve hardened like a nut in her heart.

Rachel looked at her father, put aside his hands and stood, taking a deep breath. "Very well. I see that Eliahu has forced us into this" she frowned in distaste, "arrangement. I will marry this man, because I see that I must to protect you and Annie and myself from a worse fate. And I also see that he benefits financially by this . . . marriage."

She paced the room, head down. "I will see how I am treated. If with respect and kindness, then I will repay him by being a good wife to him. But he has not impressed me so far, and if he is as he appears to me, Papa, then I will not honor him, and I will not respect the ties that bind me to him."

"Hush, my dear. Those are dangerous words."

"Yes," said Rachel. "They are."

Chapter 27

Miami, 1999

That evening, Sara wrote notes about each of the Miami Yulees she had met. Then she picked up the Miami telephone directory. She took a deep breath. The assault had left her with anger and guilt and fear. For a year she had asked herself if she had killed the man who had assaulted her. Was he alive? Did he still live in Miami? What would happen when she confronted him? She stretched her muscles and looked over at her purse. Inside was the Beretta. She could not shoot to kill, but he would not attack her again.

Tony Donnell. Would he be listed in the phone book? Was he an itinerant sailor or did he maintain an address and phone number? What if he just had a cell phone? Or unlisted number. She leafed through the white pages to the D's, then down to Donnell. There was an "A. Donnell" but that was probably a woman. Then she found "Anthony Donnell." Surely it wouldn't be this easy. She dialed the number.

A brusque voice answered. "Donnell."

Sara lowered her voice in an attempt to disguise it, but the voice on the phone didn't sound like Tony's. "Tony Donnell? You own the sailboat *Buccaneer?*"

"Yeah. The *Buccaneer*. His boat's over at Riverway Marina. Call over there."

Sara felt so relieved she could hardly respond. She croaked out a "Thank you" and hung up. She had not killed him, but was he still assaulting women on his sailboat? She needed to find out what he was up to now. She had no idea what she could do about it, but she needed to know.

And she had the Beretta. Perhaps she could terrify him as much as he had terrified her—and teach him a lesson he'd never forget.

She found the address for Riverway Marina in the yellow pages and drove to its location on the Miami River near downtown Miami. She crept past it several times until she spotted the wreck of a small sailboat, its transom backed against the chain link fence along the sidewalk. The name *Buccaneer* stood out against the splintered fiberglass. Homeport: Miami, Florida.

What had happened to the boat? Sara pulled over and scanned the yard for the monster who invaded her dreams, turning them into nightmares. She didn't see him, so she drove into the boatyard and parked her car.

Tanned, shirtless men in cut-offs swarmed around the landed hulks. Some carried hammers; others worked drills, sanders, and sprayers. Sara kept her hand on the Beretta in her shoulder purse as she walked over to the *Buccaneer*, now a wrecked and rusted shell. The mast was gone, and gaping holes in the hull opened the cabin to the weather. Sara backed away from the smell of mildew.

She looked around for the creep, but she didn't see him. She walked over to the office.

Inside, a woman at a computer behind the counter looked up. "Can I help you?"

Sara glanced around. This woman was the only one in the office. Sara cleared her throat, suddenly nervous. "Yes, can you tell me anything about," she gulped, "the *Buccaneer*, the wreck over by the fence?"

The woman made a face as she took a sip of Coke from the bottle. "Sure. They say the boat caught up on a coral reef during a thunderstorm."

Sara had not expected this. "What about the owner, the captain?"

The woman got up and walked over to the counter. Sara felt uncomfortable at the woman's obvious sizing her up.

The woman nodded and pursed her lips. "Uh huh. I'm immune to good-lookin' guys with sailboats, but I guess you weren't." She leaned toward Sara. "What I think really happened is that some woman got her boyfriend to bash him and the boat with a tire iron."

She walked back to her desk. "Anyway, he's in rehab at Hialeah Westside Convalescent Center. He lost a leg and suffered some brain damage, they say. The police are investigating. Hope he wasn't a friend of yours."

"No, he wasn't."

They looked at each other.

The woman took a long drink of soda and cocked an eyebrow at

Sara. "Good riddance, I say."

"Yes," Sara said. "Good riddance." She turned to leave but paused. "He's still in rehab, you said?"

"He'll be there awhile, I guess."

Sara returned to her car and sat there, staring at the wreck. Neither the boat nor its captain would ever sail again. Poetic justice. She smiled grimly at the thought as she started the car and drove through the gate, grateful to be on the free side of the chain link fence.

The boat and the man had been destroyed, but Sara didn't feel vindicated, only relieved. She had not killed the man or even injured him enough to stop him from luring women onto his boat and molesting them. Perhaps her lack of action had left the man free to molest other women; perhaps he would have gone free anyway. Whatever the case, someone else had rendered a more permanent justice. Sara thought about this. Had she wanted to punish the man herself? Was her urge for revenge satisfied? Was anything left unfinished here?

Yes. She needed to visit the rehab center. She had things she wanted to say to Tony. She drove to the center, parked the car, and took a deep breath.

She found his room down a long green corridor, knocked, and entered. She had been prepared to feel angry, but instead she felt pity for the emaciated cripple who lay with bandaged head on the bed. He was covered with a light blanket that showed the bulge of one leg and a flatness where the other should have been. He opened his eyes.

Sara stepped forward. "Hello, Tony," she said.

She could see the bruises on his face and the missing teeth. He would never again captivate a young woman or entice her on a sailboat.

She took out the Beretta. "I didn't like the way our last meeting ended, Tony."

He turned his head away and tried to push away from her with his good leg. "No, No!" His terrified cries were too weak to be heard outside the room.

"But I see that someone else took care of you properly." She hid the Beretta again in her purse. "So now I don't have to." She turned and left the room

As she drove away from the hospital, she felt the anger dissipate. Sara took another deep breath, feeling lighter than she had for more than a year. Now if only her panic attacks would disappear as easily.

Chapter 28

Mogador: 1786

Rachel sat on a stone bench in the courtyard, eating dates and watching her son Moses Elias draw circles in the sand around an orange tree. His older half-brothers were off somewhere with their mothers so Rachel could enjoy a moment without vigilance.

She thought back over the past four years since her marriage to Eliahu. Her tears had been shed—she had no more to weep. The trauma of the tedious, overlong marriage ceremony had been followed by the shock of finding herself the youngest and least important of the vizier's three wives. She no longer dreamed of Esther and Ada and America, and the dread with which she had faced each day since her capture had subsided somewhat, numbed by the day-to-day realities she faced in this household.

A week after the wedding, Rachel was allowed a visit from her father. She had remained stoic throughout the preparations for her marriage and the ceremony itself, but she fell apart when she saw her father, running to him and sobbing in his arms. He held her but could not console her.

"Is he treating you badly, my sweet little one?" Moses said at last.

She shook her head gulping down tears. "He is kind enough to me, Papa, but he has two other wives and holds me up to them as some sort of goad to prod their jealousy. They hate me, Papa, and they are so ignorant I have nothing to say to them. They are interested only in themselves and their children."

Her father put his arms around her, holding her tightly as she wept. She felt the comfort of his embrace. She had not meant to sadden him with her misery. He could not help her now.

"I have never known a Jewish man with three wives, Papa. How can this be?"

"Oh my dear," he replied. "It is the height of foolishness. Yes, it is accepted here in Morocco that a man can have more than one wife. But most of them have the common sense to limit themselves to one. You can see for yourself that the more wives and children a man has, the more expensive and chaotic his life becomes."

Rachel nodded and stared at the ground.

"I've heard of some men who answer their wife's arguments for more servants by bringing home a new wife instead," Moses said. "Contemptible, but there it is."

"He can have as many as he wants if he will leave me alone," Rachel said. "And, Papa," he will not buy Annie to join us even as a servant in the household. He has forbidden me to speak of her in his presence."

Moses frowned. Annie's release into Eliahu's house had been a key part of Rachel's agreement to marry him. Rachel had been shaken by Eliahu's deception, but they both were well aware of the greed and treachery that marked the man's character. "But then," Moses said one day, "all of Eliahu's qualities make him an excellent grand vizier to the king."

As the months passed, Rachel was allowed weekly visits with Moses. The comfort and joy of these visits was dampened somewhat by the details of her life in Eliahu's house. She usually greeted Moses in a reception room off the first courtyard. The room's heavy carpets and cushioned couches hushed their voices. As customary for guests, Rachel served him mint tea from glass teacups, but she said, "I know that my kind husband would forbid this courtesy if he knew of it."

"Yes, I am only your father." Moses smiled at Rachel.

She nodded. "You are my father, and I love you. You are worth the price of tea, I think, and the other two wives, for once, will not report back to my kind husband. They will wish similar favors for themselves, you see."

Over the months and years, Rachel related to her father the ways she had found to handle the daily routines and grievances that came her way in that household.

"The other wives are beginning to accept me, Papa," she told him one day. "They see that I am not a rival to them. They use me as extra hands for the work that needs to be done. They are older and they seek to exploit me, but I am glad to do any work around here. I would much rather be busy than to sit idly by and think. So I bring in water from the well, clean the vegetables, empty the wastewater buckets and even the chamber pots, Papa."

Moses reached for Rachel and hugged her. "I should have known Eliahu would use his wives in such a way."

"Yes, we are his household servants, but you said this is true in other households, is that not so?"

Moses shrugged. "It would not be my practice."

Rachel smiled at him. "But my dear Papa, you are a kind and generous man." She looked down at her hands and examined a torn fingernail.

"I am learning much in this house, Papa. It is as riddled as the king's harem with jealousy. The other wives plot to cheat each other or best one another or gain advantage for themselves or their children." She glanced at Moses and laughed. "Their efforts amuse me."

Moses took her hand and patted it. "I suppose they consider themselves superior to you because they have more years of marriage behind them."

"Oh, of course. But I am perfectly happy to stay in the background, Papa. I use my wits here, but I always show my willingness to take on extra tasks, which give me the excuse and the time and freedom to explore this house and gardens and even the town."

"Good. We must look for any opportunity."

"Papa, under different circumstances, I would find this house enchanting. It is much larger and finer than our home in Tangier." She walked over to run her fingers across the satiny wooden carvings on the walls.

Moses surveyed his surroundings, seeing the splendor through his daughter's eyes. Decorative arches of marble on each floor scalloped the edges of the two courtyards. Behind the arches were the reception, dining, sleeping, and utility rooms. In the courtyards, water splashed from the fountains into crystal pools. The scents of orange and lime blossoms in the trees filled the air. Carved columns rose from the tiled floor up to the patch of blue sky in the open air above.

A stranger would not believe that such magnificence could exist behind the decrepit clay facade of this house, but maintaining a poor facade was the way in this country where any show of wealth brought the king's greedy scrutiny.

"Have you discovered the Jewish quarter here?" Moses asked Rachel on another visit. He sat in a small reception room to the right of the foyer, sipping mint tea. "Perhaps you might find friends there. This house stands between that and the king's palace."

"I suppose so, Papa." Rachel put down the idea with her hand. "But I am not sure how to go about it unless the father of my child introduces me, which he has not. I think I would only meet the domestics in the streets, and they are ignorant and powerless." She stared down at her feet and waited as if Moses could fill the silence with other possibilities.

Moses studied the main staircase. "How is this house arranged? I should know in case I must reach you quickly."

Rachel pointed toward the back corner of the house. "My sleeping room is upstairs along the back of the house, next to the staircase that the servants use which leads to a back door." She smiled at him. "No one would see us leave—or enter—through that door, Papa. I often use those stairs." She sat back down. "The rooms of the other two wives are next to mine and they use the main stairs." Rachel motioned toward the broad stone steps rising from the first floor to the second behind the first courtyard. A carved wooden banister marched up the steps at one side while the wall was on the other. "Eliahu sleeps in a room on this floor behind the second courtyard."

"Ah, yes. That is important to know."

"I also must tell you, Papa, that I tend the courtyards. I enjoy the peace and beauty, but . . . ." She lowered her voice. "More than that, I have dug out secret hiding places in the floor tiles and the dirt. I don't know yet what use we may have for these places, but they are for the future."

Moses stroked his chin. "Very good. We must always prepare." He rose to leave. They were progressing toward their goal, he sighed, but he hoped he would see them reach it.

***

Rachel took advantage of her status as a married woman, veiled and covered by the shapeless haik, to penetrate the inner harem and talk with Annie as she went about her daily duties. Since Annie was part of the king's household and a lowly slave, she was treated as if she were a stone in the wall or, more precisely, a tile under their feet.

Annie's comforting words had helped Rachel through the early days of her marriage and the difficult months of her pregnancy. After her son's birth, Rachel drew on Annie's experience with child-rearing, and they both doted on the small boy. He was Rachel's only glow of warmth and love in a house marked by pettiness and greed. As he grew, Rachel always took him with her, dressing him poorly like herself so that they drew no attention.

When Rachel and Annie wanted to speak privately, as on this visit, Rachel left Moses Elias with the Jewish seamstresses, giving them a couple of coins for their trouble. Rachel enjoyed the short visits, and she knew Annie saw them as a lifeline since her only hope for release would be through Moses' efforts.

"Tell your father that the harem women speak of court intrigues and ambitions with no more than a glance in my direction," Annie told Rachel one day. "Their language is a smattering of Arabic, Berber, and Spanish. I am learning more and more words in those languages." Annie squinted down the passageway. "I can also use the English harem wife. She is more than happy to show her superiority by teaching me."

Whatever Annie learned, she passed on to Rachel. Rachel in turn, took this information to her father, always asking him about his efforts to help Annie. "Escape is constantly on her mind," Rachel told him, "as it is on mine."

"I've written many times to my contacts in America on Annie's behalf, my dear," he responded one day as he picked an orange from a courtyard tree. "I thought that since she is an American citizen she would perhaps be entitled to some type of ransom, but I am finding that Annie simply does not have the influential or moneyed friends or family who can help. Their government is rampant chaos stewing in indecision."

Rachel paced the walk back and forth, rubbing her hands together. "Oh, Papa. We must help her."

Moses peeled the orange. Its fragrance filled the air. "Yes, but the political situation is disastrous. The American Congress is embroiled in arguments about whether to pay tributes to prevent the piracy of American ships or to pay ransoms after seizure or to build a strong navy to protect its own shipping."

She turned to him, her eyes pleading. "They will take years to sort all that out, Papa."

Moses walked over to the fountain and sat on the edge. Rachel sat down beside him. "Right now," he said, patting her hand, "nothing can be done. We can only hope that a way may be found through that morass."

As time went on with no good news, Rachel's queries grew fewer and fewer, and now she rarely asked her father if there had been any response from America. She listened eagerly to any news, even the most meager, however, for her hope could not be extinguished.

Whenever Moses visited her, he reported on his activities, occasionally recounting incidents of Eliahu's folly as well as his astuteness to help Rachel cope with the onerous fact of being the third wife to such a man. Most often they sat close together, watching the little boy play, alone in the first courtyard while the other wives and children frequented the more ornate second courtyard.

"You should see him, my dear, striding by the mosque in his slippers." Moses chuckled in one of his visits.

"I don't understand, Papa. What is the humor in that?"

"You know we Jews must remove our shoes by a mosque. He is above such dictates of the king and is showing his power at court."

Rachel frowned, tucking her hand into Moses' arm as they walked around the courtyard. "That is dangerous, is it not?"

Moses nodded. "So far he fares better than the rest of us. The Muslims and the Christians all think they are correct in their beliefs, but at least the Muslims are above any efforts to recruit us infidels." He paused to admire a flower. "Only a few malicious ones scatter broken glass around the mosque where we must walk."

Rachel gazed down at the paved stones. "Oh, yes. I never go near the mosque."

On another visit, Moses greeted Rachel with glee. "Your husband is allowing me much greater movement around town," he told her, rubbing his hands together. "He knows that I won't leave without you and my grandson."

Rachel caught his hand and squeezed it, looking into his eyes. "Papa, if you can escape, you must do it."

Moses laughed and hugged her. "Oh, my dear, he is right. I could never leave without both of you. But I am now able to become more involved in the Jewish community here. We have at least one common bond."

"Well, yes, we are all Jews."

He waved that aside. "And most of our families were forced out of Spain and Portugal by the Catholic Inquisition."

"If we should escape, we could not go to those countries, could we, Papa?"

"Hah! Not unless our visit was officially sanctioned by the king. The inquisition still carries on its ugly work. But there is Gibraltar, you know. It is English and only nine miles across the straits from Morocco."

Rachel tucked the useful fact of Gibraltar's closeness away in the part of her mind that longed for escape.

A few days later, Rachel and little Moses Elias visited the harem women's quarters. As usual, Rachel left Moses with the seamstresses and met Annie in the hall.

Glancing in both directions, Annie pulled Rachel down a dark, little-used passageway. Annie held a finger to her lips, searched the passage ahead and behind her and listened for noises that might betray an eavesdropper. Then she said, "I have learned something that may finally turn events in our favor."

Rachel waited.

"The mother of the king's son, Moulay Yazid, boasted to me secretly of how she would be king mother someday soon."

"How can that be?" Rachel whispered. "The king is in good health, I think."

Annie peered through the dimness down the corridor in both directions before replying. "I do not think Moulay Yazid intends to wait for God."

"What do you mean?" Rachel tugged at Annie's sleeve. "Do you think he plans to murder the king, his father? Surely that cannot be so."

Annie's eyes narrowed in contempt. "He is cruel and self-centered and cares only for his own power and greed."

"He is cruel, that is true," Rachel said, thinking of the cat that Yazid had tortured to death years before.

"Rachel, I do not know this man." She paused for a moment. Rachel heard distant voices but they faded away and Annie continued in whispers. "I hear only stories, but the other harem women say he has taken some of the captives for his own estates and works or beats them until they die. He is not a good man."

Rachel tapped her lips with her fingers. "I will tell Papa. Perhaps he can protect the king from this man."

"Yes, you must. But take care. Remember that Yazid is the king's eldest son. There must be no mention of the harem women and their gossip. That may endanger them and make them fearful, and then we would learn nothing." She took Rachel's arm and began nudging her back to the main corridor.

Rachel stopped and turned to Annie, searching her face intently. "And you, what would happen to you?"

Annie looked away. "I know not, but can it be worse than this?"

Rachel stared at her. "Yes. You could be third wife to the father of my child."

Annie peered into the shadows behind her. "You must go now. They will become suspicious if we talk too quietly and too long."

They reached the main corridor arm in arm. "Oh Annie, how I wish we were in America."

Annie only nodded, and Rachel left to find little Moses, thinking again how different her life would have been in America.

On impulse, she turned her steps to the market as she walked home. Once more, she thought of escape. The difficulties she faced as a married woman leaving Morocco with a small son had led her to the decision that a necessary part of any escape would be in disguise as an Arab man with Moses Elias as an Arab street urchin. She, Annie, and Moses Elias would all need dark djellabas under burnooses with hoods. They must look like paid servants for her father.

So far, she had put off buying such garments, but today she had extra household money with her. The purchase was easier than she expected. She carried the bundle self-consciously home and left the boy playing in the courtyard while she spread the garments under her mattress. Just having them made her feel easier, but tomorrow she would transfer them to a more permanent hiding place.

***

Moses chose the next day to visit Rachel, and she told him of the plot. His eyes did not leave her face as he listened, and he stood tapping his fingers on his lips for some moments before he spoke. "I feared that such was being planned. The whispers around the medina have increased lately."

Rachel watched him. "I thought you would know best what to do."

Moses smiled at her. "Yes, my dear. I will tell Eliahu who will tell the king. I must remain in the background on something so threatening as this. I am not in as strong a position as he to be a messenger of bad news."

He saw Rachel hesitate before asking the question that was in both their hearts. "Is there any hope, Papa?"

He looked down at his feet, wishing he had better news. "I go to temple weekly, my dear," he said, "and I have sent letters to the ransom committee, but the Knights of St. John on Malta have made such a business of capturing Jews for the ransom that the funds are depleted."

"Oh, Papa." Rachel turned away. Moses could hardly bear the sadness in her voice. "We must find some way to escape. Perhaps you could look for masters of ships who can help us."

He reached over and pulled her to him. To see her so unhappy tore his heart, but he could do nothing to help and the pain of that was unbearable. "I am always searching for possibilities," he said and added to raise her spirits, "I am putting together a plan of escape, but it is too soon to attempt."

"Oh, Papa, we can be ready at a moment's notice." She told him of her purchase. "Is there anything else I can do to prepare?"

He smiled at her eagerness. "Nothing right now, my dear. We must wait until the time is right."

"Oh, it would be so wonderful to be away from here . . . ." she said waving a hand at her elegant prison.

"Yes, away from kings and viziers . . . ."

Rachel looked at him. "And husbands."

Chapter 29

Florida West Coast, 1999

Sara left Miami to drive across the Everglades on Tamiami Trail, heading for Florida's west coast and Cedar Key. She had been a week on the road but was no closer to finding Samuel E. Yulee.

The long drive west across south Florida through the Everglades soon grew tedious with slow traffic on the two-lane road. To break up the drive, she stopped at nature centers along the way, learning about alligators and spoonbills, swatting the mosquitoes, and checking the cars that pulled in after hers. The people in them seemed innocuous enough—usually older couples seeking a break for themselves and their dogs.

At Naples, she left Tamiami Trail for I-75. The interstate offered no relief to her boredom so again she scanned the billboards for places of interest. Just past Sarasota, she noticed a sign for the Gamble Plantation, off the next exit. It looked like a good place for a break and a bit of local history.

She turned onto the exit ramp and drove a mile down the road to the plantation, parking behind a pristine white antebellum mansion. It stood tall and dignified in the intense sunshine.

Here, too, she waited to see what cars followed her in. The first was a maroon Cadillac. Two older men struggled out of it. A white sedan turned in and parked over by the administration building. She could see the dark outline of someone sitting in the front seat, and Sara waited a moment to watch the driver emerge, but he or she remained in the car. Sara gave up the wait and walked over to the museum and the plantation headquarters. She couldn't believe that anyone else would be interested in what she was doing. Why would they?

A white plaque announced that the estate, now a state park, included a memorial to Judah P. Benjamin, a U.S. senator from Louisiana who joined the Confederacy during the Civil War. Sara read the plaque again. Judah P. Benjamin. He was Jewish, Sara guessed, and he served at about the same time as David Yulee—they must have known each other.

The museum offered a cool respite from the heat outside. Conscious that she was spending her grandmother's money on a serious mission, Sara felt bound to read each caption attached to the various photos and exhibitions.

Someone had come up beside her, reeking of sunscreen and sweat. Sara moved away. The man looked like a college student, but his jeans and tee shirt were torn, stained, and filthy. He chomped on a Hershey bar held in a grubby hand. Sara took a second look and found herself staring into a face that seemed familiar. Where had she seen this man before? He was looking at her as if he knew her. Then she remembered. Josh something, the man she had met at Elaine's house when she picked up the album. He had given her his address too. He lived in Cedar Key, but what was he doing here?

He grinned at her. "Wondered if I'd run into you."

Sara looked at his grubby clothes and tried not to breathe. She didn't respond.

Josh motioned to a photo on the wall. "Gamble, the man who built this place, was one of the first settlers in this part of Florida. We're just lucky the plantation was saved from developers and donated to the state."

Sara found her voice. "What are you doing here?"

"Interested. Thought I'd learn something useful for you. For me, too." He turned to walk alongside Sara.

Sara stepped back, wrinkling her nose. Josh no longer held any attraction for her. Not that he ever had, she amended.

He noticed her expression. "Spent the weekend camping," he said, gesturing to his clothes, then he went blithely on. "This place fascinates me. Can you imagine hiding out here from Union troops for four days while your friends try to find you a boat to Cuba? That happened to Judah Benjamin after the Civil War."

"Did he get the boat?" She had to ask but she hoped Josh would move on. How could he come to a public place looking and smelling like that?

"Oh, yeah. And he made it to England where he became a barrister and died a wealthy man."

"Good for him. Thank you." Sara walked across the room to a framed photo of Jefferson Davis' confederate cabinet. There was Benjamin as Davis' secretary of state and, standing in the background, Sara caught her breath, was a man identified as David Levy Yulee.

The photo seemed to make him a real figure at last—and an imposing one. Dark hair, swarthy complexion, piercing eyes. He had been a man of power and prestige even if Sara didn't agree with his cause. She studied the photo, seeking some family resemblance but saw none. Still, she felt thrilled to see an actual photo of the man.

Josh—Sara dubbed him Mr. Grubbs— followed her over, still chewing the candy bar. He gestured at the photo. "There's Judah Benjamin and that's David Yulee."

"Thank you," she said, struggling to remain polite. She no longer wanted and certainly didn't need his help.

"They were both U.S. senators, you know, and they were both from St. Thomas. Their fathers were business partners."

"You can't be a guide here," Sara said.

"Just visiting. I know you're interested in the Yulee family, so I thought I'd pass that bit of information along." He spoke nonchalantly as if his condition were normal.

Sara's instinct was to get away from him, but she steeled herself to pursue the conversation. "You seem to know a lot about Yulee."

"Yeah. Been doing some research." He took another chunk off the candy bar. "I'm going to look around some more. Give me a call when you're in Cedar Key. You've got my number."

He meandered on to the other exhibits as Sara fumbled for questions, feeling chagrined. *This possible lead fell into my hands, and I let it go.*

She searched for Mr. Grubbs, formulating questions in her mind, as she continued her own tour of the museum. When she spied him strolling over to the mansion, she followed. He hovered alongside a group being guided through the building, although most of the people shied away from him. He looked and smelled like a homeless panhandler.

Sara joined the group listening to a guide who wore the full-skirted, floor-length costume of the antebellum south. Her white, curly hair peeked out from a bonnet.

The guide noticed Sara and nodded at her before continuing. "Major Gamble obtained the acreage in a free land deal offered by the government to populate the state in Florida's early days." She paused and smiled, eyes twinkling.

"He planted his farm in sugar cane and also operated a sugar mill.

The plantation was almost totally self-sufficient, and the mansion itself is the only surviving antebellum plantation house in south Florida."

Mr. Grubbs drifted toward Sara. "David Yulee also had sugar mills in Florida," he said. "Only farther north."

Sara turned to him. "How much farther north?" After all, she was going north. Maybe there was something to learn—and see—at Yulee's sugar mills—if they existed.

"Up near Homosassa Springs. North of Tampa."

"Oh, how do you . . ." but Sara never finished the question. A shriveled little man poked her and pointed to the guide, who was motioning them forward to another room. Mr. Grubbs moved off, and Sara impatiently finished the tour, hoping to catch him before he left. But after the tour he was nowhere to be found. Sara walked back to her car, noted that the white car had not moved, took a moment to find Homosassa Springs on her map and then left the plantation without seeing Mr. Grubbs again.

So she had learned a bit more about David Levy Yulee and again nothing about Samuel E. She continued to drive north.

Just past Tampa, she left the interstate for Rt. 19, stopping by Tarpon Springs briefly, curious about the Greek heritage of this sponge-diving village. Again, she scanned the parking area as she walked to the street, and, again, a white car had followed her in. She waited to see who emerged and made a note of the license tag number. As foolish as it seemed, this time she would compare it later with the list of numbers from the motel.

After a moment, a man did emerge, tall and silver-haired, but he strode away from her as if he were late for an important appointment. From the back, he looked like the man she had seen at the condo in Fort Lauderdale—and picking a hibiscus at Elizabeth's. Sara chided herself. There must be thousands of tall, silver-haired men in Florida. He was probably just another tourist.

She walked over to the docks and bought a gyro before returning to her car. She retrieved the list of license numbers from her suitcase and compared it with the car in front of her—and found a match. She caught her breath and checked it again. There was no mistake. In front of her was a car that had been parked at the motel in St. Augustine. Her fingers trembled and her stomach turned. She started her car, peeled away from the parking lot, and sped down the road, leaving the white car parked and driverless in the lot.

This must be some kind of odd coincidence, Sara reproached herself. How would he know where she was going? Or why? Unless it was a serial killer who had marked her as a victim. She winced. That thought sent chills down her spine.

She pressed on up the road to Homosassa and Cedar Key. The weather was hot enough to scald the pavement, and her little Honda's air conditioning system labored under the assault, especially in the stop-and-go traffic of Rt. 19. The divided four-lane highway was not an interstate. Definitely not. The stores, motels and gas stations that crowded both sides of the highway gradually spaced out, giving way to a dusty growth of shrubs and trees on both sides.

She almost missed the brown sign on the side of the road. She did pass it and had to pull over and back up to read it. Fortunately, the car behind her had been moving slowly and as it passed, she thought it looked like the one in the Tarpon Springs parking lot, but it kept going down the road. A lot of white cars in Florida looked just like that one. She dismissed it and read the sign.

"David L. Yulee's Sugar Mill Ruins, Next Left," it said. Immediately following this brown marker, a green sign pointed down the same road for Homosassa Springs. Sara turned left onto a narrow asphalt road that barely held its own through the dense growth on both sides. Spanish moss hung in gray curls from the trees, and dark cumulus clouds blocked the sun, casting a mysterious gloom over the scene. Another car turned off the road behind her. It was blue, not white, and a shabby wreck, but Sara watched it nervously in her rear view mirror.

She slowed to allow the other car to pass and, she hoped, move on. Sara herself intended to stop at the ruins.

The other car passed her too fast for Sara to check on the occupant, but since it disappeared quickly up ahead, she decided that whoever they were, they weren't interested in her.

She almost passed the ruins. She expected some kind of establish-ment—visitor's center, caretaker's house, factory, or museum. None of these appeared. What did appear was a small, unprepossessing road sign announcing the "Ruins of the David L. Yulee Sugar Mill. Built 1851." And indeed, a heap of rusted machinery rested like a long-dead dinosaur on the side of the road under the oaks and Spanish moss.

This was not at all like the Gamble Plantation, but Yulee, like Major Gamble, had planted and processed sugar cane. Sara could identify the old boiler and the cane-crushing machine, but other hulks rusted beyond definition also squatted under the trees.

It didn't take long to tour these ruins. Sara returned to her car and continued on down the road for the small town of Homosassa. The road ended in a fishing camp shaded by live oaks set back from a river.

She parked in the dirt parking lot for the camp store next to the blue car that had rattled past her. She stepped warily into the store expecting a couple of "bubbas."

Two old men in faded jeans and tee shirts leaned on the counter inside, but a civilized-looking young woman with long, straight blond hair sat on a tall stool behind it. She looked up at Sara and smiled.

Sara glanced around the small store. "I came down the road to see the ruins."

"Of course. The Yulee sugar mill."

"Yes. I'm trying to find out more about him, you see."

"Sure. He and his family owned over 3200 acres around here, and they built a huge mansion over on Tigertail Island—you can see the island from here. The mansion burned down during the war."

"You mean the Civil War?"

"Yeah. The house used to be right over there." She pointed behind her as if Sara could see through the wall to the creek beyond. "There's nothing on the island now, and it's all overgrown." She nodded at the men. "Y'all got what you wanted, then?"

"Just waitin' here for our buddy. He'll be here in a few minutes."

"That's all right, then." She turned back to Sara. "Yep. Nothing on that island now."

"Oh. Too bad."

"But we have a pontoon boat that goes right by there every day. It's on our manatee tour." She was keeping an eye on the two men.

"Manatee tour?" Sara looked at her with interest. "Manatees? The endangered species?"

"That's right. We have warm springs here, and the manatees go up there for the warm water in the winter. But we always have some in there, even in the summer and fall, so we do tours."

One of the men looked up. "Them manatees are a nuisance, I say. Got too many of 'em. State oughta ease up." The other one hitched up his pants in agreement.

The clerk looked over at them with distaste. "Yeah. We only have a couple hundred. We could easily get rid of a hundred now, couldn't we?" Sara caught the sarcasm, but the men didn't.

"That's what I say," said one of the men. "You can't hardly move your boat at all what with them damn speed restrictions."

"God, you guys. Wouldn't have nothin' left if it were up to you."

Sara caught the angry glint in the woman's eyes. Sara didn't care for them either. "When is the tour?" she asked.

The woman turned to Sara. "Meet us out there on the dock at ten tomorrow morning."

Sara made up her mind. "Right. But I'll need a room for tonight."

"We have clean, comfortable rooms here in our motel. Let's get you registered."

That evening Sara called her mother.

"Thank heavens. How are you?" Her mother breathed the words as if she'd run to the phone.

"I'm fine, Mom. Just checking in."

"Well, I'm glad you did. I got a call from somebody named Elizabeth something. Said she'd talked with you in Miami?"

Sara caught her breath. "That's right, Mom. What did she say?" Maybe this was a break at last. She sat down on the bed.

"She wanted me to tell you to call her right away. Do you have her number?"

"Yes. She's on my list. I'll call her as soon as I hang up. Is everything okay there?"

"Sure. No excitement here."

"That's good. I'll call again in a couple of days. The trip's been easy so far." They spoke a few moments longer with Sara filling in the details on her visit with Elizabeth. She didn't mention the white car. "I still haven't learned anything useful, though, Mom."

Her stomach doing flip-flops, Sara said good-bye to her mother and called Elizabeth.

"Thank goodness it's you," Elizabeth said. "An odd thing happened after you left. A man knocked on my door, said he was looking for Samuel Yulee and wondered if he lived here."

"Wow. That's odd."

"Yeah. I didn't let him in. After I got over being scared to death, I told him I'd never heard of anyone of that name, and he left, but I snuck out after him and got a good look at his car."

Sara stared at the wall and felt a quiver of fear. "Good for you," she said. "What did he look like?"

"I'd say he was maybe sixty-ish, gray hair, tall, you know? He was wearing a Cuban guayabera, you know, a kind of dress shirt. He seemed nice enough, but nervous. I heard him stumble on the stairs. And, oh yeah, he wanted to give me a flower, a red hibiscus, you know, only I wouldn't open the door, then he dropped it on the landing. He was a bit of a klutz, actually."

"Stranger and stranger. Did you look for a bug in the flower?"

"Didn't see any . . . oh, you mean a hidden microphone?"

"Just a thought."

"It was only one flower, you know? I think he picked it off a bush when he walked back to my place. He scared me. Not that he looked at all menacing, and he didn't do anything, it's just that I don't expect anyone coming back here."

"What about the car?"

"It was white, Florida tags—might have been a rental, you know? An ordinary sedan. Nothing fancy."

"Did you get the license number?"

"I didn't even think of that."

"The whole thing is odd. Hardly anyone knows where I'm going or what I'm doing, but I can't imagine anyone just showing up at your door and asking about the same man I'm looking for unless they're following me."

"I thought so too. That's why I called your Mom."

"Thanks for alerting me."

"No problem."

Sara put down her phone with trembling hand. She wondered if the stranger had visited anyone else on her list but couldn't think of one she wanted to call to find out. She walked over to the bureau and picked up her purse. The Beretta was loaded, safety on but loaded. The vapory fears that had crept into this adventure now became the solid ice of certainty. She stepped over to the door and made sure she had latched the second bolt and the safety chain. Going home flitted through her mind. From now on, she must use caution.

The next morning Sara packed her bag and locked it in her car. She checked out of the motel and bought juice and a couple of doughnuts for breakfast, then strolled down to the creek, passing through the parking lot on the way. She studied the two white cars and the blue wreck lined up alongside her Honda. She peered through the windows into the white cars, not knowing what to look for, but her search revealed nothing more than the usual tourism brochures, maps, and empty soft drink cans. Their owners were nowhere in sight. The license tags did not match her list. Sara gave up and walked down to the dock and the pontoon boat.

A woman stood on the boat, bent over an outboard motor at the stern. She brushed her gray curls aside, looked up at Sara and waved. Sara waved back.

Footsteps behind her made her turn to see a man running towards her. At least he had cleaned up—she hadn't smelled him coming—and his navy blue shorts and white tee shirt weren't torn or dirty. He wore Nikes with no socks. He was quite good-looking when he cleaned up.

"What are you doing here?" she said as he ran up to her.

"Thought you'd be here, since I told you about the ruins." Josh stopped to catch his breath.

"It was an interesting lead. Now I'm here for the manatee tour."

"Yeah, so am I. Good to see you again." He extended his hand.

She shook his hand. "I stopped at those ruins. Had you been there before?"

"Yeah. Didn't need to see that again. Just chunks of junk.'

Sara nodded. "I know."

The woman on the boat called up to them. "Come on down here, you two, and let's get started. I think you're going to be all that's going on the tour this morning." Except for the gray curls, the woman resembled the cashier in the store so closely that Sara would bet they were mother and daughter.

She grinned at them as they boarded. "My name's Marie, and I'm glad to meet you. Where y'all from?"

"I'm from West Virginia," Sara said, trying not to imitate Marie's southern twang. She looked at Josh as she sat down.

"St. Thomas," Josh brushed his hair out of his eyes.

"You're from St. Thomas?" Sara asked. "The Virgin Islands? In the Caribbean?"

He took a seat beside her. "Born and bred."

"What are you doing here?"

"Tracing my roots."

Sara stared at him in surprise.

"So what brings you two to Homosassa?" asked Marie.

"I've been working up in Cedar Key," said Josh, leaning back against the rail and putting on his sunglasses. "Taking time off for a few history lessons."

"I'm interested in David Levy Yulee," said Sara. "He might be some kind of distant relation . . . maybe."

Josh folded his arms and put a foot up on the rail. "Well, he is some kind of distant relation of mine from St. Thomas. After hearing your story at Elaine's in Martinsburg, I decided to find out a little more about him. He was a significant person in Florida history, and history was my major. So you think he had something to do with the album?"

"I don't know." She shrugged. After the tour, she would talk to Josh alone. Cautiously. This link might be promising after all.

"Yulee used to live around here, I guess you both know," Marie squinted at them as she steered the boat through the creek. "We get a lot of visitors in here wanting to know more about him. You've probably heard the old story about his grandmother."

"What old story?" Sara shivered, remembering her own grandmother's secret.

"Check out your Florida history books," said Marie, eyes squinting as she peered ahead. "Seems that she and her father were traveling on a ship that was captured by Barbary pirates off Africa. This was about the time of the Revolutionary War in this country. They stripped her and sold her to the highest bidder. Somehow she escaped and got over to Gibraltar where she stayed the rest of her days. That's the story as I heard it."

"Where was her home?" Sara asked, leaning toward her.

Marie smiled over at her. "Don't know."

"You'd think she would have gone back to her family," Sara said, "once she escaped to Gibraltar."

"But she was disgraced, you know." Marie grimaced. "She'd been raped and enslaved. They wouldn't want her back."

"Yes, I suppose that's right."

Josh snorted. Sara frowned at him.

Marie turned her attention back to the creek.

Sara gazed out at the water, thinking about the story Marie had told them and feeling irritated at Josh's derisive attitude. But he was a man. What would he know? She could not imagine the horror this young girl must have felt. To be captured by pirates must have been terrifying, but then to be auctioned off to the highest bidder—that was unimaginable.

All her sympathy flowed to this young, unknown woman who was disgraced and could never again return home to her family. Sara thought of her own attempted rape and how it had changed her.

Josh leaned over and whispered in her ear, "That story's all a bunch of hog swill, you know."

Chapter 30

Mogador, 1786

Moses left Rachel's home and hurried to Eliahu's office, taking special care to note the loiterers, servants, and other men he passed in the shadowed alleys of the medina. After a last look around, he entered the office, closed the door behind him, and stepped quietly over to Eliahu, who was peering at him with narrowed eyes behind his massive desk.

"I have heard much gossip in the medina and among the guards at the fortress gates," Moses said.

Eliahu shrugged. "There is always gossip in the medina."

"But I think this is credible." Moses leaned toward him and whispered. "They speak of a plot against the king's life by his son Yazid."

Eliahu sat up straight. "You heard this in the medina?"

Moses nodded.

Eliahu pondered this, muttering, "Yes, Yazid would be the one. Perhaps I have made a mistake there. I have not paid much attention to him. He is such a wastrel."

He frowned. "Even the king is disgusted with Yazid and looks upon him as if he were a bad smell."

"I have heard that," said Moses.

"Yazid's profligate habits are a serious matter." Eliahu pursed his lips. "His massive debts have forced the king to prohibit all nations from giving aid, comfort, or refuge to Yazid."

"So Yazid is desperate, then," said Moses.

Eliahu drummed his fingers on the table. "What else did you hear?"

Moses shook his head. "I cannot add much more. I know Yazid pays some of the king's guards. They are proud to be his allies, and they whisper dreams of power."

Eliahu stroked his chin, gazing abstractedly at a wall. After a long pause, he spoke as if he were thinking out loud. "Yazid has a special grudge against us as Jews. When he needed money for his wives, he applied to the Jews of Tetuan. They refused him because they could not go against the king's command. Yazid vented his rage on his Jewish servants. One was strung up by his ankles," Eliahu shuddered, "until he died. Yazid at length wheedled money from the English because, ah, his mother is English. They hope he will soon become king and then they will seek favors from him."

Moses folded his arms and watched Eliahu. "I suppose that of all the king's sons, Yazid is selfish enough and cruel enough to plot his father's death to gain the throne."

Eliahu's mouth twisted in distaste. "He is that. We must find absolute, concrete evidence of this plot. Then we must devise a careful plan on how to bring this information to the king or we will find ourselves hanging by the ankles." He stood and walked over to peer at Moses.

Moses stepped back from him. "I will do what I can."

"Meanwhile, we will go to the king's court and see what we might learn there."

Moses felt his heart leap. The king's court! In all the years Moses had served Eliahu, he had never been allowed to show himself at court. Eliahu jealously guarded his privileges there, but this turn of events must mean that Eliahu felt the threat was credible. Moses felt Eliahu pluck his sleeve and shook his own thoughts off to pay attention.

Eliahu was studying Moses from head to foot. "You must dress for court better than this to show your respect, but modestly, you understand?"

Moses cast his eyes down at the simple black djellaba he had worn that day.

Eliahu folded his arms and nodded at Moses' dress. "You must not draw attention to yourself. That could have unfortunate consequences beyond your imagination."

"I will do as you say, but shouldn't you dress to show your power?"

Eliahu laughed in derision. "You still have much to learn, my friend. Let me tell you. Any show of wealth—and wealth is power—can lead to an investigation, and then they will confiscate everything we possess." He stared down his nose at Moses. "You have no wealth, but you are connected to me, and I prefer not to attract that kind of attention."

Moses thought of his past life as a scholar and teacher. In that life, his stature depended on intelligence, knowledge, and wisdom—and no one could steal those.

Later in the king's court, Moses watched Eliahu cast his eyes around the attendants and understood at once that he searched for clues to possible collaborators in such a plot. When Moses and Eliahu returned to the office, Eliahu said, "You must find out more."

Moses nodded. "I may be able to get the evidence we need. I hear much as I walk about the medina and the port, since I am a slave and a Jew and of no consequence. But I must have more freedom and time to roam in order to harvest these bits and pieces of talk."

"You will have that freedom, but you must, ah, report to me every morning and every evening."

"I will do that."

Eliahu waved him out of the room and closed the door. "I have much to consider," he said.

Later, Moses reported this conversation to Rachel. "I feel as if," he said, "I should sing. To report every morning and every evening is a small price to pay for gaining additional freedom and time. Now I can visit the ships alone and with more time to discuss possibilities in private with the captains."

"We are ready to leave whatever way you can manage, Papa," Rachel said, squeezing his hand.

"We'll have to see, my dear." The problem seemed to gain in difficulty as the years passed. Now he sought escape not only for Rachel and himself and Annie but for his grandson as well.

Annie. She was not as weak and passive as he had once thought. How ironic if she should prove to be their hope for rescue. Her situation in the harem had seemed hopeless, but it had possibilities. He hoped that she could ferret out more information about the plot without endangering herself.

Moses strolled down the narrow, cobbled street to the quay. His feet had toughened in the years since his march from the captive ship. He now usually wore flat, pointed Moroccan slippers on his feet, but his black djellaba and skullcap marked him as a Jew, so his walk to the port was a wary one. As careful as he was, he could not escape a blow on the head from a passing Arab who hit him in token harassment.

He stared at the ship tied at the wharf and smiled. He recognized that ship. With good fortune, his old friend, Zephaniah Kingsley, would still be master and on board.

Moses stepped forward to hail the ship. As he did, Kingsley appeared on deck, scanned the dock, and grinned. "Hello, it's my old friend Moses Levy." Kingsley walked to the gangplank. "Welcome,

welcome. Come on up here and let's have a look at ye."

Moses felt his heart lift. To see a friend and an equal after years of slavery brought tears to his eyes. Kingsley's beard had turned white, but he remained slim and his clothes looked well made as if he had prospered.

Kingsley slapped Moses on the back, "What's been happening with you, my friend," he said as he led Moses off to his private quarters.

When they entered the room, Kingsley gestured to a well-varnished oak chair around a small round table, reached into a cupboard and brought out a decanter of port and two glasses. They sipped the port while Moses told him of his misfortunes.

Zephaniah shook his head. "We risk those pirates every trip we take. They care nothing about treaties. The kings of these countries are as bad. It's a roll of the dice no matter who you are."

"Where do you go from here, then?"

"Aye, we go to Spain and Portugal, my friend. It will do you no good to go there."

"No, of course not." Moses shook his head. The Catholic inquisition had killed enough of his family.

"The king's men, they require papers of passage from all travelers, and no women are permitted to leave at all. How will you help your daughter and the other woman?"

"We did have papers of passage for all of us. They were lost when our ship was captured. Is there no way to leave this country?"

"Perhaps you could join a caravan to Tangier. The king congratulates himself on having made the roads safe for travelers. Then you might find secret passage on a fishing boat to Gibraltar and from there leave for America. God help you if you are again captured."

"But the caravan would be hard on the women and my grandson. The mountains and the desert are harsh to those unaccustomed to them, and I think they are still full of bandits."

"I suppose that is true." Kingsley stared at the ceiling. "I see of no other way to help you escape at this time. But I will think on it, my friend. I will think on it. And perhaps on my next trip to this port, things will be easier."

Moses returned to his rooms by way of his daughter's home. When they were alone, he asked in an anxious whisper, "Can you find out more of this plot, my dear?"

"Annie knows how important it is, Papa." Rachel too saw the possibilities for escape if they could use this information judiciously. "I will go to the harem tomorrow and see if she has learned anything further."

***

The evidence they required came when they least expected it. Rachel wrapped herself in a worn haik as usual to escape notice and met Annie in a barren courtyard. Together they sat on a stone bench beside a fountain that no longer sprayed fronds of water.

Annie scanned the courtyard then whispered, "I have flattered and pleased and used every other wile I could muster to ingratiate myself with Yazid's mother. We both speak English, and she is lonely. She seeks me out for conversations in her native tongue."

"I can understand that," said Rachel. She remembered those first lonely days, weeks, months, first in the harem and then in Eliahu's home, treated with aloofness and contempt by the other wives.

Annie glanced at Rachel and then put an arm around her. "The other servants told me that she has treated her son with smothering attention from birth. She feared that he would be murdered by another harem wife, seeking power for her own son."

Rachel nodded. "I am sure that fear was not misplaced." Rachel pulled her haik closer around her. "Even I have heard the story of Lalla Zara, who was the king's favorite until the other wives mixed poison in her food. I suppose they were jealous."

"But no one suspected them then," said Annie. She paused to listen to distant voices before continuing. "Lalla Zara became deathly ill."

Rachel took Annie's hand and patted it. "She survived, did she not?"

"She still suffers." Annie sighed. "I have seen her. Her skin is yellow and drawn like a rotten date, and she is weak and irritable."

Rachel thought of her son, now being entertained by the Jewish seamstresses elsewhere in the harem. He was safer there than in her own home. "I can understand why Yazid's mother would worry about him."

Annie studied her hand as she ran it back and forth on the stone bench. "The domestics all shake their heads and shudder because she went far beyond protection and good sense. She was too ambitious for her son." Annie grimaced. "She praised his every action and every word, smiling on her little treasure when he taunted his half-brothers, kicked the dogs, tortured animals."

Rachel shook her head. "My little boy would never be so cruel." Her eyes softened as she remembered the flower he had picked for her only that morning.

Annie hurried on. "But you are a wise mother. Yazid's mother is foolish. No one looks upon Yazid now with anything but fear." Annie frowned. "Yazid's guards are sworn to protect him, but I see their terror. They fear one mistake will lead to their own torture and death."

Rachel shook her head. "Then even his mother must fear him."

Annie waved that thought away. "She uses praise and approval to buy his continued regard. He boasts to her and confided his plot. I am only an insignificant chamber slave—like a flea to him—but I heard it all."

"Tell me," Rachel leaned forward.

"You know that like all the harem women, Yazid's mother cannot read or write, and her room is her own private sanctuary."

Rachel remembered the room with its mirrors, draperies, and layers of carpet. She had felt suffocated in it.

Annie spoke in eager whispers. "Her son uses the room as an over-large strongbox. He hides his papers and his plans with the one person he knows will not hurt or betray him."

Rachel nodded.

"One morning I saw him writing intently in his mother's room. He noticed me, but he was too high and mighty to think that a lowly domestic could read or in any way threaten him." She cast a knowing smile at Rachel. "I watched him roll up a sheaf of papers and hide them inside a cushion against the wall. I invented tasks that kept me hovering near the door until he had gone and the passageway was deserted."

"That was a brave thing to do," said Rachel.

Annie waved that aside. "Not brave. Desperate. I slipped into the room and retrieved the hidden papers. Then I hid in one of the back passageways to decipher enough of the Arabic to see that they offered the incriminating evidence we need."

"Yazid does plan a coup?" asked Rachel, feeling sick at the thought that the man, cruel as he was, would murder his father.

"Yazid's intentions are stated in the papers." Annie nodded at Rachel.

"The man is a dolt," said Rachel. "He must know how the eunuchs watch that place. I wonder how much he bribed them to be allowed in the harem at all."

"He probably used threats rather than money," Annie said." The old king cannot live forever."

Rachel took Annie's hand. "You must not stay here."

"Hide me with you. They may connect me with you but will not want to confront the father of your child."

Still holding Annie's hand, Rachel began walking toward the room where the seamstresses worked to find her son. "I will insist upon your staying with me," she said. "It is the price for the papers."

That afternoon, Rachel disguised herself in a haik and stood in the plaza outside Eliahu's offices, waiting for her father to appear. She smiled as she waited, unrecognizable. The caftans, haiks and veils were an excellent disguise. No one could penetrate that costume to determine a woman's identity.

Rachel watched the town clock move from two to three before she saw Moses striding down the street. She ran to him and slipped the papers into his hands. "Annie found them and brought them to me," she whispered. "She has left the harem and refuses to return. I think she would be whipped or even killed if she did. I've told her that she may stay with us, Papa. You must make Eliahu agree to this arrangement."

Moses scanned through the papers on the street. He then returned them to Rachel.

"I want you to hide these," he said. "I don't want to risk having them confiscated by Eliahu before we can make use of them. It will ensure the arrangement for Annie."

Rachel took them back in silent agreement, kissed him, and squeezed his hand as she turned to walk home.

***

Moses returned to Eliahu's offices deep in thought. Eliahu was there, scribbling in his ledgers, barely acknowledging Moses' arrival.

"Anything?" Eliahu asked without looking up.

"I have what I think will be strong evidence of Yazid's plot." Moses closed the door behind him. "And I may be able to get more, but I must have your assurance on several things."

Eliahu paused in his writing and peered at Moses. "Let me see what you have."

Moses shook his head. "I don't have it with me, and I have had to make several concessions to get it at all."

Eliahu narrowed his eyes and pursed his lips. "What do you want?"

Moses stepped forward. "First, I must have your assurance that my daughter's friend Annie will be welcomed into your household."

Eliahu sat back and raised an eyebrow. He looked like a cat ready to toy with a mouse. "I cannot make bargains without knowing what I'm bargaining for."

"I assure you," Moses gulped in eagerness, "that the information I have is sufficient to expose Yazid's plot."

Eliahu pursed his lips. "What else are you asking for this prize?"

Moses leaned over the desk. "Papers of passage for myself, my daughter, her son, and our friend Annie."

Eliahu studied Moses with amusement on his face. "Absolutely not. You forget your place. Your daughter is my wife. She and my son are my possessions. As are you, my friend. You are my slave, and you have not yet bought your freedom. Your services are still valuable to me. I cannot permit you to leave."

Moses hit his fist on the wall. "I tell you, we must leave this place."

Eliahu waved this aside and turned back to study his ledger. "Nonsense. You do well here. I will take your daughter's friend into my household, but let's not talk of you leaving Mogador."

Moses saw that this was hopeless. If Eliahu used the papers, he and Rachel would have accomplished nothing toward their own escape.

"Come, come, my friend," said Eliahu. "Give me those papers. I will see that you, ah, present them to the king yourself and perhaps he will, ah, grant you favors then."

Moses could barely hide his scorn. He knew that Eliahu feared the king's reaction to the plot. Moses would not gain favors from the king by exposing his son. He would bear the king's anger and blame. Eliahu would be spared the taint of being the bearer of bad news while accomplishing the goal of exposing the plot. And if the king were grateful, Eliahu would step in to claim the credit, but the king was as likely to be fickle, obstinate, and contrary as grateful. Moses considered withholding the papers, but he was in no position to bargain any more than he had.

"Very well," Moses said. "I will retrieve the papers. Then let us seek an audience with the king."

As he left, he thought again how life at court was like a field of traps. Eliahu had snared him and would push him to his own destruction to gain any advantage in trade, at court, with the king, or with anyone of money, position, or power.

Eliahu had taught Moses what everyone in court circles had known and cultivated for generations: That to ensure the continued good fortune of their family from king to king, they must court all the princes of the royal family as well as the king.

But Eliahu had not courted Yazid. More than that, Eliahu was another Jew who had not loaned Yazid the money he requested to pay his debts. For that, Yazid was the avowed enemy of all the Jews in Morocco.

Yazid must not become king. He was selfish and cruel and would use his power to crush and oppress. His reign would descend into chaos and terror beyond imagination. Everyone connected to the old king would most likely be murdered.

But of all the other princes, thought Moses, who would be the most likely to succeed King Muhammed ibn Abdullah? Which one would be the wisest ruler?

Chapter 31

Cedar Key, Florida, 1999

Hog swill? Sara turned to Josh, angry that he could so heartlessly brush aside the agony of a young girl captured by pirates and sold into a harem.

"What are you talking about?" Sara said, not concealing her scorn.

"That story about the abduction of Levy's grandmother. It's all hog wash, or perhaps you would say garbage, twaddle, bunkum," whispered Josh, looking out at the placid waters of the creek. He brushed aside a mosquito.

"I think you said hog swill. So what do you know about it?" Sara whispered back. She hoped Marie wouldn't hear them disputing her story. Fortunately, the noise of the boat motor covered their words, and Marie's attention was bent on steering the boat up the shallow creek.

Josh grinned at her. "I know baloney when I hear it."

Sara waved him away in disgust and gazed toward shore, watching the procession of fishing cabins pass by under the live oaks dripping Spanish moss. She sat back and felt the sun on her shoulders. Not too hot or humid yet, only a few mosquitoes out here on the water and just enough breeze to dispel the smell of dead fish and rotting seaweed. A memory of her trip to the Chesapeake surfaced, but she squelched it. Marie reached over and touched Sara's shoulder.

"There," she said, pointing ahead to a gray hulk drifting to the surface of the water. "A manatee. See there?"

"Wow! It is huge." Sara stared at the placid, floating eight-foot behemoth, ugly yet totally benign.

"Yes, and there is its baby." Marie pointed to another floating hulk, this one about five feet long.

Josh whistled. "Look at the size of those things!"

Marie brought the boat alongside the mother manatee and cut the motor. "We have to be careful not to harm these creatures, so I go real slow and careful in this creek."

She dangled a frayed hemp rope over the side into the water. Sara watched as the manatee nibbled its way up the rope to the surface. Its head rose out of the water, and it stared blandly at Sara. Sara reached down and patted its head. It felt smooth and wet. The manatee blinked and brought its tail up to float on its back in front of them.

Sara and Josh hung over the rail, gazing in silence at the manatees swimming lazily before them. Then Marie drew up the rope, turned on the motor and backed slowly away.

"They're all so scarred," said Sara.

"From boat propellers." Marie looked over the side. "But they're survivors."

Now that they were heading back to the dock, Sara asked the question that was bothering her. "That story about Levy's grandmother. . . ."

Josh snorted.

Sara continued. "I just feel for her, losing her family like that."

"That's the way it was in those times," Marie said. "Her family wouldn't have her back after she'd been raped in a sultan's harem, would they?"

Sara thought about it. Probably that was true. Even today a girl captured and raped would not be welcomed home in some families in this country, let alone in other countries where women were considered chattel. Still, it seemed so . . . cruel and barbaric, she concluded, thinking of the assault she had endured and her reluctance to tell anyone about it.

"Even more baloney," Josh whispered to Sara. She was still caught up in the tragedies so many women had faced over the centuries. She glanced at Josh, wondering whether he knew the "real story" or was just an insensitive male chauvinist.

Marie turned her attention to steering the boat. She maneuvered it smoothly alongside the dock and secured it without help.

Sara and Josh walked back to the dirt yard that served as a parking lot. The sun beat down on them now, and the humidity in the still air had risen to an uncomfortable level. Josh stopped at the blue wreck and reached in to pull out a crumpled towel. He wiped the sweat off his face.

Sara leaned against her car, arms folded, frowning at Josh. "I'm wondering what you're doing here," she said.

Josh threw the towel back in his car. "After meeting you, I became curious about my own family. David Yulee is a distant ancestor. I had some free time so I thought I ought to learn more about him—where he lived in Florida and so on. After all, he was Florida's first senator and I'm related to him." He grinned. "Maybe something rubbed off. How's your search going?"

"Not too well. No one I've met knows anything about a Samuel E. Yulee."

" Couldn't you just call the Yulees? Maybe hire a private detective?"

"Yes, I could have called them, but I thought I would learn more if I actually saw them. And a private detective? No, no, no. Anyway, my grandmother wanted me to find him. He was her brother and my great-uncle."

"I'll check with my family. They may know something. How can I reach you—if they know anything, I mean."

"You can call my mother." Sara scribbled the phone number on a piece of paper and handed it to him. If he knew anything, this connection should work—and be safe enough. After all, she didn't know and certainly didn't like this man.

"Okay, thanks," Josh said. "But if this Samuel Yulee you're looking for is connected with my family, he'd be Jewish. You're not Jewish, are you?"

Sara considered her response. "I don't know," she said. "I suppose I am," she added, remembering the rabbi's words. Her grandmother, her mother, herself.

Josh looked askance at her. "I guess there's a story there."

Sara headed toward her own car, throwing a response over her shoulder. "Too long to go into."

Josh opened his car door. "I'm driving back up to Cedar Key. You might be interested since it was the western end of Yulee's railroad. I've got a job there."

"I'm heading that way too. Two Yulees on my list live there. From the names, it looks like they may be father and son."

"No relation to me. At least, I don't think so. I've never heard of any Cedar Key connection with my parents and grandparents. We were all born and brought up in St. Thomas—the Virgin Islands, as you know."

"And I don't see any tie-in with me and my family, but we might as well get moving. Maybe I'll see you in Cedar Key." Sara turned to her car, noting that only one of the white cars remained in the small lot.

By the time she left Homosassa, Sara was hungry. Lunch time. As she drove up to Cedar Key on a lonely stretch of Route 19, she was glad that she had bought a sandwich and Coke at the little store before she left. All she needed now was a candy bar. She pulled into the next service station for gas and the possibilities in the convenience store— and to see if a white car was following her. She filled the tank, bought a candy bar, and waited in her car a few extra minutes, staring at each passing car. When she saw a white car with a lone driver, she swung out behind it, but it quickly outdistanced her, and she lost sight of it after a few miles. The relief she felt as it disappeared surprised her.

The sunny afternoon heat, flat shrubby terrain around her, and straight road ahead had a hypnotizing effect. She almost missed the left turn that put her onto a narrow causeway cutting across marshes and sand flats westward to the island of Cedar Key. She could see water ahead and sat up in anticipation.

She arrived in Cedar Key, spotted Josh's car, and parked behind it. The man was obnoxious, but he was a lead. She saw him walking ahead of her on the sidewalk and called out to him. He turned and waved.

"Just got here," he said as she caught up with him. They strode down the street together. Sara kept her eyes on the puddles and broken concrete of the sidewalk, but she was thinking about Josh's comments. Finally, she asked him, "So what was that about Levy's grandmother's capture and rape being a lot of baloney?"

Josh seemed almost eager to reply. "Her family wouldn't have rejected her. For one thing, even if she hadn't been Jewish, a lot of families—and men—would have thought she was quite a marriageable prize, having been in a king's harem."

"And Jews?"

"They would have been delighted to have their daughter back. She could always have gone back to her family if they were still alive."

A quick rush of relief hit Sara. Josh did have a reasonable explanation for his attitude, which meant that she could trust at least some of what he said.

Josh stopped. "Do you have a place to stay here?"

Sara shook her head.

"I'd offer to let you stay in my hovel, but it's pretty meager."

"I wouldn't do that anyway. Do you know anything about this hotel?"

They were standing in front of the quaint and historic Island Hotel. The square, pink building with its second floor wrap-around balcony evoked the flair of New Orleans.

"A lot of well-known people stay here," said Josh.

They walked inside and paused. Sara blinked as her eyes became accustomed to the dark, cool interior. She stumbled on the uneven wood planking as they walked over to the hotel's registration desk.

The clerk looked up. "Reservations for two?"

"No. Just for me," said Sara. "One night, I think."

Josh turned to her. "When do you plan to contact the Yulees here?" he said.

"Maybe this evening. They both live in town." Sara took a deep breath and a risk. "Want to go with me to find them now before dinner?"

"Sure. I'm curious."

After Sara had taken her suitcase to the room and freshened up, they strolled through the town. It was so small they found themselves reading street names and door numbers to find the Yulee homes. The first address turned out to be only three side streets away from the town center. The small, white frame cottages lining the street probably dated from the thirties. They squatted on sandy soil sparsely covered with grass under live oak trees.

The house Sara sought was well-kept, painted, hedges clipped, garden weeded. An elderly black man sat on the stoop, reading a newspaper. She hesitated, but Josh headed up the sidewalk toward the old man.

"Pardon me, my name is Josh Davila, and we're looking for a Charles Yulee who lives at this address."

The old man looked up. "Yep, that's right. That's me."

"We're looking for a Yulee descended from the David E. Yulee who was a Florida senator."

"Oh, you're another one, are you?" The old man stood up. "I get so tired of strangers tracking me down and askin' me a bunch of fool questions. You oughta be able to look at me and see I'm not related and I don't know nothin' about his grandma. I have nothin' to tell you. My great grampa worked on Yulee's railroad and that's how come he took the name. That's all. And don't go bothering my son neither. None of us can tell you anything about this here Yulee."

Josh backed up under the verbal assault, but he apologized for disturbing the old gentleman and walked back to join Sara.

"You heard that, I guess."

Sara was already walking away. "Yeah, but I don't know if my Samuel Yulee was actually descended from David Yulee. What was that about the grandmother?"

Josh put his hands in his pockets and stared at the sidewalk as they walked down the street. "A lot of people are intrigued by the story about how she was kidnapped by pirates and try to do a little research on their own—like you're doing. I talked to a historian at the University of

Florida who says it's a fabrication but the story persists. He says they don't know much about Yulee's grandmother, but she was simply the daughter of a merchant in Tangier who married a courtier in Morocco with no fanfare, no kidnapping by Barbary pirates or any of all that romantic stuff."

Sara shook her head but kept her eyes on the sidewalk to dodge the cracks and holes. "If they don't know much about her, then she could have been captured by pirates and maybe rescued by the courtier."

"Whatever. This Charles Yulee is obviously no relation to David Levy Yulee."

"Did you notice we're in Levy County now?" Sara gestured around her as they walked. "I suppose it was named after David Levy Yulee."

Josh stared down the road and shook his head. "David Yulee wasn't the only person of note in the family, and he wasn't the only Yulee either."

Sara paused to enjoy the red, green, and yellow stripes of an overgrown croton hedge. "These are indoor plants where I'm from." She smiled at Josh. "What do you mean he wasn't the only Yulee?"

"David's father was the one born to the courtier." Josh picked up a stone and flicked it down the road. "In Mogador, Morocco, but he grew up in Gibraltar, and then found passage to St. Thomas where he became wealthy selling timber."

Sara listened, slightly distracted by the fresh breeze coming in off the Gulf, the scent of salt in the air, and the flowering hibiscus around her—all so exotic for a West Virginia girl. "What was his name?" she asked.

"Moses Elias Levy. I guess this county could just as easily be named for Moses Levy as for his son." Josh kicked another pebble.

"Elias! That may be a link to Samuel if the "E" does stand for Elias and Samuel is descended from David Yulee." They were passing a woodworker's studio. Sara paused to admire the turned wooden bowls on a shelf by the sidewalk.

Josh waited, staring off into the distance. "I suppose so. Big 'ifs.'"

They passed the woodworker's studio and came to a crafts shop. Sara stopped to look in the display window. "What happened to David Yulee's grandmother?"

"I don't know. I think she and Moses' sister also moved to St. Thomas but stayed there."

"So how did Moses get to Florida?" Sara asked as they moved on.

"Moses and his wife Hannah had four children, two girls, two boys. David was the last child. Moses and Hannah split up after David's birth, and Moses moved here. He purchased thousands of acres in central Florida from the Arrendondo family, who had received it as a land grant from the Spanish king. Florida was Spanish back then, you know."

"Yes, I know a little history." They were passing the town museum, but it was closed.

Josh stopped and looked down at Sara. "I'm sorry. I always seem to get into lecture mode."

"That's all right. I'm finding this fascinating."

"Okay, so I'll continue then. The Arrendondos were supposed to find colonists to settle the land but weren't that successful, so they unloaded it onto Moses, and Moses was supposed to recruit the colonists. He thought Florida would be a wonderful state for Jews . . . like Israel today, you know, only he couldn't get any to come here. This was in the early 1800s, and the place was full of mosquitoes and alligators."

"He should have waited a hundred years," Sara said.

They were walking down a street near the marina. Gray, weathered buildings on their right housed gift and other shops, all closed.

Josh waited as Sara paused to stare in the windows at each one, but he continued his lecture. "Anyway, Moses had slaves to work his sugar cane fields and equipment, but he was an abolitionist and wrote anonymous pamphlets against slavery. This was the Deep South, and a man with his opinions risked being lynched or at least tarred and feathered."

"Odd that his son was a Confederate," said Sara. "How did David get to Florida from St. Thomas?"

"Moses eventually brought his two sons over to go to school in the States. David at first went to school in Norfolk, but Moses brought him back to work on the plantation. David wanted something other than plantation life under the thumb of his father so he went to St. Augustine and studied law instead."

"And became a senator," said Sara.

"Yes. And he married and had kids."

"What about the other son?"

"David's brother, Elias Levy, followed David in taking the name Yulee so his male descendants would be Yulees also."

"And I suppose they all have a bunch of descendants."

"Heaps."

"And you are somehow distantly related," Sara said, "and maybe so am I."

"Yes, so I've been tracking down David Yulee and knocking around trying to figure out what I want to do with my life."

"Yeah. I'm doing the same thing."

"Tough, isn't it?" Josh kicked a pebble. "Everyone in my family is mad at me because I quit school after I got my master's. I'm supposed to be the family academic. So now I'm living here, picking up whatever odd jobs I can get."

"Everybody said I had a great job," said Sara, "but it was tedious and boring to me."

"So your grandmother gave you a reprieve."

"Yes, I guess she did," Sara said. "Do you have any relatives left in St. Thomas?"

"Oh yeah. There are a lot of us around."

Sara thought a moment, staring at the ground, before looking up at Josh. "Would you take another look at the album I got from my grandmother? Maybe something will come to you."

"We're back at the hotel. Why don't I take a look at it now, then we'll have dinner."

Sara smiled at him and took his arm. Cleaned up, Josh wasn't too bad.

They entered the cool, dark lobby of the hotel, but as they passed the reception desk, the clerk called Sara over.

"There's a man waiting to see you." He motioned to the bar. "In there." He reached under the desk. "He asked me to give you this." He handed Sara a small bouquet of red hibiscus flowers.

Sara accepted the bouquet with a sense of panic, thinking of the stranger who had handed Elizabeth a hibiscus flower. Sara wondered if she had indeed opened a Pandora's box. She and Josh walked over to the bar and peeked into the dark, quiet interior.

Lounge chairs and low tables ranged around the room and murals of Cedar Key graced the walls. The only customer was an older man with gray hair, wearing a white guayabera, who sat at a small table perusing a menu card.

He looked up, saw them and smiled, but as he stood, he knocked over a glass of beer. Now flustered and apologetic, he stammered a hello to them as he mopped the table with a napkin. A server ran over with paper towels and motioned him to the next table. The stranger's eyes darted from Sara to Josh as he sidled over and grabbed a chair, pushing it toward Sara.

"Sit, sit," he said.

They sat.

"Thank you for coming." He sat down with them and cleared his throat. "You'll have to forgive me. I'm just not used to this kind of thing." His eyes darted around the room, and he ran a finger under his collar as if it were too tight.

"Thank you for the flowers," Sara said warily.

Josh frowned at him. "Who are you?"

"And why the flowers?" asked Sara, holding up the bouquet.

"Good questions." The stranger's hands fluttered. "I'm afraid I was starting to scare you, so I thought I'd better stop playing detective."

"Playing detective?" Sara said. "What do you mean?"

"Please, have something to drink, and I'll explain." He motioned to the server.

"I'll have a glass of Coke," Sara said.

"Beer for me," Josh said.

"Same for me," said the stranger. He turned to them. "My name is Abe Carilla. You met a friend of mine in Rockville."

"Elaine Steinitz? Or the rabbi?"

"You gave Elaine an album to translate. After you left, she called me because, you see, she thought she recognized one of the paintings in the album. A Modigliani."

"But she didn't say anything to me about it."

"She wasn't sure about the painting, you see," said Abe. "And she wasn't sure who you were and what your motives might be. She thought it safer to say nothing to you at the time."

Sara stared at him. "Safer? Why safer?"

"What if she was right? That painting disappeared during World War II. It was stolen from my family in Europe. Who took it? Where is it now? And why is a picture of it in a family album from West Virginia? She knew nothing at all about you."

Sara felt the beginning of a panic attack. For a moment she couldn't breathe and her hands shook. The server brought their drinks, giving Sara a moment to quell the fear and focus on Abe's words. She took a deep breath. "And I don't know anything about this except that the album was in my grandmother's possession when she died."

Sara stopped and took a sip of her Coke. Feeling a bit calmer, she added, "Grandma had a brother named Samuel Yulee, and before she died, she asked me to find him. I'm searching for him now. I hoped the album would help."

Abe nodded. He sat back, beer in hand. "Yes, Elaine told me."

"That's right," said Sara. "I know it sounds naïve, but it was the best idea I could think of. Couldn't you have come and asked me about all this? Why did you have to follow me and scare me half to death?"

"My mistake." Abe laughed and shrugged. "I had no idea how to proceed, but I thought if I followed you, I might find out what you were really after, and I thought that might be the painting. I hoped that the flowers might convey to you that I was not trying to hurt you." He shook his head. "The whole thing was the most colossal boneheaded idea."

"Why are you telling me all this now?"

"I was a klutz as a detective and it seemed to me that, after all, you were only genuinely searching for this Samuel Yulee. You weren't asking any questions about the paintings." Abe took a sip of beer. "I thought I might as well show my hand and see if you would show yours. I'm no good at this detective thing."

"I see," said Sara. "Well, I haven't gotten far at all."

"We thought we'd look through the album. I might recognize something," said Josh, "and maybe you will too."

Sara sat back and folded her arms. "You broke into my motel room in St. Augustine," she said, "didn't you?"

Abe shook his head. "Oh. I'm sorry about that. So you saw that, did you? I thought I was so careful."

Sara bristled. "That took a lot of nerve. You pawed through my private possessions. You had no right to do that."

"I know, I know. I'm sorry for that too. I had to know if the photo you had was of my family's painting, and I was feeling frustrated and angry, but I only looked through the album, nothing else. It cost me a bundle in bribes, but I just had to see for myself."

"And what did you think?"

"It was a picture of my family's missing painting, all right."

"That's strange," Sara said. And interesting, but how useful? She finished her Coke and pushed back her chair. "You stay here. I'll bring down the album so both of you can look through it. Tell me anything you recognize."

They spent more than an hour poring over the photos in the album.

"I didn't look too closely at Elaine's," Josh said. "Didn't think there was anything in it." Now he studied every page, whistling at some of the photos, peering closely at others, and scanning the rest.

Abe leafed quickly past the photos of people and pointed in triumph at a photo of a painting. "That one, there," he said.

Sara recognized the distinctive style of Modigliani but didn't know enough about art to identify any of the other photos.

Abe and Josh continued to study the pictures as Sara watched, alert to any clues that they knew anything about the photos. They finally looked up. Abe thoughtfully tapped his teeth with his glasses.

"You know the people, don't you," Sara said to Josh.

Josh didn't respond at once. He seemed to be considering his words. "Maybe I do," he conceded.

"Well? Why didn't you say so at Elaine's?"

"Too many unanswered questions. We decided to see how you conducted the search and what you found out. We knew how to reach you, and I hoped you would contact me for help."

Sara frowned and her eyes sparked. "So you were testing me?"

"Of course not." Josh backed away. "But you have to admit the circumstances are peculiar—and Elaine wouldn't let me study the album."

"All right. So now you are studying the album." Sara folded her arms and sat back.

Josh nodded. "I'm not sure, but at least some of them were taken in St. Thomas. I recognize the backgrounds . . . and maybe some of the people. I don't recognize the paintings at all. Why would photos of them be in a family album?"

"I have no idea." Sara shook her head impatiently and looked at Abe. "Do you have any idea why the photo of your painting should be in this album?"

"No," said Abe, pursing his lips. "The painting isn't well-known. Modigliani gave it to my uncle in return for a favor. My uncle probably loaned him some money." Abe shrugged. "Modigliani was a Sephardic Jew, you know, like my family."

"The photos are pretty old," said Josh, squinting closely at one of them.

"What about this Samuel E. Yulee I'm looking for?"

Josh looked off in the distance. "I guess I can tell you now. There is someone named Samuel Yulee in my family, but that is in St. Thomas. My mother knows all about him, I think."

Sara sat back, stunned. Was this it then? Had she found Samuel E. Yulee? "How can I reach her? Can I call her?"

Josh turned to Sara. "Could you go there? My mother would talk more freely if she met you," he said.

Sara sat back and considered the idea.

Abe looked from Sara's face to Josh's. "I think I'll trust you," he said. "I need to get back to my office, and anyway, I'm a bum detective. I'd like to get the painting back, if I can. Perhaps you'll learn what happened to it. If you do, please let me know. That's all I ask. Just let me know. If the painting's lost, so be it."

Sara stared down at the album. She took a long time to respond be-

cause, for the first time, she realized that her quest, begun as a hapha-
zard search and opportunity to travel, might have grave consequences
for some people.

Could she trust Josh? Could she trust Abe? Elaine Steinitz knew
Josh and Abe was Elaine's friend, he said, and Elaine had been referred
to Sara by the rabbi. Surely they meant well.

Were Josh and Abe working together? Were they telling her the
truth or was she being manipulated? Did they perhaps have an ulterior
motive for steering her away from Florida and towards St. Thomas?

Sara studied her hands. "Yes, you're right," she said at last. "I have
to go to St. Thomas."

But I'll be on guard.

Chapter 32

Mogador, 1786

Moses left Eliahu's offices and strode down the hot, dusty street to visit Rachel. He felt the weight of the frustrations and disappointments in his life as slave to Eliahu, but the black djellaba he now wore was of high-grade cotton and finely stitched. A floral border of silver thread made it distinctive and befitting of the vizier's assistant.

As Moses turned into the alley and prepared to knock at the heavy wooden door of Eliahu's house, his grandson threw down the stick he was using to draw in the alley dust and ran to greet him. The little boy's dark curls danced in the sun.

"Grandpapa!" he yelled, running circles around Moses.

"Ah, my little kumquat," Moses said, picking up the small boy and whirling him in a hug.

Rachel appeared in the doorway. "Papa, you have returned."

Moses looked up at her as he set the boy down. She had become a woman as beautiful as her mother, sadder, perhaps, stronger, more serious, and a firm expression in her eyes that hinted at a determination her mother had never possessed. He motioned for Rachel to join him at the central fountain in the first courtyard. They sat on the stone bench that circled the fountain. Moses scanned the second floor balcony for listeners. Finding that they were alone, he whispered to her, "I must retrieve those papers and present them to the king."

"What papers, Mama?" broke in little Moses Elias, tugging at his mother's skirt.

"Hush, little boy. Go play," Rachel said. "I must speak with your grandpapa." The boy balked but with a loving pat on his backside, he was pushed away to amuse himself in a distant corner of the courtyard.

"Is that wise, Papa? Were you able to bargain with them?"

"Eliahu refuses to bargain for them, and he refuses to release us." Moses picked up a pebble and threw it hard at the wall.

"He refuses?" Her face fell.

"He did agree to allow Annie to stay here with you. They may miss her at the palace but after so many years, no one will connect her with you." He looked at Rachel.

Rachel tapped her lips thoughtfully. "And the eunuchs will not be eager to admit that she escaped or to confront Eliahu." She picked an orange off a tree and threw it to her son.

"Yes, so that is my only achievement," Moses said, also picking an orange and peeling it as he talked. "I'm trying to decide how to proceed now. I have talked with my good friend Zephaniah Kingsley on his ship, and he will see what he can do to help us. But without papers of passage and without the king's consent, that good deed would jeopardize both him and his ship if we were caught onboard."

"I see. And the king will not be pleased to learn of his son plotting against him."

"Yes. Eliahu insists that I present this evidence myself to the king." He handed an orange section to Rachel.

"So like Eliahu," said Rachel.

"I fear so."

She turned and searched his face. "Papa, we must escape this place. We talked of the desert and the mountains. Could we not join a caravan of traders or nomads going north?"

Moses took another orange section for himself and handed the rest to Rachel. He shook his head. "Most of them take the ancient route east to Timbuktoo. Even if we found a caravan going north, we would be in much greater danger that way, and our life much harder in the going, especially if we were caught and enslaved then."

Rachel shuddered.

Moses took her hand and squeezed it. "Even now renegades and bandits still prey on caravans. The king is a fool if he thinks the roads are safe in this depraved country. And it would have to be a large caravan and even then, how would we know we could trust them?"

Rachel watched little Moses picking at the floor tiles with a stick. "If we could get to Tangier, our friends would help us."

Moses stared down at the floor. "But we would endanger them."

"We could walk there as beggars and then borrow a boat to get to Gibraltar." She stepped over to pick up little Moses and bring him back to sit on her lap.

Her father shrugged. "But we would be vulnerable to every insult and every brute and bandit we met."

"Yes, I know you're right," she said, her arms around the boy, "but I have thought and thought and cannot find an answer, Papa. It has been five years now, and still we have not escaped. Will we ever be free of this place?"

Moses glanced at his grandson. "We must," he said.

Rachel handed little Moses to her father, then ran up the steps and disappeared into the back rooms. She returned with the papers. "I hid them under my mattress." She handed the papers to him. "It's such a convenient hiding place. As long as I keep things spread out and flat and clean the room myself, it works well."

He took the papers, kissed Rachel, and hugged his grandson; then he left, his expression grave and thoughtful.

He did not return directly to Eliahu's quarters. Instead, he padded in the dust through the orange groves along the estuary of the river Ksob to the king's palace at Diabat. Moses had learned just that morning from one of Eliahu's messengers that the king's son Moulay Sliman was in residence there. Of all the king's sons, Moulay Slimon seemed the most reasonable and the most intelligent. *I should cultivate this man, but as myself, not as Eliahu's slave.*

As Moses approached the palace he was surprised to hear loud voices calling out across a field. Coming closer, he saw two men sitting in state on carpets and cushions slung over the palace gateway. Several attendants stood closely on each side of the two men, shading them from the sun with large, tasseled umbrellas. Moses recognized one of the king's sons, Moulay Omar, from a court appearance. The older, stouter man must be Moulay Sliman. The princes were dressed in simple white djellabas like any ordinary Arab townsman.

Moses saluted as he approached, but they barely noticed him. They were staring out beyond him. Moses turned to see what was so fascinating. He heard the hooves of horses and then recognized, as they came closer, about a hundred Moors on horseback in a cloud of dust.

They halted, then as the dust settled, formed themselves into rows, each comprising five to ten men on horses, one row behind the other. Confusion and chaos and more clouds of dust billowed around them. Suddenly, the first line of horsemen charged at full gallop toward the gate where the princes sat. Moses ran back around a corner of the wall, not knowing what the horsemen would do next and not wanting to be trampled underfoot. When it seemed that the horsemen must careen into the wall, they simultaneously halted and each man raised his rifle and fired into the air.

At once Moses understood that this was a competition, a fantasia, they called it. Each row represented a different tribe, vying to be the most synchronized in halting their horses and firing into the air. Moses had heard that these fantasias took place occasionally but never thought he would see one.

He stood leaning against the base of the wall and swatting flies with a stick as he watched line after line of horsemen charge, halt and fire their rifles. After awhile, the performance became tedious, but eventually, the sun drew close to the horizon and the long shadow of the palace crept over him. The men on horseback joined forces and came forward in a line. They saluted the princes and the royal party, then guided their horses one by one slowly toward some far-off field and their tents.

When it became obvious that the royal party was preparing to climb down from the wall, Moses pushed past the gate guards who, recognizing him as Eliahu's assistant, let him through.

He bowed as he approached Moulay Sliman, and then bowed again before begging for a short audience with the prince. Moulay Sliman stepped forward, his white djellaba billowing. His brother and the other men of their party stopped and stared at Moses curiously.

Moses again bowed and said, "I most humbly beg your pardon, your royal highness, but I must speak privately with you on a most urgent matter."

Moulay Sliman gestured to his attendants and stepbrother to move on. Then he turned his heavy-lidded eyes and bulky body toward Moses. "Who are you?" he asked.

"I am Moses Levy, assistant to Eliahu ben Youli, vizier to his Most Supreme Majesty, your father, Muhammad ibn Abdullah. I must speak with you on a grave matter that has come to my attention."

"Yes, yes, come forward with it. I am in a hurry." He glanced impatiently at the retreating party.

"I most humbly beg your pardon, your highness, but as the most esteemed son of his Majesty, you would know best what is to be done in this matter."

"What matter is that?"

"I have papers here, your highness, that show that your half brother, Moulay Yazid, plans to overthrow your father and take the reins of government himself."

The man's eyes fluttered and then narrowed into suspicious slits. He took the papers without comment and motioned for Moses to follow him to a bench in the courtyard under an olive tree.

Moses understood how risky this meeting was, especially since he knew Moulay Sliman by reputation only. Even though Sliman was considered a reasonable and educated man, he could interpret Moses' action as an impertinence that must be punished. Who knew what would happen with royalty?

Moulay Sliman read through the papers quickly at first, then more slowly. He rolled them into a tight scroll and hid them inside his djellaba. Then he stared across the courtyard at the king's chambers. Moses waited.

"How did you obtain these papers?"

Moses decided on caution. "I received them from a messenger who delivered them and departed before I could question him. I believe they are from a credible source. I did not know what would be the wisest thing to do with them, but if I show them to you and they are false, then perhaps little harm will be done. If I don't show them to you and they are true, then great catastrophe could befall us." Moses paused but he could not read Moulay Sliman's expression.

Trying to keep the tremble out of his voice, Moses added, "I show them to you now in the hopes that you, the most supreme of all the sons, would in your wisdom know how this dilemma might be addressed to determine the truth of the matter and prevent this catastrophe."

"But no source, my friend?" Moulay Sliman stroked his beard as he studied Moses. "If Yazid were not such a wastrel and had not offended my father a thousand times thousand times, I would not accept these papers, and I fear that you would now be begging for your life."

Moses stared at the ground and bowed.

After a long silence, Moulay Sliman nodded. "But you have done well to bring these documents to me. I have heard rumors that he planned some evil, but I did not know what. My family relays its gratitude to you and your master. I will examine the papers and find the truth of the matter so that if such a plot exists, it will not succeed. From this point forward, Yazid will be watched. To my father, I will suggest that Yazid be sent on a pilgrimage," he grinned, "to Mecca."

He stroked his beard and gazed off into the distance. "That would be good for his soul, I should think. I am sure my father will agree."

Moses bowed, not daring to risk a response.

"You have earned the gratitude of our country and myself and that of my father as well. We are indebted to you, but it would be better if my father did not learn of this plot."

"I leave it all in your hands, your highness."

"And in the power of Allah, my friend."

Moses bowed again and retreated. Staring at the ground, he trudged back to the medina and the chambers of Eliahu ben Youli. He was not eager to hear what Eliahu would say about his action.

As Moses had feared, Eliahu stood at the door, arms folded, tapping his foot. When he saw Moses, he held out his hand.

"The papers are gone," said Moses. "I found a way to deliver them that would not endanger either of us."

Elihu glared at him. "What do you mean?"

"I carried the papers to his royal highness, Moulay Sliman, in the palace courtyard at Diabat." Moses spoke slowly as he assessed Eliahu's rising anger. "He will take care of the matter and see to it that Moulay Yazid is watched. This will earn us Sliman's gratitude while keeping us away from the king's wrath."

Eliahu's nostrils flared as if he would shoot flames from them. After a moment, he spoke. "I see . . . I see that you have earned his gratitude, but you are a fool if you think that will gain you favor." Eliahu turned his back on Moses and retreated into his office, slamming the door in Moses' face.

Moses remained where he was for a moment. Eliahu was not pleased, but he could not complain since Moses' action saved both of them from the dubious gratitude of the king and the wrath of a rebellious son.

Moses had thwarted Eliahu's plans and gained the notice of Moulay Sliman, one of the most powerful of the king's sons. In retaliation, Eliahu would now hammer him with petty harassments and sneers.

Moses smiled. A small price to pay considering the prize.

Chapter 33

St. Thomas, 1999

Sara sat on the bed in her hotel room in Charlotte Amalie, the capital city of St. Thomas in the Virgin Islands. For the fourth time since her arrival the preceding afternoon, she dialed the telephone number for Josh's parents. Still no response and no answering machine. She hung up the phone in frustration. Time to try something else.

She retrieved her rental car from the hotel garage. Using the map in her guidebook, she maneuvered through the congested streets of the town. Like everyone else, she drove on the wrong side of the road because even though St. Thomas was a U.S. territory, the people here drove on the left. The traffic forced her to creep along behind the car in front of her, but she was grateful for the slow pace.

After several wrong turns, she found the Altona Cemetery, one of St. Thomas' two historic Jewish cemeteries mentioned in her guidebook. She parked her car alongside the cemetery wall and walked over to peer through the cemetery's locked and rusty wrought iron gate. At the top, a Star of David had been welded into place. She rattled the gate but it held firm. She scanned the cemetery for someone to let her in but saw no one. Her frustration was building.

The sun baked her and glared off the white pebbles that paved the ground in the cemetery. Unlike the grassy cemeteries with upright headstones Sara knew in West Virginia, this one looked more like the ruins of an ancient Grecian temple. Across the cemetery in every direction lay horizontal slabs about five feet long and a foot and a half wide. These rested on top of rectangular brick receptacles, giving the cemetery the appearance of a desolate garden of stone benches. Everything seemed to be bleached from the sun. The only shade came from stunted trees planted along the back wall of the cemetery.

Sara turned away, wiping the perspiration from her forehead and fanning herself with her hand. The heat was enervating. How could she get into the cemetery? If she couldn't get in and she couldn't talk to Josh's parents, this trip would be useless. Did Josh and Abe lead her astray? What possible clue could there be here to her grandmother's life?

Sara trudged back to her car, pondering the strange fact that despite the frustrations, St. Thomas seemed oddly comfortable and almost familiar to her, as if she'd been there before, but that couldn't be. She thoughtfully chewed her lip.

She drove back through the narrow streets crowded with tourists, business people, and locals of all color and costume. She parked at her hotel and followed the guidebook map to walk to the 200-year-old synagogue which, according to the guidebook, was the second oldest synagogue in the Caribbean. Perhaps here she might find some answers.

As she approached, she struggled with its name on the sign at the gate: Synagogue of Berecha V'Shalom V'Gemiluth Chasadim, then latched onto the English translation in her guidebook: "Blessing and Peace and Loving Deeds."

The handsome stone and brick building was a well-known tourist attraction. Sara approached it slowly, wondering what the protocol was for entering a synagogue. An elderly white man wearing a blue Cuban guayabera, beige slacks, and a black kippah on his bald head, greeted her at the door to the lobby, shook her hand, then gripped her elbow and guided her over to the guest book. She winced as each step ground sand into the floor with a rasp that sent shivers down her spine. She clenched her teeth.

Her escort gestured at the floor as they walked across it. "The sand symbolizes the ancient flight of the Jewish people out of Egypt and across the desert. We spread it on the floor in keeping with the Sephardic tradition." He spoke rapidly with a nasal twang.

Sara studied the room. Glass cases of Jewish relics and framed historic photos covered the walls. The greeter pointed to the guest book and watched while Sara signed it. As she finished, she looked up and smiled at him, hoping to ask some questions, but he was finished with her and had already turned to greet a couple who had just stepped through the door. To them, he continued talking about Sephardic Jews. It was as if he were a recorded message that must begin at the beginning and continue on to the end.

Sara listened patiently, hoping to bring him around to the cemeteries. Finally, he swept all three into a group and took them over to the books with the signatures of the original members. She saw the name

Davila there. Was this Josh's family? Had they been members when this old synagogue was formed? Was his family buried in one of the old cemeteries? She read through the list of other names and found Moses E. Levy. Was this David Yulee's father?

Pointing to the signatures, Sara shifted the conversation to cemeteries. "I would like to visit the old Jewish cemeteries on St. Thomas, but the gates are locked. How can I get in?"

The old man frowned. "Wait here," he said.

He retreated into the back offices, reappearing a moment later with a name and phone number printed on a card. He gave her the card. "She can help you," he said. "She's on the cemetery committee."

Her name was Teresa. Sara stepped outside the synagogue and called her from a public phone. Teresa sounded pleasant and willing to help. They arranged to meet at nine the next morning at the foot of the Ninety-Nine Steps.

Sara slept fitfully all night and left her hotel early to walk to the steps. She wasn't sure how long a walk this would be, but she arrived early enough to climb to the top of the steps and then back down while she waited for Teresa. She wondered what kind of person a cemetery committee member would be. Would she wear black and look grim?

Sara's question was answered a few minutes later. A dark-haired, almost plump woman dressed in a wrap-around flowered skirt and sleeveless white blouse hurried up to Sara, her sandals slapping on the sidewalk. Teresa appeared to be in her late thirties, and her hair, cut short almost like a cap, had gray streaks in it.

She squinted up at Sara. "You are Sara Miller?" she said, cheerfully waving a sheaf of papers in her hand.

Sara smiled. "Yes, I am. And you are Teresa?"

"Of course. And here," she handed the papers to Sara. "These are copies of the census and cemetery records for the Moses Levy family that you mentioned on the phone. I found nothing for anyone named Yulee."

Sara flipped through them hurriedly as Teresa guided her down an alley.

"You don't have to read them now," Teresa said. "Those are copies I made for you so you can keep them." She pointed toward a yellow Toyota. "We'll take my car."

"Thank you so much," Sara said, holding up the papers. "This is just the kind of information I'm searching for."

Even though she had only hastily shuffled through the papers as they walked, Sara had noticed that down in the list of the census records was the name David Elias Levy, son born to Moses and Hannah Levy. This must be the David who eventually became David Yulee. She put the papers in her bag as they arrived at the car.

Teresa's driving was swift and competent despite the crowded streets. Sara decided that Teresa was probably competent at everything she did. They quickly reached the cemetery Sara had seen the day before.

Teresa selected an old-fashioned iron key from a jangling ring of similar keys, unlocked the rusty gate, and waved Sara in.

As they entered, Teresa picked up a stone and placed it on a grave. "My ancestors are buried here," she said by way of explanation.

Her shoes crunching on the white limestone gravel, Sara stepped around the graves to follow Teresa to a side wall. Here, Teresa pointed out the inscriptions on the slabs lining its base.

Sara read each one slowly: Sarah Rachel Perira, 1791-1866; her husband, Joshua, 1783-1844; and their daughters, Zipporah, 1829-1865; Ramah, 1827-1850; and Julia, 1838-1866.

"According to the records," Teresa said, "Sarah Rachel Perira was Moses Levy's younger sister." She looked at Sara and waited.

Sara studied the graves. "She has my name, Sarah." There was also the name Joshua, like Josh Davila. It was all a bit spooky.

Teresa shook her head. "They were Sephardic Jews, you know. They came from families forced to leave Spain and Portugal because of the Inquisition."

"A terrible thing," said Sara.

Teresa looked at her. "Terrible, yes. In the Sephardic tradition, a child would be named for a living family relative, such as a grandparent. But many surnames were changed as Jews moved from one country to another. And refugees from the Inquisition might change their names to protect family members left behind in Spain or Portugal."

This could be part of my own family history. Sara stared down at the gravel.

"Have you ever heard of 'conversos' or 'marranos'?" asked Teresa.

"I talked to someone who mentioned them."

"In the Inquisition, Jews were allowed to remain in Spain and Portugal if they converted to Catholicism. These converts were called 'conversos' or 'marranos,' which means 'pigs' in ancient Spanish. Gives you an idea of how well you were treated even if you did convert. Many of the converted Jews left these countries anyway because the people there only found new ways to persecute them."

Sara shivered. "It must have been terrifying."

"Oh, it makes me want to weep—my own family suffered." Teresa waved a hand across her face as if to brush these dark thoughts aside.

They left the Altona Cemetery to drive to the Savan Cemetery, the other historic Jewish cemetery on St. Thomas. As Teresa parked the car, Sara saw a man in jeans and tee shirt unfold his lanky body from the shade of a banyan tree.

Teresa called to him, "Oh, good. You made it."

He loped over to join them. He carried a laptop computer carelessly in one hand and looked like a college student. "Yes, I told you I thought I could get away."

She turned to Sara, "This is Michael. Michael, Sara." They walked to the cemetery gate, which was set in a weathered concrete wall. Teresa used another key on the same ring to unlock a hefty, embossed padlock. They entered through gates that creaked with disuse. Sara scanned the cemetery. The sun was still blinding here, and the heat radiated in waves from the sand, rocks, and slabs covering the graves.

Michael squinted in the sun. "You're the one interested in the Moses Levy family?"

"Yes. How do you know about that?"

"Teresa called me. I've been studying the Jewish families here and their role in our island's history. My dissertation. Also, my friend, Josh Davila, told me you were coming here. He asked me to help. Your story might add an interesting sidelight to my research."

"Josh called you about this?" Sara stared at her feet, feeling a quiver of fear about all this unsolicited help. But Teresa was active in the synagogue, and she knew Michael, so they must be reputable people. . . . Sara crossed her fingers.

Teresa patted Sara on the arm. "Don't worry. I've known Michael for years—and his family. He's a good kid. Our rabbi is a friend of his and his family. Most of the Jewish families here know each other."

Michael grinned. "Thanks for the endorsement, Teresa. I'm harmless." He looked at Sara. "I'm writing my dissertation on Jewish families in St. Thomas and their legacy to the islands. Josh and I are both working on doctorates. That is, I am. Josh dropped out."

"Yes, he told me. Actually, I'm really looking for a Samuel E. Yulee, but the best lead I've gotten so far is David Levy Yulee. Do you know anything about him?"

"Not about him, but about his father, Moses Elias Levy. He was a prominent citizen here once."

"Oh, well, what about him?"

"Just a minute." Michael swept a hand across his short, brown hair and sat down on a stone bench in the glaring sunlight. Resting his laptop on his knee, he ran his fingers over the keyboard and brought up a file. "I'll just check my notes here and see what I can give you."

Sara waited, thinking how peculiar it was to be standing in an ancient cemetery in the intense Caribbean sunshine waiting for someone to call up the dead in a laptop file.

"Hmmm. Moses Levy. I see here that he was a fundamentalist Jew and a fanatic. Vehemently anti-slavery. He wrote tracts and lectured in America and England. Alienated his sons, both of them, for a long time."

"Yes. Josh told me about that. So he did live here then."

"St. Thomas and the Caribbean made him a wealthy man—timber mostly," said Michael. "But you can see in the census records that he was born in Mogador, Morocco. According to my notes, there's a story that pirates captured his mother, whose name was Rachel, and his grandfather, also named Moses. And I'm speculating that if the story is true, then she was probably rescued through Jewish funds. At any rate, her son, the younger Moses, father of David, married a woman named Hannah Abendanone here in St. Thomas. They had four children who lived and two infants that must have been stillborn."

"That's right," said Teresa. "I printed out the census and cemetery records about the family for you, Sara. You have them there. Will they be helpful?"

"Oh yes. It was wonderful of you. I appreciate your help."

"Not a problem," said Teresa. "Why did you come to St. Thomas?"

Sara related the events that had brought her to the island from West Virginia and Florida. "Now I'm trying to reach the Davilas."

Michael looked at Teresa. "They're in town, aren't they?"

"I'm sure they are." She turned to Sara. "That's an interesting story. I don't see how the information I gave you will help, but you never know."

"That's right," Sara said with a smile. "You never know."

"Perhaps you'd like to look through my library," Michael said.

"Your library?"

"It's papers, mostly, about the history of Jews on this island and in the Caribbean. Something there may give you a clue."

Sara was about to thank him when she thought of the sailboat on the Chesapeake. She glanced at Teresa standing unconcernedly with one hand shading her eyes from the sun.

"I would love to see those papers," Sara said, "and meet your family." Michael might turn out to be a relative.

Michael smiled. "Don't worry. My Mom will be there, and my parents are cool. They're used to me bringing home people to look through my library. They don't even mind that we sometimes sit up and talk till all hours of the night."

"Sounds like a nice family.'

"Oh, they are, aren't they, Teresa."

She smiled at him but spoke seriously. "Of course. They're quite respected here on the island."

"Come with me now and stay for supper. You too, Teresa."

Teresa looked at her watch. "Sorry. I have kids to pick up, but thanks anyway."

"Your parents won't be expecting me," Sara said to Michael as they walked back to the gate.

"I know, but we have a cook and she always cooks enough for an extra person or two. It'll be fine." He reached over and hugged Teresa. "I'll take Sara to my house, then back to her hotel. That okay with you, Sara?"

She hesitated but saw that Teresa and Michael were waiting, so she nodded and climbed into his battered Honda Civic that was even older than hers. His car probably was the best proof she had that he was a student, although with a cook in the house, it sounded like his family might be wealthy.

She saw she was right when Michael stopped in front of a pink stucco house on top of a steep hill. The views of the Caribbean were breathtaking, even where they parked, which was alongside a one-lane road that met another coming from the other side of the house. She joined Michael on the verandah, feeling nervous but curious.

A woman came to the door as they entered the house. Michael waved a hand and introduced Sara. "Another researcher, I see." She smiled and held out her hand to Sara. "I'm Michael's mother, Louise Andrade, but please just call me Lou."

She wore a rainbow-colored sundress, and her short, wavy gray hair and raspberry red lipstick evoked a sense of youthful energy. Sara liked her at once. She was different from the washed-out, passive nature of her own mother, although her own mother was loving and kind—and probably worrying about her right then.

"Sara is visiting the island, Mom," Michael said as he kissed his mother on the cheek. "Trying to find out something about her grandmother's past and it all has to do with the Levy-Yulee family. I might have papers here that would help. If we find her grandmother's family, I'll have a great addition to my dissertation."

Louise folded her arms and regarded Sara. "That's interesting."

Sara couldn't help feeling that Louise was sizing her up.

"And who was your grandmother? Maybe I knew her."

"That's just it. I don't know. We don't know anything about her early life except that she was in a Nazi concentration camp—and we only found that out after she died. She had a tattoo on her arm."

"She was in a concentration camp?" Louise studied Sara. "Where was she before that?"

"We don't know. We don't even know for sure what her name was before she married my grandfather. It was down as 'Smith' on the marriage certificate." Sara felt embarrassed to say it. How ridiculous to think it would be Smith. She fumbled on. "Smith doesn't sound either German or Jewish. It could have been Schmidt, I guess, but even so. . . " Why hadn't her family caught on to this before?

"Your grandmother, what did she look like?" Louise became as alert as a terrier staring at a mouse.

"Whitish hair, wispy curls, thin."

"I mean, when she was younger. Do you have any pictures of her?"

"Oh. The only pictures I have of her date from when she married my grandfather and afterwards. Some of them show her when she was fairly young. And I brought her wedding photo with me, but it's at the hotel. Why? Do you have any idea who she might be?"

"No, no. Just curious, that's all," said Louise. "Sara, I'd like you to come for dinner this evening. I'll ask our friends, the Davilas, to join us. We'll all be interested in your problem. Is that all right with you?"

Sara breathed a happy yes. At last she was meeting people who might help. "I would enjoy that. I met Josh Davila in Florida. He said his mother might have information about the family."

Michael was stepping toward the hall. "Sure, Mom, go ahead. Come on, Sara."

Sara held back. "I've been trying to call them, but no one answers."

"They have an art gallery in town, my dear. Most likely, they were there. I've been meaning to have them over for dinner, and this sounds like an excellent opportunity." Louise reached for the phone.

Sara followed Michael to his office down the hall on the first floor, passing the living and dining rooms, both spacious with high ceilings and long windows open to the Caribbean breezes. The house felt comfortable to Sara even without air conditioning.

Michael's office was paneled in teak with floor-to-ceiling book-shelves on one wall and a bank of filing cabinets on another. A comfortable room made for work. He pulled open a file drawer and withdrew a folder thick with papers. "I think this is the one." He handed it to Sara.

She opened the folder with care. Aging news clippings hung out the sides like tongues from thirsty dogs.

"I've been collecting local articles about residents for years, especially if I knew they were Jewish. I recently added Yulee to my searches, once Josh . . . that is, once I learned the connection," Michael said. "You know that the name Levy is like the name Smith. Hordes of them, but what information I have is all in that folder."

Halfway through the pile of clippings, Sara found one that mentioned a Samuel E. Yulee who had received a soccer award, but the date was just four years ago, and the man was young, too young to have been a contemporary of her grandmother. He could have been named after his father, though. Or grandfather. She showed the clipping to Michael.

"If I remember right, this Samuel Yulee is in college somewhere, I think in Pennsylvania. I only cut that out because he got the award and I didn't. Keep looking."

"But what about his family?"

"He's one of Josh's relatives. You can ask his parents tonight."

Sara continued to search. No other clippings referred to a Yulee, much less a Yulee named Samuel.

"Do you have anything else?" she asked. "The man I'm looking for would have been alive before World War II, and my grandmother was probably born around 1920."

"What you have there is what I've collected so far. I know it's disappointing, but let's see what Josh's parents say tonight."

Sara thanked Michael and Louise as she left to be driven back to her hotel. "Don't forget dinner," said Louise. "Six o'clock."

"I'll pick you up," said Michael. "Traffic here is crazy, and this place is hard to find on your own. It's better if I drive you."

Sara hesitated, but Louise smiled at her and so Sara agreed.

Dinner. And with Josh's parents. This might be the break she needed. Now that she seemed on the brink of discovery, she wondered if the possible revelations might be painful. Whatever happened, she could not turn back.

As she emerged from the hotel that evening to meet Michael, a tropical breeze made her skin prickle with anticipation. Would this be the night she learned about her grandmother's past? She slid into the car, hugging the album close to her heart.

Chapter 34

Mogador, 1790

Moses picked his way down the narrow street, barely noticing the flies that rose in a swarm as he stepped around the piles of dung and garbage. He held a letter for Rachel and smiled at the thought of giving it to her.

As usual, she was the one who answered the door. Moses silently applauded her desire to know who visited the house and why. "I want to learn his business too," she had once remarked to Moses.

Her face brightened when she saw him. "Papa, I am surprised to see you so early." She took him by the hand and led him into the first courtyard to sit under an orange tree.

"I have a letter for you from your friend Esther." He held it out to her.

She opened it hungrily. "It has been months since I heard from them. We share so little now. They are horrified at my situation, and now they are both married too—under happier circumstances."

Moses nodded. "Yes, and America is still thousands of miles away." He gazed at his daughter as she read. She was still a young woman but serious and thoughtful beyond her years. Nine years had passed yet the fire to escape still burned within her as it did in him.

Rachel folded the letter and placed it in her pocket. She peered up at her father. "You do not hear from Moulay Sliman, Papa? It has been four years since you spoke to him about Yazid. The coup did not happen, Papa, and because of you."

Moses frowned at the courtyard tiles and shook his head. "So far, my dear, all my efforts to ally myself with Moulay Sliman have failed. He has no interest in a mere assistant to a vizier and seems to have forgotten that I saved his father's life. Such is the gratitude among princes."

Moses saw the fleeting look of disappointment cross Rachel's face. He knew she tried to hide it, but the same feeling lurked in his own heart.

He changed the subject. "But see what came in the mail pouches for me." He opened a leather folder and brought out a thick printed document. "This is also from America. I wrote an acquaintance in New York for a copy of a Bill of Rights they seek to add to their Constitution. I have been waiting months for this. I have read and reread it, Rachel. This is a wonderful document."

He riffled through the pages, and then spread them out across the leather folder open on his knees. "This is the Bill of Rights that the states are insisting upon. And look here, the first one, calls for freedom of religion. These good and wise men mean to separate church and state."

"But, Papa, what does that mean?"

"Rachel, you know what the Catholic Inquisition has done to our people. That kind of horror can happen when religion and state are united in the government." He spoke seriously. Even here Jews and Christians are mistreated because Islam is the state religion. "

"And yet we are people too."

"Yes." He saw her sad eyes watching him. "Here, here, my sweet little one, we progress. I have hope. My circumstances have changed for the better. Even though I am still an assistant to," Moses flicked a fly off his arm, "your kind husband, I have made alliances with the wealthy merchants in the town, and they often call upon me for advice and assistance."

"I know, Papa. They pay you well, and I hide the sums you give me. They are here in the caches I have hollowed out under our feet." She dug at a tile with her toes.

"Good." Moses smiled at her with pride. "Good."

"But why do you stay with the father of my child, Papa? Surely you can buy your freedom now?"

"Yes, more than you know. The merchants in town have even come forth and offered to lend me the money to free myself, but I have refused them."

"Refused?" Rachel frowned.

Moses took Rachel's hand and patted it. "They would expect repayment on their terms. I would only exchange one form of servitude for another. I prefer earning the money and hiding it rather than entrusting it to your husband for my freedom. If I remain where I am,

Eliahu's closeness to the royal court allows me a few miserable crumbs of power. Not enough yet since even Moulay Sliman refuses to grant me any significance, but if I persist and remain close to Eliahu, I might eventually have the opportunity to acquire the papers of passage and the means for all of us to leave Morocco."

"I pray it will be soon, Papa."

Moses nodded. "As do I, but if I cannot acquire the papers soon, then we will have to find a way to smuggle ourselves out of the country."

Rachel smiled. Moses saw a mischievous twinkle appear in her eyes. "Annie and I are ready, Papa. We only need an hour's notice." She hopped up. "We have the materials to disguise ourselves as Arab men. And we are preparing Moses Elias as well." She paraded in front of him standing tall and taking long resolute steps.

Moses chuckled. "Yes, an excellent plan, my dear. I am confident that you and Annie can perform your parts well. I still need to obtain the necessary papers—especially for non-existent men, but for Arabs, perhaps bribes will be enough. It is the way of going that concerns me now."

An hour later, Moses walked back to Youli's office by way of the ramparts to see what ships were in port. Today there were none, and he walked on.

Moses knew that something must be done soon. The country was on the brink of disaster. The people around him were edgy and tense. Tempers were short, sparking angry brawls that broke out like wild fires here and there in the streets. Rumors had paralyzed almost all business as everyone waited for the latest word from Rabat or Marrakech.

Was the old king dead or alive? No one knew. Even Eliahu, with his spider's web of sources and gossips, did not know the truth.

As eager as Moses was in scrambling for news, none that he received was trustworthy. A rumor saying the old king was dead quickly followed another saying he was alive and well. No one knew for certain since the king traveled frequently from city to city in Morocco. Even his servants could not be trusted for the truth because their heads might roll no matter which story they told, so they remained mute whenever queried on the subject. Meanwhile, every report made a lie of the previous one.

Eventually, the mayor called a meeting of the merchants and officials of the town. A number of soldiers and guards were included as well. Moses arrived with Eliahu who whispered, "I mean to influence whatever critical decisions are made that affect my own security."

Moses could hear the rumble of arguments and debates as a servant led them into a narrow room along the inner courtyard where the men waited for the mayor's arrival. They were seated, Arab fashion, on dark red cushions along the back wall. In front of the room lay a mattress covered with white linen that was reserved for the mayor.

Moses and Eliahu joined the Jewish merchants wearing black djellabas or caftans who whispered among themselves as they squirmed on the cushions along one side of the room. The Arab merchants and government officials in white djellabas huddled in small groups toward the other side. The soldiers and guards stood near the doorways while servants offered glass cups of hot mint tea to each man assembled there.

All were speculating on the rumors and impending crisis. Several were willing to propose strategies that might defuse a crisis, and Moses listened thoughtfully.

Eventually, in the leisurely way of this country, a servant appeared to announce the imminent arrival of the mayor. Moses was an active man, still lean and fit, for which he was grateful, hearing groans from the older and more obese men as they all rose in greeting.

The mayor, a tall, stout man wearing a white caftan and heavy gold sash, strode in followed by two minor clerks. He recognized the assembly with a brief nod, and then despite his bulk, he sat gracefully on the mattress. The others returned to their cushions.

Exuding power and control, the mayor did not speak at once but waited while the servants again served cups of tea to everyone there. Moses sat quietly against the wall but he could see the subtle nervous tremor in the mayor's fingers that betrayed his tension.

After several minutes, the mayor raised his teacup to his lips and began. "Gentlemen," he said, "we have an extremely volatile situation building here."

A loud clamor began as the assembly all spoke at once advancing their own opinions and suggestions. The mayor held up his hand for silence and continued. "We do not know if the king is alive or dead. As long as there is this uncertainty, I have a measure of control. If it is confirmed that the king is dead, there will be chaos throughout the country. We must squelch the rumors and plan for the protection of our city. We have much to fear, my friends."

Again, a loud clamor arose, but Moses stood, stepped forward and bowed. He commanded attention and speaking above the crowd, he said, "Your Excellency is wise. I suggest we assume the king is alive and act as if we are preparing for his forthcoming arrival. We can make a public show of acquiring and storing as much food and drink as we can manage while countering any threatening rumors with cheery faces and merry anticipation of the king's arrival and ceremony."

Two other men rose behind Moses and began to argue. The mayor listened a few moments and then held up his hand. He stroked his beard, apparently deep in thought, and after several moments, spoke to Moses. "Your plan is an excellent temporary measure to buy us time to gather more information." He looked up and raised his voice to address every man there. "Mogador is strongly fortified. As long as we are well-provisioned, we can hold out against our enemies. Therefore, I order every merchant in town to store extra food and water in his cellars in anticipation of a supposed visit by the king."

His expression left no room for argument, but a sallow, pock-marked young man stepped forward and spoke with a haughty sneer, "We're already squelching rumors as fast as we can, but they spring up again like weeds. We need to do something stronger than that."

The crowd broke into a clamor of agreement and dissent. The mayor again held up his hand for silence. "If the Berbers in the villages surrounding us learn the old king is dead," the mayor stopped to look at each man there, "they will rejoice and then surround our city. They will prevent all commerce in and out, gradually weakening us and draining our resources until we no longer have the will or ability to fight."

He drew himself up and slammed one hand on the other for emphasis. "Provisioning our storerooms as if for the king's arrival will prepare us for a long siege."

"But your Excellency," an Arab merchant ventured, "on Fridays, all the village folk—and most of these are Berbers—come into the city to pray. Each man has his own weapon."

A guard chimed in. "They come in with swords, daggers, firearms and who knows what other weapons."

"Yes," Moses added. "That is a dangerous situation. If the Berbers sense any uncertainty, especially on a Friday, they will take advantage of it."

"You are right, my friends," said the mayor. "We all know that an old prophecy decrees that this city will be delivered over to its enemies on a Friday. We will counter this threat by ordering the city gates to be closed while the people are praying." He paused. "And I will relocate the open market outside the city walls."

Several of the venerable white heads in the room muttered under their breath.

"I will also order that all weapons must be surrendered before a person enters the city," the mayor continued. "You are the most powerful people in Mogador. I count on your support in this crisis. We must pretend all is well."

The heads nodded.

"Gentlemen, these are dangerous times. If we learn the king is dead, then I will no longer have the king's mandate to be your leader and protector."

More dismayed whispers filled the room. The men cast surreptitious glances at the others around them.

Moses felt Eliahu stir. Was the man going to volunteer himself as leader? Moses wondered if even Eliahu had that kind of audacity.

Moses watched Eliahu gather his wits and prepare to rise, but one of the soldiers rose first. Moses took a second look. It was the guard who winked. This man had so unaccountably aided him in the early days of his misery in Mogador, bringing him first to Eliahu who rescued him from the docks and then to Annie who reassured him that Rachel was unharmed.

The guard stepped forward and said, to the obvious approval of his comrades behind him, "Your Excellency, I believe I speak for all of us here. We are agreed that in any event you should remain as our commander."

Cheers rose from the men assembled there. The guard raised his hand to quiet them. "We shall obey you as we have in the past." He stepped back to more cheers.

Moses smiled, relieved that Eliahu had not been given the chance to manipulate the meeting for his own benefit. Moses whispered to Eliahu, "I think the mayor has acted wisely. He now knows he has the full support of his men and of all of us here.

"Yes," said Eliahu grudgingly. "He has succeeded through this speech in finding—by some miracle—such a fickle group to be of one mind."

The meeting was adjourned, and the assembly broke up. Moses walked alongside Eliahu to return home and begin preparations for what might happen next.

As feared, Friday market days were filled with tension. Moses encountered guards and soldiers everywhere he walked. Some stood alone as sentries while others lined major avenues like protective walls as the masses of Berber tribesmen grew, crowding the streets throughout the town.

Moses, like everyone else in town, waited for news of the king.

Chapter 35

St. Thomas, Virgin Islands, 1999

As Sara slid into Michael's car that evening, the memory of the sailboat she had boarded so lightheartedly a year ago flared in her mind. She looked over at Michael who returned her look with a smile. "I'm looking forward to this evening," he said.

"So am I," Sara said and shivered.

Michael reached over and patted her hand. "Don't worry. My parents and Josh's parents have known each other for eons. They're all pretty nice people, and maybe they'll be able to help."

"I hope so," said Sara, but she felt tense and nervous and sat quietly as Michael bantered on about the other drivers on the road and the buildings they passed. Before long, Michael pulled up in front of his house and beeped.

Michael's father, Daniel, opened the door. "Welcome," he called to them as they approached.

"My Dad, Sara," Michael said by way of introduction. "Daniel Andrade."

"Pleased to meet you, Sara," Daniel said, holding out his hand.

His broad smile and white teeth shone in the tanned face, but Sara noticed that the smile covered a swift appraisal. She shook his hand and managed to stutter, "I'm glad to meet you too." She hadn't expected to be so nervous.

"This way." Daniel held out an arm to guide her down the hallway to a verandah where Louise Andrade and another couple sat. Josh's parents, Sara realized at once. The Davilas. Michael came up behind and waved a hello to everyone.

Josh's mother walked over to Sara. "My name is Sarah, too," she said and gestured to the other man. He stood.

"And this is my husband Benjamin."

Her unsmiling gaze intimidated Sara, but she managed a greeting to both of them. Then she took the chair Daniel held out for her as Sarah and Benjamin returned to their seats. Sara looked up to see that Sarah Davila was staring at her. She looked away quickly, and Sara sat back.

She supposed that both Louise and Sarah were in their fifties. Both were slim and wore flowered sundresses, but Louise was attractive and vibrantly alive while Sarah seemed serious and quiet. Sara thought of the matronly West Virginia looks of her own mother. Her plain country dress and style contrasted dramatically with the sophistication of these two women.

The older men repeated a tropical island look in their blue guayaberas. Daniel sat back, crossed his legs, and said nothing. He seemed heavier both in weight and disposition than Benjamin, who appeared lean and fit as if he spent a lot of time on a tennis court. Of them all, he looked the most relaxed and waved at Sara with a laugh. "So you're the young lady Josh has told us about."

"I guess so," said Sara. "He was helpful and suggested that I come here to talk with you."

"Yes, he didn't tell us much, my dear." Benjamin looked at the others. "But we are all most interested to hear what it's about."

The evening breezes swept across the tiled verandah, bringing with them the scent of rain and sea. Lightning flashed in the distance. Sara was glad she could gaze at the house rather than the ocean, but when, by chance, she turned her head and saw the ocean extending out into the distance, she didn't feel even a hint of the panic that usually came over her. *How odd.*

Sara glanced at Michael. He rocked back in his chair, arms folded.

"We're pleased to meet you," Sarah Davila said stiffly but with a hint of a smile. "Josh told us that you'd be visiting our island."

"Thank you. It's beautiful here."

"We love it," Sarah said.

"Our families have lived here for generations." Louise waved her hand as if to encompass the entire island.

"Louise's family came as pirates," Daniel sat back and winked at Sara.

Louise laughed. The tension broke.

"Yes, yes, yes. My ancestors were scoundrels—pirates and slave traders." Louise turned to Sara. "Anyway, by the early 1800s, the pirates were put out of business and by 1848, the slave trade in St. Thomas was discontinued, so all that was a long time ago. We've been a most respectable family since."

Sara didn't know how to respond to this, so she took a safer route. "All your families must have been here a long time. I noticed several Davilas in one of the cemeteries I visited this morning."

"They're my family," said Benjamin. "And yes, we've been here for centuries." He brushed his silver hair back.

Louise suddenly stood up and walked back into the house. "Excuse me. I forgot I'm the hostess."

She returned carrying a tray loaded with bowls of cashews and mango chunks and glasses of chilled white wine.

Sara took a glass, grateful for the diversion. She felt as if they all expected something of her, but she had no idea what to say next. She caught Sarah again studying her face as if she were searching for something. Sara stared down at her hands. She saw no resemblance to her family in any of their faces.

The lull in the conversation grew uncomfortable. At last, Sara broke the silence. "I'm surprised we both have the same first name. Josh didn't tell me."

"Oh yes," Sarah dismissed the comment with her hands. "I'm named after my grandmother. We're Sephardic Jews, you know. It's our custom to name a baby after a living relative." She looked at Sara expectantly.

Sara fumbled for a response, but then Sarah went on, "Tell us more about what brings you to our island."

Sara drew a deep breath. "Josh said you might have information on a person I'm trying to find."

"And who is that?" Sarah was looking at Sara but had reached for Benjamin's hand.

"A man named Samuel E. Yulee."

"And who is he?" Sarah said the words so casually that Sara knew they were important.

"He's my grandmother's brother. Before she died, she asked me to find him." She told them about the Nazi branding on her grandmother's wrist and the strange request.

"But why did she wait so long?" Benjamin asked.

Sara shrugged. "I'm not sure except that she thought her brother had been killed in World War II and then suddenly began thinking he was still alive. She was always a bit peculiar. She never wanted to look back. I now think that she was running away from something." She paused to take a breath. "And then she was hit by a car and killed."

Sarah Davila's eyes never left Sara's face. "So you had no idea your grandmother was Jewish?" Sarah raised an eyebrow at Benjamin.

"No, none at all."

"And you had never heard of this Samuel E. Yulee before?"

"I guess my grandmother's maiden name was Yulee, but we thought it was Smith. We don't know anything about her life before she married my grandfather." These were not casual questions. Sarah and Benjamin Davila knew something about this. She was sure of it.

"When was that?"

"When was what?"

"When did your grandparents marry?" Sarah asked.

"Right after World War II ended, in 1946."

"So, considering the number on her wrist, she must have been liberated from a concentration camp."

"I have to believe that's right."

"If she'd been in a concentration camp, she would normally have been taken to a displaced persons camp when she was liberated. Then the authorities would have conducted a search for her family," Benjamin said. "But I suppose if she married an American soldier right away, then she would have come to the states with him. Where did you live?"

"In Martinsburg, West Virginia. My grandfather was from West Virginia, and there's a large VA hospital in Martinsburg. He was always going in for treatments."

"I see." Benjamin said, with a distant gaze as if his thoughts had flown to a far-off place.

"Tell me about your grandmother," Sarah said. "What was she like?"

Sara sat back, hoping the interest in her grandmother meant something. "I remember her as being kind to me when I was a small child. As I grew older, I thought of her as quiet and a bit secretive—of course, that might be hindsight. But she did live with us for years after our grandfather died. I loved her. I think we were alike in some ways, but she seemed so grim and sad. She was pretty much a recluse, and she didn't like strangers. I guess I just didn't realize . . ."

"No. How could you," Louise broke in, reaching forward to pat Sara's hand.

"But," Sara said, "I did find a clipping in Michael's files this afternoon. It had a photo of a Samuel Yulee from a couple of years ago. He was way too young to be the man I'm looking for, but with the same name, he might be related, and Josh told me that a Samuel Yulee might be related to you." She looked at Sarah.

Sarah shrugged. "I think I remember someone of that name . . .

vaguely. I don't know. I'll check on it and see what I can find."

"I brought the album my grandmother left. I thought we could go through it and see if you recognize any of the people and places in the photos."

A maid appeared in the doorway. Louise stood. "I see dinner is ready. Let's go in, shall we? We'll look at the album after dinner."

As they walked into the dining room, Michael held Sara back and whispered to her, "I told you it would be all right."

Sara felt relieved that so far the evening's conversation had shown interest, although she wondered what was behind Sarah Davila's odd attitude. She smiled at Michael and took her place next to him at a large table set with gold-rimmed, cream-colored plates on a turquoise tablecloth. A crystal chandelier hung over the table and a large window opened onto a tropical garden showing the muted colors of dusk.

Crystal goblets of water were set at each place and Daniel bustled around pouring wine. Once they were seated, a maid brought in bowls of soup.

Michael sniffed at the soup and grinned at the maid. He turned to Sara. "Cold cucumber and dill. My favorite."

Sara felt more at ease until she noticed Sarah staring at her.

Sarah picked up her wine glass and peered over it at Sarah. "What do you do?" she asked a shade too casually.

"I'm not sure." Sara didn't want to answer this question. "I graduated from college with the idea that I might go to law school so I took a clerical job in a law office and stayed way too long."

"You didn't like the work?" Benjamin asked.

"It's not for me, but I don't know what to do next. I'm using this trip for soul-searching too. You know, who am I? What do I want to do with my life, that sort of thing."

"And what are you learning?" Benjamin asked.

Sara thought a moment. "I need something with scope. The people in that law office had been there forever and were too comfortable with their routine."

"Sounds bo-o-o-oring," said Michael.

"Believe me, it was—for me anyway," Sara said. "I want more than that."

"What possibilities interest you?" Sarah asked, her fork halted midway to her mouth.

Sara took a deep breath. "I want to do something meaningful. I just don't know what yet."

"Sounds like a Greenpeace recruit to me," said Michael. "Or maybe the Peace Corps."

Sarah shook her head. "I don't know. I just want to do something I like and feel good about. So where are you going when you get your doctorate?" Sara's eyes flashed.

"Actually, I like my routine. The dull life of a history professor sounds just right to me."

"Not all that dull," put in Daniel. "You can travel, study, trace interesting sidelights. . . ."

Louise turned back to Sara. "How did you happen to meet Josh?"

Sara described meeting Josh at Elaine's and then later at the Gamble Plantation. "He was tracking down David Levy Yulee, and I was searching for Yulees. He said the family was from here before Florida and that you might know something about them."

"When they were here, they were Levys, you know," put in Sarah Davila.

"I know. I heard the stories about the pirates and Morocco and the governor's daughter."

"You probably think the pirates were just some novelist's fantasy," said Benjamin. "But piracy was a major part of Morocco's economy for hundreds of years, not to mention Tunisia and the whole Barbary Coast."

Michael looked up from his plate. "There's a Jewish prayer for people captured by pirates," he said.

"Yes, and at one time," added Benjamin, "we had funds to ransom Jews who had been captured. The pirates and others took advantage of that."

"We've told you something about our pirates in the Caribbean," added Daniel. "In fact, in the early days, our government here on the island actually welcomed them because the merchants could benefit from the sale of the pirates' booty. We also had a slave trading post."

"That's all pretty loathsome," Sara said.

"Yes," Benjamin said, "but interesting."

"I like the fact that my ancestors were pirates," Louise said. "That's why I married Daniel."

Sara saw the twinkle in Louise's eye and knew she'd just heard an old family joke.

After dinner, they moved to the living room. Sara picked up the album and placed it on the coffee table. They all gathered around as she opened it and went through the book page by page.

When she came to the photos of the artwork, Sara pointed to the Modigliani. "This is the one identified by the nervous little man I met in

Cedar Key. Abe Carilla."

No one around the table claimed any knowledge of the painting and the name evoked no response.

Several times, Sara thought she caught a surprised look of recognition on Sarah's face or Benjamin's, but at the end, they only shook their heads.

"Some of those pictures look vaguely familiar to me," Sarah said, "but I'm just not sure. Perhaps I could borrow the album and check some of those photos with ones in my own albums?"

"I don't know . . . ." How far could she trust these people?

"We'll return it to you," Sarah said. "What if we have you and the Andrades over to our house for dinner in a couple of days? That will give us time to compare the photos, and then we can return the album to you."

"That's a good idea," Louise added. "Daniel and I could ask around town about this Samuel E. Yulee."

It was settled. They would meet for dinner at the Davilas home on Thursday evening, which would give them all two days to see what they could find out.

Sara had hoped the evening would be more productive, but it seemed to her that they had, well, pumped her for information without reciprocating with much of their own. After the dinner date was set, her attempts to bring the conversation back to her search were graciously but deliberately avoided.

As Michael drove Sara back to the hotel, she felt torn between misgivings and hope and kicking herself for letting them borrow the album. She had been lulled into liking and trusting these people, but she didn't really know them at all. Dumb, dumb, dumb. What if this promised dinner party never took place? What if they denied all knowledge of the album?

She stopped. It was done. She felt that in her place her grandmother would have done the same. Anyway, the dinner date was set, and at that dinner, she was going to get more than she gave when she met the Davilas and the Andrades.

Chapter 36

Mogador, 1790

Days passed, and the people of Mogador returned to their daily routines. Rachel now kept to the little-traveled side alleys for her errands rather than risk encountering the increasingly frequent brawls in the main streets. In the medina, shopkeepers laid out their wares, but the usual good-natured banter was replaced by a taciturn grimness. Once Rachel climbed the ramparts and saw for herself the watchful, greedy eyes in the Berber camps spread out across the fields. Everywhere she walked, she could feel the fear, anxiety, and dread of a civil war that lurked in everyone's heart.

Mogador was heavily fortified, well-planned, and to the south of the royal cities, but the wealthy now employed extra guards for their homes and plastered shut any outside windows, all doors but the front door, and their counting houses. Some had buried their money under the floor tiles.

The grim atmosphere turned Rachel's thoughts to escape and a growing impatience with her father's lack of action. Almost ten years had passed, and still they remained in this barbaric country. Surely by now her Papa could have arranged their escape. She knew he feared for them, but he was too cautious. They were ready to leave now.

These thoughts usually brought her around to considering her feelings for Eliahu, the father of her child. He doted on little Moses—more than on his other, older children. She supposed he felt proud to father a child at his age. She could not love such a man and perhaps knowing her feelings, he could not love her. But sometimes, in the intimate moments, as rare as they were, he would whisper tender words to her, and those words over the years had stirred in her a kinder regard toward him—but not enough to entice her to want to stay. She frowned and shook her head. No, she would not miss him.

But optimism and hope can prevail even in adversity. Her father now lived in Eliahu's home. Under peaceful conditions, Eliahu would have refused such an arrangement, but now he insisted upon it, looking at Papa as an extra man, extra hand, extra eye to maintain their security. Whatever Eliahu's reasons, Rachel was able to spend much more time with Papa and for that, she was grateful.

Rachel felt only a detached interest as Eliahu's house, like all the others in town, took on the look of a barricaded fortress. Watching the hired help prepare the house for a siege, she thought they were the ones to watch. Most were renegadoes earning extra money as private guards while not on duty guarding the town. They were a nuisance and always underfoot.

Except for one. This one was taller than the others and clean-shaven, and he wore brown breeches, shirt, and vest. He looked like an Englishman, and he spoke English as well as Arabic. Rachel did not know his name, but she pointed him out to her father one day, and he whistled and said, "The man who winked."

"I don't know what to think of him," he told Rachel. "He made it possible for me to meet Eliahu and so to become Eliahu's assistant. And he was the one who arranged that meeting with Annie after both of you were taken away from the rest of us captives. Annie told me you were alive and well. I am so grateful to this man."

"Well, then," Rachel said. "I will be grateful too. But why does he help us?"

"I don't know. I don't understand him at all, but I find him interesting. I've rarely seen him despite the years I've lived in Mogador. Even when I did see him, it was only a glimpse, like a flash of silver fins in dark water. I try to catch up with him, but then he disappears."

Moses stroked his beard. "Now that he works here, we will become better acquainted with him. Perhaps he might once again be able to help us. Perhaps there is some way we can help him."

***

The opportunity came the next day. While sitting in the courtyard, Moses saw his grandson run out of his mother's room, down the stairs and then trip on a loose tile. Moses rushed to him, but the guard who winked appeared, gently picked up little Moses, and soothed his tears, softly murmuring, "There, there, it's all right now . . . sh . . . sh."

"He speaks in English and is a renegado," Moses thought to himself. "But I've seen him at prayers, bowing towards Mecca, so he must be a Muslim. He reads, so he must have some education. He is a puzzle, that one."

As they soothed the little boy, Moses took advantage of this proximity to introduce himself.

The guard nodded. "Yes, I remember you."

Moses' attempts to thank the guard for his help so many years before were brushed aside with a wave of the hand, leaving Moses at a loss for what to say next. Finally, in exasperation, Moses said, "Please tell me your name."

The guard bowed and smiled. "My name is Adam Mohammed. My parents are from Morocco although they moved to England and I grew up there."

"How do you come to be here in Morocco?"

The guard sat down on the edge of the fountain. Moses took a seat alongside.

"I've always been an adventurer," Adam said. "It seemed natural to come here. It is the home of my ancestors, and it feels good to pray to Allah in a Muslim country."

"Yes, I see . . . ."

From then on, Moses sought Adam out for little chats. He became an amiable companion. Little Moses Elias also looked to Adam as a willing audience for his jokes and games. Even Rachel came to regard Adam cautiously as a friend.

And as Moses and Rachel considered plans for escape, Moses wondered about Adam. He had helped before. Could he be trusted to help again?

Several weeks later, Moses at last learned the king's fate as he stood on the wharf, counting and checking the barrels of freight being unloaded from a ship. The captain was leaning on the ship's rail, smoking a pipe, and sending tendrils of scented smoke towards Moses.

Moses paused in his counting. "In your travels, have you heard any word of our king?"

The captain took out his pipe in surprise. "You don't know? After all this time?" he said in wonder. "We had a special commission to pick up several members of the royal family and take them to France." He replaced his pipe and puffed at it before continuing. "We have come here from that delivery. They were fleeing the country."

"Fleeing the country!" said Moses. "But that means . . . ."

"Yes. They told us the old man had hemorrhaged and died while riding in his carriage. It was a natural death."

Moses shook his head. Yazid then had no hand in his father's demise.

"The coachman," added the captain, "didn't know there was a problem. He kept driving down the road. When the carriage arrived at the palace in Rabat, the old king's servants found the king half off the seat, lying in a pool of blood. The servants were afraid for their own lives, so they conspired to keep his death a secret. They buried him in a place known only to themselves."

"And the royal family took advantage of the delay to escape."

"That's the way it seemed to me," the captain said.

Moses ran back to Eliahu's offices shaking with this news. As Eliahu listened, his eyes narrowed in a strange thoughtfulness. He sat at his desk staring at nothing.

The minutes passed. Moses waited and watched Eliahu's cold, expressionless façade as he drummed his fingers on the desk. He was dressed in the dark wool djellaba he customarily wore. A gold medallion hung from his neck and glittered with the flickering light from the lamp on his desk.

"I know what you think," said Eliahu at last, looking over at Moses with calculation in his eyes. "You think that if the new king is Moulay Sliman, he will grant you the papers you need to leave Morocco." He snorted. "Let me tell you what happens when the king dies.

"Once the people learn the old king is dead, our entire country will be open for looting and pillaging. No woman or maiden will be safe. Murderers will stand at every crossroads to kill and rob. The caravans are stopped. There is no food. And this destruction will go on until the entire country is laid to waste, and one of the king's sons is strong enough to gain control.

"And who knows what horrors he will wreak on us as he fights for that control. When he gets it, his rule will be by oppression and force. This king had ten sons. Who knows for sure which one it will be? We are fortunate that the old king lived so long." He paused.

"We can only wait to see what our destiny will be," he added and resumed drumming his fingers on the desk.

A loud knock sounded on the door. At a tense gesture from Eliahu, Moses walked to the door and ushered in a tall young Arab in a simple white djellaba stained with dirt and sweat and smelling of donkey. Moses recognized him as the courier they had sent to Rabat.

Eliahu rushed to him. "What news? What news?" he asked.

The Arab wiped his brow and silently held out his hand. Eliahu pressed three coins into it, then repeated, "What news?"

The man bowed. "They still spread word that His Royal Highness, Muhammed ibn Abdullah, is alive." He paused. "But Moulay Yazid has seized control."

"Moulay Yazid." Eliahu stuttered the name and collapsed on a couch against the wall.

"How can that be?" Moses said, stunned.

"Yazid has placed his men throughout the medinas in Rabat, Fez, and Meknes. They guard everything and have forced the other princes into their quarters. No one is allowed in or out." The messenger paused as if to summon strength to continue. After a few deep breaths, he went on. "Moulay Yazid has taken control of the royal coffers, the estates, and the ships. He has his men everywhere—and he has the support of many of the people."

"Fools," said Eliahu. He stood up and leaned toward the messenger, piercing him with his stare. "What of Moulay Sliman? Where is he?"

The messenger wrung his hands. "They say he is imprisoned within his apartments in Rabat. Perhaps he is dead already. I tell you no one can move in those cities except Yazid and his men."

Eliahu and Moses looked at each other. They had taken little pains to court Yazid. "Now see where we are," Eliahu sneered. "You delivered Yazid's plan for a coup to Moulay Sliman. That bought us four years of peace, my friend, but now it appears your bet was on the wrong horse."

Moses studied Eliahu without expression. Moses knew what Eliahu was thinking. Could he deflect Yazid's hatred onto Moses, while he, Eliahu, retained his own power and position as grand vizier?"

Moses could almost see the plot taking shape in the ooze of Eliahu's mind. Moses' own thoughts clicked rapidly through a series of alternatives. If Yazid became king, almost certainly there would be reprisals against the Jews.

Eliahu dismissed the messenger and paced back and forth, grinding his teeth so fiercely the noise sounded like carriage wheels on stones.

Moses used the moment to put forth his plan. "We must leave this country immediately."

Eliahu snorted and waved his hand in dismissal. "We cannot leave without official permission."

Moses walked over to Eliahu's desk and studied the papers on it. "Could you not create an official-looking document from the king?"

Eliahu stared at his desk. "I suppose I could," he said, "but not if the guards know the king is dead."

"That is why we must hurry. They do not know yet, and most of the guards can barely read. They wouldn't know one document from another."

Eliahu stroked his chin. "Perhaps such a plan could get us passage out of this country—until it is safe to return." He picked up a pen.

Moses held his breath, not daring to risk a distraction, but the silence was broken by a rap on the door. The messenger reappeared, out of breath. He leaned against the wall, panting, and finally spoke to Moses.

"I cannot leave the city. The gates are locked, and the guards interrogate and beat anyone on the streets. I must go home now to protect my family." He turned and disappeared into the courtyard.

Eliahu dropped the pen. Moses rushed over to him and urged him to keep writing, but when courage and daring were needed, Eliahu shrank away and instead rushed to the door.

"We must return home, arm, and barricade ourselves." Eliahu was halfway across the courtyard before Moses could say another word.

He followed Eliahu out into the medina, but instead of taking the short and direct route to Eliahu's house, they scurried in the shadows along walls like rats in an alley, fearing the unruly mobs that now roamed the streets. When they reached Eliahu's house, Rachel and the other two wives and the children greeted them in surprise.

Eliahu brushed aside their questions and darted from door to door, checking their security. The heavy front door, four inches thick, was made of cedar from the mountains, a hard and tough wood. In times of civic order, it was latched with a light, thin plank in deference to the women. This time, Eliahu brought in iron bars from the storeroom and set them in place to bolt the door.

Moses leaned against a column and watched, but his mind was racing through the possibilities. Was it true that Yazid was now the ruler? And if so, could they count on peace? Or would the chaos that Eliahu predicted destroy them and their country? He must alert the mayor.

Unlike Eliahu who was distrusted and sometimes discreetly shunned, Moses found himself welcome in most households. Later that night, he crept out of the house and kept in the shadows as he walked to the mayor's house. The servants allowed him into the official reception room where he was served hot mint tea and left alone to wait. He felt too agitated to sit so he paced the floor and wrung his hands until the mayor at last returned home.

"Your Excellency," Moses began but the mayor interrupted him.

"Please, Moses, we are friends, no?" He snapped fingers at the servant who disappeared into a back room. "What urgency brings you here at this time of night?"

"I came to tell you that the king is indeed dead, and that Moulay Yazid has been recognized as his successor in Rabat, Fez, Meknes, and Tetuan."

The mayor sank heavily onto a couch. "Indeed." He stroked his beard. "How do you know this?"

Moses relayed the captain's story and the messenger's report. He paused as the servant reappeared with fresh glasses of mint tea for the two men.

They waited until the servant left the room, then the mayor rubbed his hands as if they were cold. "I have been waiting for any news that sounded like the truth." He stood and walked over to a mahogany desk along the wall, took out pen and paper, and wrote two notes, then rang the bell for a messenger. He looked up at Moses.

"I am sending this information to the leaders of our city but suppressing it for everyone else. I wish you to suppress it as well. I am also writing my friend in Fez for confirmation." He stared above Moses' head.

"When this news is confirmed," the mayor added, "I will wait for the people to come out of the mosque after prayers and then wave at them an official-looking document, announcing the succession of Moulay Yazid. I will act as if I am bringing good news to the people, and then, my friend, I'll declare that day to be a holiday. A deception, I know, until we see how things lay."

Moses nodded to signal support for the mayor's plan as he stroked his beard. It seemed weak, but it might stave off the chaos they all feared.

The mayor followed through on his word, but after his announcement to the people, every ship resting in the harbor hurriedly finished its business there and departed. Eliahu with his forged documents had at last been willing to leave his home and all he could not carry away, but it was too late. Even the Dutch ships, which had provided a refuge for several local families during the uncertainty, now insisted that these refugees disembark despite the desperate pleas of the men and women onboard. The harbor became deserted except for the rats, but so far the city remained quiet.

As the days passed, horror pervaded the country. Refugees from other cities trickled into Mogador, bringing with them reports of murder, rape, and pillaging. Moulay Yazid's reign of terror had begun, and it was vented not only upon the Jews, for the real and imagined slights they had visited upon him, but upon other Muslims and Christians as well.

Moses, and sometimes Eliahu, met with each newcomer to the city, seeking reports of Yazid's actions and whereabouts and news of any other members of the royal family. One refugee, a Jew from Rabat, trembled so much he could barely speak and sat on Eliahu's couch covered with a rug as he whispered his story. "I was with the vice consuls who were dressed in their finest as they traveled to meet the new king in Rabat. I was behind answering a call of nature when I saw my friends seized on the road, stripped, and tied to the tails of the soldiers' horses." The man closed his eyes and shuddered. "I will never forget their screams as they were dragged toward the city, their blood leaving red trails in the dust."

He drew the rug tighter around him to quell the trembling, but his fingers could not hold the cup of mint tea. Moses gently took it from him and set it on the table. The man continued. "I could do nothing to help. Nothing."

Two days later, Moses opened the door to a filthy man dressed in rags. "My friend Moses, do you not recognize me?"

Peering through the dirt and rags, Moses reached out to the man and pulled him in. "It is Jacob ben Mali from the king's court. What has happened to you?"

"The king's court no longer, my friend. I am much in disfavor. I have lost everything. I am too exhausted even to weep."

Moses brought him into the reception area. "Sit, my friend. Rest." He waved at a servant who had appeared in the doorway. "Bring us some tea and fruit." The servant disappeared.

Jacob's eyes burned into Moses. "Yazid's men have murdered my wife and plundered my house. I watched them arrest the old king's finance minister and nail his feet to the floor. I would have been next, my friend, if I had not escaped."

Tea and a platter of fruit arrived. Moses poured and handed the cup to Jacob who drank it quickly as if it were an unwelcome interruption then he spoke.

"The Jewish communities of Tetuan, Larache, Arcila, al-Qasr al-Kabir, Taza, Fez, and Meknes are no more. The people raped and murdered, their estates plundered. Every Jewish man employed by the late king that Moulay Yazid could capture was hung by his feet at the gates of Meknes until, even after, he died. I watched this horror from hiding, hardly daring to breathe lest I, too, become a victim.

"Even the old king's treasurer Mordecai Chriqui was handed over to the executioner after he refused to convert to the Muslim religion. You remember Jacob Attla?"

Moses thought back to his days in Tangier. Yes, of course he remembered Jacob Attla.

"He did convert, but, my friend, it did not matter. He was hung by his feet until dead."

Jacob leaned back against the wall and closed his eyes as if spent.

"You must rest," said Moses. He helped Jacob to his feet and with the servant's help, took him to a back room. "The servant will bring water for bathing and new clothes for you and a hot tagine for your supper. I must report this news to my master."

Jacob sank down upon the mattress and began to shiver. He dragged his face up to stare at Moses and through blistered lips, he whispered, "The horror is just beginning, my friend."

Chapter 37

St. Thomas, Virgin Islands, 1999

The phone's shrill ring jarred Sara awake. She turned over and stared at it, not sure at first where she was. The hotel room. St. Thomas. She reached over and picked up the receiver.

"I thought you might like a tour of St. Thomas," Michael said, hearty with enthusiasm.

"I'd love it," Sara answered, smiling at the suggestion. "I've been planning to visit the local museums and library. You probably know where these places are and how to ask about the records."

"Sure. And we can see highlights of St. Thomas too. I'll pick you up at ten."

Sara opened the door to her balcony and watched the warm breezes ruffle the draperies as she dressed. She was learning that the morning warmth soon turned hot, so she slipped into a light blue sundress and sandals. At ten, she was standing on the hotel's front steps chatting with the parking attendant when she saw Michael's car drive into the hotel lot and park. As he loped her way, she walked down to meet him. The jeans and white polo shirt he was wearing suited him. She liked this guy.

He greeted her with a grin and turned to walk alongside. They sauntered down the hotel driveway to the street.

"We can hike over to the Davilas' art gallery this morning," he said, looking down at her, "but we can take our time since it's so early."

As they window-shopped the streets of Charlotte Amalie, Sara laughed repeatedly at Michael's irreverent anecdotes about the shopkeepers, the political scene, and the social butterflies of the town.

Laughing felt good.

As they pushed their way down the crowded streets, Sara noticed one or another passerby nodding at Michael or greeting him with a smile or quick remark or a question about his mother or father. Any doubts that lingered about Sarah and her confiscation of the album disappeared when they reached the Davila Art Gallery.

The front show windows displayed dramatic works of modern art. Inside, the yellow pine floors and white walls gave the gallery a bright, airy, cool feeling. Original paintings and sculptures by local artists covered the walls. Each piece was labeled with a typed note card providing biographical notes about the artist.

"I'm impressed," Sara whispered to Michael.

Michael called Benjamin's name, and he emerged from a back room.

"Hello, hello. Welcome to my little shop," he said, smiling at them both. He was wearing white shirt and shorts and looked as if he were heading out to play tennis. He appeared as relaxed and good-humored as he had the night before.

"I wouldn't say 'little.'" Sara gestured at the walls. "It's pretty large, and you have so many lovely pieces." Sara didn't know much about art, but the exhibits all seemed well-crafted by skilled hands and included interpretations of scenes around the islands.

"Do you think so?" He seemed delighted at Sara's trite praise. "Thank you. My wife would have liked to take you around, but unfortunately she had things to do at home today."

"I'm showing Sara the town," Michael said. "We'll be going to the library after lunch."

Benjamin glanced at his watch. "Speaking of lunch, it's almost noon. How about joining me? We'll just go to the café next door. They have great food." He led them to the door.

The cafe had blue tiled walls and floor and was crowded with locals. Several of them waved greetings at Benjamin and Michael. Benjamin ignored the menu and ordered conch fritters, hamburgers, and iced tea for the three of them. Sara's annoyance gave way to appreciating the adventure of eating conch. Never in West Virginia. Afterward, as Benjamin waved them on their way, he called out, "Don't forget dinner at our house tomorrow night."

Sara grinned. "I'm looking forward to it." She warmed to his friendly attention, but his wife's odd treatment of her last night still left her feeling like an interloper.

The historic museum and library did not provide much information. The staff was eager to help, but they had no files specifically on the Yulee family, and there were too many Levys to contemplate. The reference librarian directed them to a file drawer containing folders of newspaper clippings and magazine articles, but after an hour, they still had found no reference to Samuel E. Yulee. Sara listlessly picked up the last folder, grateful it was the only one left, and almost missed a yellowed newspaper article with a photo of a group of local citizens. The caption included the name, Samuel E. Yulee. She read it again. Samuel E. Yulee. She looked over at Michael and pointed to the photo. "There he is!"

Michael took this find in stride. "So he is. What's the date? September 20, 1958. Man, that's a long time ago."

"Yes, and he looks like he's maybe 40 there. I see he was part of the local tourism council then. Do any of the other names in the caption seem familiar to you?"

Michael studied the caption. "Yes, I know most of them, but some are no longer with us." He scanned the article. "Here, look at this. There's a Benjamin Davila on the council too, but he must be the father of the Benjamin we know."

"Sounds like Samuel was a prominent citizen, don't you think? Your parents and Josh's might have known him." Sara watched Michael's face for his reaction.

He shrugged. "I suppose so, but after all, this picture was taken a long time ago."

"That's true," Sara said slowly. She quelled the panic that threatened to derail this important finding, forcing herself to attack Michael instead. "I think the Davilas—and you—know more than you're telling me."

Michael reared back. "Whoa. Not me. But if you think that, why don't you ask the Davilas tomorrow night?"

"I will." She brought the photo closer to her eyes. She supposed there might be a resemblance between this man and her grandmother. Excitement grew in her heart and she felt goose bumps on her arms. She was close; she knew it.

Michael returned Sara to her hotel. "By the way," he said, "I have to run errands tomorrow, but I'll pick you up for dinner at six. Okay?"

"Yes, of course," Sara agreed absently. She didn't expect anyone to take care of her. She needed the time to think. She did feel the Davilas knew something they weren't telling her. And she thought it odd that Benjamin Davila had not mentioned knowing a Samuel Yulee. Why would they withhold information when they must understand how important it was to her?

Didn't they trust her? Maybe they thought she was taking advantage of her grandmother's legacy as an excuse to travel. They might see it that way. Sara felt a bit guilty, knowing that she was enjoying an adventure that sprang from her grandmother's death and bequest. Then she chided herself. She was carrying out her grandmother's wishes and may have succeeded in finding her grandmother's brother. Tomorrow Sara would know.

The next day, on her own, Sara strolled the streets of Charlotte Amalie, trying to imagine her secretive, West Virginia grandma growing up in such a cosmopolitan, tropical, sun-washed city. How could she have stood to live year after year in the bricks and shingles of a cold railroad town in West Virginia? Sara placed her hopes on the dinner that night.

Later, as she waited for Michael, she again felt tense and anxious. When he picked her up, she could not help the tremble in her smile and the queasiness in her stomach.

Listening to Michael's banter on the drive calmed her and to her delight, she found that Josh had returned home and was there when she and Michael arrived. He greeted her shyly with a glance at his parents as if seeking their approval. As a result, she felt awkward at meeting him again but managed to smile a hello and then covered her confusion by admiring the Davila's home.

Like the Andrades' house, it was perched on a mountain with a sweeping view of the sea in every direction. The house itself branched like a tree with rooms stretching off on both sides up a circular staircase—an art lover's home—custom designed, custom built.

Benjamin and Sarah Davila's greeting was friendly but subdued. Sarah seemed much warmer to her tonight than when they had first met. Sara followed them, Josh trailing behind, up to an open deck on top of the house where Michael and his parents were already seated. Louise and Daniel greeted her with smiles while Benjamin busied himself with pouring wine for everyone. He passed the glasses around and then pulled up a chair to join them.

No one seemed willing to speak, and the ocean views around Sara were bringing on the panic attack that lurked in her subconscious, ready to pounce. She took a deep breath and then noticed that everyone was staring at her with a quiet air of expectation. Sara felt awkward and tongue-tied.

At last, Sarah Davila broke the uncomfortable silence. "We were pleased to meet you the other night, Sara." Everyone stared at Sara.

"And now we feel we must speak with you seriously." Sarah put up her hand as Sara sought a response. "No, let me say what I must say. We needed to know more about you, you see." She coughed. I called your home yesterday, Sara, and I talked with your mother."

Sara sat up, startled. She had never expected this.

"And today I talked with the rabbi you consulted. Your story seems to be true. It agrees with what your mother said and what the rabbi said also. You yourself come with an excellent reference from your supervisor. Yes, I talked to her, too." She paused, looked down at her hands and examined her fingernails.

She looked over at Sara. "So we feel we can trust you."

Sara frowned and scanned the other faces in the group. Everyone was tense and watching. "I'm glad I passed your . . . test," she said in a cold, stiff voice.

Sarah reached over and patted Sara's hand. "We felt we could trust you the other night, and we liked you at once. We loved your enthusiasm, but you must know that we had to check. There are important reasons why we must be careful."

"I told them you were okay," added Josh, staring at the floor with his hands in his pockets and his legs stretched out in front of him.

"But I don't understand." Sara said, wondering where all this was leading. She was realizing that, deep down, yes, she did feel enthusiastic—even happy. She saw Josh watching her and smiled.

Benjamin broke in. "Probably we're being too careful. It all happened so long ago."

"Yes," said Sarah, holding up her hand to shush him, "but we can't be sure."

Benjamin sat back and studied Sara. "I can tell you that the photos of art in your album are all photos of original paintings and sculpture. I checked our files and found most of them listed there as ones that passed through my parents' hands. They helped in getting art out of occupied countries during World War II, you see."

"Then, after the war," added Sarah, looking at Sara, "our families found ways to return the artwork to the owners or their heirs where possible." She sat back and paused to sip her wine.

"But the one your friend in Cedar Key recognized," said Benjamin, leaning forward, "that one I did not find listed. I suppose it has disappeared into someone's private collection. The route from Europe to here was a sea of sharks. Dangerous and uncertain." He threw up his hands.

Then Sarah set down her glass and added, "Samuel E. Yulee and your grandmother lost their parents in World War I. My great grandparents were related to the family and adopted them. Ruth, Samuel, and my mother all grew up together and were very close. We thought of

Samuel and Ruth as uncle and aunt, although they were not related to us."

"So you knew them!" Sara gasped. Her hand flew to her heart, and she took a deep breath as she stared at Sarah. "I can't believe it." Was this the end of her search? Was this to be her family?

Sarah reached over to steady Sara. "Yes, and I think that your grandmother may have been my Aunt Ruth, but I never met her. She had been lost before I was born."

Sara took several deep breaths. Tears sprang to her eyes. Louise walked over to put her arm around Sara. Benjamin picked up the wine and refilled everyone's glasses while the other men stared at their hands.

Sarah patted Sara's arm. "Yes, I believe so. I know this is hard . . . such a shock for you."

Sara shook her head and attempted a smile. "What a strange story." She took a sip of wine. "I'm all right now," she said to Louise who returned to her seat. "But why did my grandmother keep all this a secret?"

Everyone began talking at once, but Sarah held up her hand to silence them. "I suppose we'll never know," she said, "but we thought your grandmother was dead. Samuel certainly thought so until recently. They were separated during the war and sent to different concentration camps. Your grandmother may have heard a rumor or saw something that led her to believe he had been killed. My mother grieved for Ruth and told me so many stories about her that even though I never met her, I felt as if she were still a living part of our family." She stopped and lifted her glass.

Josh, still sitting back with his hands in his pockets, smiled at Sara. "I even know a lot of the stories," he added. "I just didn't connect them with your grandmother."

"She never wanted to look back," said Sara, glancing at all of them. "It was too painful for her."

Louise murmured, "Of course." The men relaxed and sat back.

Sarah gazed out at the darkening sky. "The war must have changed her. My mother always thought of Ruth as courageous, although most of the family called it headstrong. I'm afraid she was too forthright and honest. She always said what she thought. She was fearless, rushing into dangerous situations and—most of the time—escaping without a scratch. She and Samuel knew what was happening in Europe and wanted desperately to help."

"So," said Benjamin, standing up at the bar and refilling his glass, "in 1939, they went to Denmark, after Denmark signed the nonaggression pact with Nazi Germany. They both knew some Danish, you see."

Louise interrupted. "Denmark owned St. Thomas until 1917, which I'm sure you know, and Danish was often spoken here."

"Yes," said Sarah. "In Denmark, Ruth and Samuel became involved politically. We're not sure how because when the Nazis invaded Denmark in 1940, our family lost track of them. In fact, we had given up both of them as lost for years."

"So then," Benjamin continued from his stance at the bar, "one day Uncle Samuel showed up back here. It was in the late forties. He was broken in body and spirit, and it took years to help him recover from the horrors of the concentration camps. He is okay now, and elderly, you understand, but self-sufficient since he retired long ago and has good investments."

Sara looked around the room as if Samuel were hidden there. "But where is he? May I see him?"

Sarah shook her head. "Your journey is not over. He now lives in Gibraltar where he hopes to see your grandmother, his sister Ruth, again."

"But why would Samuel hope to see Ruth there?" Sara asked.

Benjamin stared down at his glass as he spoke. "Before they separated and were captured by the Nazis, they made a pact to meet in Gibraltar if they were freed and after the war was over." He shrugged. "Apparently, they had unfinished business to resolve. We know it's useless and hopeless, but after Samuel's wife died, he lost his will to live. They had no children, you see." He took a sip of wine.

Sarah leaned forward. "Then one day he came to us and said that he had decided that Ruth might be alive after all. He insisted on moving to Gibraltar, and Gibraltar is not a bad place to spend one's last days."

Benjamin smiled at his wife before turning to Sara. "So he is there, living in a quiet hotel and everyday he goes to the tourist office where he hopes to receive word from Ruth." He finished the wine with a flourish.

"How sad," said Sara.

Sarah nodded. "But now you can tell him about Aunt Ruth and bring him back home," She leaned toward Sara. "You must do this. We all miss him here, and he needs to be with us. Take the album to show him so that he will have proof."

Sara picked up her purse. "I will. And I do have my grandmother's wedding photo with me—I thought it might help."

"I'm sure it would." Sarah held out her hand. "May I see it?"

Sara retrieved it from her purse and gave it to Sarah Davila who gazed at it as tears came to her eyes. Brushing them away, she said, "Yes, that looks like the Aunt Ruth I've seen in family photos, but there's no spark, no spirit in her."

"I know. She was a kind, loving woman," said Sara, "but I never knew her as she really was . . . before the war and the camps."

Sarah looked up. "But she had a good life, didn't she?"

Sara put the photo back in her purse. "We loved her, but I always felt that something in her life was missing."

"And indeed, it was. The Nazis took it away."

"But now," Sarah Davila gazed at Sara through her tears, "we have found you. A part of Aunt Ruth is back with us."

She reached over and squeezed Sara's hand. "And, my dear, I think she asked your mother to name you Sara. Like Rachel and Elias and Moses, it is a name that is repeated again and again in our family."

The men, silent witnesses to all this emotion, broke in with a cheer. Josh now sought to lighten the atmosphere. "So what do you think, Sara, shall we go to Gibraltar?"

"Do you want to go too?" Sara said.

"But of course. How else will you know Uncle Samuel and he know you? I'm the best liaison you could have."

"That's true, Sara." Benjamin said. "We'll hate losing you right away, but perhaps it would be best to finish your quest since you are now so close to an answer."

"I guess so. I'll check on airlines tomorrow. Luckily, I brought my passport with me since I didn't know where I'd end up."

"Excellent," said Sarah Davila. "Now we would like you to stay with us."

"I would love to," said Sara. What a charming family. She liked all of them. Now she felt as if she had roots . . . and substance. *Grandma endured the Nazis for years. I only endured that jerk on the sailboat for a few minutes. But Grandma survived, and so did I.*

She thought of the strange panic attacks. They had almost disappeared. Could they have been related to the assault? A huge weight in her heart had lifted when she found that she had not, after all, killed the creep on the sailboat.

But then she thought of Rachel Levy, her distant ancestor, a girl caught by pirates and enslaved. What was she like? What kind of horrors had she endured? And what kind of life did she live after she escaped? Did she ever make it to America?

Sara looked up to find them all staring at her. Then they laughed, and the spell was broken.

"And now," said Sarah, standing and gesturing to the stairs, "it's time for dinner. Afterwards, we'll go through that album again." Sarah started down the stairs, holding Sara's hand as she followed. "This time I'll tell you about the people and the places in it. Your family, Sara."

"I thought you recognized the people in those photos!' Sara said. She thought of her family back in West Virginia. Her mother would like these people, but would her brother? How would he manage this revelation of his Jewish roots and new family? He could not argue with the truth. At heart, he was a decent human being, but how would his girlfriend react? Would her reaction sway her brother? Martinsburg was a small town with dozens of churches and only one synagogue.

The question was beyond her. She shrugged.

But her feet danced on the stairs.

Chapter 38

Mogador, 1791

Moses stared out past the small harbor islands to the ocean beyond. No ships lay in the harbor below. Few ships ventured into the now scarlet waters of Morocco.

Yazid's bloody excesses had reached almost every community throughout the country. Only the gates of Mogador still held strong against his thugs. Even so, most families in the country could name at least one family member murdered by Yazid's order. No one was safe, and no one knew what person or group would next be targeted for torture and murder at Yazid's whim.

Moses turned back toward the medina. He trudged along, reluctant to endure once again the confrontation and abuse to come.

It began as soon as Moses entered Eliahu's office.

"What?" said Eliahu, looking up from the papers on his desk, pen in hand. "You have still not managed to contact Moulay Sliman?"

Moses did not bother to reply.

"Do you even know where he is?" Eliahu sneered.

Moses shook his head. Eliahu had become even more overbearing and offensive than usual, a sign of the tension everyone felt these days.

"We know that he has escaped his palace prison," Moses said at last. "And we know he is at large, recruiting men and money to support him in opposing his half-brother."

"Yes, I have heard this." Eliahu's eyes flicked to a large chest in the corner. "That coffer of gold bars is for him so that he will recognize me as his friend and supporter." Eliahu pursed his lips. "You know he has enlisted the support of other Jews in this country. They call on me daily to join them."

"I agree that it is critical that Moulay Sliman receive this money," Moses said with quiet intensity as he stared at Eliahu. Then he added, speaking each word distinctly, "We are all in fear for our lives from Yazid."

Eliahu frowned and turned back to his papers.

Only that morning, Moses had hidden behind a pillar and watched Eliahu oversee his servants struggle to load a chest into a carriage pulled by two horses. Two horses. A very heavy chest then. Moses then heard Eliahu instruct a cadre of ten renegados to escort the carriage to Yazid's palace in Rabat. Moses had caught his breath at such treachery. Eliahu was sending the monster a gift. *He hopes to position himself advantageously no matter which way the wind blows.*

Moses had crept away in disgust at Eliahu and fear for the men escorting such wealth.

Two days later, as he passed the fortress gates, he stopped to watch a guard accost a filthy beggar clinging to the gate bars. The beggar's djellaba was so ragged it barely hung on his body. In one hand he clutched a rolled piece of paper. His eyes pleading like a dog's, he reached out with this hand to Moses.

"Please, sir," he said in a cracked, dry voice, "I come from Moulay Slimon, who seeks your help."

Immediately, Moses halted the guard's bullying and took the piece of paper. He unfolded and read it, and then called on the guard to help carry this ragged and exhausted human being into the courtyard.

They set the stranger on the ground under a jacaranda tree. Moses sent the guard for water and bread. The stranger held up his hand as he caught his breath. Moses waited until the guard returned, and then filled a cup with water and gave it to the stranger with a piece of bread. The stranger took the cup in shaking hands, spilling some as he gulped the water. He tore at the bread with his teeth.

After he had eaten and drunk, the man sat, eyes closed, motionless as if to collect energy from the air and bodies around him. Moses waited. At last the stranger spoke, this time coherently.

"My name is Abbas ibn Karim ibn Abdulazz. I am come here from His Royal Highness, Moulay Sliman. I made my way through the defenses of Mogador to reach the grand vizier, Eliahu ben Youli. I am messenger sent to receive the monies held here for Moulay Sliman. I have here letter with his seal on it. His Highness's forces hide in the mountains, waiting for this support."

Moses brought Sliman's messenger to Eliahu, who greeted him with an excess of fawning attention and led him to a low couch next to a table laden with a pitcher of water and bowls of dates and nuts. He snapped his fingers at a servant to bring mint tea.

"I have the camels and mules ready for you," said Eliahu. "They wait only the loading of them."

"Perhaps you would like to refresh yourself," added Moses. "We can have clean clothes for you and a bath."

The messenger looked at Moses with gratitude. "Yes," he said. "I would like to depart here in better condition than I arrived."

"Of course." Eliahu flicked his fingers at Moses who saw this as permission to withdraw.

After giving the orders to prepare a bath for their guest, Moses strode to his own room where he drafted a letter to Moulay Sliman, reminding him that Moses had helped him defeat Yazid's earlier coup attempt. He now asked that in return, Moulay Sliman prepare the official papers of passage for himself and his family. He hid this letter in his cloak. Moulay Sliman was, Moses felt, at least an honorable and good man. Yazid was a horror and an abomination.

When Moses returned to Eliahu's office, the messenger had returned from his bath and was dressed in clean robes. He was earnestly sharing his news.

"You know that Yazid ordered all Jews to be struck down," he said. "As a result, members of some of the finest Jewish families in Morocco have been slaughtered."

Moses could feel the terror. If he and Rachel had remained in Tangier, they too might have been victims of this insanity.

The messenger continued. "Yazid's men climb through windows, dig up floors and wells, tear down walls and plunder everything they fancy. If it is of little or no use, they demolish it. They rip the gold earrings from the women's ears and the bracelets from their wrists. They strip the men naked, rape the virgins and defile the married women." He paused.

"There is no escape, my friends. The anguish, the pleas, the cries of the Jews only increase the viciousness against them."

Moses sat stunned by such horror. He silently blessed the mayor who had foreseen this catastrophe and had kept the town under control. The mayor was even now occupied with directing his soldiers in guarding the town gates and holding back the rebels. The countryside swarmed with every kind of thief and opportunist seeking to profit from the chaos.

"Where are Yazid's forces now?" asked Eliahu.

"They still range in the north, but they will soon direct their attentions to the south," the messenger replied. "The town of Mogador was the old king's pride. Do not think that Yazid has forgotten that. Your mayor is wise, my friends, and you may thank Allah that the town is fortified well."

"What are Moulay Sliman's plans?" said Eliahu.

"That I cannot tell you, but he is gathering his forces and his support. Moulay Yazid rules by terror but I must tell you, my friends, that of all the countries of Europe, only England favors Yazid. When our old king was alive, England alone acted against his orders and gave Yazid the money to pay his debts. England now supports Yazid in this war."

Moses rubbed his chin. He had feared that the English king would make such a foolish choice.

"Yazid holds a grudge against all the nations but England. His mother is English." The messenger clutched his robe. "There is such chaos that anyone with an enemy can kill him without fear of punishment, and debtors scoff at their creditors. No law governs our people."

Eliahu paced back and forth. "Even here the uncertainty is felt, and the fear of retribution by law grows weak. Order must be restored to our country—and soon."

"Yes." The messenger nodded. "But each day the forces of Moulay Sliman grow stronger and gain more support as reasonable men seek to restore law and justice."

He yawned. "My friends, my eyes are heavy, and I find it difficult to continue. Might I be led to a bed and night of quiet sleep? I will be off with the horses in the morning."

Moses felt chagrined. They had seized all they could from this man without consideration. "I will show you to your room."

As they entered the dark passageway, Moses withdrew the letter hidden in his cloak and said, "I offer my services to your master with whole heart. Please give him this letter and let him know this. I remain here with my family, but I support him. He has only to tell me what I should do."

Eyes half closed, shoulders slumped, the messenger took the envelope and followed a servant off to the bed.

Instead of returning to the office, Moses hurried to Eliahu's house. He found Adam Mohammed reading a book by the courtyard fountain and sat down beside him.

Adam closed the book and smiled at Moses. "You look most serious, my friend."

Moses scanned the courtyard for possible listeners. Seeing none, he turned to Adam and whispered, "I need you to take on a task that might be dangerous and must remain secret, between the two of us."

Adam looked at Moses with a question in his eyes.

"A messenger from Moulay Sliman rests in Eliahu's offices. Come with me now so I can show you where he is. I want you to stand guard outside his room and then to continue on as one of the guards when he returns to the camp of Moulay Sliman. You are to take note of the camp's location, its size and the morale of its men. If Moulay Sliman is present, and you are able to see him, I want you to take him our offers of help. Then return and report only to me."

Adam stared at him. "This is between you and me, I gather. You will assure my superior that my absence is under your authority?"

"Yes, I will insist that this is official business should that become necessary. I hope it will not. You will return in a day or two. Your absence will not even be noted."

"And that is a sad comment on my existence, my friend, but I will do as you ask. I am as concerned as you about the current state of affairs." He put his book into his satchel and rose to follow Moses with an air of quiet amusement.

As they walked back to the messenger's room, Moses reflected that he had just had the longest conversation he'd ever had with Adam who had been stationed at Eliahu's house for weeks now. Moses often made friendly overtures, but Adam's response was a brief comment, then he would walk away, pull a book out of his pocket and read. Moses could not detect bitterness or anger in the man, just a quiet disposition that seemed to prefer solitude. Moses also noticed that Adam stood aloof from the other guards and did not engage in their banter.

Moses continued to find the man a puzzle. Still, Adam was intelligent and reliable. Moses felt he could be trusted.

Abbas left early the next morning with mules and camels heavy with the money and supplies contributed by the town's leaders. Two armed guards accompanied him as escorts. Adam rode alongside.

Moses watched them leave. He brushed his concerns about Adam aside. If Moulay Sliman would present Moses with the necessary papers of passage for himself and his family, he would be in a stronger position to negotiate passage on a ship in port—if the captain would take on passengers and if the ship were going to a friendly port. It was so difficult to put all the necessary pieces in place at the same time. Here it was, almost ten years after their capture, and still Moses had not worked out all the details successfully enough so they could actually make an attempt to escape.

If they could not obtain the papers, then Rachel and Annie would not travel as women. He knew that whenever possible, the two women observed the way Arab men carried themselves, how they talked, how they acted, how they wore their clothes and hair. Knowing that Arab men were proud of their beards, Rachel had made false beards by cutting inconspicuous strands of her hair and sewing them to cloth stained with tea. The beards would pass in the dark if the hood of a burnoose was drawn loosely across their faces.

"Let us show you, Papa," Rachel said one afternoon. "Wait here."

Moses sat in the first courtyard. After a few moments, two Arab men and a ragged Arab boy walked down the stairs. The boy broke into giggles and ran to Moses.

"See? It's me, Grandpapa." The little boy laughed and danced around Moses.

Rachel grabbed the boy. "No, no, you must be quiet and stay with me." She turned to Moses. "See, Papa? We practice, we criticize each other, we watch." She laughed. "You know that Arab men squat to pee like women? We did not think we needed to practice that."

Moses smiled. Even though the sun streamed into the courtyard from above, Rachel and Annie's faces were obscured by the hoods. They did indeed look like Arab men, and at night, in the dark, no one could identify them.

"Should we shave our heads before we leave, Papa? Like the Arab men and leave only a long topknot? We have debated this many times, but what do you think, Papa?"

Moses reached over to adjust Rachel's hood. "You mustn't shave your beautiful hair. It will take weeks to grow back and then you would have no choice but to remain in disguise. I think that wearing a hooded burnoose will suffice. Then you can resume as women once we are safe."

Rachel looked at Annie. "We will travel at night."

"Just wrap the hoods closely around your chins and keep your heads down," Moses said. "No one will know. You must act like beggarly servants paid to handle the donkey and carry sacks for me."

"When? Papa, when? The father of my child no longer pretends any affection for me. He criticizes my every word, every action. And he threatens to leave Mogador and take my son. Papa, you must not let that happen. Please, Papa. We must escape soon." She did not mention her other fear. Eliahu still insisted on his marital privileges, as infrequent as they were. She felt the signs that she was again with child.

"I agree. Everything is in readiness." Moses knew now that waiting for Captain Kingsley was a vain hope. Kingsley was still only the captain of a ship owned by others who had no interest in Moses' dilemma. Moses had approached other ships and other captains, but most of them shied away from such a risk. Despairing of help from that quarter, Moses also watched the fishing boat fleets and had thrown out lines of camaraderie to the fishermen and their families. They were rapidly becoming the more logical route to escape.

In his bantering with the fishermen, Moses sought to learn from them of the hazards they faced in the coastal waters of Morocco. He had gradually gained a good understanding of how to navigate the coast and now needed only a boat large enough to carry his family and their provisions.

He, Rachel, and Annie saved every Spanish doubloon and English pound they could manage. Since neither he nor Eliahu nor any other courtier or administrator received an official salary, all requests had to be accompanied by bribes or other fees. Moses often received these payments himself and held them in secret. He was used to a more honest way of earning money but fell in with the local practice. The result was now a substantial sum hidden in his room and in Rachel's secret caches.

Often he and Rachel would take long walks, and they would discuss their plans and possibilities.

"Whenever I visit the docks on business," he told Rachel one day as he accompanied her to the market, "I take extra time to visit the fishermen. I have become well known to them. I grant favors when I can and buy their catch."

They stopped at a fruit vendor's stall. Moses picked up an apricot and nibbled on it. "I spend hours talking with them. Casually, you understand. I pick up what information I can about the men and their families. I know whom to trust among them, and I have found one in particular who has shown himself to be honest and reliable."

"Wonderful, Papa. Who is he?"

"Afonso Cavaka. He is a Portuguese, I believe. He also has a pleasant family and the best-maintained boat among all of the fishing boats at the docks." He waited as Rachel chose carrots and cabbages. "They often invite me to join them in their meals."

"Well, then," said Rachel, paying the vendor and placing the vegetables in her market bag, "we can travel with him on his fishing boat."

"Perhaps not on his fishing boat, but on our own." Moses smiled as they continued walking through the market.

Rachel stopped in astonishment. "You have bought a boat, Papa?"

Moses chuckled at her amazement. "I secretly commissioned the man to purchase and rebuild a fishing boat for us."

"A fishing boat." Rachel nodded, walking faster toward the wharf where the fishing boats were docked.

"It's not here," Moses said, surveying the harbor. "And it does not look like most of the fishing boats in the harbor, but it's large enough for all of us and it can move by sail or oar. There's a cabin to protect us from the weather and storerooms below. My friend scraped the paint and dirtied the sails to make it appear in bad repair. He uses it himself." He peered down at Rachel. "His comrades ask questions, but he told them a tale about receiving it from a far-off uncle who no longer needed it. They all know it now—including the port authorities."

Rachel looked out to sea and searched for a fishing boat in bad repair, but the boats she saw were only dark shapes in the distance. "Are you sure it will be safe, Papa?"

He picked up a pebble and skipped it on the water. "It is sound and seaworthy, tough enough to withstand the trip up the coast and large enough for all of us, I think."

"Now that we have a boat, Papa," she said, taking his hand and walking alongside, "where will we go? I fear sailing across the ocean in a small vessel."

"We would not attempt that. A good question, my dear, and I have given much thought to it."

"Then where, Papa?"

"Our goal should be the English colony of Gibraltar. It is not more than fourteen miles across the straits from Morocco—after we sail up the coast. I am still an English citizen, and I could establish myself there with the help of Gibraltar's Jewish community."

He did not mention that England had that awkward agreement with Spain that no Jews were to be allowed in Gibraltar, but England ignored the agreement. Jews were too important to Gibraltar's economy to be excluded so, Moses had decided, this would not be a concern.

"I wonder about the guard Adam," Moses said, glancing at Rachel. "He could be a useful companion on the voyage and a strong ally in protecting ourselves and the boat as we sail up the coast."

"But Papa, he is so reticent in talking about himself and so aloof that we don't know anything about him. And," she insisted, "Annie and I work like slaves here. We are both strong. You can teach us how to sail the boat. We don't need Adam's help. I am afraid that if we tell him our plans, he will find it more lucrative to reveal them to Eliahu than to leave everything here to go with us.

"I know you like him," she added, "as do I. But he is a Muslim. We may all be lost if we err in judgment and place trust in this man none of us knows well and who may have allegiances elsewhere."

Gazing at his grandson playing in the fountain, Moses reluctantly agreed.

Chapter 39

Gibraltar, 1999

Sara watched through the plane porthole as they landed at the Gibraltar airport in the late afternoon. She searched for the famous mountain, the Rock of Gibraltar, but she was on the wrong side of the plane. Instead, she watched the airport buildings loom and then saw the cars lined up behind a red traffic signal to let their plane roar down the runway.

"Are we landing on a street, for Pete's sake?" she asked, pointing this out to Josh.

He leaned over to look out the porthole. "Oh. Yeah. This airport is on the isthmus connecting Gibraltar to Spain, and the landing strip crosses the main road to Spain. Gibraltar is only about two and a half square miles." He grinned at her. "Space is tight."

Then the plane turned and came to a stop, and Sara saw the wooded slopes of the famous "Rock." She scanned the mountain side, looking for signs of the caves and fortifications that had kept Gibraltar a British colony for hundreds of years, but from this angle, the Rock appeared to be simply a green and benign symbol of power. Josh nudged her and they prepared to disembark.

They made their way through passport control and customs and then out into the waning sunshine. A cab took them down a boulevard lined with palms and orange trees, and Sara sat back, feeling the warm and balmy breeze that swept in from an open window. The Mediterranean was just beyond the buildings on the right—she could smell the salt air as they rode in the cab, but she did not feel a panic attack coming on. She was tense enough without that.

In less than ten minutes the cab stopped in front of a small, plain building with a facade of white marble. Sara read the elegant brass sign by the door, which identified the building as the Hotel Linea Mar. Pink and orange bougainvilleas climbed trellises set in narrow strips of grass on each side of the front steps. A young woman in a gray maid's uniform was sweeping the steps and opened the door for them with a smile.

Sara could not control the queasiness in her stomach. She wondered what would happen when she met Samuel. What would he be like? She concentrated on the scent of fresh roses in the dark, mahogany-paneled lobby. As if he understood her nervousness, Josh took her hand and squeezed it as they walked to the reception desk to register. She smiled at him.

"This hotel looks okay for one we picked out of a guidebook," he said.

They checked in, deposited their suitcases in their rooms, and then met again in the lobby to find a restaurant for dinner. They walked past a strip of stores but no restaurants and came to an intersection. Sara glanced up to see cable cars rumbling above her to the top of the Rock and back down to the station in town.

Sara looked over at Josh. "Tomorrow," she said.

He took her arm as they crossed the street. Sara started in surprise at his touch, but she found she liked it. She liked Josh and she liked his family. She felt a kinship with them, even though whatever actual relationship there was must be distant. She smiled at him. He squeezed her arm.

The cruise ships in the harbor and the famous mountain behind the hotel, the Rock, dominated the landscape. Sara could not believe that she stood in its shadow. Despite the fatigue she felt after the long flight, a feeling of joy bubbled up from her heart. She danced a few steps and clapped. Josh laughed with her.

In the next block, they found an Italian restaurant. The menu was in English, and they both ordered the antipasto followed by lasagna and salad. The waiter poured bottled water and left. Sara looked over at Josh. "So, what now, then?" she asked. "Are you going to call Samuel?"

He shook his head, playing with the fork by his plate. "No, I don't think so. We'd have to negotiate with the concierge to get him to the phone, and I don't want to explain this complicated story to him on the phone. I've got his address. We'll show up there tomorrow morning early."

Sara nodded. "I'm worried about how he'll react to my grandmother's death. We should be there."

The waiter appeared with their dinners, but Sara felt too apprehensive to eat much and left half of the food on her plate. They walked back to the hotel and then parted for their rooms.

The next morning, they caught a cab for the short trip down the coastal road along the Mediterranean to the pensión where Samuel lived. The orange trees along the street glistened in the bright morning sunshine. Sara brought the album and her grandmother's photo, but kept her eyes averted from glimpses of the Mediterranean to stave off any lurking vestiges of a panic attack. She was nervous enough about this meeting.

The cab pulled up in front of a building that looked more like an American colonial mansion of white wood and columns than a guest house. A long porch with rocking chairs spanned the front of the building. "Si, Si," the cab driver assured them. "That is the Pensión Palma del Mar."

When Josh and Sara walked into the foyer, the concierge, a brisk, older woman behind a small desk peered at them over her bifocals. The long-sleeved black dress she wore made her look like a dowager duchess, and she spoke in a clipped British accent. "You're here to see Samuel Yulee? Splendid. I'm glad he has such good company this morning." She smiled at Sara and gestured at a doorway. "He's in the breakfast room, luvies. Just go through there."

They walked through the doorway into a courtyard covered with a glass roof that let in light but kept out weather. The aroma of coffee made Sara's mouth water even though tea was her favored drink. Red ceramic tiles zigzagged across the floor, and a fountain with a dolphin statue sprayed tinkling fronds of water into a small circular pool. Large, clay urns planted with flowers and ferns brightened the room. Several elderly men and women sat around small tables eating breakfast here. She watched Josh survey the room and then focus on an elderly man sitting alone behind a pillar.

"Uncle Samuel!" Josh called out, pulling Sara along with him. Everyone in the room stopped eating and stared at them.

Samuel looked up surprised and as he recognized Josh, a gentle smile spread out on his face, a face stern and careworn as if he had weathered a lifetime of storms. "Josh!"

He rose stiffly and limped forward to hug Josh. His navy blue suit, red sweater, and full head of wavy, white hair gave him a dignified but robust appearance despite the limp and stooped posture. "What brings you here, my son?" he asked.

"I have news for you, Uncle, but first I want you to meet Sara Miller." Josh reached out for Sara's arm and drew her closer. She smiled at Samuel, searching for a family resemblance. She felt her nervousness subside.

Samuel shook Sara's smooth hand loosely in his gnarled one, the fingers bent with arthritis. "How do you do, Miss Miller? Sara, is it? Sit down, sit down."

As he sat down himself, he gestured to the empty chairs at his table. Josh and Sara joined him. She studied Samuel's face. His nose, it looked like her brother's nose. And the eyes, they could be Grandma's eyes.

The hovering server came forward and interrupted Sara's thoughts. Josh touched her arm. "Coffee," he said to the server.

"I am delighted to see you," said Samuel, "but I hope your coming means good news." He looked at Josh with a raised eyebrow and turned to grin at Sara.

He thinks we're engaged, Sara thought, watching Josh's eyes dart around the room as if he sought an escape. "It does, Uncle Samuel," Josh cleared his throat, "and on the other hand, it doesn't."

Samuel waited, glancing at Sara with a puzzled look. "Your mother, she is well?"

Josh nibbled at the pastry. "Everyone at home is fine and asks after you. We all miss you."

Samuel stared at Josh as if to read his mind. "Well, then, that is good. Now tell me, what is this good, maybe bad, news?"

Josh softened his voice and placed a hand on his uncle's arm. "We have word of Aunt Ruth, Uncle Samuel."

The smile left Samuel's face. His eyes blinked. It almost seemed as if he had stopped breathing. "You have heard from her? Is she well?"

Josh shook his head. "No. The news there is not good."

Samuel looked down at the table, his hands trembling. After a pause, he said, "What is it, then?"

Sara had watched joy and hope flit by on Samuel's face, but this final question carried heartbreak in it. She could not stay silent a moment longer. She leaned toward him and placed her hand on his. Looking into his eyes, she said, "I am your sister's granddaughter."

Josh sat back as if relieved to let Sara take over. "Sara brought us the news," he added.

"Yes, I am sorry to tell you that Grandma Ruth died two months ago," Sara said. She waited, still holding his hands and looking into his face, trying to convey her own love for her grandmother to him.

"I see." Samuel withdrew his hands, leaned back in his chair and stared at the clay pot of flowers behind Sara.

After a moment, Sara said, "She never told us about you or her family in St. Thomas. Nothing. Until she died, we never knew she had been in a concentration camp. She must have suffered terribly in the camp and perhaps thought you had died there. I think the memories were too painful for her and she lived with the fear that it would happen again."

Josh stepped in. "But before she died she asked Sara to find you."

"You are my legacy," Sara added.

Samuel cast his eyes down at the table. After a long pause, he looked up to examine Sara's face as if searching for a remnant of memory. Then he stared off into the distance. "So," he said. "So."

Sara looked at Josh, but they both remained silent, giving Samuel time to absorb the news.

"So," Samuel turned to Sara. "And you are her granddaughter."

"Yes." Sara smiled at him.

He sighed and fingered his napkin. "So did Ruth have a good life then?"

Sara patted his arm. "I believe so, yes. She married my grandfather in 1946. I have her wedding picture here." She brought it out and showed it to him.

"Yes," Samuel said, tears in his eyes. "That is Ruth."

He dabbed at his eyes with the napkin and drew a deep breath. "So it is over." His voice cracked, and they waited for him to compose himself. Finally he said, "She never told you anything about me or our family in St. Thomas?"

Sara shook her head. "She never talked about anything in her past. I learned about you in a letter. She asked me to find you."

Samuel sighed. "Yes, the same thing happened to me. I started feeling that Ruth was alive, and so I decided to come here . . . just in case."

"That is so strange," Sara said, reaching for her coffee. "I wonder why that happened? You both must have been close."

"Yes, we were. We'd been orphans, you know, adopted by Josh's great grandparents. I searched for Ruth after the war but nothing came of it. And then I met my Harriet. She was wonderful." He paused a long moment.

Sara waited, her hand on Josh's.

At last Samuel continued, brushing at his eyes. "After she died, I had nothing to live for. Coming here seemed like something to do." He shrugged and pushed his plate away. "I am no longer hungry."

Sara leaned toward him. "I am glad to meet you, Uncle Samuel."

He looked up with sad eyes and smiled at her. "And I am pleased to meet you, Ruth's grandchild."

Sara caught her breath, unable to speak for a moment, afraid to bring up more painful memories yet knowing that she must. She gulped and began. "After Grandma died, we found a valise hidden in her room. Inside were a bunch of strange receipts and Jewish items like a menorah and a . . . I think you call it a mezuzah. We never even knew she was Jewish."

"She didn't tell you she was Jewish?" Samuel's eyes searched her face.

"No," said Sara.

"So you were not raised Jewish?"

"My grandfather and his family were all Methodist . . . I think. But we never belonged to a church . . . or synagogue. Grandma distrusted organized religions, you see."

"Oh, well then, you are Jewish." Samuel sat back. "Ruth told you nothing about us? Or our religion?"

"No, she didn't. She kept saying she wanted only to go forward, not back. I think she was much more fragile than we ever considered. We knew nothing about her family, where she came from, or anything about her life before she married our grandfather."

"Oh, what she must have suffered." Samuel put his head in his hands.

Sara frowned. "Well, really, she had a good life with us."

Samuel did not raise his head so his voice was muffled. Sara leaned forward to hear him. "No, no. I mean what the Nazis must have done to her. They broke her spirit and made her forever afraid."

"Yes, she did always seem afraid." Sara sat back and considered this idea. "Even when there was nothing to be afraid of. I thought that she was probably shy."

"Shy!" Samuel raised his head and snorted. "Ruth was never shy!"

Sara looked at him. "I would very much like to know what Ruth was like."

Samuel sat up and thumped his cane, his eyes fiery. He stabbed at the air with his finger. "She was brave and outspoken, and she stood up for what she believed. Even when it meant certain disaster—and it destroyed her. That's what Ruth was like."

Sara leaned back in her chair away from that stabbing finger. Samuel was talking about a woman she never knew. Could he mean Grandma? "My grandmother was a sweet and loving woman . . ." Sara said in confusion.

Samuel snorted again. "Sweet! Oh yes, she was sweet. That sweetness covered her fury and her drive, and she used it like camouflage when she needed to. That's why she survived so long in Denmark. She protected me with it too."

Sara felt her world shift. Like seeing the other side of an optical illusion, Sara remembered how her grandmother would appear so docile and, yes, sweet, but her eyes gave her away in brief glints. She had seen those sparks, thought there was something her grandmother wasn't saying but had been too self-centered to see beyond the facade. No one in Sara's family had known Ruth Rachel for the woman she really was. Sara had been closer to her grandmother than anyone else in the family. She had sensed this hidden self, and perhaps her grandmother knew that. Perhaps that was why she had charged Sara with the task of finding Samuel.

"What did happen in Denmark?" asked Josh at last.

Samuel took a deep breath that seemed to calm him. He shook his head. "We were both young, stupid, and naïve. We wanted to help the desperate Jews in Europe, but we made mistakes. We knew the Nazis were closing in on us. I was working with the resistance. . ."

He leaned back in his chair with his hands in his pockets and spoke as if the subject bored him. "We were with Zionist organizations to help Jews smuggle their art and jewelry out of Europe to safe areas. Their property was stored until the rightful owners could claim it."

"My grandmother worked with the resistance?" Sara's mind reeled with the revelations. Samuel was talking about her loving, apron-wearing, West Virginia grandma.

"Yes. I told you. She was a brave woman. We kept up a façade of being innocent, fairly dumb tourists from the islands," he paused. "I suppose it wasn't much of a façade, more like the truth, but we were able to gather information we could pass on. Only the Nazis came too close." He shrugged.

"We escaped Denmark and made our way here to Gibraltar, planning to go on to England. I wanted to make one last trip to Marseille and there I was captured. Ruth had also planned a trip through France. I never saw or heard from her again. I thought she was dead until just recently." He glanced at them and sighed. "That's why I came here, because we agreed that we would meet here if we got separated."

Sara picked up the album and placed it on the table in front of Samuel. "Do you recognize this?"

Samuel stared at it a moment, then opened it to leaf through the first several pages. He closed it again and looked at Sara.

"Ruth gave this to you?" His gaze was so intense that Sara knew the album was important.

"It was among the items in the box she left for me. I don't know what it means. I don't know what this means either." She placed the receipt in front of him.

Samuel was silent for a long time. Sara glanced at Josh. He examined his fingernails. They waited.

"This album is for me," Samuel said at last. "It is . . .unfinished business. It is why I waited for her here."

Josh sat back. "Why here, though? Why not home?"

"I will tell you why, but not now. You must join me for dinner this evening, and we will continue this," his eyes flickered, "discussion." He gestured to the attendant and pointed to his cup. Then he turned to Josh. "Now, talk to me, Josh. Catch me up on what you're doing."

Josh stared at the tablecloth and spoke in a low voice. "I left school, Uncle Samuel."

Samuel sat back and waited until coffee had been poured. Sara could feel the tension in the air and felt sorry for Josh. Samuel merely added cream and sugar to the coffee, took a sip, and brushed the napkin across his lips before responding. "I see. You left school."

Josh flinched. "I needed some time. I'm not sure what I want to do."

"You don't know what you want to do?" Samuel raised an eyebrow.

Josh shook his head. There was a pause as if Josh waited for criticism and a lecture, but none came.

"Well, well. Then you must find what you want to do." Samuel turned to Sara. "I'm glad to meet you, my dear," he said. "Tell me about your family. About Ruth's family."

The conversation continued through breakfast. Samuel at last tossed his napkin aside and rose. "I would like to show you Gibraltar today, my children, but alas, I cannot. I have an appointment that I must keep." He gestured at the server who hurried forward with a slip of paper that Samuel signed. Josh pulled out his wallet, but Samuel waved it aside.

Sara and Josh walked with Samuel to the elevator. As they turned to leave, he stopped them with his hand.

"But also, you must rent a car for tonight. We have a special place to go after dinner."

As Sara's mind buzzed with the questions she wanted to ask—Rent a car? Special place? Where?—Samuel hugged Josh, kissed her on the cheek, and then entered the elevator, shooing them on their way. They began walking toward the door.

***

Samuel held the elevator door open and, one finger tapping his lips, he watched Josh and Sara walk past the concierge and out onto the sidewalk. He stepped out of the elevator and waited in the lobby until he saw them go off in a cab. Then he limped out the door on an errand of his own.

Chapter 40

Mogador, 1791

Moses enlisted Rachel's help in locating where Eliahu hid the wealth he had accumulated over the years. Through deduction, guesswork, and exploration, she found the cache in a hollow carved out under the floor in Eliahu's private quarters. Eliahu had disguised the excavation with the same blue and white tiles that covered every floor in his house. The seam around the removable tiles was not discernable except under careful scrutiny, but Eliahu also covered the area with carpet.

One afternoon when Eliahu was out of the house on a time-consuming errand, Rachel revealed the cache to Moses. Together, they pulled aside the carpet and plucked up the tiles to expose the rough brown sacks and heavy gold bars that lay in the cache. Moses looked up at Rachel. She nodded at him. They both knew that part of this stash must leave with them when they escaped. Moses opened the clinking sacks—they contained Spanish doubloons—then counted the sacks and the gold bars to assess their value. Together they replaced the carpet and tiles and returned to the courtyard.

As they parted on other errands, Moses whispered to Rachel, "Watch the cache but don't touch it until we are prepared to leave."

The siege of the country by Moulay Yazid's thugs persisted, but so far, Mogador remained strong in its defenses. The weeks crawled by, and the reports of horrors elsewhere continued to render the entire town tense and wary.

Despite the uncertainty of the times, Eliahu's arrogance and pride could not be denied for long. One day, Moses looked up from his desk to find Eliahu staring at him, lips pursed. Then Eliahu inclined his head as if he had reached some decision and said, "I believe, my friend, that I can turn, ah, these despicable events, ah, in our favor."

Moses regarded Eliahu but said nothing and waited.

"Yes. I have devised a plan, ah, to regain my former position with, ah, the new king, his royal majesty, Moulay Yazid."

Moses sat up. "What? This man who murders, tortures and robs Jews and anyone who displeases him? You would attempt to gain his favor?"

Eliahu frowned. "He is only doing what he must to gain control. He is forced into this . . . and perhaps he has bad advisors. He needs the advice of, ah, seasoned administrators. He needs my . . . our . . . assistance. I am a man of, ah, consequence. I have power and ability. He must know how much I increased the wealth of his father. He can use me to, ah, further consolidate his power and his wealth." He glared at Moses under his thin brows, as if daring Moses to contradict him. Moses stared at Eliahu in disbelief.

After a short pause, Eliahu continued. "Besides it is better to join his side now and prosper than to hold off and be vanquished as the enemy." He shuffled the papers on his desk as if the discussion was over.

Moses could not let this insane idea pass. "But Yazid is not ruled by reason . . . ."

"Please spare me your opinion. I am leaving tomorrow for Rabat, for I hear that he is in residency there. I will arrive with a full caravan of camels and horses and gifts and, ah, guards."

Moses just stared at the man. If Eliahu could see opportunity in the current catastrophe, if he could align himself with such evil, then Moses, slave or not, would refuse to condone it. He saw only disaster in such folly.

Eliahu would not be dissuaded. His departure was indeed taken the next morning and hastily, as if he wanted no contradictions or second thoughts to interfere. Moses stood by, saying nothing, his face expressionless, his arm around Rachel. He did not expect to see Eliahu again, but none of the other wives or children suspected that this journey might mean anything more than a long absence.

Rachel was cool in her farewell to Eliahu, but the other wives wailed and wept as he left. Their children joined in the general wailing while little Moses Elias stood thoughtfully at his mother's side, holding her hand.

Even Adam Mohammed watched the procession from a doorway, alone, the only guard to take any interest in the comings and goings of the family. Moses looked at Adam, who cocked his head at Eliahu and raised an eyebrow. Moses shook his head, feeling grateful that Adam had been spared this perilous journey.

Once Eliahu had set out, Moses had a clear field to prepare his own plan. And now, at last, the time was right. All the pieces were in place. The fishing boat was ready to sail. Moses thought they could leave that night, but when he went to speak to the fisherman, Afonso Cavaka, he met Afonso's neighbor on the road.

"Afonso is not here," the man said. "He visits his uncle's family in Agadir and will return in a few days."

Moses trudged back to Eliahu's house cursing his bad fortune. To be ready at last only to face another setback was but one more tedious frustration.

He debated whether he should take the boat and sail it north himself. At last he decided that since Eliahu could not be expected to return for a fortnight—if all went well, which it probably would not—then they could afford to wait for a week. A major advantage to this plan was that the boat was supposed to belong to Afonso. To have someone else take it away from the dock would raise questions that might interest the guards. Better to have it all seem like a normal fishing trip by a local, well-known fisherman. Once they arrived in Gibraltar, the fishing boat could then be presented to Afonso as a gift for his help and his agreement to remain quiet about the arrangement.

Moses now had to talk to Rachel and Annie without the prying eyes of the other wives and their children. With two other women and six other children in the household, privacy was scarce. Fortunately, the other wives saw themselves as ranking high above Rachel and Moses in social standing and power and so paid little attention to them.

He entered the house unobserved and walked on to his own room at the back of the second courtyard. He uncovered the cache in his room that hid his earnings, removed five heavy, clanking sacks and laid them under a covered stool in a corner. He draped a filthy old haik over the stool as well and studied the effect. *Good.* It would serve until they departed.

He found Rachel and Annie playing with Moses Elias in Rachel's room. Moses gestured Rachel aside, leaving Annie to distract the boy. "Rachel," he whispered, "prepare to leave in the next few days."

He smiled as he saw joy brighten her face and continued. "Retrieve all the money hidden in your caches in the courtyard and hide it with the stack under the stool in my room."

"Mama! Grandpapa! Catch me!" Moses Elias ran past them and down the steps. Moses followed him, gave him a hug, and waved at

Annie. The boy ran back to Annie, and Moses returned to his room.

Each morning, Moses visited Afonso's cottage, carrying additional supplies—food and water in small bundles and urns—with which to stock the boat. He hid them in covered clay jars behind the cottage. All was in readiness for the fisherman's return, but day after day dragged by with no sign of him.

From the cottage, Moses went to Eliahu's offices to wait for word from him. As the days passed, he began to fear that Eliahu would return unexpectedly and make their escape more difficult.

Eliahu had been gone six days when Moses received word of Eliahu's fate. An acquaintance arrived in Mogador and asked to speak to Moses in private. In Eliahu's office, over cups of mint tea, this acquaintance, a thin man named Jacob Ezratty, told Moses the story. "Eliahu exceeded the gods in arrogance," Jacob began, adjusting his djellaba as he shifted in his seat. He laughed without humor. "You will find this difficult to believe."

Moses grimaced and shook his head but said nothing.

Jacob picked up his tea cup and continued. "Eliahu sent word to Moulay Yazid of his presence in the town and desire to speak with him. Instead of the polite invitation Eliahu expected, Yazid sent his guards to seize and beat him."

Jacob took a sip of tea, peering at Moses over the cup. "After the beating, Eliahu was brought before Yazid in the large ceremonial courtyard of the palace at Rabat. There, Eliahu bowed to the ground and stammered some obsequious praises to Yazid." Jacob shrugged. "Yazid only looked at him in contempt. Then Yazid raised his gun, aimed it at Eliahu's toes, and shot him in the foot." Jacob took another sip as if to punctuate his story.

"Shot him?" Moses looked up. He was not surprised.

Jacob nodded. "All this was only a beginning. While Eliahu cowered in pain on the ground, Yazid shouted at him, claiming that Eliahu had turned the old king against him. Then, my friend, Yazid gave Eliahu a choice: to die as an Arab or to die as a Jew." Jacob touched his forehead and sighed.

"And Eliahu was in pain and terrified," said Moses, staring down at the carpet.

"Yes, and despite being beaten and shot, Eliahu was still not willing to believe that Yazid was indeed his enemy." Jacob patted his hands on his knees and took a deep breath. "Eliahu's conceit was boundless."

"He had steeped himself in power." Moses flicked a speck off his djellaba, thinking of Eliahu's arrogance.

"Eliahu denounced his religion, my friend. He told Yazid that he would rather die as a Muslim."

Moses shook his head. "As if that would help him."

"It did not. Ten times Yazid repeated his demand, 'Choose whichever you wish, to die as an Arab or a Jew.' And ten times, Eliahu stated his wish to convert to Islam." Jacob stared at the wall and shuddered. "Yazid finally tired of this game and ordered Eliahu out to be shot and dragged through the streets by horses. I saw him shot with my own eyes. Eliahu is dead. There can be no doubt."

Moses shook his head. The folly of Eliahu to think he could survive a meeting with such a dangerous foe.

After seeing Jacob off to continue his journey, Moses hurried to Eliahu's house. He found Rachel on the steps and took her by the hand, leading her out the door into the alley. There he whispered the news to her.

"Oh, Papa." Rachel covered her eyes and stood silently for several minutes. Moses put his arm around her. She had been forced into the marriage, but she was at heart a loving woman. He knew she felt the pain and horror of such an unspeakable death.

They agreed not to say anything about Eliahu to the other wives. They would learn the news soon enough, and then there would be squabbling and turmoil as ownership of house and possessions became subjects of debate.

Moses and Rachel knew that they could delay no longer in making their escape. Because of Eliahu's display of wealth, it would only be days before Yazid's forces would turn their attention to Mogador. Once that happened, more guards would be placed at the gates, and no one would be allowed to enter or leave. Even then, the town might not be able to withstand the assault.

Moses walked to the fisherman's cottage and found, by some miracle, that the man and his wife had returned. They were still unloading their donkey when Moses appeared.

Afonso waved at Moses, but his wife shooed the children into the cottage.

"How was your visit, my friend?" Moses said in Portuguese.

"It was good," the fisherman replied, also in Portuguese. His trade had leathered and deeply tanned his skin and faded his blue eyes, but kindness, humor, and interest shone out of them. He wiped his hands on the striped and stained djellaba he wore. "My uncle and his family remain in good health, although they are not happy at the current state of affairs in this country."

"They are not alone," Moses replied.

"Yes, I look at you, and I see the tide has turned, my friend."

"You are right. We must depart. We dare not delay much longer. Eliahu, my master, has met his fate and the new tyrant's forces will seek our lands to plunder."

"Yes, yes. I understand, but we have just returned from a tiresome journey. We are weary, my friend, and the journey north to Gibraltar will be long and difficult. I must rest."

"You must refresh yourself, but I beg of you, let us leave tomorrow night, after midnight. You will be rested then, surely. I tell you we dare not delay much longer."

"Tomorrow night, then. I will wait for you at the quay. Meanwhile, my woman will load the boat with the provisions you have left here."

"Excellent, then until tomorrow night, my friend," agreed Moses, seeing that nothing more could be done. "My gratitude to you and your family." He saluted the fisherman.

After little Moses Elias had fallen asleep that evening, Moses motioned to Rachel and Annie to join him in the courtyard for a secret conference. They took care to appear as if they were casually enjoying the evening air. The other wives and children could interrupt at any moment.

Moses drew them close and whispered, "We leave tomorrow night. I have made arrangements, and we dare not wait longer."

"Oh, wonderful, Papa." Rachel's smile lit up her face. She clapped her hands.

They went over again, for the hundredth time, every detail of the plan they had been refining for years. Each one's part was critical. They paused as Adam Mohammed sauntered by, but he didn't linger. Moses watched him leave with misgiving.

"I don't understand him," said Rachel. "He seems to watch everything. I know he is kind to little Moses, but what does he want?"

"I like him well enough," Annie said, "but he says so little that he worries me."

Moses thought back over the years. Adam Mohammed had helped bring them together after their capture. He seemed to be educated but where did his allegiance lie? With the current king of Morocco? With the mayor? They did not know and that uncertainty made Adam too big a risk to include.

The wait was tedious and irritating, but they carried on as usual to avoid raising the suspicions of the other wives. Somehow Moses, Rachel, and Annie managed to get through the next day, doing what they could to make whatever final preparations were necessary so their departure that night would go smoothly. They planned to leave as soon as all was quiet and still in the house.

As evening approached, Moses crept into Eliahu's quarters, listening for approaching footsteps from the other wives. He quietly removed the carpet and tiles, but during a pause, he heard Adam accost one of the wives with a question. Their footsteps trailed away. How fortunate that Adam distracted her. Moses had no excuse for being in Eliahu's room, much less taking apart the floor.

With Eliahu's cache exposed, Moses tore open each of the twenty sacks hidden there to make sure they contained coins and not sand. He had feared that Eliahu would take this stash of gold coins and bars with him to Yazid's court, but apparently Eliahu had emptied caches elsewhere for that purpose. Moses removed five of the sacks, leaving fifteen for Eliahu's first two wives. They should live well with these if they did not squander them.

Under the sacks, thirty solid gold bars lay neatly stacked. Moses took five of the bars and laid them alongside the sacks. He left the cache uncovered so the other wives would find it and have money on which to live. He felt a momentary twinge of conscience at the thought of robbing his son-in-law but dismissed it with a grimace and wave of his hand. Eliahu had taken all the monies that could have been used to ransom Rachel and instead made the money her dowry for his own benefit. Furthermore, Moses himself had served this man as a slave for ten years. No amount of money could compensate for the years he had spent with Eliahu.

***

Later that night, when all was quiet in the house, Rachel and Annie crept to the storeroom off the first courtyard and away from the sleeping rooms to retrieve a small cart often used to haul foodstuffs from the market. To avoid squeaks and clatter, they carried the cart across the courtyard and into Eliahu's room at the back of the second courtyard. Rachel lined the cart with rags to muffle the sound as Moses laid first the gold bars and then the sacks of coins onto the rags.

As they loaded the cart, Rachel looked over at Annie and pointed to the wheels. Annie nodded. Taking a long strip of cloth, she wound it over the wheels to muffle their sound on the stones. Rachel then slathered the goat butter she had retrieved from the kitchen on the wheel axle and moving parts to grease them. They covered the gold with a cloth and wheeled the cart quietly over to Moses' room, also on the first floor across the courtyard.

Rachel joined Moses as he tossed aside the haik and together they picked up the sacks, one by one to avoid the clanking of coins, and carried them to the cart. Then Moses brought the gold bars and placed them on top of the sacks. The cart axles bowed under the weight.

While Moses loaded the cart, Rachel and Annie secreted themselves behind the folding doors in Rachel's room. Rachel pulled back her mattress and picked up the garments she had hidden for so long. They dressed in the white tunics Arab men wore, then helped each other wind their hair into tight knots that could be hidden under the hood of the burnoose. Using a thin mixture of gum arabic that Rachel had made from the oozings of the acacia tree, she affixed the beards to her chin and Annie's. Each woman threw a burnoose over her head and pulled it down to cover the tunic, then drew the hood down over her brows and across her chin to obscure her face.

They rejoined Moses as he wheeled the cart into the courtyard. He motioned to the guards on duty and sent them away from the house on the somewhat flimsy pretext that they were to check at the town gates for news of Eliahu. Rachel watched them, but if they thought this was odd, they didn't say so. She knew that they accepted Moses as an authority and would obey him.

This left the way clear for her, now dressed as an Arab, to bring out the donkey she had bought earlier that day from one of the tradesmen in the medina and hidden in the storeroom along with the cart. She led the donkey to the courtyard near the front door. On its feet she had wrapped heavy carpet to dull the clatter of its hooves on the tiles and stones, and she had bound its jaws shut. She tied the donkey to the door handle next to the cart, and then waited there for her father to return.

They transferred the gold sacks and bars to the donkey's panniers for Arabs did not use carts. Moses walked over to the storeroom and disappeared. He emerged with sacks of dried fruit and dates to cover the treasure. He went back and this time emerged with bread and spare clothes. Then they added more bags of clothes and other personal items to take with them. The pannier on each side of the donkey bulged, but the donkey took the weight placidly.

Meanwhile, Annie tiptoed down the stairs with little Moses Elias rubbing his eyes. He was dressed in a ragged djellaba. Rachel bent down to him and put a finger to her lips. "We have practiced this, my sweet little boy. You must come along with us and not say anything. Keep your head down."

Moses Elias said nothing, but his brown eyes grew large and luminous as he followed his mother.

Before they set out down the street, they grabbed each other's hands and squeezed for good fortune, and then Moses picked up the cart handle and wheeled it back to the side building for storage, removing its rags from the wheels so that no clue would be left.

They stole through the door and out into the street. Behind them, one of the other wives called out to them once, but she did not repeat the call, and they did not stop.

The carpet muted the donkey's hooves but caused the animal to slip occasionally on the stones so they progressed slowly down the quiet, dark streets of the town. Rachel felt they were being followed but saw no one whenever she looked back. She glanced at her father and saw that his jaw was clenched and that he too looked behind them again and again. If they failed to escape, they would surely all lose their lives. Even if they weren't Jews and even if Jewish women weren't discovered masquerading as Arab men, the mere fact that her father led a donkey carrying a fortune would be enough reason to murder them all.

The donkey balked and shied but added a touch of authenticity to their promenade along the street toward the port. Rachel looked down at her own costume, then over at Annie. They both looked sufficiently like Arab men so that all of them escaped the notice of casual passersby.

In the darkness of an alley, just before they reached the gates, Rachel removed the carpet from the donkey's hooves and the cloth around its jaws. The guards would be sure to wonder why the donkey's hooves and jaw were muffled and that would lead to questions.

Rachel saw Moses peer through the darkness down the street behind them.

"What is wrong, Papa?"

"I don't know. I can not shake the feeling that we're being followed."

"I feel that too, Papa," she whispered. "But no one is there."

Moses shook his head, and Rachel heard him muttering to himself. "I have the   documents—surely they will pass as official permissions."

Rachel nodded in encouragement. "And we are prepared to bribe the guards."

"Yes. Most of the guards know me. I don't think they will be a problem."

But they did become a problem. Rachel saw them whispering among themselves as she and her father approached. One guard gestured to the town clock while the other halted them at the gate. He refused to let them pass. She watched her father proffer the documents, but the guard balked, unwilling to accept the dubious documents or the bribe Moses offered. The guard's questions were drawing the attention of other guards.

Rachel drew in her breath and gripped her son's hand. Unless the gates were opened immediately, They would all be questioned . . . and searched.

They must not be searched.

Rachel drew closer to Moses and Annie as she desperately sought a strategy to get around the guards.

"Here, what's this now?" The voice was authoritative—and familiar.

Adam Mohammed sauntered down the road toward them.

Rachel watched in disbelief as Adam drew the guard aside. The two mumbled together and then, miraculously, the guard opened the gates and saluted as they walked through onto the quay.

Adam now strode easily by their side. He took the donkey's reins from Rachel, but he made no comment about her unusual appearance. She dared not look at him.

They walked down the quay to where a woman stood wrapped in a black haik. She pointed down the side of the quay. A stone ramp descended along the seawall to a platform just above the water where a boat bobbed in the darkness. A man stood by the boat with a torch that cast a dim light on the boat and the platform. Moses gestured to Rachel to halt on the quay while he and the man bounded down the ramp and disappeared into the boat below. Only a sliver of a moon shone over them, and the torch lights of the guards at the gates did not reach this far.

Rachel waited nervously for Moses to reappear. Adam stared out to sea. Little Moses reached down to pick up pebbles. As her eyes adjusted to the darkness, she could make out shapes around them—the pilings, their fishing boat, the fishing boats anchored near the shore.

After a few minutes, her father jumped back onto the ramp followed by the fisherman who waved at them and then turned back into the boat, which creaked from side to side in the gentle waves flowing into the bay from the ocean.

Moses gestured to Rachel for all of them to walk down the ramp to the boat. "All is well. We are ready to leave as soon as we load the boat."

The smell of dead fish, rotting seaweed, and sewage assailed them. With open mouth and wide eyes, Moses Elias clung to Rachel's burnoose, while she kept her hand on his shoulder. Annie led the donkey down the ramp with one hand and covered her nose with the hood of her burnoose with the other. The donkey, finding itself in such unfamiliar surroundings, resisted, and Annie had to pull and coax, increasing the tension Rachel felt. Finally Adam slapped it on the rear and it jumped forward, then half slid, half walked down to the platform.

For a long moment, Rachel dubiously regarded this tiny boat, but despite the darkness, she could see that it was sturdy and roomy. Hearing a shout from down the quay, Rachel picked up little Moses and clambered aboard. Annie followed.

Moses and Adam began lifting the bags out of the panniers and carrying them across the gunwales into the boat, setting them down in the center of the deck. Moses whispered to Rachel to put them below. She and Annie began taking the bags into the cabin.

As Rachel finished clearing the deck, she watched Moses lead the donkey back up the ramp and pull it over to the fisherman's wife. He placed the reins and several coins in her hands and bent to kiss them in gratitude before turning back to the boat.

Adam untied the furled sails. Moses joined the fisherman in freeing the boat from the dock and raising the sails. Then the fisherman took the tiller and began guiding the boat out beyond the islands and the bay into the sea.

Adam turned to Moses and Rachel, now sitting on benches against the gunwales in the open cockpit. Rachel had her arm around little Moses, restraining him from trying to reach down over the side to the water. She looked at Adam. "We would have been exposed if you had not intervened, but why did you help us?"

Adam smiled at Rachel. "I, too, am tired of Mogador," he said.

A slight smile appeared on Rachel's face as she looked at him. "So are we," she said.

"Me too," added little Moses.

Adam laughed and kneeled down to him. "And so we seek new adventures."

"Yes," Rachel said. "In Gibraltar. And from Gibraltar, perhaps we will finally find our way to America."

She settled back on the hard seat and kissed little Moses Elias. The night was clear and there was a light breeze, just enough to send the boat on its way. She retrieved a fragment of blue tile from under her tunic, kissed it, and tossed it into the sea. At last she was leaving Mogador and Morocco, not for America yet but for Gibraltar and a new beginning.

It was 1791. It had been ten long years since she had last seen the outer wall of Mogador. She was now a widow with a child, and she felt inside her a new life growing. She looked over to see Annie smiling at her. Rachel smiled back. A good and faithful friend, Rachel thought. She snuck a peek at Adam, who stared out at the sea ahead. She still did not know what to make of him, but he, too, had become a friend and an ally.

She turned her face into the wind and gazed out at the ocean to the west. "If I have another child and if it is a girl," she said to herself, "I will name her first after myself as the only living woman in our family. Then I will give her a second name in memory of my mother, and I will call her by that name."

"I will call her Sarah."

Chapter 41

Gibraltar, 1999

As Sara and Josh left the pensión and walked back to the center of town, Josh muttered, "I wonder what Uncle Samuel has up his sleeve."

Captivated by the bright Mediterranean sunshine and fresh scent of the rain-splattered oleanders, Sara replied absently, "Maybe he was just being eccentric."

Josh snorted. "He's always been that, but this is something more. He has something planned, all right."

Sara stopped at a sidewalk kiosk to peruse the touring opportunities, but she said, "He should be back in St. Thomas with his family."

The weather was balmy and warm, perfect for touring, and the kiosk vendor had no trouble persuading them to buy tickets for the complete tour of Gibraltar. They joined several other tourists in boarding a white jitney, which whisked them first to the cable car station for a trip to the top of the Rock of Gibraltar. Since Gibraltar is a British colony, the guide spoke excellent English, but Sara noted that he spoke to the driver in Spanish, which made sense. Spain was right next door.

As they climbed out of the jitney, the guide motioned toward the mountain beside them. "This, ladies and gentlemen, is the famous Rock of Gibraltar, which you have all come to see," he began. "It dominates the straits between Spain and Morocco, being a little more than three and a half miles long and 1,394 feet high."

The guide herded his charges over to the cable car station. Sara was not eager to enter this precarious cage, but the guide enthusiastically pushed her in with the others, ignoring her protests. She endured the trip with her eyes shut, gritting her teeth as the cable car swayed and lurched. But the ride was worth it, Sara decided. From the café at the top, they could see Morocco just fourteen miles away across the Straits.

At first Sara took quick peeks across the Mediterranean, expecting the suffocating feeling of a panic attack that usually occurred when she looked at the sea. As the moments passed with no adverse reaction, she took a deep breath and stepped closer to the rail in front of her. She shook her head, not believing at first, then she began to grin and the grin bubbled into a laugh.

Josh tore his eyes away from the magnificent scene in front of him and turned to stare at her. "What's going on?"

"Nothing." Sara laughed. "I think I just broke a curse."

"What do you mean?"

"I'll explain later." She tugged on Josh's sleeve. "We can see Morocco over there. Now I understand why my ancestor, Rachel . . ." She saw the blank look on Josh's face and added, "The one captured by pirates, David Levy Yulee's grandmother . . ."

Light dawned on Josh's face. "I can see why she came to Gibraltar after escaping from Morocco," he said. He snapped his fingers. "And Gibraltar belonged to Great Britain too, not Spain, where the Inquisition persisted."

"I wonder if she ever made it to America," Sara whispered to herself.

Josh smiled at her and took her arm. "They're heading down again." He was already leading her toward the steps back to the cable car.

Sara stepped aboard the wavering cage with more confidence this time. At the halfway platform, the cable car stopped, and the passengers were instructed to jump across the gap between the swinging cable car and the platform and walk up to the road where their bus waited. Sara jumped without hesitation, but Josh hovered a moment and Sara saw a spasm of fear cross his face. She watched him close his eyes, take a deep breath, and jump. He shook his head, and she snuck a look at him, touched by his vulnerability. She took his hand as they walked over to where their guide waited among a group of small, cinnamon-colored animals, the Barbary apes.

"They're actually tailless monkeys," the guide was saying, "And we take excellent care of them." The guide handed crackers to Josh and Sara and motioned toward the apes. "A legend says that when these apes leave Gibraltar, Britain will lose this colony."

Sara's amusement at the small apes changed to apprehension as one jumped onto her head and held out his hands. Josh handed her a cracker to feed the animal as one of the local photographers took yet another photo of a tourist in Gibraltar with an ape on the head.

They climbed back on board the jitney for a trip to Europa Point, the southernmost tip of Gibraltar. A 160-foot-tall lighthouse stood on the point while a mosque with tall minarets had been built nearby. A king from Morocco had contributed the funds to build the mosque, insisting on minarets so tall that he could see them from across the straits. Sara again felt awed at the closeness of Morocco across the water. She could even make out Morocco's Rif Mountains in the haze, but what was more important to her was that when she looked across the Mediterranean to the opposite shore, she did not feel even a faint queasiness.

As they rode the bus back, Sara turned to Josh. "For some reason, I used to have panic attacks," Sara crossed her fingers—she hoped that the panic attacks were over with— "when I looked eastward at the ocean or the sea or even a lake."

Josh took her hand and squeezed it. "I thought there was something like that going on, but you seemed to recover all right. I get panic attacks myself sometimes," Josh said. He gazed off into the distance, his expression remote and pensive.

"You do?" Sara asked, feeling closer to Josh. This was one more bond between them. "I thought I was pretty weird."

"I guess maybe we both are. I'm afraid of heights too." He looked at her out of the corner of his eye, as if to gauge her reaction.

"Yes, I noticed that at the halfway platform."

Josh turned back to Sara and whispered, "I think I know what my panic attacks are about. With yours, maybe you should consider your family's history."

The tour ended back at the town center where they found a small tearoom for lunch, then walked down the street past souvenir shops, pharmacies, cafes, and banks to find a car rental agency. Sara insisted on paying for the rental but let Josh drive. They were both impatient to see Samuel again.

When they returned to the pensión that evening, Samuel was waiting for them outside, leaning on his cane. He signaled to them to stay in the car. Sara watched as he scanned the area around them like an elderly James Bond and then snuck behind a thick hedge of crotons beside the door. They saw his head poke up. Again he surveyed the area before shuffling to the car, now carrying a shovel. He threw it in the back seat and climbed in after it.

"Okay." He grinned at them. "Let's go."

Sara peeked over at Josh, wanting to laugh. He caught the glance, shrugged and smiled. "Where to?" he said.

"The Garrison Restaurant. I know it, and we can talk without being disturbed—or overheard."

Sara hid her amusement. The old man had quite a sense of the dramatic. Josh followed Samuel's directions, and they were parked outside the restaurant in a few minutes. Sara noted its elegant landscaping and natural wood exterior. Expensive, she concluded.

A valet took their car at the door, and they walked into a darkened foyer. Sara heard soft music that mingled with the bubbling sounds of a lighted aquarium to her left. A tuxedoed maitre d' greeted Samuel by name and then seated them at a table overlooking the sea. Sara could hear the surf crashing against the rocks below, but the sound was muted enough by the window glass for them to converse easily. They were alone in the dining room. It was much too early for most of Gibraltar's population to even consider dinner.

"Uncle Samuel," began Josh, "what is this all about?"

"Sh, sh, let's not talk about that. Tell me, Sara, what do you do? Are you in school?"

Sara stared at him, wondering what to say. "I graduated from college," she ventured, "and thought I might want to go to law school, but now I don't think so."

Sam cocked his head at her. "You have another idea then?"

Sara could see that Josh was listening intently as if her plans concerned him. "I'm not sure what I'm going to do next. I'm mulling over several possibilities, though. I'd like to hear what you're thinking about doing."

Having thrown the conversational ball back into their court, Sara sat back and listened as the two men, the old and the young, caught up on their lives.

Samuel was not to be hurried. They finished their seafood dinners, and then Samuel insisted on brandy and coffee. Sara joined them in the brandy because Samuel's subterfuge was making her nervous. He was deliberately delaying them, dawdling over his meal, insisting on dessert, asking question after question about family and friends and business. The meal went on and on. Sara listened with half an ear as she watched the sun go down and the Mediterranean take on a deep velvety blue with the darkness.

At last, even Samuel could linger no longer. He checked his watch, surveyed the sea, stood, and nodded at Sara and Josh.

"We'll go now," he said.

They walked to the car. Samuel sat in the front seat with Josh so he could direct him. Sara sat in back with the shovel.

"I hope no bodies are involved with this," she said.

Samuel laughed.

They ascended a narrow, winding road that carved its way in a zig-zag path up the mountain. They eventually came to a small parking area on the side of the road, and Samuel told Josh to pull over. Samuel seemed distracted and worried. He twisted around and scanned the parking area through the back window. Then he focused on Sara. He pointed to the shovel. She reached over and picked it up.

They left the car and followed Samuel across the deserted parking lot to a tall iron gate painted a white that shone in the moonlight. Samuel limped up to the gate, dug in his pocket, and withdrew a heavy iron key and a can of household oil. He squeezed oil into the lock and the gate hinges.

Then Samuel slipped the key into the lock and turned it quietly. He opened the gate just wide enough for them to squeeze through and closed the gate behind them. They stood in a small, overgrown cemetery built into the slope. Narrow, white steps wound their way up the hill to disappear into the darkness. On the left inside the gate stood a bench, also painted white, against a white wall where a dry, bowl-shaped fountain protruded out over the steps. Plaques paved the ground, their edges overgrown by the grass that threatened to engulf them. All was quiet. Sara looked around. Even crickets paid their respects here. The cloying perfumes of night-blooming flowers filled the still air, and branches from unpruned trees brushed her arms as she followed Sam and Josh up the steps.

Sara watched the two men pick up a few pebbles and place them on a grave. Josh noticed her watching him. "Old Jewish custom," he said. "We probably have ancestors here."

Samuel pulled a light out of his pocket and flashed it on the plaques, revealing worn Hebrew inscriptions that Sara could not read. Once she stumbled against a post and found, as she brushed off the cobwebs, that the post supported a bird feeder. She peered ahead at Samuel in the darkness.

Samuel stepped around the grave plaques and limped forward.

He turned once to look back at Sara. "It pays to be a hard-working volunteer at the synagogue, my dear. I am in charge of this cemetery, which is the oldest Jewish cemetery in Gibraltar." He paused. "You see that we have no standing headstones here but instead the flat plaques. We follow the Spanish and Portuguese tradition."

They climbed up a few more steps. Samuel mumbled incoherently. He stepped forward across the grass and stopped at a simple grave plaque. He shined the light onto the inscription. It was weathered but still readable.

He pulled a pebble out of his pocket and placed it on a gravestone. Then he reached over and tugged Josh's arm. "This is where your many times great grandmother, Rachel Levy Youli, is buried." He turned to Sara. "And she was yours also," he said. "She was a resourceful and intelligent woman, and she would have been unknown to you, Sara, if you had not come searching for me.

"And over there." Samuel pointed to the stone next to Rachel's. "That was Rachel Levy's father, Moses Levy. He was an assistant to the vizier of Morocco."

"But I don't understand," said Sara. "Is this the Rachel Levy who was captured by pirates?"

"Oh yes. That story." Samuel poked his cane into the earth around Rachel's gravestone. "Actually, I think her father arranged her marriage to the vizier. It was probably to advance his own position with the vizier and the court. That was often done in those days, I understand."

"And her father is buried next to her, so she didn't lose her family after all," Sara murmured. She laid the shovel aside and knelt to brush off the lichens in the Hebrew letters on Rachel's grave plaque.

"Is that part of the story too?" asked Samuel. He leaned on his cane.

"I thought so," Sara said. She traced the letters on the plaque with her fingers. She considered the accounts she'd heard of Rachel and her son Moses and his son David and listened to Samuel who was peering into the darkness around them as he spoke.

"I don't know about that," said Samuel, "but now I can tell you the rest of the story." He paused and flashed the light around the cemetery as if searching for eavesdroppers before he continued. "In World War II, the Germans wanted Gibraltar because of its location, you know, being the gateway to the Mediterranean. If they had captured Gibraltar, they would have won the war." He punctuated this by shining the light towards the sea, and then brought it back to the ground at their feet.

"Your grandmother Ruth feared they would succeed, but she had international connections, and they gave her an office here. She used it as a central shipping point for the Jewish art and other valuable objects she received from all over Europe. She felt that if she couldn't rescue the Jews themselves, she could at least rescue their possessions." He sighed and shook his head. "We were such idealists."

He stared at the ground as if remembering the times long past. Then he looked at Sara. "Your grandmother was scrupulous in her business methods, you know. She always provided a receipt and kept a copy for her records. Many times there was no one to send a receipt to and just as often, the art and artifacts were never reclaimed. It was a tragic business."

"But what happened to the art then?" asked Sara, standing up alongside Josh.

Josh picked up a stick and tapped the plaque with it. "That's part of the story I know a little about," he said. "She shipped it to my grandparents in St. Thomas, who paid the duties, and then stored the pieces until they could be reclaimed or otherwise disposed of."

"It's all so incredible to me," said Sara.

Samuel shrugged. "Those were incredible times—and dangerous too."

Sara stood by Rachel's grave, absorbing this story. She was still readjusting her image of her grandmother. Of all the possibilities that had come to mind when she thought of her grandmother's legacy, she had never considered that her grandmother had been a courageous and enterprising heroine. To learn this about her grandmother was the most wonderful heritage she could have received. This was her true legacy. This and her new family, and it was much richer than she could ever have imagined.

She woke from her thoughts, startled, to the bizarre fact that she and Josh and Samuel now stood in an ancient cemetery in the middle of the night.

"But why are we here?" she asked.

"Because there was one treasure that we received under odd circumstances from people in France that Ruth did not know. Don't worry. We weren't going to steal it. Ruth had given them a receipt and kept the copy, which she managed to send with a few personal items to a friend in America."

"That's right," Sara said, "but even the rabbi couldn't read it."

"We were so rattled by that time," Samuel said, "that I'm afraid we weren't writing or thinking clearly. We had planned, you see, to go to America before we returned to St. Thomas. But first, I wanted to make a few more trips to France and left Ruth here to handle this last piece of art. She had reservations about it; that's why she hid it here in Gibraltar for safekeeping until we returned rather than shipping it as we usually did." He hit the cane hard on the ground.

"Then I went back to Marseille and was captured. All our plans were blown apart. You know the rest. I never learned what happened to Ruth until now."

"You mean the artwork is still here?" Sara looked around the cemetery. Josh stared at the shovel.

"Yes. I was waiting for Ruth," Samuel's face turned sad for an instant, "or for you," he added, smiling at Sara.

"It's here then?" Josh asked, picking up the shovel. He pointed to Rachel's plaque.

Samuel stepped back. "Careful now. You don't want to break it."

Josh pushed the shovel into the dirt at the edge of Rachel's plaque. He dug around it carefully, then drove the shovel under it to pry it out of the soil and lever it aside.

Underneath was a cavity, now riddled with wormholes and lined with pieces of wood long decayed into mulch. Inside this cavity lay an oblong box covered many times over in some putrid material. Josh reached down with both hands to pick it up. The slimy material disintegrated as he touched it. An acrid smell filled the air.

"Oilcloth," Samuel said.

Scraping away this long-useless covering revealed the flaking, rusted iron of a metal case about two feet long and six inches wide. A gray paste oozed out of its cracked seams. Josh slid the shovel under the box to support it and Sara held it on the shovel as Josh pulled it out of the hole. They laid it aside as they filled in the hole and replaced the gravestone.

"You never know when someone might visit this place," Samuel said, "but the grass grows fast and should soon cover all marks of our visit." As he spoke, he reached into a coat pocket and pulled out a plastic bag.

"Here," he said. "Wrap it in this."

Together they eased the disintegrating metal case into the bag and then wrapped the extra plastic around it. They looked at Samuel.

"Let's get out of here," he said.

They drove to the hotel, and all three went up to Sara's room.

Samuel sat on the bed. "I knew about this case, but I had no identification for it. Only Ruth had the receipt. She knew who owned it, but I didn't. I didn't know what to do about it, and after the war, I was stuck in a displaced persons camp until they could get me back to the family in St. Thomas. So I left it here where you found it, which is where Ruth put it, and went back to St. Thomas. I wanted to forget about it at first, and later I hoped that by a miracle I would learn something that would give me its provenance."

Sara laid newspaper on the floor and placed the plastic bag on it. Josh pulled the case out of the plastic bag and set it on top. Sara scraped off the dirt and the rust and used a towel to clean the long, narrow case underneath.

She looked up at Samuel. He nodded. So tense her fingers shook, she fumbled with the catch on the lid, but it fell apart in her hands. She didn't know what to expect but after the drama of digging up the case, bringing it back to her room, and now opening it, she was looking for an exciting discovery.

Instead, a repellent smell like the squashed bodies of a thousand grubs wafted out across the room. She and Josh sat back away from the case. Samuel stooped down and peered into it, then reached inside, murmuring, "Oh, see what she did, oh, see what she did."

He dipped into the gray ooze and pulled out an oblong package covered with more disintegrating oilcloth. He removed the wrappings to reveal a glass tube about two feet long and two inches in diameter. He smiled and shook it at Sara and Josh. "See what she did! Here it is, and I think there is no damage."

Sara looked at Josh. "But what is it?" she asked, her voice a whisper. A shiver crept down her back and she felt the goose bumps on her arms. Samuel's excitement thrilled her.

Samuel took the glass tube into the bathroom. Sara heard the sound of the faucet running, then a loud pop followed by shattered glass falling to the floor. Samuel emerged carrying a nondescript roll of stained canvas.

"See what she did!" he crowed.

"What, Uncle?" asked Josh impatiently. "What did she do?"

Sara stared at the roll of canvas as comprehension dawned.

Samuel grinned at them. "She had a glassmaker seal this canvas in a glass tube, and then she wrapped it in oilcloth to protect the glass from breaking. Then she put it back into the metal case and filled it with sand and borax to keep out the insects and mold. Only she didn't think her homemade preservation technique would have to last more than sixty years! She was a smart one, she was." He shook the roll of canvas at them.

"It looks like a painting," said Sara.

"That's right. Go ahead," Samuel said. He noticed their grubby hands. "Wash your hands, then let's take a look at it."

Sara scrubbed her hands hard, noticing that Josh did the same. She shuddered at the thought of the ooze and the grubs. When they returned, Samuel handed the roll to Sara, and then sat down on the bed.

"Wait." Josh wrapped the case and its revolting contents back into the plastic bag before laying fresh newspaper on the floor. He rewashed his hands while Samuel placed the rolled canvas on the newspaper.

Sara and Josh knelt to unroll the canvas, still flexible despite its age, and lay it flat. "This should be done by an expert," Sara said, pointing to the fine cracks spreading across the painting.

"But, Uncle Samuel," said Josh, "what is it?"

Peering at Josh intently, Samuel said, "Study it."

Sara sat on her heels and scrutinized the painting with Josh. She heard him catch his breath.

"Why, I believe this painting is by . . ." He stopped and stared up at Samuel. Samuel said nothing but waited.

"I think this painting is . . . it must be, I think," Josh swallowed and stammered, "I think it's a Rembrandt."

Samuel nodded. "Yes, I believe so, but it could be by one of his students, or it could be a fraud."

Sara stared at the painting. It was certainly old, and she supposed age had darkened the colors. The cracks across the face of it didn't help. Cleaned and framed, it probably would rival Rembrandt's early portraits she'd seen in the National Gallery.

Samuel used his cane to point. "Yes, you see? The signature here?" said Samuel. "Rembrandt lived in the Jewish section of Amsterdam for awhile, and I think this is . . . well, it looks like one of his studies of Rabbi Saul Levi Morteira. Here the rabbi is made to look like a Moor . . . . " Samuel's gaze moved slowly across the painting. "Pick it up carefully," he instructed Josh, "and turn it over."

Josh picked up the canvas and turned it over. On the back was a pencil drawing. Samuel studied it for several minutes. Then he whistled. "I think this is the same subject, only here he is dressed like Abraham. This must have been a quick study for a future painting." He looked at them expectantly.

"But Rembrandt wasn't Jewish, was he?" Sara asked, not able to take her eyes off the painting.

"No, but while some Christians in Amsterdam regarded Jews as a misfortune, he did not and was friendly to them. He would use leaders from the Jewish community to sit for him."

Then he added, "You realize this painting, if it's authentic, may be worth millions."

Sara and Josh sat back on their heels and gazed reverently at the painting.

"Ruth told me that she had acquired something special. She said it should be ours, but why would she say that?" Samuel took the canvas out of Josh's hands.

Sara watched as Samuel turned the painting over to gaze again at the

Moorish figure. Then he peered closely at the lamp and curious dishes and scarf placed on the table beside the figure before returning the painting to Josh and pointing to the floor.

Josh again spread the canvas on the newspaper, holding the edges down gently with his hands.

Samuel looked at Sara and Josh over his glasses and then down at the painting. "See those objects there? And that scarf?"

Josh and Sara bent close to the painting.

Samuel grinned. "We have that same lamp and scarf at home. They've been handed down in our family for generations. They came from Morocco, you know." Samuel paused. "She must have thought ours are the same as in the painting."

Josh looked up. "I recognize the lamp and the scarf. Do you suppose they are the same? The ones we have are antique, but they've been preserved although I'm afraid the scarf will disintegrate if we try to touch it."

Samuel shrugged. "Rabbi Saul Morteira may be a distant ancestor of ours. Like us, he was a Sephardic Jew but his family fled Portugal and went to the Netherlands. Our branch of the family went to Morocco and England. I suppose that somehow we might have acquired and protected those items. I don't know."

Sara sat on her heels and stared at the painting. He was talking about her ancestors. Their family. Her family.

"Ruth must have recognized these objects," said Samuel. "Maybe she even learned about this connection from the owner of the painting. But she didn't tell me about that or even who owned the painting." He stopped and stared at the wall across the room. "Why didn't she tell me?"

"Aren't we drawing a lot of conclusions here?" asked Sara. "This subject, even those objects in the painting, may not have any connection at all. And those objects may have been common souvenirs."

Samuel looked back at the painting. "You could be right."

"The only clue we have about the painting is the receipt from my grandmother."

"That's true. Now that we know it was for this Rembrandt, perhaps we will be able to decipher that receipt." Samuel paused. "And we can look through the lists of paintings stolen during the war, but I think I am right about those objects. When you return to St. Thomas, you must ask Sarah to show them to you."

"So you really think that is the same lamp and scarf?" Sara asked.

"Yes, I do. I don't know who owns this painting or where it should go now—except we must place it in a bank vault while we search for the owner." Samuel stared down at the floor. He looked up, first at Sara and then at Josh.

"I am an old man. Ruth is gone." He sighed. "It seems to me, my dears, that this enigma belongs to your generation. Ruth bequeathed it to you, Sara, and I give it to you, Josh. I think," he paused, "yes, I think that all the questions are now yours to answer."

"But we can't read the receipt." Josh rolled up the canvas.

"I will work with you on that. I can compare it with a list I've kept of people we helped." He tapped his cane on the floor. "You can also check with associations that help Jews recover stolen art."

"Maybe Abe Carilla will help." Sara looked at Josh. "It's not his painting, though."

"Who? Who is this Abe Carilla?" Samuel asked.

"He recognized one of the paintings in the album my grandmother gave me. He said it belonged to his family but has disappeared," Sara said. "It wasn't a Rembrandt—more modern."

"I knew a Carilla once . . . long ago," Samuel said, shaking his head. "When the paintings left our hands, we could not help what happened after that." He shrugged and watched Josh roll the canvas into a plastic bag.

Sara felt stunned. She had already received a rich legacy by learning her family's history. Of all the possibilities that had come to mind when she thought of her grandmother's legacy, she had never once considered this kind of challenge. This kind of . . . .adventure.

But as she thought about it, she realized that her grandmother had known her well. Her grandmother's heritage ran through Sara's entire psyche. Sara thought of her ancestor, Rachel Levy, just a girl, younger than Sara herself, but captured by pirates and forced to live in slavery in Morocco. Rachel never had the life of freedom that Sara enjoyed in America. For a moment, Sara could feel Rachel's sadness, but Rachel had escaped Morocco and perhaps her life was happier in Gibraltar. Perhaps she did make it to America or . . . or St. Thomas.

Sara remembered Josh's comment about her family history. Perhaps, Sara thought, the panic she felt as she faced the sea to the east was another part of her heritage. Her family had endured the pain and horror of slavery and tyranny carried down through the generations. Perhaps the assault on the boat triggered inherited memories. Sara smiled at that. Inherited memories. What an idea!

What would her brother think of this development? Would he be elated at the thought of a new family and the discovery of a Rembrandt or even more upset at the now confirmed Jewish connection?

Once she had thought her grandmother was a passive, simple homemaker. Perhaps her brother and her mother would surprise her too. Sara studied the painting.

"But who is the real owner of this painting?" she asked. "How can we ever find him or her?"

Josh cleared his throat. "I am confounded. We can begin with the receipt and those organizations Uncle Samuel mentioned, but what an incredible project. We have a difficult job ahead of us, Sara."

"You're right." Sara nodded. "We must find the rightful owner and return it."

She looked at Samuel. He smiled at her and then at Josh.

"I leave that to you," he pointed his cane at her. "Now I can go home, back to St. Thomas and my family. It is not a good ending to Ruth Rachel's story. No, it is not. But at least she has been found."

"And I have found my family." Sara took Samuel's hand and squeezed it. She grinned at Josh. "I think we've got a fascinating challenge ahead of us."

"Yes." Samuel paused at the door. "It is now your turn to carry on and your task to find the owner."

Josh grinned back at Sara, looking into her eyes. He took her hand. "And who knows where this will lead."

Samuel turned to leave, but as he walked out the door, he peeked back at Sara and at Josh with a faint smile on his lips. Then swinging his umbrella, he whistled his way down the hall.

Epilogue

Rachel Levy, Eliahu ben Youli, Moses Levy, and David Levy Yulee all existed at one time, but this is a work of fiction, and I have taken liberties with Rachel's story.

Chris Monaco, author of *Moses Levy of Florida*, asserts that Moses Levy's mother, Rachel, was not a captive English slave and questions whether her name was actually Rachel. He says that she was a Sephardic Jew from Tangier, probably the daughter of a merchant, known for her beauty and wisdom. Little else is known about her, but Barbary pirates did plunder the ships in the Mediterranean and the Atlantic, and they did rob, kidnap, and enslave the unfortunate on those ships.

According to Monaco, Rachel had two children, Moses Elias, born in 1782, and Rachel, born in 1798. The real Eliahu ben Youli did have three wives who bickered constantly about their connubial rights.

In 1790, Eliahu smuggled Rachel and his son Moses Elias Levy to Gibraltar. His son eventually immigrated to St. Thomas and became a wealthy man. He brought his mother and sister to St. Thomas, and they are buried there. Although there are various accounts of what happened to Eliahu, including the one inflicted on Eliahu described in this novel, Monaco notes that Eliahu died in Gibraltar sometime between 1798 and 1800.

When King Muhammed ibn Abdullah died in 1790, his oldest son Moulay Yazid took control and conducted a reign of terror and chaos for two years until his stepbrother Moulay Slimon amassed the forces to kill Yazid and return order and reason to the country.

The accounts of Moses Levy's adult life and David Levy Yulee's life in my book are factual.

I am grateful to Chris Monaco, who provided much useful information as I searched for Rachel's story. His book, *Moses Levy of Florida*, is a well-researched, interesting, and readable account of Moses Levy's life and brings together the fragments of information about Levy and Yulee that are scattered all over Florida and elsewhere.

If you enjoyed this book, please write a review on Amazon.com and tell others about it.

Eileen Haavik McIntire may be reached through her email, eileenmcintire@aol.com and her blog, eileenmcintire.wordpress.com

CPSIA information can be obtained at www.ICGtesting.com

261014BV00001B/4/P